AF271341

AFRICA
A HISTORY

Alvin M. Josephy

HORIZON • NEW WORD CITY

Published by New Word City, Inc.

For more information about New Word City, visit our Web site at
NewWordCity.com

American Heritage Publishing
Edwin S. Grosvenor, President
P.O. Box 1488
Rockville, MD 20851

1

AFRICAN BEGINNINGS
J. DESMOND CLARK

For centuries, people's imaginations have been captured by attempts, usually fanciful, to establish the exact locality of the place of origin of the human race - the paradise of ancient mythology. Scientific research of the last few decades, carried out by archeologists, paleontologists, and workers in allied disciplines, is making it increasingly likely that the legendary birthplace was somewhere on the African continent, probably south of the Sahara.

Africa today is the home of many human cultural traditions, ranging from simple hunting societies to elaborate urban civilizations - a result of interaction over many millenniums and the selective use of the potentialities of the different environments. Indeed, the single most powerful influence on the lives of men, as of other creatures, is the environment in which they live. Temperature, rainfall and its distribution throughout the year - in short, climate - together with the kind of plant communities, the associated animal life, the availability of surface water sources or of economically important minerals not only shape the tenor of man's daily life but have been significant influences on his biological evolution.

Animals and plants are adapted to living in a particular habitat through natural selection and competition. Some creatures have succeeded in adapting to several different ecological niches, but by reason of man's culture and technology, only he and some life forms dependent upon him have been able to make adjustments that permit him to live anywhere he wants to in the world.

Humanity's emancipation from environmental controls has been a comparatively gradual process, though one of steadily quickening tempo. For nine-tenths or so of human history, however, the rate of biological and cultural progress was extremely slow, almost imperceptible; only in the past few thousand years has man developed the abilities that make possible today's sophisticated urban civilizations. Nonetheless, man remains an integral part, though by far the most influential part, of the many different ecosystems in which he lives, and he now has it in his power to destroy or to conserve and improve them. Moreover, from the beginning, man's relationship with his environment was one in which he always had the freedom to choose how he could make best use of the natural resources and which of them he should select.

It is the possession of a rational intellect and of culture - the ability to manufacture artifacts and the skill to use them - that gives man the opportunity to exploit the resources offered by the different habitats, and this finds expression in the patterns of behavior that control the lives of every human community. Depending on social, legal, and religious sanctions, all of which affect the way a population reacts to innovations and the pressures of external influences, a culture may be sympathetic or conservative in its acceptance and modification of new beliefs, tastes, or technologies.

In any community, the cultural tradition is made up of the social structure, the economic pattern, the learned ways of behavior, and the influence on these of technology and material culture - all of which are handed down from one generation to the next. For example, in Africa, the peoples south of the Sahara may be separated generally into two geographical culture areas: those in the south and east, where hunting, wild food gathering, and the herding of livestock determine the culture; those in West Africa and Equatoria, where the economy is based on cultivation by sedentary populations. The ways of life of the peoples in each of these main culture areas are broadly similar except where historical interaction has brought about some modification or displacement.

The concept of culture areas is of great value for the study of cultural evolution. Except in the latest, prehistoric periods, however, little evidence, other than the less perishable parts of the material culture, has survived. But as research becomes more advanced, archeology - the science that seeks to interpret these material remains - is able to provide a time perspective for some of the culture areas. An understanding of the main geographical regions of the continent is not only essential to an explanation of the varied ways of life of the African peoples today but is even more important for understanding the evolution of man and his culture in prehistoric times and his preference for and selection of some habitats rather than others.

Geographically, Africa can be divided roughly into a highland and a lowland zone by drawing a line from the mouth of the Congo River in the west to the Ethiopia-Sudan border in the east. South of this line, High Africa comprises mainly an interior plateau, most of it between 3,000 and 5,000 feet above sea level, but with higher ridges and mountains. The bedrock is formed of pre-Cambrian crystalline metamorphic rocks that also commonly obtrude, and some of them provide important sources of mineral wealth. North of our imaginary line, Low Africa composed largely of plains and basins of sedimentation in which are found the younger sedimentary rocks of Cretaceous and early Tertiary periods, is generally between 500 and 2,000 feet above sea level.

In the depressions on the plateau are large, relatively shallow lakes and swamps containing a seemingly inexhaustible supply of fish and, formerly, large numbers of hippopotamuses. The major rivers have their sources in the higher mountain ranges, from which they descend to undulating savanna, meandering in broad, deep valleys until they reach the escarpments, where they fall in a series of rapids and waterfalls, often through narrow gorges, to the coastal plains. Thus, the rivers are never navigable for any great distance from their mouths. This feature was directly responsible for the general failure of alien peoples - travelers, traders, soldiers, and geographers - from classical times into the nineteenth century to penetrate the interior and relay knowledge concerning the country and its inhabitants to the outside world.

The eastern part of Africa is split by a huge trough, or fault, that runs nearly the whole length of the continent. This is the Great Rift Valley, which starts in Asia, in Syria, and continues southward down the Red Sea, through Ethiopia into Kenya, Uganda, and Tanzania, and finally loses itself beneath the alluvial sediments in the lower Zambezi valley in Mozambique. In Kenya and Uganda, the trough splits into the Eastern Rift and the Western Rift; in a shallow basin on the plateau between the two branches lies Lake Victoria, Africa's greatest lake.

The bottom of the Great Rift lies at extremely variable elevations. In the Danakil section of the Ethiopian Rift the bottom drops in places to nearly 400 feet below sea level, but southward the floor rises in a series of steps until in Kenya, in the Eastern Rift, the elevation is over 5,000 feet. The volcanic rocks and sediments of the area support short grasses and thorn bushes, which are highly favorable to wild game and the pastoralist way of life.

The Great Rift is a technically unstable zone where compression and tension of the earth's crust have pushed up the land bordering the trough into high ridges and mountains. The deeper portions of the trough are filled by great lakes, some of which, such as Lakes Tanganyika and Malawi, are among the deepest and longest in the world.

Although there exists now only one active volcano in the rift zone (Ol Doinyo Lengai in Tanzania), there are numerous dormant and extinct ones, two of which Mount Kilimanjaro (19,565 feet) and Mount Kenya (17,040 feet) are perpetually snowcapped. Another huge snow-covered mass - this one a crystalline rock thrust of nonvolcanic origin - is the Ruwenzori range. Its highest peak, Mount Stanley, rises to 16,795 feet. The vegetation zones of the rift run in belts around the mountains, changing with altitude from rain forest at the foot to alpine tundra near the top, and the scenery is some of the most beautiful and varied in the world. The rich fossil record preserved in the Great Rift Valley is due to the accumulation of deep sediments in the bottom of the trough and to the rapid burial of land surfaces by ash and dust from the volcanoes.

Elsewhere in Africa, the climate and vegetation zones generally fall in a similar system to the north and south of a central, equatorial region of high rainfall and evergreen forest, though altitude, monsoons, and other factors have modified this pattern, especially in the eastern and southeastern parts of the continent. Africa is not the all-over forest-covered steaming jungle that popular belief often assumes it to be, and the zone of rain forest is now greatly restricted as a result of some 2,000 to 3,000 years of cutting and burning by man. Most of the continent is covered by a wooded savanna where deciduous trees predominate. The farther from the equator, the longer the winter, or dry season, lasting up to six months or more. The ubiquitous green cover, stretching over mile upon mile of undulating plateau, varies in the thickness of its tree communities from a nearly continuous canopy with only sparse grass beneath, or the gallery forest, to parkland, where the grasses predominate over scattered bush.

The savanna zone north of the equatorial forest is known as the Sudan belt, and that to the south as *miombo* woodland. These savanna lands are the home of a mammalian fauna uniquely rich not only in the great variety of its species but in the size of the herds of its gregarious animals: antelopes, buffaloes, horses, elephants, and many others. The variety of this "Ethiopian fauna," as it is called, indicates the continuing favorability of the habitats in which the animals evolved over many millenniums and which we now think were also the original home of man himself.

To the north and south of the savanna belts, the climate becomes drier, supporting only sparse grass and low bushes - steppelands. In turn, these give way to true desert, the Sahel grading to the Sahara in the north and the Karroo to the Namib and Kalahari deserts in the southwest.

All these tropical and subtropical regions of Africa enjoy a summer rainfall system; but in the north, along the coast of the Mediterranean, and at the southern end of the continent south of the Great Escarpment, or Drakensberg range, the country is fed by winter rains and experiences a much more temperate climate.

There is evidence for considerable past fluctuation in these vegetation zones, with their closely adapted animal communities, in response to changes in rainfall, temperature, and the intensity of winds and ocean currents. Plant and animal species and even communities, now isolated sometimes by hundreds of miles from the main center of distribution, are evidence for a previously more extended and continuous spread of these forms at a time when the climatic conditions favored this. Such changes in the habitat of prehistoric man were of considerable importance in influencing his biological and cultural evolution and thus inducing variations in the pattern of his behavior. It becomes of great importance, therefore, to be able to reconstruct past habitats in order to understand the way of life of the human populations.

There are many ways in which it is now proving possible to reconstruct Africa's past habitats, and these involve scientists in a number of different disciplines. The sedimentary history of a lake basin, a river valley, or a cave is interpreted by geologists and soil chemists. Botanists identify the microscopic pollen grains of plants, sometimes preserved in muds and silts recovered from the basins of existing and former lakes and rivers. Zoologists and paleontologists examine the assemblages of animal bones to determine to which point in the time scale these belong. By comparison with the general habitats and behavior of similar species and communities today, they can deduce what type of faunal community might have existed at that time.

It is essential to be able to arrange all these data into a logical, historical sequence within an established chronological framework. Since 1950, several methods have been developed by physicists and chemists to provide a radiometric time scale of the greatest significance. Two methods are of particular importance for African prehistory. The first is that of potassium-argon; it is based on the measurable amount of argon in rocks rich in radioactive potassium (K40), which, over time, decays at a regular rate into the isotopes of calcium (Ca4o) and argon (A40). This method is valuable for measuring the age of rocks and of formations of volcanic origin, both those that are geologically very old and quite young - as recent as 250,000 years or less.

Of more universal use, but more limited in time range, is the radiocarbon method, based upon the measurement of the radioactive isotope of carbon (C14), which remains in a plant or animal organism after death. Animal bone, or shell, or charcoals from hearths are, in varying degrees, suitable substances whose age can be determined, back sometimes to a maximum of 60,000 years. The time scale thus achieved provides the basis for understanding the rate at which man's biological and cultural evolution took place.

The prehistorian is in much the same position as

a man trying to reconstruct the picture of a jigsaw puzzle of which half the pieces are missing. It is both challenging and exciting, and the degree of success is determined by recognition of the pattern and the significance of the missing pieces. For the more recent periods, the record is obviously much more complete than it is for the beginning, where little evidence of man, other than stone and bone, is preserved. However, much can be learned from the tools and waste material at the sites where they were manufactured, the dispersal of dwellings, the disposition of bone fragments from meals, and from other kinds of artifacts.

It is also fortunate for the prehistorian that Africa has preserved in contemporary society a number of different ways of life, techniques, and tools, the origins of which lie deeply buried in the past. Of course, the present way of life of all these economically simpler societies, such as the hunting-and-gathering Bushmen of the Kalahari Desert or the Pygmy peoples of the Ituri forests, has been affected by contact with peoples of more complex institutions and technologies so that no *direct* comparisons between ancient and modern societies are possible. But, through analogies, archeologists can construct models that make it possible to surmise how prehistoric man behaved.

Another means to rediscover the past, though of more limited extent both in space and time, is the interpretation of the rock art of the Late Stone Age, some of which is incomparable for the liveliness of its styles and its portrayal of events and customs. Later in time other sources, such as historical traditions passed on by word of mouth, the evidence of linguistics by which the history of a language can be deduced, and, finally, written documents, all combine to create a better understanding of the past.

When it is assembled, all this evidence provides a record of man's activities that covers some 4 to 5 million years. It shows that Charles Darwin was right when he suggested in his *Descent of Man* that it was somewhere in the tropics, perhaps in Africa, that man the toolmaker first evolved, and leaves no doubt that man shares a common ancestor with the great apes, or Pongidae.

This ancestor, who lived at some distant time as yet not precisely identified, must have been a small, unspecialized apelike animal, probably similar to the subfamily of fossil apes known as *Dryopithecus*, a term meaning "tree ape." The earliest of these dryopithecines was found in sediments of the Oligocene epoch of the Tertiary period (28 to 30 million years ago) in the Fayum depression not far from Cairo in the Nile Valley. This fossil, named *Aegyptopithecus zeuxis,* is a quadrupedal ape with a tail and an apelike tooth pattern. *Aegyptopithecus* was an arboreal ape, as were later forms found in East Africa, and dates from the

Miocene epoch (about 20 million years ago); the Miocene apes, however, show some modification of the hand and forelimb, suggesting that they may have been partly terrestrial. A smaller species, known as *Dryopithecus africanus* (sometimes less formally referred to as Proconsul), appears to have been adapted to living in gallery forest along the streams and in the savanna, while a larger form, *Dryopithecus major,* occupied the forests on the slopes of volcanoes.

In 1961, the Kenya-born British prehistorian Dr. Louis Leakey found pieces of an upper jaw and two isolated teeth in late Miocene deposits at Fort Ternan in western Kenya that have since been dated to 14 million years old. This fossil, which he named *Kenyapithecus wickeri*, showed unmistakable human characteristics of the hominid branch of the Hominoidea family, from which man and apes are descended. Later it was demonstrated by Dr. Elwyn Simons of Yale University that Leakey's discovery differed in no essential respect from *Ramapithecus punjabicus,* a form discovered earlier in India. Although the India fossil is unfortunately known only from fragments of the upper and lower jaw, the modifications of the face and the tooth pattern that these exhibit have given rise to the suggestion that *Ramapithecus* (to which species the East African find was subsequently assigned) was not only a hominid but a tool user. A further indication was the discovery at the same site of a long bone that had been fractured in a manner suggesting crushing; close by lay a piece of lava with a battered ridge on one side. Proof of man's tool-using ability, however, must rest upon the discovery of limb bones showing whether *Ramapithecus* was a quadruped or a biped.

Professor Sherwood L. Washburn of the University of California postulated the likelihood that the earlier hominids were knuckle-walkers like the apes. This would not only allow for more specialized use of the forelimbs for manipulating objects but would suggest, as does the estimated size range, that *Ramapithecus* lived mostly on the ground.

The place of both the dryopithecine apes and the more advanced *Ramapithecus* is yet to be conclusively determined. Some physical anthropologists consider the dryopithecine apes to be ancestral to the chimpanzee and gorilla. If so, they probably lie close in time and not far removed biologically from the common ancestor of apes and man. However, certain recent biochemical studies have cast doubt on this theory. These studies, based on the analysis of blood serum proteins and on the chromosome composition of the higher primates, suggest that species have evolved at a constant rate and that man and the African apes split off from a common ancestor as recently as the Pliocene epoch (some 5 million years ago). If this were the case, then *Ramapithecus,* a savanna dweller, would be an aberrant ape that left no descendants. It is to be hoped that the search of more recently discovered Pliocene formations in East Africa will provide evidence to show whether the long chronology for the time of separation of the hominid and pongid lines, suggested by the earlier fossil finds, or the short one based on the biochemical studies is likely to be the correct evaluation.

By the beginning of the Pleistocene epoch (some 3.5 million years ago) there were present in the savanna land of East Africa, and probably also of South Africa, hominid forms known as australopithecines, or man-apes. There can be no doubt that through natural and social selection processes, which bred out the less desirable genetic characteristics and encouraged the increase of those more highly favored, the man-apes became ecologically well adapted to life in the open savannas. They were possessed of an upright carriage, using the forelimbs for tool manipulation and the hindlimbs for bipedal locomotion. It can be inferred that these fundamental changes were brought about by the greater potential of the woodland and grassland environments, with their wider opportunities to experiment and the greater excitement of a life in the open over one in the forests.

These hominids are the best known of any of the fossil ancestors of modern man, being represented today by several hundred specimens. The first of these fossils was found in 1924 at Taung in the northern part of the Cape Province in South Africa in brecciated cave deposits that were being exploited for limestone. Here, uncovered by a blast, was found the cast of the greater part of a juvenile skull; it showed characteristics that, in the opinion of its discoverer, Dr. Raymond Dart of South Africa, placed it midway morphologically between the apes and the oldest definitely identifiable human fossils.

Some believed Dart was wrong and considered the skull to be that of a fossil ape. Others, including Dr. Robert Broom, also of South Africa, thought that "In *Australopithecus* we have a being also with a chimpanzeelike jaw but a subhuman brain. We seem justified in concluding that in this new form discovered by Professor Dart, we have a connecting link between the higher apes and one of the lowest human types."

A few years later, Dart was proved correct when Broom discovered the first adult australopithecine fossil at the cave of Sterkfontein in the Transvaal. Systematic investigation of similar limestone caves at other sites in the Sterkfontein area and in the Makapan Valley in the northern Transvaal produced a number of other man-ape fossils in association with many bones of animals.

On the basis of the fossil fauna, the earlier South African deposits could be no younger than the Lower

Pleistocene and might be as old as 2 million years or more. The later deposits appear to belong in the Middle Pleistocene and could be half as young again. The earlier sites - Sterkfontein, Makapan limeworks, and Taung - contained the remains of a small, slender form, *Australopithecus africanus*; whereas, at the later sites - Swartkrans and Kromdraai - only a robust form was present. At Swartkrans were also found the remains of a more advanced hominid, which has now been shown to represent an early form of *Homo* species. It is this form that is believed to have been the maker of the stone tools found in these breccias. No implements of flaked stone have yet been discovered with the gracile form *(Australopithecus africanus)*, but what are claimed to be clubs and cutting, piercing, and chopping tools have been found among the many thousands of bones of other creatures in these deposits.

The australopithecines were small-brained hominids with cranial capacities of between about 435 and 530 cubic centimeters - around the average for the gorilla and about one-third the size of modern man. Their rather muzzlelike face shows a number of apelike features, but the tooth pattern is essentially human, as are many features of the brain case. The head was centrally placed on the spinal column. The pelvic girdle and bones of the lower limbs show that the man-apes walked upright on two feet, and the arms and hands show that they were capable of simple toolmaking.

Australopithecus africanus measured an average four feet six inches tall and weighed about sixty to seventy pounds; *Australopithecus robustus* was taller, about five feet in height, and weighed about 130 pounds.

It appears now most likely that the Transvaal caves were not the dwelling places of the man-apes but rather the sites where carnivores, possibly leopards, brought their victims. In this case, the australopithecines were not the aggressive hunters that some have claimed them to be.

East African discoveries that have been underway since 1959 have enhanced our knowledge of these earliest hominids. There, australopithecine fossils are known from a number of different localities in the Lake Rudolf section of the Rift Valley (Omo, Lothagam, Kanapoi, and sites on the east side of the lake), from Lake Baringo (Chemeron) in Kenya, and from the Olduvai Gorge and Garusi in northern Tanzania. The oldest of these fossils dates from about 5 million years ago, and by the beginning of the Pleistocene, both a slender and a robust form were living in the Lake Rudolf rift. The oldest stone tools, made some 2.6 million years ago, are from Koobi Fora on the east side of Lake Rudolf. At a nearby site have been found one well-preserved skull of the robust australopithecine and parts of another representing a more gracile form. Stone tools are also present at one layer in the Omo beds, about 1.8 million years old, and in the bottom of the 350-foot sequence of Pleistocene lake sediments at Olduvai Gorge.

Olduvai is unique for what it can tell us about early man. Here, since 1931, Drs. Louis and Mary Leakey have recovered the remains of a number of hominids associated with concentrations of animal bones and stone implements. These lay on land surfaces that had been rapidly covered either by ash and dust from periodic eruptions of the nearby volcanoes or by the rising waters of the lake, thus sealing the remains in a remarkably fine state of preservation.

The base of the Olduvai sequence begins about 1.9 million years ago, and in the lowest level (Bed 1) *Australopithecus robustus* was found together with a more advanced form named *Homo habilis.* The name implies the ability to make tools, and it is the association of this form with evidence of stone toolmaking that has justified including it with *Homo* rather than with *Australopithecus.* His remains are known from six sites and include three fairly complete craniums and lower jaws, together with bones of the lower leg, a nearly complete foot, and a number of the bones of the hand as well as isolated finds of teeth.

Homo habilis was possessed of a larger brain (640-650 cubic centimeters) than either of the australopithecines. However, in the remainder of the skeleton, so far as can be observed, the differences are not great. *Homo habilis* resembles *Australopithecus africanus* in its slender build, and since it is of a later date, it could have evolved from the latter form; as yet, no certain identification of a slender australopithecine has been made at Olduvai. Alternatively, the evidence can be interpreted as showing three distinct and evolving hominid lines of which only the third, *Homo habilis*, survived to become a competent toolmaker and to be the ancestor of modern man.

The remains that are found at Olduvai provide almost the only evidence for the technological capabilities and activities of the Lower Pleistocene hominids. Concentrations of animal bones, split to extract the marrow, and numbers of stone tools, together with the waste resulting from their manufacture, can be seen as their living places or home bases, to which were brought back the results of hunting, scavenging, and other gathering activities to be shared among the members of the group. Sometime in a previous epoch, therefore, most likely in the Pliocene, which immediately preceded the Pleistocene, some of the ancestral hominids turned from a largely vegetarian to an omnivorous diet in which the hunting of animals became the most significant activity. In fact, it is likely that the need for sharp cutting implements to skin and dismember a carcass was the factor that made these groups take the momentous step involved in working stone to make tools.

The home bases were more than the transitory sleeping places of the hominids. The numbers of individual animals and species represented there suggest that the sites were occupied for several days at least. They were also the places where the juveniles were taught the skills and behavior that made for the successful perpetuation of the species, and it is now apparent from a study of the age when the young's permanent teeth erupted that they were dependent upon their parents for about the same time as those in simpler societies are today. The nature of the learned behavior can be gauged from several different lines of evidence - from the morphology of the fossils themselves, from artifacts, and from what is now known of the behavior of the gorilla and chimpanzee, the latter in particular.

Studies of free-ranging groups of chimpanzees in wooded savanna (by the English ethologist Jane van Lawick-Goodall in the Gombe Stream Reserve in western Tanzania) and in forest (by English zoologist Vernon Reynolds in Uganda's Budongo forest and by others in West Africa) show that these animals live in highly sociable groups that are continually changing in composition. They do not indulge in any regular defense of territory, and they use some twenty-three different calls, together with facial expressions and gestures, for communication. They manufacture and use simple tools - peeled sticks and grasses for extracting termites from their nests, sponges for sucking water contained in hollow trees, sticks for breaking open the nests of tree ants or for defense; they also throw stones and regularly weave sleeping platforms. These observations, in combination with the fossil evidence, provide a basis for assessing the capabilities of *Australopithecus* and other early hominids, since what the chimpanzees are capable of doing, the australopithecines were biologically equipped to do appreciably better, and much else besides. Already it is probable that we can differentiate between the activities of the males and females, the males engaging in hunting and the females and young gathering wild plant foods.

It is, however, man's tool-making ability that places him above all other forms of life, and his first great step in the manufacture of simple stone tools required a mind capable of inventing and transmitting a rudimentary knowledge of how stone is fractured so as to produce sharp fragments, or flakes, from the parent lump, or core, and a hand that could do the work. Such tools belong to what is called the Oldowan industry (after the site at Olduvai), and they consist of choppers, flakes for cutting, and rounded, many-faceted lumps for pounding or breaking bone to extract the marrow. Sometimes a flake will show a small amount of fashioning to form a scraper, or more rarely, a bone fragment may show signs of having been employed as a tool. These represent domestic equipment used at the home base, and there has been little, if anything, found to support the view that man was from his earliest beginnings the armed aggressor he has become today. Stones and sticks for throwing at game are likely to have been the only weapons, if such they can be called.

Fossils of early hominids in South and East Africa, and another in the basin of Lake Chad, show them to have been widely spread over the savanna and drier regions of the continent by the beginning of the Middle Pleistocene (about 1 million or more years ago), about the time that the australopithecine forms had given place to the biologically more evolved *Homo erectus.* So far, australopithecine fossils have not been found outside the continent of Africa; however, *Homo erectus* forms, with their toolmaking skills, were widely distributed throughout all the inhabited regions of the Old World.

Two fossils from Olduvai (classified by archeologists as Hominids 13 and 16), the one from the upper and the other from the lower part of Bed II, were originally grouped with *Homo habilis;* but they have been shown to have more evolved features, indicating that they could be forms intermediate to *Homo erectus.* As known from sites in China and Java and from a third example found in the middle of Bed II at Olduvai (Hominid 9), the skull of *Homo erectus* shows quite a variation in cranial capacity (therefore in brain size), ranging from about 750 to over 1,000 cubic centimeters, with a longer, broader, and thicker skull, a larger palate, a low vault, and projecting brow ridges. *Homo erectus* was taller and had larger bones; indeed, there appears to be little difference between the rest of the skeleton and our own. This Olduvai specimen is probably about 500,000 years old, though the earliest of the *Homo erectus* fossils probably is as old as 1 million years or more.

At a site on the edge of what was once a small lake at Ternifine on the Algerian plateau, *Homo erectus* is represented by three lower jaws and one of the side bones of a skull. These jaws are massive and lack a developed mental eminence, or chin, but the pattern of the teeth is not markedly different from that of modern man. Biological changes of the magnitude that occurred between the australopithecines and *Homo erectus* typically take about 8 million years to effect in other animal species, but in the case of these ancestral human fossils, they seem to have transpired in not more than 1 million years. There is small doubt that the reason for the evolutionary speedup lies in man's cultural abilities and the attendant potential for improving his way of life. Once the great initial step had been taken - and it is likely to have been a comparatively sudden invention whereby the finished stone tool was envisaged in the rude block or cobble from which it was to be manufactured - it was inevitable that the innovator's descendants would dominate the less gifted species and that genetic changes would be further accelerated.

At much the same time as *Homo erectus* appears on the African scene, there also appears a new bifacial technique for making stone tools, and we find the first characteristic tools of the Middle Pleistocene: the hand axe and cleaver. They were made from boulders fractured into large flakes; the pieces were then retouched and shaped on both sides with a hammer stone or by striking them on a stone anvil. This Acheulian industrial complex (named after a site in France) lasted for more than 750,000 years. Sites are found throughout Africa, southern Europe, and Asia. The bifacial tools often show considerable skill in manufacture, and the degree of symmetry and finish of some of the later ones reveal the beginnings of an aesthetic appreciation among the makers.

Camping and flaking sites of Acheulian man are known in almost all parts of the continent with the exception of the primary rain forest, showing that by this time, the hominid populations were able to live in a number of different ecological niches. The sites are nearly all in the open, close to water, and cover larger areas than do those of the makers of the Oldowan industry. Many hundreds of hand axes and cleavers may be found on the living sites, along with a range of other tools, and it would seem that the number of individuals making up the social group had by now increased and that some of the camps were revisited seasonally.

The stone tools still appear to be domestic equipment rather than weapons. We know from sites in Europe that simple pointed wooden spears were in use by this time, and a site at the Kalambo Falls in Zambia has produced a wooden club as well as primitive digging sticks.

The makers of Acheulian tools were more competent hunters, if the increased variety of species of animals and greater number of carcasses represented by the bones found at the dwelling places are acceptable as evidence. Improved methods of communication (signs and grunts), and so, more efficient group hunting techniques, were probably the chief factors behind the extended "awareness" of *Homo erectus.* At Ternifine, many large and medium-sized animals had been dismembered and eaten, and their bones thrown into the water from the lakeside camp. At Olduvai and other East African sites, there seems to have been some definite selection of the animals that were hunted, and at one of these, near the top of Bed II, herds of sheeplike and giraffelike creatures (both now extinct) were apparently driven into a muddy stream and there killed and butchered. At another of these artifact concentrations in Kenya, the remains of some eighty giant baboons have been found among the food waste.

The different tool kits and the activities they represent suggest that individuals were now beginning to communicate with each other by means of some form of language. This protolanguage was, no doubt, essentially connected with staying alive and securing the immediate necessities of the moment, but, nonetheless, it provided the foundation on which language as we know it developed in the Middle Pleistocene. However, the fact that at this time, one cannot see any regional specialization suggests that man continued to make only rather limited exploitation of the resources of his habitat. Similar living patterns existed wherever the Acheulian, or hand-axe, industry is found.

Homo sapiens makes his first appearance at about much the same time in Europe and Africa, about 150,000 to 200,000 years ago. European forerunners of modern man *(Homo sapiens sapiens)* are associated with Acheulian hand axes at Swanscombe in the Thames valley in England, and it seems likely that the fragmentary skulls and tools found at Kanjera on Lake Victoria were also those of *Homo sapiens*. Most of the other fossils are unassociated finds. Recently, two almost complete craniums have been found from late Middle or early Upper Pleistocene sediments in the Omo valley in northern Kenya and probably date to about 200,000 years ago. Though they represent the oldest *Homo sapiens* fossils from Africa, they do not look alike. Clearly, there was considerable genetic variability within a single population at this time.

A similar situation is exhibited by the later (about 50,000 years old) human fossils from the Mount Carmel caves in Israel, where both modern and primitive *sapiens* features are present in the same population. However, wherever it was that modern man originated, perhaps in southwest Asia or perhaps distributed over a wider area, it would seem that his intellectual and cultural abilities were such that the *Homo erectus* form was replaced with remarkable rapidity. By 50,000 or 40,000 BCE, Neanderthals (*Homo sapiens neanderthalensis)* were present in North Africa, and a closely connected race of Rhodesioids (*Homo sapiens rhodesiensis)* in the southern part of the continent.

We can now see clearly for the first time the beginnings of a broad, regional specialization in stone tool manufacture. The cultural pattern of the North African population was not unlike that of the other contemporary peoples in Europe and Asia in that they made much use of light cutting and scraping equipment, such as has been associated with hunting camps and the working and flensing of skins. South of the Sudan, modifications of the old Acheulian bifacial technique continued in use, together with a quantity of light wood-working equipment. In the open grasslands of the Horn and the South African Highveld, an evolved expression of the Acheulian tradition (the Fauresmith) is found, while in the forests and woodland savannas of Equatoria and West Africa, now occupied permanently for the first time, many heavy-duty and denticulated (toothed) flake tools (the Sangoan tradition) are found. It has been suggested that the Sangoan tools may be those of a carpenter, reflecting a growing use of wood and such byproducts as bark and resin. The working of wood with stone tools is made appreciably easier by the discovery of a technique of controlled charring with fire and scraping. Utensils can be hollowed out by this method, and weapons and tools made with comparative ease.

Firemaking also has important implications for codifying the social behavior of the groups. Evidence from sites in the Far East and Western Europe shows that fire was definitely used by *Homo erectus* in the colder regions close to the ice sheets during the Middle Pleistocene. None of the Acheulian sites in Africa shows indisputable use of man-made fire before the Upper Pleistocene (about 70,000 years ago). It is from the end of the Acheulian also that we begin to find many occupation sites in caves and rock shelters, and although weathering will have destroyed much of the older evidence for cave occupation, these kinds of sites appear to have been more frequently sought from this time onward.

About 40,000 to 50,000 years ago, therefore, three "races," or subspecific forms, of man were present on the continent: Neanderthals in North Africa; Rhodesioids in southern Africa; and a stock tentatively identified as the ancestors of modern man to be seen in the Kanjera and Omo fossils from East Africa. However, by about 35,000 years ago the Neanderthaloid and Rhodesioid populations had been largely replaced, it would seem, by modern man *(Homo sapiens sapiens)*. The disappearance of these Neanderthaloid populations is most likely to have come about, not as a result of wholesale replacement, but through long-term natural and social selection.

The tool kits are now more complex and exhibit a diversity of regional variations within several more general patterns, but it must be in the greatly stimulated intellectual life that the superiority of these Upper Pleistocene races lay. Whereas in the time of Neanderthal and Rhodesian man it is possible to see the beginnings of a concern with abstract beliefs, ritual, and a superior technology, these find full expression only with the coming of modern man.

It seems probable, though as yet the evidence is insubstantial, that the distinctive success of *Homo sapiens sapiens* lay in his possession of language, in the true sense of the word, without which man's life could never be complete. After 35,000 BCE, we have evidence of consciousness in art, music, ritual, as well as care for the dead and a counting system. More sophisticated tool kits speak of more efficient and extensive exploitation of the natural resources of the habitat, and the increased number of sites that are known to belong to this time suggests an overall increase in population density.

The fossil record for the Upper Pleistocene in Africa is not a particularly complete one; though a number of fossils are known, mostly from the drier parts of the continent, their precise age is often a matter for dispute. However, by about 10,000 BCE, the relatively unspecialized ancestral stock of modern man in Africa, which is generally identified with the Kanjera type, had undergone genetic changes, resulting in the appearance of the large and small Khoisan, or Bushman, types, the robust and gracile blacks, and perhaps also the tall, long-headed Afro-Mediterranean stock.

The large Khoisan type was probably the oldest, dating to about 17,000 BCE, and the most unspecialized. It had evolved in the more open savanna and grasslands of southern and East Africa, even as far north as Khartoum. The small Khoisan - the Bushman proper - appears to have evolved out of the larger type in the southwestern parts of the continent only some 11,000 years ago.

The earliest remains that show black characteristics come from the West African forest country and the western branch of the Great Rift Valley. The first of these, from a burial site in a rock shelter at Iwo Eleru, near Benin in Nigeria, dates to about 9000 BCE. The second, at a site on the shore of Lake Edward, discloses skull fragments that are more robust, but with limb bones that show the slenderness of the West African blacks; these date to about 6500 to 6000 BCE. Unfortunately, the rain forest is not favorable to the preservation of bone, so the ancestry of the black is imperfectly known as yet.

The Afro-Mediterranean type appears at about the same time in the Eastern Rift at Gamble's Cave, and both black and Afro-Mediterranean are present in the Sahara after 5000 BCE, being known from a number of burials and settlement finds.

In North Africa, the population of the Maghreb, during the closing stages of the Upper Pleistocene and later, is known from many remains found buried in settlement middens and in caves. The physical type was tall and robust and is known as the Mechta el Arbi stock - from the name of the shell midden in eastern Algeria where some of the first remains were found. These people show a general likeness to the type of man from the Cro-Magnon shelter in southwest France (of a much earlier date), but the associated cultural remains are different. The oldest Mechta el Arbi skeletons date from about 10,000 BCE, but there was also present in northwest Africa by about 6000 BCE a more slenderly built type representing an early Afro-Mediterranean stock that would ultimately dominate the area.

Both of these local races were associated with stone tools known as microliths, made by using parallel-sided flakes, or blades. These microliths included various kinds of scraping, grooving, and cutting tools, many of the last devices having the back blunted so that they could be held in the hand or, since many of the blades are quite small, mounted in a series. An ingenious notching technique was used to reduce long blades to sections of the required length. The sections were trimmed to various shapes to form the barbs of spears and arrows, the blades of sickles, and so on. Several sickle handles of bone have been found in the Maghreb, one with the microliths still in position, though the tree gum, or mastic, with which they had been held firm had long since disappeared. Microliths became considerably more common after about 15,000 BCE. They are indicative of fundamental changes in the technology, and it is hardly surprising that their use spread rapidly.

It has been suggested that technical innovation of this kind must have been accompanied by population migration, but this is not necessarily the case. Since hunting-and-gathering populations maintain regular contact between their various component groups, an innovation, if it is a sufficient improvement on the existing system, is likely to spread and be quickly adopted. Its progress is especially rapid if it concerns more efficient ways of food getting, for this allows more leisure to devote to intellectual pursuits. In this case, it was a change to lighter equipment: Microliths were easy to make, they could be quickly hafted, or mounted, in the most effective manner. The bow and arrow were invented somewhere about 9000 to 8000 BCE, and because of greater efficiency in some types of country (for example, low grass savanna), were widely, though not universally, adopted.

From the beginning of the Upper Pleistocene epoch, the coastal regions of North Africa were the home of cultural traditions that differed from those found south of the Sahara. The North African Neanderthals were associated with industries known as Mousterian, in the pattern of those found in the Levant and in Europe. It is as yet unknown whether Mousterian technology (successor to the Acheulian tool culture and also named after its earliest discovery site in France) developed independently in each area or whether some population movement was involved. By about 40,000 years ago, however, we find present in northeastern Libya a blade industry typologically in the Upper Pleistocene tradition of the north side of the Mediterranean basin. This would seem to have been an introduction from outside the continent, but, since it is known from only two caves in the Jebel Akhdar, it is unlikely that it was widely distributed, nor can it be seen to have had any profound influence on the essentially local traditions of the African Middle Stone Age or on the contemporary North African industrial complex. This last culture - known as Aterian - developed out of the Mousterian and spread throughout the Sahara; it is distinguished by the use of different kinds of tanged, or stemmed, points, suitable for inserting into handles or attaching as heads of spears, and similar projectiles.

Several local industries based on blades, sometimes employing microliths, have been found in the Nile Valley north of Aswan, and it seems probable that there was not a little interaction between Egypt and the Levant from about 15,000 BCE onward, and possibly earlier. The effect of this is also manifest throughout most of northwestern Africa. The similarities between the two regions, however, remain at the general level rather than the specific. As in the Mousterian, it was more probably the knowledge and innovative behavior that spread, rather than any significant group movement. Some of these blade industries are found south of the Sahara: one site on Somalia's northern coast; another in the East African Rift, where it is associated with a fishing and hunting economy about 7000 to 6000 BCE; and others in Ethiopia.

It is from the desert-confined Nile Valley at this time that there comes the earliest evidence of intergroup warfare. Two cemeteries in the Jebel Sahaba area of the Upper Nile contained a number of burials that had microliths associated with skeletons in such a way as to suggest death as a result of injury. Some even had broken microliths sticking in the skull, pelvis, and thigh bone. It was probably economic pressure on an increasing population of culturally distinct units that brought about the need for each group to seek to preserve its own territory intact and steal some of its neighbors'. Since groups could exploit, but not move permanently into, the desert, it would seem that defense of the more desirable flood plain by force of arms was necessary. Another outcome of this economic pressure was the much greater use of wild cereal grasses, as seen in the large numbers of grindstones in the equipment inventory of some of the hunting camps. Large quantities of wild grain could be harvested by means of primitive sickles, and when stored, could serve as a main food source for several months.

The savanna and forest lands south of the Sahara do not appear to have experienced similar economic pressure, and, indeed, these have always been among the richest natural environments in the world. Most of the Bushmanoid and early black populations that exploited the unlimited plant and animal foods of these habitats would have had little cause to encroach on each other's territory. Those occupying the West

African savanna and forest were also hunters, made microlithic tools, mostly from quartz, and had both axes and adzes. They experimented more specifically with wild plant foods, so that by perhaps about 3000 BCE, if not earlier, selective genetic processes had resulted in the development of early forms of African domestic cereals.

In the Congo Basin, the characteristic stone implement was a trapezoidal piece of stone that could be used in several different ways. It could be fashioned into the head of an arrow to cut the hide of prey, leaving a blood spoor; it could also be used as sickle or knife, as a chisel for hollowing or a drawknife for smoothing wood.

In East Africa and the southern African savanna and steppe, the population was mostly of Bushman, or Khoisan, stock. Here also many of them used microlithic stone tools, including scrapers and hand adzes - tools of the woodworker. They made arrow points, link shafts, and ornaments of bone; ivory and shell were commonly used for beads and pendants. Among other regional groups, larger scraping tools and pounding and grinding equipment were common, and the microlith rare or absent. In Zambia and Malawi, for example, there was an emphasis on grinding equipment, presumably because of the greater reliance on plant foods; in the Highveld of South Africa, the emphasis was more on cutting and flensing equipment and on bone arrow points, showing the greater importance of game herds to the hunting groups there.

The rock art of Africa gives us a good indication of the activities and beliefs of these hunting-and-gathering peoples. The pictures are engraved on rocks or painted in caves or rock shelters. Women are shown gathering wild plant foods, sometimes with the aid of a digging stick on which was occasionally set a stone with a hole pierced through the center for weight. The all important occupation of the men was hunting, and many paintings are scenes of stalking with animal-head disguises or the killing of antelopes, elephants, giraffes, and hippopotamuses with bows and arrows, and less frequently, with spears. Honey-gathering was another male occupation. Dancing and social get-togethers also played a part in the way of life that one authority has called the "master behavior pattern of the human species."

Still more complete information about the prehistoric life patterns can be collected from the example of modern survivals of primitive hunters, though their continued existence has often depended on accommodation to more advanced neighbors. The later Bushmen of the Drakensberg range in southeast Africa persisted, a dwindling population until the 1870s, when they finally succumbed to the pressures of Bantu and European farmers who had taken over their hunting lands. On the other hand, the Bushmen of the central and northern Kalahari demonstrate successfully how hunting groups can make a living out of dry, near-waterless country. The relatively unattractive character of their environment to other, economically more advanced peoples has saved them. So, too, the Hadza people demonstrate how much leisure the rich, though dry and tsetse-ridden, game country of the Lake Eyasi Rift in Tanzania permits to those hunters with six-foot bows. The Pygmies of the Ituri forests, and to a lesser extent the Nderobo of the montane forests of Kenya, show how hunting peoples can adopt and develop a system of exchange relationships with their Bantu agricultural neighbors.

A rare instance of peoples who have made few apparent modifications of the hunting and gathering way of life are two communities of Ova Tjimba people, who were discovered in the Baynes Mountains in the extreme north of South West Africa. Their only contact has been with pastoral Hottentots, and they still make and use stone tools - the only people in contemporary Africa known to do so. A wealth of information exists here for the archeologist and ethnographer to link directly the past and the present.

Elsewhere in Africa, in the region of the many lakes that existed in early post-Pleistocene times in the southern Sahara, as also along the seacoasts, man turned from strict hunting and gathering to exploiting the food resources offered by the water. Special equipment was developed at the close of the Pleistocene, and we find spearheads, barbed harpoons of bone, and fishhooks and gorges of bone and shell. Abundant fish and shellfish could be caught in tidal weirs, and stranded sea mammals supplied quantities of meat, as on the South African south coast. In the lakes and rivers, fish and shellfish were taken, and the hippopotamus and other water mammals were hunted with spears and harpoons. Some of the waterside camps, such as those just mentioned and others on the Upper Nile at Khartoum or on Lake Edward must have been near-permanent settlements. Today, some of the Batwa peoples of central Africa (for example, those living in Zambia's Bangweulu and Lukanga swamps) persist in a way of life that can give an idea of what some of these late prehistoric fishing camps were like.

There would have been small reason for the sub-Saharan peoples to exchange the hunter's way of life for that of the cultivator, especially if the farming tools were not effective ones for dealing with the tropical woodlands and forests. The strong excitement of the hunt can be seen the world over by the amount that is still done today even in the most sophisticated societies. This is primarily the reason why farming came to sub-Saharan Africa fairly late in time.

As yet, no evidence has been found of food producers anywhere on the continent before about 5000 BCE, several millenniums later than their first appearance in southwest Asia. Whether domestication of plants and animals is, in fact, later in Africa will not be known until further work on settlement sites of this time has been carried out, especially the Nile Valley, where circumstances were most favorable.

The Nile Delta is only some 300 miles from southern Palestine, where the incipient stages of domestication go back to 7500 BCE and further, and it is difficult to understand what barrier could have prevented the spread of the experimental techniques that were already widely dispersed in the Near East. Was it the abundance of natural food supply? Perhaps so along the Nile, but this cannot have been the case in other parts of North Africa. Was it the fact that the Nile was then flowing in a channel now covered by many feet of alluvial sediment and that these earlier stages are buried and have escaped detection? Or is it that the evidence is already present in the archeological record but has not yet been recognized as such? The initial steps toward domestication form the substratum of urban civilization and have manifested themselves differently in the New World from the way they have in the Old. So, too, the first advances may have been different in Africa from the now well-known pattern of southwest Asia's agricultural revolution; remembering the trend in the use of wild grains after 15,000 BCE in the Nile, it seems not unlikely that earlier farming settlements, making use of local grains, may eventually be found there.

The settlements at Merimde in the Delta (dating to about 3600 BCE), at Badari in Upper Egypt (about 4000 BCE) in the Fayum depression (about 4500 BCE) are of groups of farmers cultivating emmer wheat, barley, and flax. Flint-bladed sickles in wooden handles were used for harvesting the grain, which was then stored in basketwork silos. These people made pottery and lived in permanent and semi-permanent villages. Bones of cattle, sheep, and goats, probably domesticated, have also been found. At Badari, careful burial of animals suggests the emergence of animal cults, which later became a feature of the religion of dynastic Egypt.

Whether the first farmers in the Nile were migrants from Asia or of indigenous African stock has been much debated.There are a few cultural traits that suggest connections with Asia (for example, some of the pottery, a type of barbed harpoon, and notched arrowheads), but most of the material culture exhibits a characteristically African tradition of bifacial stone flaking, as in the axes and adzes, the sickle blades, knife blades, and scrapers. Sheep and goats as well as cereals, however, must have been introduced from elsewhere since there are no wild forms known in Africa from which they could have come. This is not the case for the cattle, for two wild species were present in northern Africa; cattle bones, said to date to 5400 BCE, have been found in the Sahara. The bas-reliefs in the tombs of the Old Kingdom in Egypt (3200-2900 BCE) show what appear to be experiments in domesticating native species of gazelle, hyena, ass, and various birds. How far back this goes is not known; with the exception of the ass, these experiments came to nothing, presumably because of the greater potential of the Asian domesticates.

By 5000 BCE, there were certainly domesticated sheep or goats, though not cattle, in eastern Libya, but we have as yet no means of knowing whether the people also cultivated grain crops. It is interesting that, except for the introduction of pottery and a more refined manner of making flint tools, the material culture of these early farmers shows little change from that of the immediately preceding hunting population. It is likely that the new economy resulted from the diffusion of outside ideas, rather than from a substantial change of population. In the same way, northwest Africa probably acquired domestic animals, wheat, and barley about the same time that the Sahara was also populated by nomadic pastoralists with herds of sheep and cattle.

All these peoples have been described as being in possession of a Neolithic economy: They owned livestock and sometimes cultivated plants, made pottery, and ground and polished their stone axes and other implements to produce tougher cutting edges. There is little or no substantial evidence of cultivation by the Saharan pastoralists before about 1100 BCE, when bullrush millet was being grown by the Neolithic peoples living in defended villages at the western edge of the Sahara along Mauritania's Dar Tichitt escarpment.

The Sahara at this time, as during most of the Upper Pleistocene, was a much more favorable place to live than today. Up to about 2000 BCE, the large Ethiopian game animals abounded and were regularly hunted, as is evidenced by the many different forms of arrowheads that occur in large numbers at desert sites. The grazing by lakes and swamps and in the wadis supported not only wild game but large herds of cattle besides. Cattle bones have been found dating from the middle of the sixth millennium BCE in the Acacus caves in the Saharan desert of southern Libya and from 2000 BCE in the Dar Tichitt. The people were mostly nomadic, living in easily transportable dwellings, probably made of mats or skins laid over a bent wood framework. Sometimes, as in the Tassili caves of Algeria - among the greatest storehouses of art in the world - these pastoral peoples are portrayed as blacks, at other times they are shown as Afro-Mediterraneans.

These Neolithic pastoralists spread throughout the Sahara, and it can be expected that they made contact with the hunting communities living in the savanna belt to the south, where much of the country was unsuitable for livestock because of the tsetse fly. Intradesert movement, evidenced by the wide distribution of certain traditions (for example, that of the dotted wavy line pottery motif), would also have led to the spread of knowledge of domestication. Since, however, the wheats and barleys are winter rainfall crops and do not do well in the tropics (other than on the high plateau of Ethiopia) except under irrigation, local cultigens had to be developed.

Although evidence for the stages of incipient agriculture south of the Sahara still has to be found and documented, it is clear from the stone tools that have been uncovered that there must have been from about 3000 BCE onward considerable experimentation. At first, this was random, but later, it was planned. Eventually, by hybridization and selection, indigenous wild prototypes were converted into staple West African and Ethiopian food crops. How long this took is unknown, but it was the essential basis for all large-scale settlement.

Dry rice in Guinea, sorghum and bullrush millet in the Sudan savanna belt, yams in the forests of West Africa, and the indigenous teff (a grain) and ensete (African banana) were cultivated similarly in the highlands of Ethiopia, as were also emmer wheat and barley, which presumably spread from the Upper Nile. Sites in northern Ethiopia and rock art depicting long-horned cattle suggest the likelihood that food production had spread to Ethiopia by at least the beginning of the second millennium BCE, if not appreciably earlier.

In the first millennium BCE, perhaps due ultimately to the desiccation of the Sahara and the consequent exodus of peoples, pastoralists appear in the Eastern African Rift with herds of sheep and cattle, introduced probably from the southern Sudan and Ethiopia. These herdsmen were long-headed Afro-Mediterraneans who buried their dead in communal graves under stone cairns or sometimes cremated them in caves. They had ground stone axes, made several different kinds of pottery, and used pestles and curious thick platters and bowls made of lava, probably for cooking food. They made a range of implements from obsidian, the black volcanic glass.

As their handiwork shows no obvious break with local tradition, nor do the physical remains of the people themselves suggest a new physical type, it seems likely that it was the economy rather than the population that changed, as in Libya and West Africa. Some of these early peoples may even have penetrated into the southwestern parts of the continent, where they introduced cattle and sheep.

Some of the large Bushmanoid peoples, including ancestors of the Hottentots now living there, were not slow to become pastoralists themselves.

The bushlands are yielding a unique record for the understanding of our human origins. The seemingly unchanging and limitless expanse of Africa's savanna lands would appear to have been the cradle of mankind, and it was here about 2 million years ago that the first technological advances were made that led to the complex civilizations of the twentieth century.

By 8000 BCE, the ethnic and linguistic maps of the continent as we know it began to take shape. Berbers occupied North Africa and the Sahara, and Ancient Egyptians the Nile Valley. Sudanese blacks lived in Nubia. Other blacks lived in the West African savanna, the Sahara, and the rain forests. Long-headed proto-Nilotes and proto-Kushites inhabited the drier parts of East Africa and the Horn. To the south in the savanna grasslands were the Bushman races, who spoke Bush and Hottentot languages; and small-statured black peoples occupied the equatorial forests.

Each had its individual cultural tradition and developed those skills and patterns of social and economic behavior that were dictated by the record of the past and the exigencies of the surroundings. So there emerged the naturalistic art of the Bushman hunters; the plastic art of the West African potter;

the simplistic, but highly symbolic, skills and craftsmanship of the artists in wood carving in the equatorial and West African forests; the self-sufficiency and knowledge of animal husbandry of the Berber peoples. Each was, in turn, affected by contact with peoples of different races and different traditions in other culture areas, and so the way was paved for the appearance of more complex civilizations in the more strategically situated and economically richer parts of the continent. These new civilizations and cultures were also influenced by external factors, but they were, nonetheless, essentially African, with their roots buried deep in the land of Africa.

2

CIVILIZATIONS
OF THE NILE
MARGARET SHINNIE

The advance from a life of food gathering and hunting to one of agriculture brought far-reaching changes to the people. Nomadic life, with its urgent search for food, was replaced by permanent agricultural communities and a greater sense of security. Villages gradually gave rise to towns and the organization of forms of government, and the reliability of seasonal crops and animal herding provided leisure time in which to practice all the arts and crafts, a noticeable feature of this stage of man's development.

Agriculture probably came to Egypt from western Asia, where it had been practiced since about 6000 BCE or possibly earlier. Although the Nile Valley is particularly well suited to agricultural pursuits, the earliest known farming settlements there date from as late as about 4500 BCE. By about the middle of the fourth century BCE, however, the Egyptians had become dependent on agriculture.

Once this advanced stage of life had been established in Egypt, more sophisticated social and cultural achievements rapidly followed, partly because farming was so unusually easy in the Nile Valley: Grain scattered on the silt deposited by the river's annual flood grew of its own accord and had only to be harvested. It has been calculated that by sensible exploitation of his land, an Egyptian farmer could produce three times as much grain as was needed for his domestic purposes. As a result, society could support craftsmen, officials, priests, and landowners. Another reason for Egypt's progress was that the Nile Valley, enclosed by infertile land, was slightly remote and easy to defend except in times of internal weakness. Lastly, because of its location, Egypt could share in the advances of the countries of the Levant, whose perpetual struggles with one another may well have given rise to technical achievements that they, involuntarily perhaps, placed at Egypt's disposal.

Although ancient Egypt seems separate from the rest of Africa, isolated in the narrow valley of the Nile and unique in its culture and achievements, there was nevertheless contact with other African peoples - with Libyans to the west and with Kushites and the inhabitants of Punt to the south and southeast. In the earliest days of Egyptian agriculture, the neighboring Sahara was not the arid expanse of desert that it later became. Climatically, there was a wet phase. The Saharan rock drawings make this clear, for the many animals portrayed, including cattle, would not be able to exist in the current environment. The people of the Sahara were not only pastoralists but also hunters, who must have hunted over land that was savanna. About 3000 BCE, the wet phase came to an end, and desiccation set in, accelerated perhaps by overgrazing as the aridity increased. It is not unlikely that the Saharan people learned the practice of animal herding and domestication from Egypt, and as the encroaching desert forced them to search farther and farther for better grazing lands, this knowledge was carried slowly to other areas by peoples whose identity is still something of a mystery. (In 1907, the remains of three previously unknown cultures were discovered in the region of Aswan; they were designated as A-, B-, and C-Group people.) The C-Group people, who moved into Nubia from the western desert about 2300 BCE, may have been one of the tribes forced southward; others may have gone toward the fertile banks of other great rivers. At Ntereso in northern (modern) Ghana, arrowheads of a type common among the Saharan people were found much farther south than had been earlier supposed.

Traces of the various peoples who lived in the Nile

Valley are prolific, and it is hardly possible to walk along the banks of the river without treading on antiquities - almost every part of the river's bank was inhabited at some time or other. For most of its course, the Nile flows through a valley made cultivable by the deposit of silt that the flood brings down from the Ethiopian highlands following the summer monsoon rains. In a year of heavy flood, enriched soil extends some way up the wadis, thus providing further areas for cultivation. Back of the valley lies the desert sand, and at various places, particularly in Upper Egypt and the northern Sudan, a barrier of rocky cliffs separates the flood plain and the desert. Proceeding south into the area of annual rains, the desert lands and the scrub and seasonal grazing lands of the central Sudan give way to wide savannas, and even farther south, near the headwaters, to tropical forest. There is a barrier to river travel in the south in the shape of a tangled mass of floating papyrus and aquatic grass, known as the sudd (meaning in Arabic "obstruction" or "dam"), which even today must be cleared if boats are to pass. It has always been possible to travel overland, however, though the terrain might seem uninviting for such a trek.

Although the Nile would appear to be a natural link between the lands and peoples along its banks, river travel south of Aswan is made difficult by a series of cataracts or, more properly, rapids. The First Cataract at Aswan and the five more cataracts in the Sudan are all unnavigable; even small boats have frequently met with disaster in their attempts to negotiate the currents. All these natural barriers probably impeded the Egyptians from penetrating as far south as they might otherwise have done, but they did have constant contact with Nubia (the lands along the Nile south of the First Cataract) and are known to have traveled as far as the Fifth Cataract.

The earliest agricultural settlements in the Nile Valley are those discovered in the Fayum in Middle Egypt. Here, on the edge of a lake, were village communities that grew wheat and barley - staples of their diet - and possibly herded livestock. Tools and weapons of stone and spear points of bone indicate that they engaged in hunting, which must have played a large part in their lives. They made simple, rough pottery for cooking and storage - useful rather than beautiful - the shapes patterned on leather bags and baskets familiar from times when there was no pottery. If there was a more rudimentary agriculture at an earlier time, evidence of it has either been buried deep in the Nile silt or eroded away by subsequent exploitation of the land for farming and grazing.

Later settlements, whose inhabitants had more sophisticated skills such as carving bone and ivory into spoons and combs, decorating pottery with painted designs, and grinding jars out of alabaster and basalt, have been discovered at various places, the best known being Merimde, Badari, and Naqada. Much of this work reveals a growing appreciation of artistic design and expression, and there must have been craftsmen with tools adequate to practice it. There is also evidence that trade with outside peoples was beginning, for copper objects and fragments of cedar and juniper wood (materials not indigenous to Egypt) suggest contact with other lands, probably by an overland route that presumably crossed Palestine to Syria and the more advanced cultures of western Asia. Arrowheads of a type found widely in the Sahara were also found at Merimde, so there must have been contacts with people to the west of Egypt as well. Malachite, used in the preparation of eye paint, may have come from Nubia or Sinai.

Much farther upstream, in and around Khartoum, hunting and fishing and food-gathering communities lived on the riverbank. Two sites that date from the fourth century BCE have been identified, similar in many ways to those of Egypt, but later by 1,000 years. Neither crop-growing nor animal-herding was practiced, though there is a possibility that at the later site, Shaheinab, the domestication of animals had just begun, as evidenced by the discovery of bones identified as those of a domesticated goat. Similarities in the stone tools of this village with some of those of the Fayum villages suggest contact between them, even though the Egyptian influence would have taken about 1,000 years to take hold in the Sudan.

Up till this point in time, 3500 BCE in Egypt and a little later in the Sudan, these small farming communities grew and developed their skills without much contact with the civilizations around them (particularly the more advanced cultures of Mesopotamia). Although agriculture presumably came to Egypt from western Asia, further influences are not apparent at this stage, despite some evidence that small trading activities were beginning. Another factor limiting the development of Egyptian technology was that many of the raw materials, such as hardwoods and metals, essential to the more advanced techniques of Mesopotamia, were not available in Egypt. Vague references in the later literature of early dynastic Egypt allow the inference that these small settlements were products of a social system essentially African in character, with a rainmaking god-king as leader. It was probably similar to practices that still survive in parts of southern Sudan, where the leader is invested with the power of bringing rain and is ritually killed when his powers begin to wane. (In Egypt, it was not so much the bringing of rain that was desired as the control of the Nile flood, which itself is dependent on rain far upstream.)

Physically, the Egyptians at this time were typical North Africans, lightly built, brown-skinned people. They were predominately of Afro-

Mediterranean type, though in Upper Egypt, skeletons of blacks have been found. (By pharaonic times, a mixing of peoples would take place, and the careful depiction in the tomb paintings of skin color, facial features, and kinds of hair make it clear that there were Afro-Mediterranean, Southwest Asian, and black types among them.) The people of early Khartoum were blacks, and they shared a distinctive custom of the modern southern Sudanese, that of extracting two incisor teeth. The custom is still observed today to signify manhood.

The next period, starting about 3400 BCE, was one of great development in Egypt; it contained all the fundamental advances that would lead to the brilliance of the Old Kingdom. The most impressive features almost certainly arose out of contacts with Mesopotamia and are well seen at the Nile settlements of Hierakonpolis, Naqada, and Gerza. While it had been possible earlier to make trading ventures by overland routes, the development of a seagoing ship was vital in encouraging and widening the scope of such activities. At this time, seaworthy ships capable of sailing the tideless Mediterranean Sea were probably first used; they were most likely built in a well-wooded area such as the Lebanon. Other innovations found at prehistoric sites included a distinctive wavy-handled pottery, which is related to similar ware from Palestine. Still other innovations came seemingly from Mesopotamian sources: for example, building with sun-dried mud bricks, thus making possible more substantial houses than the earlier light reed or matting huts; using cylinder seals as amulets to protect personal belongings; and, most important of all, developing a pictographic form of writing. Though Egyptian writing was entirely different from that of Mesopotamia, it may well have been inspired by the concept of literacy derived from that culture. Trade, however, was not all in one direction, and Egyptian wares found in Palestine testify to the passage of their goods into wider areas.

During this period, the first small states probably emerged in the Nile Valley (on the evidence of ruins found, it looks as though they fell into conflict.) Towns grew up and some of them were apparently fortified. Excavations at Naqada have revealed part of a town wall standing below the enveloping sand, and a little clay model found in a tomb shows a similar wall being guarded by soldiers. Rectangular-shaped townhouses were built of mud brick, though no doubt in the countryside the traditional reed or matting huts, usually approximately circular, persisted, as they still do today. Technological skills increased, and the working of flint reached a standard of perfection that has never been surpassed; the thinnest of knife blades were finished with regular ripple flaking, showing a mastery over material that is truly astonishing.

Toward the end of this period, about 3100 BCE, the coalescing of small towns gave rise to two main states: Lower Egypt, from the Mediterranean to the apex of the Delta; and Upper Egypt, from the south to the First Cataract. These became unified under the first pharaoh, Narmer, but the duality of two states continued down through Egyptian history. In times of internal dissension, the rivalry between Lower and Upper Egypt asserted itself until a powerful leader came to the fore with the ability to reunite the country. The pharaoh was known as Lord of the Two Lands, and his two-tiered crown expressed this duality, the white miter of Upper Egypt being superimposed on the red crown of Lower Egypt. Our conventional division of Egyptian history into dynasties is that given by the third-century BCE Greek historian Manetho, who also gives the names of royalty and some account of events occurring in the various reigns. The dynasties, in turn, are conveniently grouped into kingdoms: the Old Kingdom (2664-2155 BCE); the Middle Kingdom (2052-1786 BCE); and the New Kingdom (1570-1075 BCE). The periods between the kingdoms, called Intermediate Periods, were times of confusion and dissent, and it is in the three kingdoms that the mainstream of Egyptian history and culture developed.

Preceding the Old Kingdom was a time known as the Archaic Period, which was one of great development in many fields, and Narmer was the first known king of this period. His monuments have been found at Hierakonpolis, Abydos, and in the robbed tombs at Saqqara near Memphis. He also built a city called White Walls (later Memphis) as his residence; it was to become one of the great cities of ancient Egypt. Throughout the Archaic Period, trade with the Levant increased. Wood, in particular, was imported and employed in building. Another major import was copper, turned to new uses for making tools, vessels, and even statues. Expeditions penetrated far south, and a rock-cut inscription of the First Dynasty pharaoh Djer near the Second Cataract in Nubia records an invasion and conquest of local tribes, though it may be a rather boastful description of a successful raid. Technical skills increased, and building became more magnificent, large stone blocks being hewn for funerary monuments and temples. In the making of smaller scaled artifacts, craftsmen became more competent, not only at making jars and ornaments but also statues from various kinds of stone. The potter's wheel was introduced and ceramic styles became more varied. Most important of all, however, was the use of writing and the manufacture of a kind of paper from the papyrus reed, so that records could be kept, instructions sent, and all the business of state noted down.

During this time, foundations were laid for the role of the king, the pharaoh of Egypt, as a divine god-king who embodied the spirit of ancient Egypt. Originally, simply the most powerful among regional leaders, he became associated with divine functions, in particular, the control of the Nile flood, which meant life to the country. (The powers of the Nineteenth Dynasty pharaoh Ramses II were thought to be so great in this respect that he was credited with the ability to affect rainfall in the far country of the Hittites.) A well-known stone plaque, the Palette of Narmer, found at Hierakonpolis, shows the contemporary view of the pharaoh: the typical stance, huge in proportion to the other figures in the picture, smiting his enemy before the hawk-god Horus, and treading on two captives beneath his feet. Even at this early time, the extraordinary power of the pharaoh was evident.

The seeds sown during the Archaic Period came into full flower in the Old Kingdom. An impression of peaceful development, together with a broadening of trading activity, is conveyed. Royal burial customs became elaborate, as illustrated by the Great Pyramids of Giza (about 2600 BCE). Organizing a sufficient labor force, and conceiving and carrying out the architectural plans, testify to the prosperity and order of the country and to the divine omnipotence of the pharaoh, who could command such resources for his personal use.

From the pyramids and from temple reliefs and wall paintings much can be inferred of religious beliefs. For example, the tomb structure - be it pyramid for the royal or rich, or brick-lined grave for the poor - was seen as a house to live in forever, where objects serviceable or precious in life were placed with the dead for use in the afterlife. Gods other than the pharaoh appear in the reliefs, most commonly Hathor, protectress of the City of the Dead, and Osiris, god of the dead, and the pantheon became established. Much of the artistic endeavor of the time must have been devoted to funerary building, and wall paintings and reliefs on tombs and temples show aspects of daily life, of the running of the country estate and country crafts, amusements, and even the arrival of the tax collector. Statues were also placed in tombs; they were carved of wood or limestone and often painted, and many appear to be realistic portraits, for physical defects are not disguised, and there is little suggestion of flattery.

Trading activities were more venturesome, and expeditions were sent to Kush (the Egyptian name for Nubia), to Punt, probably along the coast of the Gulf of Aden, and into the Levant. Egyptian penetration into Palestine is revealed in tomb reliefs, which show Asian fortresses being stormed. At Byblos in the Lebanon, a temple was built by the Egyptians as early as the Fourth Dynasty, about 2600 BCE, perhaps for a local community of their people, implying peaceful contact with this great trading center.

Nubia was invaded on several occasions, and early in the Fourth Dynasty, the Pharaoh Snefru launched an invasion that cost the Nubians 7,000 prisoners and 200,000 head of cattle. It subdued the local population for some time to come. The wealth of the country was exploited, particularly gold, and at Buhen, near the Second Cataract, an Egyptian settlement was established that was in effect a trading post, and at which copper smelting was carried on. Nubia had been settled by a population archeologists call the A-Group people for lack of more information. Such evidence as there is suggests an appreciable increase in the population of Nubia in the third century BCE due to settlement by the A-Group people, who may have drifted in from Egypt or from Saharan areas. Physically, they were similar to Egyptians, and their culture was much like that of predynastic Egypt, based on small agricultural communities. They were probably not subject to a central authority, though each community would have had its leader.

The basis of Egyptian interest in this land was trade, and Mernera, a pharaoh of the Sixth Dynasty, sent four peaceful expeditions into Nubia, led by a nobleman named Harkhuf, that were of a more ambitious nature than before. The purpose was to open up communications with a country called Yam, whose exact geographical location is uncertain, though it must have been south of the Second Cataract. Harkhuf's fourth journey took place in the time of Pepi II, then a young ruler, who was delighted with the offer of a Pygmy. He wrote to Harkhuf, giving instructions for the care of the Pygmy on the journey northward and adding: "My Majesty desires to see this Pygmy more than all the gifts of Sinai and Punt." All control of Kush was lost, however, during the period of anarchy that followed the Old Kingdom, and the Egyptians withdrew into their homeland.

Up to the Fourth Dynasty, power and government had been centralized in the pharaoh, aided by officials whom he chose and to whom he delegated various responsibilities. During the Fourth Dynasty, the post of provincial governor and some local offices came to be accepted as hereditary, and the holders of these positions were conscious of their power. It needed only an old or a weak pharaoh for the whole structure of government to collapse under the jealous ambitions of an anarchic elite. This situation caused the downfall of the Old Kingdom. At the death of Pepi II, an old man, reputedly a centenarian, who had ruled for many decades, a formidable blow was dealt to the achievements of the Old Kingdom. A vivid account is given in *The Admonitions of the Prophet Ipuwer:* "Behold, they that had clothes are now in rags. . . . Squalor is throughout the land: no clothes are white these days. . . . The Nile is in flood yet no one has the heart to plow. . . . Corn has perished everywhere. . . . Men do not sail to Byblos today: What shall we do for fine wood. . . . Laughter has perished. Grief walks the land, mingled with lamentation."

All the artistic achievement of the Old Kingdom withered, and much of the work of craftsmen ceased to be practiced except in poor and debased forms. Various leaders made unsuccessful attempts to restore peace and order. Finally, a powerful family from Herakleopolis managed to unite Middle Egypt and also bring the Delta under its control. However, Upper Egypt seems to have maintained virtual independence, ruled by the Theban princes. (Thebes was the most important city in that area and the capital of Upper Egypt in times of disunity.) The Herakleopolitans (Ninth and Tenth Dynasties) made an impressive attempt to restore order out of chaos, expelling numbers of Asian and Libyan settlers from the land around the Delta, fortifying their northeastern frontier, reopening trade with Byblos, and re-establishing Memphis as the capital city. Nevertheless, there was sporadic warfare with the Thebans throughout this time, fortune favoring first one side and then the other. After a decisive battle in about 2061 BCE, the Thebans defeated the people of Herakleopolis, and Mentuhotep I became pharaoh of a reunited Egypt. This marks the birth of the Middle Kingdom.

During the time of conflict, a secular literature grew, in which appeals were made to the peoples' feelings by means of artistic expression. At a time when the divine guidance of the pharaoh was lacking, this had a particular relevance. Elegant and poetic as it was, much of the writing was inspired by a deep pessimism, an expression of the tremendous misfortune that had befallen a land bereft of its god-king. Titles such as "An Argument between a Man Contemplating Suicide and his Soul" or "The Complaints of the Peasant" give a hint of the sense of depression experienced. "The Instructions for His Son, Mery-ka-re," thought to have been written by one of the Herakleopolitan kings, is concerned with promoting a code of conduct based on moral principles. "Do right," he says, "as long as you are on earth. Calm the afflicted, oppress no widow. . . . Do not kill; but punish with beatings and imprisonment. . . . Leave vengeance to God. . . . More acceptable to Him is the virtue of one who is upright of heart than the ox of the wrongdoer. . . ." But another piece of advice praises the art of speaking, "for power is in the tongue, and speech is mightier than fighting."

The Middle Kingdom was a period of further expansion and development in all fields of activity. It was nor entirely peaceful, for a bout of anarchy intervened before long and abated only when Amenemhet, who had been a governor of the South, claimed the throne as first pharaoh of the powerful Twelfth Dynasty. A prophecy attributed to the time of Pharaoh Snefru had forewarned that a period of disaster in Egypt would come to an end only "when a king shall come from the South called Ameny" but this prediction was contained in a papyrus of Twelfth Dynasty date and is more likely to be a piece of royal propaganda aimed at supporting Amenemhet's ambitions.

About this time, a determined effort was made to subdue Kush. A series of remarkable forts was built to control the river passage and quell any insurrection by the local population. The southernmost of these was at Semna, above the Second Cataract; some were built on the eminences along the banks of the river and some on islands in it. The fortifications were strategically placed so that should any be attacked, it could call for help by signaling with a beacon to its neighbors. They served as trading posts as well as military garrisons, for the purpose of Egyptian excursions into Kush was as much for trade as to secure the southern frontier of Egypt. An inscription of a governor of Middle Egypt says that he followed his lord when he sailed south to overthrow his enemies: "I passed through Kush in sailing southward and reached the borders of the earth. I brought back tribute. . . . Then His Majesty returned in safety having overthrown his enemies in Kush, the vile." Efforts to subdue Kush reached their peak in the time of Sesostris III (1878-1843 BCE), who rebuilt where necessary and consolidated the line of forts, and whose connection with the area was so close that he was later worshiped as a local god.

The people of Kush at this time were the earlier mentioned C-Group people, a cattle-owning people living in small communities. Although their culture was dissimilar from that of contemporary Egypt, it had, nevertheless, affinities with the pastoral civilizations of late predynastic Egypt, including a distinctive pottery, much of it black with incised geometric designs, by which their settlements are easily recognized. Their animals were of such importance to them that they sometimes buried the skulls of cattle around their own graves and scratched pictures of them on pots. The C-Group were a non-black people, and their settlements and cemeteries have been found from Kubanieh near the First Cataract to as far south as the area of the Third Cataract. One concludes from the number of fortresses built that they were extremely troublesome to the Egyptian forces occupying their land. In an inscription at the fortress of Semna, Sesostris III instructed his men "to prevent any Nubian from passing downstream or overland or by boat, [also] any herds of Nubians, apart from any Nubian who shall come to trade at Iken or upon any good business that may be done with them." (Iken was the name of the fortress at the Second Cataract.) Even their most trivial movements were reported back to Egypt, and the almost daily accounts end with, "All the affairs of the king's domain are safe and sound."

At about the same time, around 1900 BCE, a trading

post was set up at Kerma in the neighborhood of the Third Cataract, but whether by the Egyptians or by the local people is not known, though it was certainly a native entrepôt. The remains of the material culture found there are entirely different from that of the contemporary C-Group people. A spectacular burial mound revealed the interment of an important chief with the accompanying sacrifice of over 300 others, mostly women and children. The pottery of Kerma, a fine, highly polished, black-topped red ware, was unique, as were the little ivory and mica figures of birds and animals, which seem to have been used decoratively, the former as inlay for furniture, and the latter attached to leather caps. In the rooms around the trading post were found a variety of raw materials together with manufactured objects, including fragments of Sixth Dynasty alabaster jars, which had no doubt gone out of fashion in Egypt and were foisted off on the natives of Kush in trade. Various Egyptian statues, including one of the Lady Senuwy, wife of Hepzefa, a governor-general of Kush and prince of Asyut, and a fragment of a statue of Hepzefa himself, were discovered; these had probably also been passed in trade.

While the southern border of Egypt had been secured to some extent by deliberate expansion and subjugation of the native population, the northeastern border, which was frequently crossed by Asians, had still to be strengthened. To this end, a series of fortified positions, named the Walls of the Prince, was set up along the frontier; but there was no attempt to conquer land or peoples, merely to define the frontier and protect it. Egypt's main interest in Palestine and Syria was undoubtedly a commercial one, though there are evidences of occasional wars; there was, however, much interchange of products of countries in the eastern Mediterranean, including Crete, most of which was conducted through an entrepôt city, such as Byblos.

After the death in 1797 BCE of Amenemhet III, the last great ruler of the Middle Kingdom, the strength and prosperity of Egypt declined. After about 1785 BCE, a number of Asian names appear in the king lists, and evidently by about 1750 BCE, an Asian people, the Hyksos, had established a principality at Avaris in the eastern Delta. Hyksos control spread over Egypt, and Memphis, the capital city, was seized. Egyptians continued to rule Upper Egypt from Thebes, paying tribute to the Hyksos and holding an uneasy independence only as far north as Asyut. The Theban rulers had apparently also lost their hegemony to the south of Aswan, the land being ruled by a prince of Kush, probably from Kerma. His people had stormed and destroyed that great system of fortresses guarding the First and Second Cataracts and had evidently made an alliance with the Hyksos. Kamose, "a mighty king in Thebes," writes: "I should like to know what serves this strength of mine, when a chieftain is in Avaris, and another in Kush, and I sit united with an Asiatic and a Nubian each man in possession of his slice of this Egypt, and I cannot pass by him as far as Memphis."

Kamose decided to deliver Egypt from Asian power and set out to crush the Hyksos, along the way meting out ruthless destruction to the towns that had "forsaken Egypt, their mistress." He also captured a messenger traveling southward to the chieftain of Kush. The letter he was carrying from Apopi, the chieftain of Avaris, makes clear the alliance between the two: "Why have you arisen as chieftain without letting me know? Have you [not] beheld what Egypt has done against me, the Chieftain who is in it, Kamose the Mighty, ousting me from my soil . . . come, fare north at once, do not be timid. . . . Then will we divide the towns of this Egypt between us."

Kamose did not live to see the final destruction of Hyksos's rule. His younger brother, Ahmose, carried on the war, eventually bringing about the fall of Avaris and the expulsion of the Asian invaders. He also killed the king of Kush, thereby regaining control of Upper Egypt. By about 1570 BCE, through these successes, Egypt had regained its strength and Ahmose I became the founder of the Eighteenth Dynasty and the New Kingdom - in many ways the most glorious period of Egyptian history. The result of the Hyksos invasion was not a total loss to

Egypt in that new ideas and techniques had come with it, among the most important of which was the horse-drawn chariot. The Thebans adopted not only the chariot but the Hyksos designs in armor and weapons in clashes with the enemy.

Ahmose I set to work to re-establish his kingdom and secure it from further invasion. The subduing of the states of the Levant as far as the Euphrates was to continue under his successors. The states of Palestine and Syria were formed into dependencies through treaties with the rulers, whose sons were removed to Egypt as hostages for guarantee of good behavior. On the whole, this was a policy of indirect rule rather than one of colonization, and it was quite different from the treatment meted out to Kush.

Once again in power, the pharaohs waxed supreme and complacent. By 1370 BCE, however, the Hittites of the Anatolian plateau had become strong enough to present a direct challenge to Egypt. No effective answer was given, and Akhenaten, a somewhat eccentric pharaoh who was on the throne at the time, was entirely abstracted by his new religious ideas, which were apparently monotheistic. As a result, Egyptian influence in Syria waned.

Early in the twelfth century BCE, masses of peoples, known in Egyptian texts as the Peoples of the Sea, migrated through the Levant in search of land; they spread destruction wherever they passed, causing further loss of Egyptian power and prestige. Though Egypt did manage to protect its own borders, all its possessions to the northeast had to be sacrificed. Egypt remained a conservative element in the fast-developing world of the Mediterranean. Throughout the New Kingdom, the power of the pharaoh was identified with military conquest and the preservation of Egypt's borders, a concept that could not be satisfied once strong enemies and new iron weapons successfully challenged its supremacy.

On the western borders of Egypt, the Libyans became troublesome, and on more than one occasion attempted to settle on the rich Delta lands. Driven out of their territory by the incursions of Sea Peoples, and possibly also by increasing aridity of their own lands, the Libyans were so harried that they were difficult to repel. Even after Pharaoh Ramses III of the Twentieth Dynasty crushed them finally, parties of Libyans still infiltrated Egypt. Many became mercenaries in the army, later forming a special military caste that grew strong enough to provide two dynasties among the rulers of Egypt.

The abundance of archeological discoveries from the New Kingdom makes its civilization seem very real - even the shrunken forms of dead kings can be seen, their names known, their possessions studied. The splendor of the tomb of Tutankhamon - rich in alabaster, gold, and precious ornaments - gives an idea of the luxury and art of the period, as do the fine temples and sculpture. This was a time of massive architecture and colossal statues, much of which still stand as testimony to the power of the pharaoh. But the basic wealth of Egypt was in agriculture, and the tomb paintings frequently depict agricultural pursuits. The wealthy occupant of the tomb is shown inspecting his fields, vineyards, and gardens. But there were also fishing trips and wild fowl hunts or picnics and entertainments in his house, accompanied by his servants and slaves or on appropriate occasions by his family. The gulf that separated the rich from the poor, the landlord from the peasant, is clear.

After the Twentieth Dynasty, about 1075 BCE, Egypt again fell into lawlessness and decay. Over the centuries, Libyans, Kushites, Persians, Greeks, and Romans dominated, each group holding power for as long as it could. The Libyans formed the Twenty-second and the Twenty-third Dynasties. Having been soldiers in the army, they set up a military dictatorship; but it ended in dissension and instability, to be succeeded in time by a line of Kushite kings.

The pharaohs of the New Kingdom had brought Kush under direct government control. The territory was put into the charge of a governor, "King's Son of Kush," residing probably at modern Amarna, a town on the east bank of the Nile well above the Second Cataract. He was appointed by the pharaoh and was directly responsible to him. The frontier was extended beyond the area of the Middle Kingdom forts to a point south of the Fourth Cataract. Towns and temples and military garrisons were established, and the names of many of the rulers are to be found carved on temple walls and columns in the land of Kush. Frequent raids by Egyptian forces were needed to keep the population under control, both the riverain people, with whom they were mainly in contact, and the desert tribesmen, who never became imbued with Egyptian influences. In time, the riverain Kushites became completely Egyptianized, adopting Egyptian religious practices and becoming part of the land of the pharaohs. Kush supplied many products that added greatly to the wealth and luxury of Egypt, in particular, gold, ebony, ivory, cattle, and slaves.

Under the New Kingdom, Kush prospered and became culturally and economically part of Egypt, their people serving in the army and government. Many Egyptian priests, traders, and officials settled in Kush and gave the Kushites a lasting flavor of their culture. At Jebel Barkal, a religious center devoted to Egyptian theological beliefs was probably controlled by an Egyptian priesthood.

But by the end of the Twenty-second Dynasty, profiting from the weakness that had overcome Egypt, Kush became effectively independent, although maintaining its traditions and orthodoxy. Napata, on the east bank of the Nile just downstream from the Fourth Cataract, was the great city of Kushite-Egyptian culture and became the capital of the independent state of Kush. About 750 BCE, a Kushite king, Kashta, felt himself powerful enough to gain control of Upper Egypt, and his son Piankhi (751–716 BCE) completed the conquest of the country, though this was not accomplished lightly and the Kushite armies had to penetrate Egypt on more than one occasion to achieve their objective. Piankhi made the mistake of withdrawing to Napata, having, as he thought, subdued the Egyptian princes. As a result, it was left to his brother and successor, Shabako (707-696 BCE), to establish power over the whole of Egypt and assert Kushite administration. Shabako became known throughout the ancient world as King of Kush and Misr (Egypt), and he and his successors formed the Twenty-fifth Dynasty.

The Kushite kings, imbued with an orthodox, slightly old-fashioned view of Egyptian life, a reflection of their remoteness from the sources of their adopted culture, were probably welcomed by some in Egypt: by the Theban priests, who saw the possibility of re-establishing their own power under the piety of the conquerors; by those who foresaw a return to the good old days of law and order under the traditionalist usurpers. Indeed, the Kushite kings proved themselves to be pharaohs in the old manner, larger-than-life majesties, who left a fine record, both in Egypt and in Kush. They, too, were responsible for temples, colossal statues, inscriptions in Egyptian hieroglyphs - extremely valuable in relating the events of the period - and they were able to establish a measure of law and order that gained them the respect of other rulers.

In time, the Assyrians replaced the Hittites as the dominant power in western Asia. In the reign of Pharaoh Taharqa, in 671 BCE, the Assyrians descended on Egypt. The king was forced to retreat to Thebes from the residence he had established at Tanis (Avaris) in the Delta. A second invasion in the reign of Taharqa's successor, Tanwetamani (664 653 BCE), drove the pharaoh out of Egypt and back to his own domains. The descendants of these Kushite kings were to rule in their own land for nearly 1,000 years, maintaining a state with its own complex culture.

The Kushite capital was moved from Napata to Meroë, located above the Atbara River, probably in the sixth century BCE, perhaps because of the sack in 591 BCE of Napata by the Greek mercenaries of an Egyptian pharaoh, Psammetik II. An equally likely reason for the move was the fact that Meroë lies in an area of annual rainfall (approximately 4 inches), and grazing for the huge herds of Kushite cattle was more certain.

The Greeks called the Kushites "Ethiopians," which

means "burnt faces," implying a darker skin color than that to which they were accustomed. The term does not denote any connection with the modern state of Ethiopia. The Kushites were probably much like modern Sudanese, a varying mixture of the light brown-skinned people of North Africa and the blacker people from farther south. In Egyptian tomb paintings, they are always shown as darker than the Egyptians themselves. Kushite art, too, makes it clear that there was a difference; the royal ladies of Kush are shown as markedly plump women, and both male and female portrait subjects often are characterized by tightly curled black hair. The culture of Kush, though always overlaid with characteristic Egyptian influences, became more individual after the removal of the capital to Meroë, partly because links with Egypt were more tenuous and partly because lively and more essentially African influences were at work. At one time, the Kushites were literate to some extent in Egyptian language and hieroglyphs (though this may have been the prerogative of the priesthood only), but lack of close contact with Egypt caused this skill to decline. The shapes of signs were altered and sometimes given different phonetic values, and finally, a new script was developed. While the phonetic values of the new signs are known, they express a language that cannot as yet be interpreted. Except when Meroë is mentioned in the writings of other peoples, knowledge of its culture has to be inferred from material remains.

Many standing monuments of the Kushites can be seen today: the ruins of the city of Meroë; the pyramids where members of the royal family were buried both near Napata and near Meroë; temples; reservoirs for catching water during the rainy season. The greatest concentration of monuments is in the "Island of Meroë," not actually an island but the stretch of country between the Nile and Atbarah rivers that was the heartland of the state. Southwest of Meroë is the famous site at Musawwarat-es-Sufra - a complex of temples built, altered, and rebuilt over a period of 1,000 years. It is a most spectacular place, where temples, once plastered with sparkling white gypsum, were set in a small plain surrounded by black hills, and it is thought to have been a place of pilgrimage, for there were no dwellings other than a single house, presumably that of a priest.

Objects found in Meroitic pyramid tombs show the influences of pharaonic and Hellenistic Egypt, but also, especially in the pottery, the spirit of Africa. In the Egyptian fashion, objects both, precious and useful were placed in the graves: gold and enameled jewelry, beads of all kinds, glass, silver and bronze vessels, bells that were buckled to the necks of cattle, both decorated and plain pottery, quivers, arrowheads, spears, bronze and silver lamps, wooden and ivory boxes, furniture, wrappings of cotton cloth, and scatters of animal bones indicating the sacrifice of cattle and horses. The royal pyramid tombs, the majority looted before archeological excavation, must have been rich in these objects. The mound graves of the common people, with a burial chamber cut deep into the ground, offered up pottery, beads of stone and glass, traces of basketware and fragments of cloth, a hunter's favorite weapon, or a child's toy. In the royal tombs, many of the objects were ones that had been imported from Egypt and are some indication of the wealth of the royal personages and of the continuing trade with Hellenistic and Roman Egypt. But the presence of local ware also expresses their appreciation of their own, less sophisticated products, including their beautiful decorated pottery, both that showing Mediterranean influences and that more typically African - such as can be found in many parts of the continent still today.

Little is known of the social organization of Kush in Meroitic times. However, it is clear that royalty was revered, probably as divine beings as in Egypt. Also, there was possibly an elite priesthood, again in the tradition of Egypt. The importance of the royal ladies, as evidenced by temple reliefs and by reference to Candace, queen of the Ethiopians, in the Acts of the Apostles ("Candace" is a Meroitic word meaning "queen" or "queen mother"), suggests that it may have been a matrilineal society; in that case, succession to the throne would have been through the female line, a not uncommon African practice. As in Egypt, there may also have been brother-sister marriages, though it is more likely that they were marriages of cousins, an arrangement still considered desirable in many parts of Africa today. Indeed, cousins are referred to and thought of as brothers and sisters in some African societies. Religion was obviously an important part of life, as shown by the devoted work, both architectural and artistic, in temples; they were all built of hewn sandstone blocks in contrast to the sun-dried brick dwellings, royal or common.

The greatest achievement of Meroë, however, was the practice of ironworking. Iron was first introduced into Egypt perhaps by Greeks who had settled there or perhaps by the Assyrians, who used iron weapons in war. The Kushites seem to be the first people of sub-Saharan Africa to have used iron, starting perhaps about 500 BCE, though this may be due simply to the accident of where excavation and study have taken place. The Kushites were fortunate in having iron-bearing sandstone in their hills and the wood for charcoal with which to smelt it. So precious was this metal reckoned that an iron spearhead, wrapped in gold foil, was buried in the tomb of King Taharqa. Mounds of iron slag abound at Meroë, and smelting as well as forging were practiced on a fairly large scale. Whether this knowledge passed from Meroë to other parts of Africa, as has often been argued, cannot yet be established.

Apart from raiding bands of desert dwellers, Kush was left largely alone and grew into a state that stretched from the borders of Egypt between the First and Second Cataracts to at least as far south as Sennar in the modern Sudan. Meanwhile, Egypt had fallen prey to yet another invader. The Persian conquest of Egypt in 525 BCE, when Cambyses defeated Psammetik III, hardly affected Kush, though the Persians made an unsuccessful attempt to invade the country.

Subsequently, the Greeks, led by Alexander the Great, occupied Egypt in 332 BCE. The Greeks were not strangers in Egypt, their forebears having lived and worked there for some centuries as merchants and soldiers, and having been allowed to establish a trading center of their own at Naukratis in the Delta. Ptolemy, one of their victorious generals, was left in charge of Egypt. When the Greek Empire broke up at Alexander's death, Ptolemy became the ruler of an independent kingdom. Attempts at peaceful integration were made: The Greeks worshiped Egyptian gods, and upper-class Egyptians learned Greek. But the peasant population was oppressed and resentful at having to hand over to the foreign ruler half their produce as rent for their land. The ruling dynasty of the Ptolemies encouraged trading ventures, setting up new ports on the Red

Sea coast and extending trade toward the east. (Ptolemy II completed the last link in a series of canals reaching from the Nile to the Red Sea.) They introduced currency into Egypt, where barter had been the common practice, and Alexandria, said to have been planned and laid out by Alexander himself, became a center of learning and crafts, among the greatest in the ancient world.

During the period of Hellenistic power in Egypt, Kush appears to have enjoyed particular prosperity. The Kushites maintained friendly relations with the Greeks, and one of the Kushite kings, Arkamani (about 218-200 BCE), called Ergamenes by the Greeks, is said to have acquired a smattering of Greek learning. He is known to have joined Ptolemy IV in some temple building; the number of buildings erected in Kush and the luxury of the objects found in the royal tombs illustrate the degree of security known. Somewhat later, Netekamani and his queen, Amantari, also built extensively, including two temples at Naqa, a town some distance from the Nile. The first structure, the Lion Temple, shows Apedemek, an indigenous lion god or god of war, who, on this occasion at least, had three heads and four arms, causing speculation about possible contacts with India. (A number of local gods had been added to the Egyptian pantheon some time after the capital was moved to Meroë. Whether they were of long standing or not is unknown.) By contrast, the second temple, known as the Kiosk, is strikingly Roman in style, and though decorated with Egyptian symbols, it seems strange so far south in Africa.

Roman occupation at the death of Cleopatra in 30 BCE brought no relief to the discontented peasantry of Egypt. Their country became merely a province of the Roman Empire, exploited for its grain supplies and paying taxes to the colonial governors. The middle classes became poor, and the poor, destitute. It was not surprising that Alexandria's intellectuals and malcontents began to look at the teachings of a new religion. By CE 330, when Christianity was the religion of the Roman Empire and the Christian capital was Constantinople, not Rome, most of Egypt had already been converted, and Alexandria had already been a great center of Eastern Christianity for almost 200 years. Later, at the Council of Chalcedon in CE 451, the patriarch of Alexandria declined to subscribe to the orthodox doctrine. The Church was divided over doctrinal issues, and Egypt became more secluded from its neighbors, its indigenous Coptic Church no longer a participant in the mainstream of the Christian world. Kush, too, became more remote as its contacts with the northern neighbors declined. Further, it was harried by desert tribesmen and by a new power to the southeast, Axum, whose strength was already being felt.

To explain the rise of Axum, one must go back

to 700 BCE, when bands of immigrants from the Yemen began to cross the Red Sea and settle among the people of the Ethiopian highlands. They mixed with the local population, and there is no evidence that they did so violently; their impact seems to have been cultural. They were sophisticated farmers who understood terracing and the intricacies of irrigation and employed such tools as the plow. They spoke a Semitic language, Sabean, and inscriptions in Sabean characters have been found, though there are enough departures from the language used in Saba (Sheba), to show its local development. The earliest inscriptions and monuments so far discovered date from about 500 BCE. By the third or second century BCE, one group of them, the Habashat (from which came the later name Abyssinia), established a strong kingdom with its capital at Axum and developed their own language, Ge'ez. This was one of the Ethiopian kingdoms that grew out of the synthesis of Yemenite and local endeavor. There is not much information about its early days, yet we know that their religion was analogous with that of southern Arabia: worship of the divinities Astar, Mahrem, and Beher, the divine symbol being a disc resting on a crescent, the Sabean moon god's symbol.

When the Ptolemies began to extend their trade empire, the Axumite state became of immediate importance, being well placed to take advantage of the new commercial development. Its main port was Adulis. The Ptolemies wanted to acquire elephants for war purposes, and among other trade goods were rhinoceros horn, tortoise shell, and the various perfumes, incense, and spices for which this area had been famous as the probable Land of Punt to which Hatshepsut sent ships. Much of this trading activity was in the hands of Greeks, and Greek became the language of commerce and diplomacy in Axum. Greek and Jewish traders from the Levant settled there from about the first century CE, and later, inscriptions on coins and monuments were in Greek. By the fifth century CE, the state of Axum had probably become the main trading center for the Mediterranean-Indian Ocean routes. It may have been the Greeks who first brought Christianity to Axum; sometime in the fourth century, it had become the official religion of the country, as it still is, being retained with great tenacity in the fastnesses of Ethiopia.

The culture of Axum was largely south Arabian in character, modified by local tradition, but uninfluenced by contacts with Egypt or Meroë. The buildings of Axum, of which there are remnants visible today, were characterized by stepped walls. Stone thrones or their pedestals, column bases and capitals, and fragments of columns, all testify to architectural achievement. Most impressive of all are the tall steles, some sixty feet high, which recreate in stone many-storied wooden buildings typical of Axumite architecture; these were probably funerary monuments.

Ambition led the rulers of Axum to extend the boundaries of their new kingdom and to regain the land of their ancestors. About the first century BCE, their agents are found in the Yemen, making alliances with various tribes in an attempt to regain control in southern Arabia, though it is not clear whether they achieved a position of direct rule there. At later times, invasions were made culminating in that of King Afilas toward the end of the third century CE. The Axumites also sought to subdue their immediate neighbors and claimed to have taken their power to the borders of Egypt by the third century CE.

An inscription found on a stele of one Axumite king, Ezana, relates that about CE 350, he and his army invaded the kingdom of Kush, which had been a source of perpetual annoyance to him. He burned and destroyed their cities, "both those built of bricks and those built of reeds," causing as much devastation as possible and chasing the Kushites for twenty-three days. The nomads, called the Red and the Black Noba according to Ezana, had been particularly troublesome, interfering with his officials and messengers and fighting among themselves, which they had promised not to do. "Twice and thrice they had broken their solemn oaths," Ezana says. So, he claims, he attacked and scattered them also. This may be an overboastful account of the event, especially as recent excavations at Meroë show no sign, so far, of sudden destruction or burning; but, equally, there is no doubt that the power of Kush waned at about this time, and it was no longer a viable kingdom.

Once Meroë had ceased to be a power, wandering bands of tribesmen, the Noba and the Blemmyes, both from the desert areas beyond the Nile, mingled with the Kushites and assimilated their culture. From Roman accounts, they seem to have been a rather intractable people, and at a time when Egypt was already virtually a Christian country, they won special dispensation from the Romans to worship the Egyptian goddess Isis at the temple at Philae, the last remnant of pharaonic religion in the Nile Valley.

Rich tombs of their rulers at Ballana and Qustul in Egyptian Nubia were filled with amazing objects showing a strong flavor of pharaonic culture allied to Byzantine splendor: jewel-studded crowns of Byzantine style, decorated with pharaonic religious symbols such as the uraeus, or sacred serpent, the ram's head and plumes of Amon, the eye of Horus; iron furniture and inlaid wooden boxes, bronze vessels and hanging lamps, vessels of silver and glass, elaborate and beautiful horse trappings, pottery, linen shrouds, and fragments of rugs on which the dead had rested. Many were luxury imports from Egypt; indeed, the decoration of a cross on some of them implies their manufacture at Byzantine hands. To accompany him in death, the king's retinue, his queen, slaves, and guards, his dogs and horses, were sacrificed with him. This was not an Egyptian or Meroitic custom in which the necessity of providing servants for the afterlife had been circumvented by placing in the tomb little figures called *shawabtis,* which were thought to come to life to perform their services. The people of Ballana and Qustul, known to archeologists as the X-Group, had acquired a marked overlay of Egyptian-Meroitic culture, but certainly retained features of their own culture. Eventually, they and the peoples of the Sudan as far south as modern Khartoum became Christian under the teachings of the Byzantine Church.

Egypt made little attempt to influence other parts of Africa beyond Kush; rather, it held them at arm's length, concentrating all its effort in its own domain. Whether this was equally true of Kush cannot yet be seen. Except at Axum, where three undoubtedly Meroitic bronze bowls were found, and in the kingdom of Darfur in the western Sudan, where a Meroitic stone thumb ring is thought to have been found, almost nothing of certain Egyptian or Sudanese origin has so far been discovered in any other part of Africa. (A single faience bead in the Coryndon Museum in Nairobi could be Egyptian, but it is of doubtful provenance.)

As yet, there is little archeological evidence for the passage of ideas, either for their actual conveyance or for the direction in which they flowed. The Nile Valley may have sent knowledge of agricultural and metallurgical techniques upstream and out across the deserts and savannas, or they may equally well have been independent inventions elsewhere.

It is not known when agriculture started in West Africa, for example, either in the Sudanic belt or in the forest areas to the south. Agricultural techniques were transmitted slowly - it appears to have taken about 1,000 years for the practices in use in the Fayum to reach Shaheinab. Moreover, the crops which grew well in Egypt - wheat and barley - were not suited to climates farther south, so that different grains, mostly sorghum and other millets, had to be cultivated, and these are still the main crops of the Sudanic belt. Farther south in West Africa, yam cultivation took the place of grain, calling for different tools and techniques, and there, particularly, agriculture may have been a separate invention; but because it leaves no traces - no grains, no bins, no grinding stones - knowledge of when it started may never be discovered.

Information about events and human development west of the Nile is much more limited, partly because the societies there were illiterate and partly because less investigation has been undertaken. Such cultural traits as are common between the

Nile civilizations and those to the west of them may be a product of common African thought, as divine kingship for example, or may have been transmitted by the Saharan peoples over a long period of time. Although it has frequently been suggested that Meroë was the center from which the knowledge of ironworking spread throughout Africa, this skill might more easily have reached West Africa by trans-Saharan routes from Phoenician Carthage, where ironworking was well known, or it could have been independently discovered. The earliest iron-using communities yet discovered in West Africa are those of the Nok culture, named after a village on the Jos Plateau of north Nigeria. In the course of open-cast mining operations at Nok were found some remarkable terra-cotta heads of men and animals, together with iron and stone tools. A second site of the same people, at Taruga, produced an iron-smelting furnace. There is no doubt that iron was smelted and worked there from about 300 BCE, a date obtained by radiocarbon methods.

The working of iron gave its users improved weapons and more control over their environment; it was also instrumental in enabling them to establish trading centers, which in time developed into an important feature of the western Sudan. The basis of trade was gold, produced in an area to the southwest of the Sahara and transported by desert caravan to North Africa. The middlemen in this operation - those who met the caravans, brought the gold from the producers to them, and arranged an exchange of goods - were the ones who set up the trading centers that later became the great medieval states of the western Sudan. The earliest of these was Ghana, a state that grew up in southern Mauritania; its connection with the present Republic of Ghana is only indirect. Nothing is known of its beginnings as yet, and it is first mentioned by Arab travelers about CE 800; but according to local tradition, which was written down in the sixteenth and seventeenth centuries, it was already flourishing by the seventh century, and its early days may well reach further back into history.

While a great deal is known about ancient Egypt, the history of the civilizations of the rest of Africa is only now emerging. There are many tantalizing threads to follow, though they may never be fitted into the tapestry: the possibly Indian influences in Kush; the stone terracing that transformed the agriculture of Ethiopia and is seen also at Zimbabwe in southern Rhodesia; the bronze casting by the lost-wax process known in ancient Egypt and used again, much later, by the West African artists of Ife and Benin; the facts behind the statement by the medieval Arab geographer Al-Masudi that the sons of Kush, having crossed the Nile, separated, and some "very numerous, marched toward the setting sun," to mention but a few of them. Little is known of the comings and goings of peoples or of the interchange of ideas and techniques across this vast continent. Literate Egypt, with all its achievements, overshadows the rest of Africa; but more research, exploration, and excavation may help to redress the balance.

3

THE BARBARY COAST
STUART SCHAAR

Two distinct geographical regions found in North Africa: in the east, Egypt and Cyrenaica (eastern Libya); in the west, Tripolitania (western Libya), Tunisia, Algeria, and Morocco. The western region juts out of the Sahara, forming an erratic quadrilateral surrounded by water on three sides. To medieval Arab geographers, who saw the Sahara as a vast sea of sand, the western portion of North Africa, with its many oases, seemed an island of refuge, and so they named the region *jazirat al-maghreb*, "the island of the west." Egypt and its geological appendage Cyrenaica, separated from the Maghreb by one of the most desolate stretches of the Sahara, more often than not shared a common history. Yet, though sand and sea have at times acted as barriers isolating the Maghreb from sub-Saharan Africa, Egypt, and Europe, these same barriers also served as bridges for the diffusion of new ideas and technology and as highways for invaders, traders, and missionaries.

The Western Sahara, the massive Atlas Mountains, and the Mediterranean Sea have molded the Maghreb into a unit. The Sahara is more than just sand; it comprises high, arid mountains reaching to 10,000 feet, deep depressions similar in appearance to those on the surface of the moon, salt flats, high steppelands, moving dunes, and fertile oases that support large settlements. Life depends on underground rivers and natural springs scattered throughout the vast desert, and sudden rains, at times followed by flash floods, make even the most arid regions bloom.

To the north of the Sahara, the Atlas Mountains, called by different names from west to east, stretch out between Morocco and Tripolitania and keep the desert sands from invading the fertile, densely settled coastal plains. (The Jebel Akhdar range in Cyrenaica, though geologically distinct from the Atlas range, also serves the same protective function.) The Atlas peaks are highest in Morocco, reaching 13,600 feet. Their maximum elevation in Algeria is 7,600 feet, less than 4,500 feet in Tunisia, and 2,500 feet in Tripolitania, becoming hills. The coastal plains start out as a narrow strip in Tripolitania and widen to between fifty and 100 miles as they extend westward, reaching their widest expanse on the Atlantic coast of Morocco, an area of abundant rainfall.

Rainfall in North Africa becomes irregular and unpredictable in duration and intensity as one moves from west to east, and water sources become less plentiful. Cyrenaica consists of oases surrounded by desert, and other than the Nile Valley, the Suez region, and some scattered oases, Egypt is all desert. Most of the North African population has therefore lived in dispersed plains or oases, separated from one another by gorge-like valleys or inhospitable deserts. Internal communications have been especially difficult in Morocco and Algeria because of the ruggedness of the mountains and the hazards of crossing valleys.

As large portions of the Sahara, Morocco, and Algeria have traditionally been inaccessible, especially the Atlas chain and the more northerly Rif and Kabylia, mountains, the Berber peoples of North Africa tended over the centuries to seek safety from foreign conquests in mountainous and desert zones. As they escaped from conquerors, they trekked westward so that, according to one recent estimate, 45 percent of the Moroccan population speak Berber, 30 percent do so in Algeria, and less than 1 percent do in Tunisia. Other Berber-speaking people live in the Siwa oasis in Egypt near the Libyan frontier and throughout the Sahara, and some are located south of the Niger River.

Notable among the desert dwellers are the Tuareg, who are the only modern Berber people known to have an alphabet. When other Berbers wish to write their language, they have on rare occasions in recent centuries composed their works in Arabic script. The language used in antiquity by the ancestors of the Berbers, containing an alphabet of twenty-three consonants, has long been forgotten, and although the Tuareg have partly derived their own dialect and writing system from it, knowledge of the Tuareg alphabet does not help them to decipher hundreds of Berber inscriptions that date from Roman times.

Where the Berbers originated and how they got to North Africa remain mysteries. Ancient inscriptions, which seem to have been written by the ancestors of the modern Berbers, have been discovered in the Sinai Peninsula and in the Nile Delta, leading some scholars to conclude that these people migrated into Africa from southwest Asia. More recent analysis of African languages lends some credence to this view. Linguists, notably Joseph Greenberg, have grouped the numerous Berber dialects, which vary from region to region, with the larger Afro-Asiatic family of languages, along with old Egyptian, Somali, Galla, Hebrew, and Arabic.

Whatever the outcome of future research into the

problems of when and if these intruders conquered North Africa from other people, it is known that by the fifth century before the Christian era, when written sources were available for the Maghreb, the Berbers had already spread throughout the northern third of the continent. There they had come into contact with a darker-skinned population. According to numerous Greek and Latin texts, these dark-skinned people, known generically as Ethiopians in antiquity, occupied the majority of the oases in the Sahara until the first few centuries of the Christian era. Supposedly, they formed nations and moved about as they pleased.

These black people shared a common culture; they traced their earlier history to Neolithic fishing-and-hunting communities located along rivers near marshes and dominating the Sahara. It seems that these people migrated after a wet phase, between approximately 5500 and 3000 BCE, when the Sahara began drying up. Those moving south would have mixed with the Sudanese population. Migrants to the north and those remaining on oases presumably later intermarried with the ancestors of the Berbers and Egyptians of North Africa and the Galla, Somali, and Beja of the East African Horn. Such migrations and communications over once-navigable rivers probably aided in the diffusion into surrounding areas of social and cultural institutions.

The most powerful of the ancient desert dwellers,

the Garamantes, whose skin color is still a matter of controversy, lived on the Wadi Ajal, a populous 100-mile-long chain of oases located south of the Tripolitanian coast in the desert region known as the Fezzan. As Herodotus noted, from at least the fifth century BCE, commercial relations between the Tripolitanian coast and the Fezzan flourished. The intervening routes offered few obstacles to communication; thus, the Garamantes were placed at the heart of an important crossroads that connected Egypt, the coast, and the south. Their commercial empire, with its center at the town of Germa, extended westward to the town of Ghadames and possibly reached southward to the central Sudan around Lake Chad. Their forts protected trade routes, and the horses that they bred were used to police the desert. United into a kingdom since at least Roman times, they served as the chief middlemen in the central Saharan trade.

Just as some Saharans mixed with the Berbers, so did other peoples, for in antiquity, Phoenicians, Greeks, Egyptians, Persians, Romans, Vandals, and Byzantines controlled parts of the Maghreb. Yet, despite these contacts, the Berbers remained aloof from external controls and influences. Long distances and the difficulty of the terrain limited communications and restricted the number of permanent settlers who came to the Maghreb. Although oxen and horses crossed the Sahara during the first millennium BCE, the desert ceased to be an impenetrable barrier in the Maghreb only after the second century CE, when the use of camels became widespread.

The stereotyped prejudices that classical writers developed about the North Africans tended to heighten Berber isolation even more. Many authors viewed them scornfully as uncivilized, violent, and passionate people who lacked subtlety. Although some Greek and Latin literary sources at times portrayed them as courageous, sober, and persevering, most writers reproached them for sensuality, apparent cruelty, turbulence, laziness, love of raiding and pillaging, and double standards of truth. Since the Berbers lived outside the pale of classical civilization, the Greeks and Romans considered them barbarians, from which the name "Berber" evolved to designate the light-skinned inhabitants of North Africa. The Arabs later called the area they inhabited Barbary. (Alternatively, the area was known by the Greek name "Libya," after the Lebu Berbers.)

Barbary entered written history about 1100 BCE. The first foreign settlements were made by Phoenicians from the city-state of Tyre in present-day Lebanon, who were drawn west by the prospects of gaining access to silver, copper, tin, and lead in the Iberian Peninsula. In the last quarter of the ninth century BCE, these Middle Easterners founded Carthage (*Kart Hadasht,* or

"New City"), and within three centuries, this tiny settlement had grown into a city-state, asserted its independence from Tyre, and organized the other Phoenician colonies in the western Mediterranean into a powerful Punic Empire under its leadership.

Toward the start of the fifth century BCE, Carthage became the first maritime and commercial power in the western Mediterranean. It had set the limits to the expansion of the Greeks, restricting their activity in southern Spain and sweeping them out of Sardinia and the African coast west of Cyrenaica. Despite gigantic efforts and the establishment of several strongholds in western Sicily, Carthage had failed to destroy Greek colonies in the eastern regions of the island. This enemy presence was a threat to the whole system of Carthaginian dominance: Sicily served as an ideal staging base to launch invasions against North Africa and as a gateway to both Spain, with its metal production, and Sardinia, where African Berbers had settled. The Sicilian and Sardinian colonies also provided Carthage with precious wheat supplies, which they exacted as a tithe on produce, and soldiers. Both were critically needed during African revolts and invasions, when the city-state was deprived of local agricultural resources and manpower. All attempts by Greeks and Romans to drive the Carthaginians from Sicily were therefore resisted fiercely; it became a cornerstone of Punic foreign policy to maintain a foothold there.

Carthage had escaped the westward onslaught of Iranians when the Phoenicians, vassals of Persia between 538 and 332 BCE, refused to join in the invasion of Carthage because, in the words of Herodotus, "of the close bond which connected Phoenicia and Carthage, and the wickedness of making war against their own children." King Cambyses of Persia conquered Egypt in 525 BCE, but failed to conquer both the Nubian country to the south and the site of the oracle of Amon-Re at the Siwa oasis in Egypt's western desert. It fell to Darius I (521-486 BCE) to pacify the sprawling Persian Empire, torn by revolt, and to organize Egypt into one of twenty satrapies ruled from the Middle East. Darius, after extending his realm beyond the Indus River in India, sent his troops as far as Euesperides (Benghazi) on the Cyrenaican coast and annexed Cyrenaica in 515 BCE. The Greek towns of Cyrene and Barca were joined to the Egyptian satrapy and helped pay the 700 talents in tribute offered annually. Neighboring Libyans added gifts, and the Nubians were required to bring to the Persians every second year two quarts of gold, 200 ebony logs, five young boys, and twenty elephant tusks.

The combination of Persian power to the east and Greek hostility in Sicily forced various Phoenician settlements in North Africa to unite with others in southern Spain, western Sicily, Sardinia, the Balearic Islands, and Corsica, all under Carthaginian leadership. Carthage also sought to protect itself through alliance with the Etruscans of Italy in the sixth century BCE, but in 474, the Greeks defeated these allies. Earlier, they had repelled an invasion of the Greek mainland by King Xerxes of Persia (485-465 BCE) and the Carthaginian attempt to conquer Sicily. Also, the Greeks of Marseilles closed ports of Gaul and Spain to Punic ships. Athens even attacked the Phoenician coast in 459 BCE, but its ambitions were soon checked when it supported an unsuccessful rising in Egypt. The Greek historian Thucydides in his *History of the Peloponnesian War* describes the events that followed: ". . . a Libyan king . . . on the Egyptian border . . . caused a revolt of almost the whole of Egypt from King Artaxerxes [Persian ruler from 465 424 BCE], and placing himself at its head, invited the Athenians to his assistance. Abandoning a Cyprien expedition upon which they happened to be engaged with two hundred ships . . . they arrived in Egypt and sailed from the sea into the Nile . . . making themselves masters of the river and two-thirds of Memphis . . . and the king sent . . . a Persian to Lacedaemon [Sparta] with money to bribe the Pelopennesians to invade Attica and so draw off the Athenians from Egypt. Finding that the matter made no progress, and that the money was only being wasted, he . . . sent . . . a Persian with a large army to Egypt. Arriving by land he defeated the Egyptians and their allies in a battle, and drove the Hellenes out of Memphis. . . . The Libyan king, the sole author of the Egyptian revolt, was betrayed, taken and crucified."

Thenceforth, until 332 BCE, the moment of Alexander the Great's invasion, Egypt remained under nominal Persian control; but periodic revolts broke out, and as early as 404 BCE rulers of the satrapy asserted their independence.

Throughout the fifth and fourth centuries BCE, Carthage fought the Greeks for control of Sicily. By 375, Carthage had won control over the western third of the island, which it retained more or less for a century. But continual wars weakened both belligerents, benefiting an expanding Rome.

However, the wars served to accelerate the introduction into Barbary of Hellenic influences - to a slight degree in religion, but significantly in the arts, military science, and weaponry. A large number of rich Carthaginians settled in Syracuse; many members of the Punic aristocracy served in the army or in Sicilian diplomatic posts and came into direct contact with Greek civilization. In the fourth century, splendid works of art were brought as booty to Africa from Sicily. An important Hellenic colony settled at Carthage, Greek cults spread, and Greek mercenaries joined the Punic army. Carthage could no longer remain aloof.

During the turbulent first half of the fifth century

BCE, Carthage's trade with the Mediterranean world had declined, and outlets for selling raw materials and precious metals dried up. This commercial depression, combined with the necessity to use its silver and gold to pay for mercenary troops and its initial stalemate in Sicily, had also turned Carthage inward to Africa. By the middle of the fifth century, it had built a land empire so that fifty years later, despite numerous Berber revolts against Punic expansionism, the new territory (corresponding to northeastern Tunisia) provided the bulk of army recruits; by the early third century, with the assistance of Numidia (corresponding to parts of present-day Algeria and western Tunisia), it raised adequate grain to feed Carthage's population of about 400,000, including slaves and foreigners.

In the century after its founding, Carthage had paid an annual tribute to the neighboring Berbers as a form of rent for the soil it occupied. During a part of the sixth century, it had freed itself of this burden and ceased to pay anything for many years. But toward the end of the century, it had to submit once again. Sometime around 475 to 450 BCE, Carthage permanently revoked the obligation. This was accompanied or followed by the growth of a sizable settlement beyond the city so that by 400 BCE, Carthage reached its greatest extent. At the same time, the Carthaginians settled sites along the Barbary Coast between Cyrenaica and the Atlantic and established regular commercial relations with the Berbers.

In the western Mediterranean, Carthage sought to reserve for itself the exclusive exploitation of vast markets and supplies of raw materials. From the fourth century, its dependencies save Sicily were closed to all but Punic merchants. The Punic fleet even sank ships that navigated toward the Strait of Gibraltar, and to discourage foreign exploration, sailors or merchants invented imaginative tales of the dangers and obstacles in the Atlantic Ocean, including encounters with gigantic sand bars, impassable fields of algae, enormous sea monsters, and thick fogs. Herodotus, taking his information from Carthaginian sources, describes how Punic traders bartered merchandise for gold along the same Atlantic coast: "The Carthaginians also tell us that they trade with a race of men who live in a part of Libya beyond the Pillars of Heracles. On reaching this country, they unload their goods, arrange them tidily along the beach, and then, returning to their boats, raise a smoke. Seeing the smoke, the natives come down to the beach, place on the ground a certain quantity of gold in exchange for the goods, and go off again to a distance. The Carthaginians then come ashore and take a look at the gold; and if they think it represents a fair price for their wares, they collect it and go away; if, on the other hand, it seems too little, they go back aboard and wait, and the natives come and add to the gold until they are satisfied. There is perfect honesty on both sides; the

Carthaginians never touch the gold until it equals in value what they have offered for sale, and the natives never touch the goods until the gold has been taken away."

About 470 BCE, Hanno, a member of the Carthaginian ruling class, supposedly led a group of settlers on a voyage of colonization along Africa's Atlantic coast, ostensibly to consolidate the gold trade, a major Punic enterprise. It now seems well established that Hanno's description of his voyage was not, as has long been thought, a Greek translation of an inscription on a Carthaginian temple; rather, it was the product of pure fantasy mixed with some facts drawn from earlier authors and was composed perhaps as a school exercise in the first century BCE. A Greek geographer of Asia, known as the Pseudo-Scylax, writing about 338 BCE, also reports that Phoenicians exchanged perfume, Egyptian stones, and Athenian pottery for animal skins, hides, and tusks, all of which could have been found in the region corresponding to present-day Morocco. He, like the author of the document describing Hanno's voyage, omitted to mention the gold trade, which the Carthaginians did not readily publicize. Doubtless, some Punic colonies beyond the Strait of Gibraltar traded in gold on a small scale until Roman times. According to a source that the Greek geographer Strabo mistrusted, this trade ended prior to the first century CE, when the Pharusians and the

Nigrites attacked. (They were nomadic horsemen and archers about whom we know little more than that they lived south of Morocco.) Strabo relates that they destroyed more than 300 trading posts on the Atlantic coast.

Punic merchants rarely, if at all, had direct commercial relations with the Sudan. Instead, as previously stated, the Garamantes played the role of middlemen, supplying Carthage with precious stones known as carbuncles and possibly slaves, whom, according to Herodotus, they "hunted" in horse-drawn chariots in the Sahara south of the Tripolitanian coast. One series of rock drawings shows these chariots were in use from the Fezzan to the Niger Bend, but nothing indicates that Carthage received gold from the Fezzan. Rather, the weight of evidence suggests that Carthaginian gold came entirely from the Atlantic coast, and even this source seemingly ceased to be active by Roman times.

Finds of tomb jewelry attest that Carthage had gold objects in quantity during the seventh and sixth centuries BCE. Although they had stopped burying such valuable commodities in their graves by the fifth century, the reliable historian Thucydides informs us that the enemies of Carthage believed they possessed a great deal of gold and silver. But supplies of these metals did not suffice to underwrite the Sicilian wars of the fourth century BCE. During this period and in the following century, Carthage passed through a financial crisis. During the First Punic War against Rome (264-241 BCE), the North African state lacked money to the point that it had to double taxes on Berber subjects, taking from them fifty percent of their harvests, and even then could not pay its mercenaries. Only the conquest of the entire Iberian Peninsula, beginning in 237 BCE, provided large amounts of silver to pay off the Roman indemnity and later to fight the Second Punic War (219-201 BCE).

With commerce as the main source of Carthaginian riches, land never became a major concern of the ruling class, whose members remained basically wholesale merchants and shipping magnates. Commercial needs, therefore, dictated foreign policy. By force or by treaties or by founding colonies, the state opened up new markets for the merchants and, where possible, organized monopolies and negotiated reciprocal trade agreements. It also assured the liberty of navigation against pirate attacks.

By the fifth century BCE, about 300 of the wealthiest Carthaginians shared in the control of the state through the agency of the senate. Although they were divided into rival clans, they came to terms with each other in order to maintain stability for trade. Short wars increased the senators' fortunes and filled the treasury with booty. Conquests also benefited the ruling families by expanding markets, eliminating competitors, producing new administrative posts, and, in Africa, extending their private property. However, senators disdained long wars. Besides being costly, such drawn-out struggles disrupted trade and fortified the position of ambitious generals.

In addition to two *sufets,* executive officers who held office for a year and presided over the senate and an assembly of citizens, the Carthaginians appointed generals as commanders in chief on extraordinary occasions, usually for the duration of a war. They, too, were traditionally chosen from the upper class. Fearing that popular commanders might usurp their power and establish tyrannies, the senators generally chose mediocre men for these posts. By the middle of the fifth century BCE, a court of 104 judges, chosen from the senate, supervised and oversaw the activities of the generals. In the third century, a few members out of an executive body of at least thirty senators accompanied officers overseas to exercise control over political decisions. The fear of sentences passed by the high court dissuaded the best men from assuming a command, and more than one incapable or unlucky general was fined, had his property confiscated, lost his life, or faced exile, as a result of senatorial action.

Below the senate was an assembly of citizens

composed of retail merchants, manufacturers, administrators, and employees of large firms, who depended on the senatorial aristocracy for their jobs and livelihood. We do not know the exact number of citizens within the capital of Carthage (estimates range in the area of 80,000) or how many among them qualified for membership in the assembly. Citizenship could be granted to foreigners whom the state judged worthy of the honor, and Phoenicians from the Middle East and citizens of other Phoenician or Carthaginian colonies also probably enjoyed rights of citizenship in Carthage.

Until the late third century, the citizen assembly scarcely affected government. If the senate and the *sufets* agreed on policies, there was no need to submit issues to any other body. At times, a popular vote took place in the assembly even when the two executives and the senators agreed in order to obtain general support for hazardous ventures. This procedure gave citizens the illusion of participation. In return for their collaboration, citizens paid no taxes in peacetime, and after the sixth century BCE did not have to serve in the army. Contingents were then drawn from among Carthage's disfranchised subjects and government-financed mercenaries. It had become cheaper to use precious metals to hire mercenaries than to withdraw a large number of citizens from wealth-producing trade. Moreover, there were far too few citizens in Carthage to provide for the defense of the empire. Two serious army defeats would have wiped out their forces, so that if Carthage had relied on a citizen army, it might have disappeared long before 146 BCE, when Rome ultimately defeated Carthage because of its greater manpower reserves.

Besides the citizens, the population of Carthage included Libyans, who had migrated to the city from surrounding rural areas to find work, and also slaves, who were imported from all over the Mediterranean, the Sahara, and farther south. Most Libyans and all slaves had no political rights in Carthage. Merchants, commercial agents, and artisans also flocked to the city-state from Sicily, Italy, and Greece. Fusion with the citizenry was not easy, but Carthaginians did intermarry with other peoples. Mixed marriages were especially frequent with Libyans, less perhaps in the capital than in the coastal colonies. No source indicates how many Libyans became Carthaginian citizens.

In urban centers, slaves were employed by the Carthaginians as servants in rich families or as workers in artisanal shops, commercial houses, and state arsenals. On the sea, they manned merchant and war galleys. A few blacks served as slaves in the cities or regions of Barbary close to the coasts, but it does not seem that, at this time, they furnished enough manpower to play an important role in the working of the agrarian estates of the aristocracy.

North Africa was well enough populated with poor Berbers to provide a cheap local supply of farm labor, and rich Carthaginians certainly used war prisoners and victims of piracy to cultivate their fields. We do not know, however, if these captives were purchased by their masters or loaned out by the state. The rural Berber population rarely had slaves. They were too poor to buy them, and if any were acquired in warfare, the Berbers were better off selling their captives than feeding them. Besides, women did most of the hard labor among the Berbers. It is possible that Punic merchants sold black slaves to Greeks and Italians, but in smaller numbers than those that reached the Mediterranean by way of Egypt.

The slaves who cultivated the suburban estates of the rich had little to lose by revolting against their masters, and there were periodic uprisings in the fourth century BCE. They therefore had to be watched carefully. Also, a part of the free Libyan population that had migrated to the cities joined urban riots in rare periods of crisis, often just for the chance to raid the homes of the rich. To offset rebellious reactions, the ruling class responded with utmost ferocity and cruelty when threatened.

Meanwhile, Rome was regarding Carthage with increasing jealousy. The potential for a clash between the two had become evident in 268 BCE, when Carthage took over the Sicilian seaport of

Messina, across the channel from the Italian coast. Between 264 and 241 BCE, the two powers fought the First Punic War, which ended in the destruction of the Carthaginian fleet. Carthage finally had to evacuate Sicily and pay Rome a heavy indemnity. To compensate for the loss of Sicily, Sardinia, and Corsica, the Carthaginian general Hamilcar Barca led a campaign to conquer Spain beginning in 237 BCE. The booty and the precious metals sent back to Carthage from the Iberian Peninsula enriched the treasury, and the conquest opened new Spanish markets to Carthaginian commerce and industry. His son, Hannibal, became the most famous of the Barcids. While in his mid-twenties, he provoked the Second Punic War with Rome. With the vast silver mines and manpower of Spain at his disposal, and backed by the popular support of the Carthaginians, he crossed the Alps in 218 BCE, leading his soldiers and elephants into Italy. In order to prevent revolts during these war years, he sent Spanish soldiers to Africa and Berbers to Spain. These men did not get along with the population among whom they lived, but while serving as hostages, they kept the peace.

Hannibal's fortunes were reversed in 203 BCE when, after fifteen years of military campaigns on the Italian peninsula, he was forced to return to Carthage to oppose the Roman legions of Publius Cornelius Scipio, thereafter known as Scipio Africanus. Hannibal was defeated and ultimately forced to flee Carthage when he attempted to reform its government structure. He then served several Hellenistic princes, among them Antiochus III of Syria in his unsuccessful resistance to Rome. Finally, to avoid being handed over to the Romans, he committed suicide in 183 BCE, apparently by taking poison.

Thus, despite Hannibal's efforts, Carthage lost the war. It gave up Spain and its colonies along the North African coast and had to pay Rome another heavy indemnity. By 200 BCE, Rome had become the center of the Mediterranean world, and Carthage was relegated to the status of a weak dependency of the Latin state. Fifty years later, Rome, jealous of Carthage's continued commercial success, provoked the state's leaders into violating the peace treaty and sent its army to enforce stiffer demands. The Carthaginians surrendered, but when the Romans insisted as a condition of future peace that they raze their city and build a new one inland, the Carthaginians locked the city's gates. This was the beginning of the Third Punic War. Legionnaires destroyed Carthage in 146 BCE, and the people who survived, an estimated 50,000, were sold into slavery, bringing a once-powerful state to an ignoble end.

Like later North African conquerors in antiquity, the Carthaginians had settled in urban clusters located mainly along the Mediterranean. Such cities as

Carthage, Utica, and Lebda (Leptis Magna) served as pockets of cosmopolitan influence, but being artificial, albeit glorious, creations, they scarcely affected the way of life in the hinterland. Moreover, as stated earlier, from the fifth to the mid-third century BCE, Carthage prohibited outsiders from sailing into the western Mediterranean, so the chances to renew and enrich the culture through foreign contacts were restricted. Adaptation to external influences took place only gradually; it was most successful when Berber dynasties molded foreign practices and beliefs to local conditions. Mediterranean civilization reached the Berbers largely through the efforts of Berber kings, who ruled over large, loosely administered states in the shadow of Carthage and Rome.

Since the end of the second millennium BCE, kingship was hereditary among the Lebu, a Berber people living west of Egypt in an area that is now part of modern Libya. In the next millennium, iron and the horse were introduced into North Africa, two innovations that enhanced the military and technological strength of those who possessed them. Most probably, Berber states were formed by the unification under one authority of diverse lineage groups. Originally, chieftains were necessary only in time of war. When circumstances warranted it, an assembly of family elders met and decided on common action. In case of external threat, they would choose a chief for the duration of the hostilities or for a year. But such a chief might abuse his authority or refuse to give up his office once peace was restored. If a loyal following grouped around him or if he amassed allies, he became a prince, though he would still have to respect the autonomy of the lineages that supported his authority and consult with their representatives. Once he consolidated his personal power through victorious warfare, a prince could impose himself on others, making his territory and his lineage the center of a rudimentary state. The chief would have then become a king and would, in all likelihood, establish a dynasty.

Kingly rule was constantly challenged in antiquity. Berbers in the mountains, who in their inaccessibility were almost immune to nomadic raids, periodically pillaged the kingdoms of the plains. Also, internal rivalries among ambitious chiefs and pretenders abounded. To limit treason and rebellion, kings held members of powerful families as hostages in their retinues. They also chose wives from among the daughters of the chiefs and kept the sons of rural notables in their bodyguard. When a ruler died or was deposed, crises erupted, and the interregnums were marked by civil wars. Being menaced from all sides, these kings had to work diligently to maintain authority over their subjects. Ultimately, sovereigns sought ways to enhance their legitimacy and celebrated the "divinity" of former kings.

The main wealth of Berber kingdoms came from the agricultural produce of the sedentary population living on the plains. Monarchs, therefore, favored agriculture in order to increase tax yields, and whenever possible, they forced nomads to settle. A primary function of the kings was to protect farmers against nomadic raids and town dwellers against foreign invasions. They needed at their disposal both mobile forces to police their territory and regular troops to man strategic garrisons and to fight in wars for and against Carthage or Rome. These forces watched over nomadic displacements and helped to collect taxes on transhumant livestock. Even when they could not enter turbulent areas, Berber princes could control dissidents by threatening to close down regional markets, where the population came to buy and sell. The rulers developed commercial relations and guaranteed the flow of goods within their realms. Sales and market taxes, as well as custom dues, probably helped to fill the treasury. Since rural taxes were paid in kind, kings served as the greatest merchants of their states. They exported wheat, wool, skins, livestock, horses, wild animals, carbuncles, ivory, wood, marble, and some slaves.

In the third century BCE, three large kingdoms dominated the Moroccan, Algerian, and Tunisian hinterland. To the extreme west (corresponding to modern Morocco) were the Moors (*Mauri* in Latin), who lived in the kingdom of Mauretania.

Moving eastward from the Moulouya River, there were at least two Numidian kingdoms, that of the Massaesylins, centering on the province of Oran, and that of the Massylins, smaller in size and bordering on Carthage.

The Massaesylin king Syphax, who died in 201 BCE, was the first Berber monarch about whom we have any detailed historical information. According to the Roman historian Titus Livy, he was the "wealthiest of the African princes," and before the Romans defeated him in 203 BCE, he controlled all but the Saharan regions of the country that is now called Algeria. He had two capitals: Siga in the extreme west of Oran province; Cirta (modern Constantine) in the east. Both Rome and Carthage tried to make Syphax an ally, but for a time, the king believed that he could play the arbiter between these adversaries. He imitated Hellenistic monarchs by wearing a crown and minting coins engraved with his image. Recognizing his importance, one of the most powerful Carthaginian families gave him a daughter to marry.

Syphax lost his territories to Masinissa, an heir to the Massylin throne and an ally of Rome. Masinissa, who died in 148 BCE, was one of the greatest Berber personalities in history. This intelligent, fearless, and subtle man is shown on contemporary coins as a king in his forties or fifties, with sharp features, wide eyes, thick eyebrows, long hair, and a pointed beard. He led an extraordinarily vigorous life, so that at eighty, he still could jump on his horse without aid and ride bareback. At the age of eighty-six, one of his wives bore him a son, bringing the total of his male progeny to at least forty-four. Several of them survived him when he died at the age of ninety. His kingdom was divided among three of his sons, and his dynasty ruled Numidia for a century, then transferred to Mauretania to reign for sixty years more.

In Spain, Masinissa had seen Roman legions in action, and he predicted that the Latins would reign over all of Libya. He wisely allied his kingdom with Rome against Carthage and King Syphax, who was at this time aligned with the Punic state. In return, Rome allowed Masinissa slowly to absorb the maritime colonies that had once belonged to Carthage, leaving him a free hand to conquer Berber subjects. In this way, he extended his kingdom from the frontiers of Cyrenaica to the Moulouya River. Conveniently, this expansion into Carthaginian territory also provided Rome with the pretext to destroy Carthage in the Third Punic War.

Masinissa possessed a palace at Cirta, where, in the manner of the Carthaginians, he gave lavish banquets complete with silver dishes, gold baskets, and Greek musicians to entertain his guests. Although he was raised in the tradition of the Berbers - indeed, his mother had been a popular

Berber prophetess - he knew the refined culture of Carthage, where he perhaps spent some of his early years. He married the daughter of a leading Carthaginian and gave his sons a Greek education. The Carthaginians of high rank so respected kings such as Syphax and Masinissa that they did not believe they were lowering their social status by giving their children as wives or sons-in-law.

Berber kings helped to diffuse Carthaginian religious practices throughout Barbary. From earliest times, the Berbers were nature-worshipers; they had developed cults venerating the sun, mountains, water, trees, and other natural phenomena. Phoenicians, who worshiped nature gods, probably contributed elements to these cults, and certainly, Berber influences entered Punic beliefs when Carthage expanded into North African territory in the fifth century BCE. Even after Rome conquered Barbary, the Carthaginian deities of Baal Hammon, the lord of harvests, and Tanit, goddess of life and fertility, still had a large number of devotees, though their names were Romanized respectively as Saturn and Caelestis. Inscriptions discovered at Constantine and its suburbs, in the heart of Numidia, prove that the Berbers, like the Carthaginians, at times sacrificed their first-born children before the Romans prohibited the practice. Rationale for this custom lay in the belief that the virtue of the gods must be maintained by a continual supply of blood. The practice fit into the general character of the Punic religion, which accepted the premise that man was weak and had to submit to capricious and powerful gods who demanded to be appeased.

A large number of Berbers, especially women, still follow magical rites that apparently have their origins in antiquity. These include ceremonies invoking the gods of fertility and incantations to produce rain. Others accompany birth, marriage, and death. Women still tie rags to trees and gather stones, only to throw them away, thus transferring evil to other objects. From the Stone Age, Berbers have worn amulets, which they believe give protection through a genie, or jinni, who deposited some of his power in the object. The fear of the evil eye, the practice of anthropolatry (the worship of men), the belief in genies, and the ritual sacrifice of animals are also holdovers from pre-Islamic times.

In the maritime colonies and over a large part of Tunisia and eastern Algeria, the population spoke Punic. Army veterans and merchants gradually spread the language throughout the Maghreb, beyond the towns and regions under direct Carthaginian control. To Berber princes, Punic was the lingua franca, since the people they ruled spoke a multitude of Berber dialects. Under Rome, neo-Punic, a development of the old Carthaginian language, was gradually replaced by Latin in the cities, but in some rural areas, it died out slowly and was not extinguished until the beginning of the third century CE.

The Berbers adopted new agricultural and stockbreeding techniques from their Carthaginian mentors. However, outside Punic Tunisia, olive-tree cultivation, grain farming, and viticulture hardly spread before Roman times; most other North Africans continued to raise livestock. The Phoenicians also taught the Berbers how to use bronze and iron in the manufacture of tools and other objects. Exploitation of a copper mine in Numidia only began under the Phoenicians, and Barbary lacked tin to make bronze.

Carthaginians brought Greek and Italian ceramics and Egyptian glassware into Barbary; however, most of these goods were probably beyond the purchasing power of the Berbers, who manufactured their own pottery. They also produced clothes of wool and leather, and ambulant or local blacksmiths supplied them with their iron weapons, plows, utensils, and tools. It was most likely that Carthage furnished Berber princes and chiefs with luxury goods such as ornamented weapons, fine textiles, jewels, perfume, and rugs. Less expensive merchandise was probably sold to veterans who had served in Carthaginian armies. Goods supplied to the general populace in the interior were handled through the intermediary of Berber princes.

Direct relations were established between Carthage and Egypt after Alexander the Great's conquest of the East and the founding of Alexandria in 332 BCE. Alexandria was made the capital of Egypt by Ptolemy, one of Alexander's Macedonian generals and founder of the Ptolemaic dynasty. From the end of the fourth century, Carthage competed with Alexandria as Africa's chief trade center, exporting to the burgeoning Hellenistic centers.

Egypt also challenged Carthage on the political front. In 310 BCE, an independent Ptolemaic governor of the Greek cities of Cyrenaica plotted with a tyrant of Syracuse to annihilate the Punic capital. In return for his aid, the governor was promised all of Carthage's North African possessions, but the Syracusan killed his co-plotter and the scheme never materialized. During the first war against Rome (264-241 BCE), Carthage, lacking money to pay its mercenaries, asked King Ptolemy II of Egypt (285-246 BCE) for a loan of 2,000 talents. Although the monarch refused, the fact that Carthage could approach him for such a large sum attests to the close ties between the Nile Valley and the Maghreb.

Other evidence of these connections can be seen in Egyptian styles of architecture and art, which entered the Maghreb with the Phoenicians, who themselves had borrowed heavily from the older civilization of the Nile Valley. The Phoenicians introduced such Egyptian construction procedures as placing blocks of stone on one another without mortar, baking large bricks in the sun, and making stucco. The Carthaginians also borrowed Egyptian weights and measures, including the cubit - a linear measure based on the length of the arm from the elbow to the fingertip. Phoenician merchants who had commercial establishments on the Nile Delta and formed an important colony at Memphis initially imported Egyptian pottery, statuettes, ritual razors decorated with Egyptian divinities, gold work, seals, scarabs used as amulets, and small pendant masks, many of which later Maghrebin artisans copied locally. The cult of the Egyptian sun god Amon-Re spread from Thebes into the Siwa oasis. The Greeks of Cyrenaica knew him under the name of Zeus, and Berbers accepted him as a great nature god.

The Roman emperors, however, regarded Egypt as their private domain, and except for its trade, attempted to keep the Nile Valley isolated from the rest of the empire. An experienced businessman known for his loyalty to the emperor was usually chosen as the Egyptian prefect and acted as the personal representative of the imperial household. To ensure Egypt's isolation, no member of the Roman senate could enter the province without the permission of the emperor.

Under Roman rule, the senate was entrusted

with administering a truncated version of the old Carthaginian Empire - a political unit known by the Latin name "Africa" and encompassing an area of some 5,000 square miles. Initially, the senators showed little interest in "Africa." Masinissa's heirs controlled and policed that part of Barbary bordering on the new possession, and some coastal cities enjoyed for a time autonomy and exemption from taxation. Few Romans settled in the province; those that did, viewed their sojourn as an opportunity to make a quick fortune, which they hoped to spend in Rome.

After surveying its newly conquered lands, Rome allowed small holders to continue farming, but compelled them to pay taxes. The province barely brought in as much revenue as was needed to pay the cost of administration. Rome confiscated estates belonging to the Carthaginian aristocracy and distributed some of them to Roman war veterans and other deserving citizens, who mostly had to work their plots by themselves or with the aid of a few slaves. Rich absentee landlords employed overseers to supervise slaves or freemen to cultivate their property.

Berber kings were at first allowed considerable independence by the Romans since the central government wanted rulers at their disposal who facilitated commands, organized contingents to fight in wars, and cooperated readily in selling wheat to Latin merchants. These kings policed frontiers and facilitated the penetration of Roman commerce into their territory. But they were allies who had to be treated well and were not humble or docile vassals.

Masinissa's grandson, Jugurtha, broke with dynastic tradition and opposed Rome in the Jugurthine Wars (111-105 BCE). In an attempt to wrest all of Numidia from Rome, he bribed a number of Roman senators. When the plot was revealed, Jugurtha was summoned to the capital, where he is quoted as saying, "Rome is a city for sale, and doomed to perish if it can find a purchaser." The Roman historian and politician Sallust provides some clues to Jugurtha's charisma. He writes: "As soon as Jugurtha grew up, endowed as he was with great strength and handsome looks, but above all with a powerful intellect, he did not let himself be spoiled by luxury or idleness, but took part in the national pursuits of riding and javelin-throwing and competed with other young men in running; and though he outshone them all he was universally beloved. He also devoted much time to hunting; and was always to the fore at the killing of lions and other wild beasts. His energy was equaled by his modesty: he never boasted of his exploits . . . [later, when fighting in Spain] by dint of hard work and careful attention to duty, by unquestioning obedience and the readiness with which he exposed himself to risk, he won such renown as to become the idol of the Roman soldiers and the terror of the enemy. He was in fact both a tough fighter and a wise counselor - qualities extremely hard to combine. . . ."

Another Berber king, Juba II, who died in CE 23 or 24, married Cleopatra Silene, the daughter of Antony and Cleopatra. This legendary couple, who really lacked the proper administrative ability to make Egypt a profitable province, had provided Rome with the pretext for annexing Egypt. Juba, although an Algerian, had been raised in Rome and was given the best Greek education possible; he became an art connoisseur, and wrote or compiled at least fifty works in Greek, none of which, unfortunately, has survived. Pliny the Elder wrote that during the forty-eight years Juba was king of Mauretania his "glory as a scholar was greater than his reputation as a sovereign." Indeed, he had great difficulty in maintaining the loyalty of his subjects and was confronted with a series of Berber revolts that ultimately were crushed through Roman intervention. Apparently, he carried his cultural affinities and friendship with Rome to extremes, antagonizing his subjects. Even when he attempted to establish himself as a living god, he failed to enhance his legitimacy adequately enough to prevent rebellions.

It was his wife, Cleopatra Silene, who probably introduced the Egyptian cult of Isis, the mother goddess of fertility, into Mauretania. The same cult also spread to Tripolitania. Latin soldiers introduced the popular Egyptian god Sarapis (the Ptolemaic amalgam of the two male fertility symbols, Osiris and Apis the bull) into the Berber pantheon. The success of these cults stemmed from the vagueness of Egyptian doctrines. Since Egyptians viewed their gods as mere symbols of cosmic or ethical forces, they could be easily syncretized with the most popular local deities. Ornate Egyptian rituals and mysterious ceremonies must have intrigued initiates, but at the same time the Osirin influence injected optimism into their religion and promised the faithful immortality and life after death. The Berbers easily associated Sarapis with Baal Hammon or Saturn, and Isis with the Punic goddess Tanit. Under Christianity, statues of Isis would readily become identified with the Virgin Mary, and some Isiac rituals would find their correlatives in Christian practice.

By CE 40, Rome had extended its control over Numidia and Mauretania and extinguished the Berber dynasties. The Roman senatorial aristocracy, sometimes by means of small payments and with the connivance of the state, carved for themselves vast holdings out of former Berber crown lands.

In the majority of cases, the new owners lived in Italy and leased their land to companies; these, in turn, sublet plots to North Africans, who at first became hereditary occupants, and by the fourth century, serfs. The Berbers paid rent to the companies, and both master and farmer paid taxes to the state. The chief exception to this pattern was the domains of the emperor, acquired through bequests, purchases, or confiscations. Those who leased estates from the Crown paid as rent one-third of their produce, usually wheat. However, if they were slaves, they worked the imperial domains without compensation. Over the centuries, more and more acreage would come under these latter systems.

By CE 50, Rome faced the problem of depopulation at home and could not spare settlers for Africa. The emperors, therefore, had to send experts to teach Africans how to administer their holdings. They had to depend on the local population to run the bureaucracy and serve in the army. To garrison the province of "Africa" after CE 150, the Romans recruited the Third Legion from 5,500 locally born sons of legionnaires. In addition, until about the end of the fourth century, they used about 7,500 Berber auxiliaries in Numidia and 15,000 in Mauretania to keep the peace. During revolts, locally conscripted irregulars swelled these ranks. Much earlier, Rome had fortified its North African cities and allowed the people to arm themselves in case of Berber or pirate attacks. Large farms also had their citadels.

Under the empire, not only did Roman Africa

contain several large and beautiful cities, among them Carthage, Leptis Magna, Volubilis, and Dougga, but the Romans created a special municipal spirit. This cosmopolitanism permeated several hundred small towns (numbering more than 450 in the fourth century) each with 3,000 to 10,000 people, who prospered and possessed municipal councils, forums, temples, baths, and other amenities. Town dwellers, including merchants, artisans, and farmers, came to believe that municipal life was the highest and, ultimately, the only form of civilization. This ideology, stemming from the practice of granting citizenship to urbanites, made city dwellers feel superior to that part of the rural population that lived in the remote regions and set them apart as an elite. Although most townsmen had some Berber ancestry by the fourth century and although the most famous of their countrymen, Septimius Severus of Leptis Magna, reigned over the Roman Empire from CE 193 to 211, the Romans only had a limited success in incorporating large numbers of Berbers into urban civilization. They succeeded most in those areas where Carthaginian and Numidian cities had previously flourished.

By organizing the imperial cult, Rome won the support of the urban aristocracy and, through their influence, a majority of the subject population. Every town elected delegates from among the upper class, who celebrated the cult at the provincial capital once a year. At that time, every province chose a single priest from those delegates who, among other things, presented local grievances to the governor and could, if he had a complaint against this high official, carry his case directly to the emperor.

The closer a peasant lived to a municipal center, the more fully Roman magistrates protected his legal rights. In isolated regions, the rural population was forced to submit to local lords, though at times, when their grievances went unanswered, sharecroppers would stage a strike by remaining at home and refusing to work. This put pressure on imperial or private landlords to come to terms, improve conditions, reduce the number of corvées, or lower taxes.

Rome preferred that taxes and rents be paid in kind, and collectors assembled revenues in warehouses throughout Barbary. After the African garrisons received their rations and collectors removed their share as salaries from these stores, the remaining stocks were dispatched to ports and transported to Rome. From 125 BCE to the time of Julius Caesar, who died in 44 BCE, a sector of the population of Rome received a monthly allotment of five free bushels of wheat per man from the state. Shortly after 63 BCE, about 320,000 citizens were receiving a dole. In 46 BCE, Caesar reduced the number to 150,000, but in the time of Augustus (63 BCE - CE

14), the number had risen to 200,000. In addition to distributing these handouts, the state sold cereals at reduced prices. At the beginning of the empire, the Maghreb and Egypt each provided one-third of Rome's wheat supplies while other provinces such as Sicily and Sardinia produced the rest. When Sicilian and Italian agricultural yields declined, Barbary's surplus provided enough grain to feed the entire city of Rome, including those receiving free food, for eight months out of a year; the Egyptians contributed enough to cover the remaining four months. After the foundation of Constantinople in CE 330 and the takeover of Egypt by eastern emperors, Rome depended on grain from the Maghreb alone.

When oil became scarce in Italy during the second century, the people of the Maghreb increased the acreage devoted to olive trees. Initially, Romans disliked the strong taste of African oil, but as production methods improved, both Romans and Egyptians imported large quantities for cooking, bathing, and fueling their lamps. Although the grain trade, mining, and marble quarrying had all been Roman state monopolies, commerce in oil remained in private hands. Not only did peasants in eastern Barbary become rich from their olive trees, but a large number of middlemen thrived as never before. In the second and third centuries, these businessmen invested their wealth in numerous public monuments. By the second century, a local ceramic industry had developed in the olive-producing areas so that Roman Africans, instead of importing luxury-quality pottery, as they formerly had done, were able not only to satisfy their own needs but to become exporters of pottery.

As the Romans developed techniques for growing olives in dry country, they extended cultivation into semiarid zones. They planted trees several feet apart, destroyed all weeds near them, kept the ground clean, and painstakingly worked the soil so that it would absorb all available moisture. (At the end of the nineteenth century, the French in southern Tunisia, learning from the archeologists, applied these techniques with gratifying results to land that had reverted to scrub over the centuries following Roman occupation.) The Romans also employed engineering specialists called *aquilegi*, whose task was to seek out water sources. Hydraulic devices allowed them to take full advantage of rain and spring water, and to conserve water use. They erected dams and dug wells and cisterns. Dikes diverted water to the plains, where canals and trenches carried it to fields, while aqueducts supplied the towns.

The Roman expansion of agriculture into southern zones far from the Barbary Coast provoked serious clashes with the nomadic population of the Maghrebin steppe and desert. Their constant movement and pillaging brought them into contact with their neighbors to the north and south, and, like the strongest Berber kings before the Christian era, imperial Rome tried unsuccessfully to extend its domination over them.

By the first century CE, the political situation between the Romans and the Maghrebin nomads had become critical. Forced into restricted areas, somewhat like reservations, they demanded more and better pasturage for their goats and sheep. Between CE 17 and 24, the southern part of North Africa from Roman Mauretania to Tripolitania rose up under the leadership of the Numidian Tacfarinas. His defeat signaled the temporary victory of the sedentary population over the nomads.

The Garamantes, too, caused Rome much trouble in the Fezzan. In addition to raiding "Ethiopians" in the south, they attacked coastal settlements along the Gulf of Sidra, aided Tacfarinas, and offered a haven to other fugitives. For these acts, the Romans punished them several times. Short of permanently occupying the Fezzan, Roman governors stopped the Garamantes from further pillaging and, to ensure communications in the Sahara, formed a protectorate over them. Evidence of Roman presence on the Fezzan oases has been unearthed: traces of Roman-style irrigation and remains of Roman merchandise. Rome certainly received tusks from the Garamantes by way of the overland Saharan route to compensate for dwindling supplies of ivory in Barbary by the fourth century CE. Toward the end of the first century, a king of the Garamantes had led some Roman officers into a Sudanese region that he dominated. However, this and another expedition were exceptional.

The official limits of Roman occupation in the Maghreb stopped at the northern boundaries of the Sahara. In southern Numidia, Romans hardly entered the desert areas, and in Mauretania, they stayed away from it completely. From CE 24, and for more than 200 years thereafter, Rome either settled colonies of veterans in the south and the far west or founded military posts on the edge of the desert to control the nomads. Their frontier defenses, or *limes,* which extended through Numidia from Tripolitania, consisted of ditches, walls, camps, forts, lookout towers, and road networks.

Beginning in the second century, Rome also imported as guards Syrian nomads with camels. Known for their speed and their ability to go without water for up to ten days, the *mehari,* or riding camel, made it possible to cover greater distances between wells than horses or oxen could, thereby adding to the mobility of the nomads. Besides rendering the chariot obsolete in the Sahara, these camels facilitated the disruptive raids of nomadic fugitives, whose migrations and conquests would continue into the Islamic period.

For a long time before the Roman conquest, ancestors of the Berbers living in the Libyan region of the Sahara had dominated the habitable oases. From the end of the second millennium BCE, if not earlier, they had attempted to settle in Egypt, but they never presented major threats to the inhabitants of the Nile Valley. In the Roman period, as the following passage from Strabo's *Geography* shows, Egypt lived in peace with its neighbors to the west and south: "Now Aegypt was generally inclined to peace from the outset, because of the self-sufficiency of the country and the difficulty of invasion by outsiders, being protected on the north by a harborless coast and by the Aegyptian Sea, and on the east and west by the desert mountains of Libya and Arabia . . . and the remaining parts, those towards the south, are inhabited by the Troglodytes, Blemmyes, Nubae [Noba], and Megabari, those Aethiopians who live above Syene. These are nomads, and not numerous, or warlike either, though they were thought to be so by the ancients, because often, like brigands, they would attack defenseless persons. As for those Aethiopians who extend towards the south of Meroë, they are not numerous either, nor do they collect in one mass, inasmuch as they inhabit a long, narrow, and winding stretch of riverland . . . neither are they well equipped either for warfare or for any other kind of life. And now, too, the whole country is similarly disposed to peace."

Strabo, however, refers to incidents following Rome's conquest of Egypt in 30 BCE, when Kushites revolted and raided Syene (Aswan) in a series of attempts to seize lower Nubia. Rome retaliated and sacked Napata near the Fourth Cataract in 23 BCE, but moved no farther south. Instead, a garrison was stationed at Premnis (Qsar Ibrim). According to a papyrus dating from the second half of the first century CE, Romans and "Ethiopians" clashed somewhere in the eastern desert, but no other sources recorded the specific incident. Was there a connection between this skirmish and the decision of the Roman emperor Nero to send the Praetorian Guard on a mission to Meroë about CE 61? Perhaps future archeological finds will provide an answer to this question.

In Hellenistic times, when the Ptolemies established the Nile Delta as the hub of an international commercial network, contacts between Egypt and Nubia had been the rule. The Egyptians received through Nubia gold, ivory, ebony, panther skins, incense, gums, slaves, and wild animals in exchange for manufactured goods, wine, corn, and olive oil.

Under Rome, commerce and travel between Egyptian rule and Meroë continued, but gradually slackened. The Meroites sent some ambassadors to the Romans, and occasional envoys probably returned these visits. Meroite pilgrims mixed with Romanized Egyptians at Philae, the site of the temple to Isis, and Egyptian artisans had a hand in temple building in the south. However, by the third century, Meroitic rulers were no longer being buried with imported luxury goods, and pyramid construction had deteriorated - signs of the decline in Meroë's power.

At the end of that century, when Roman control over Egypt weakened, the Blemmyes, mounted on camels, began to infiltrate the Upper Nile Valley. Their raids forced Rome to evacuate Nubia in CE 289 and to relocate its southern border at the First Cataract. Seven years later, Emperor Diocletian called in a people known as the Nobatae (perhaps the same people as the Noba mentioned by Strabo) to protect the southern frontier from further Blemmye incursions. Early in the fourth century, Meroë collapsed as a result of conflicts with the Nobatae, and Axumite raids under King Ezana (about 320-360) would help to extinguish the dying kingdom. During his reign, Axum converted to Christianity and established close links with the Alexandrine patriarchate and the Byzantine Empire. Meanwhile, Axum also had indirect commercial ties with India and must have competed successfully with Meroë for control of the caravan routes to Central Africa.

Following the destruction of Meroë, Nubia

experienced a period of political fragmentation. The former enemies, Blemmyes and Nobatae, united forces and toward CE 450 attacked the temple site of Philae. Rome, in turn, defeated them by 453, forcing them to give up Roman prisoners and pay an indemnity for the damage they committed. In return, the nomads were allowed to visit the Isis sanctuary and even carry her statue back periodically to Nubia. When these nomads broke the peace a few years later, another Roman expedition punished them, and Rome agreed to pay them a subsidy for a period of 100 years to keep the peace.

The Roman territories in North Africa, excluding Egypt and Cyrenaica, covered only about 140,000 square miles during the period of its strength. This relatively small area, mainly the fertile, "useful" zone in the north, represented less than 10 percent of the present-day Maghreb, but it contained most of the Maghrebin population of approximately 6.5 million people. The region was divided into four provinces during the high empire: Africa Proconsularis (Tunisia and coastal Tripolitania), Numidia (eastern Algeria), Mauretania Caesariensis (western Algeria), and Mauretania Tingitana (northern Morocco). But even this proved too large an area to control effectively. At the end of the third century, Rome amputated about one-third of its territory around Tripolitania and in the west, leaving intact a region relatively safe from the nomads. Rome also regrouped the provinces: It joined Egypt and Cyrenaica with other eastern holdings, and for administrative convenience, attached Mauretania Tingitana to Spain and divided the rest of the Maghreb into seven smaller provinces.

Numerous revolts in the far west taxed the Romans during much of the third and fourth centuries, but the emperors never attempted to restrict the movement of nomads in and out of the Mauretanias. Most mountainous zones also escaped Roman control. By CE 253, mountaineers began raiding their lowland neighbors; they continued their attacks on and off until the end of the century. About CE 370, the Berber prince Firmus, based in the mountainous region of Kabylia, a perennial stronghold for dissidents, led a destructive revolt that spread through Numidia, and the Romans imported troops from Europe to crush the rebellion in 375. A revolt that lasted from 396 to 398, led by Firmus's brother Gildo, proved to be less serious and was easily put down. Both, however, represented Berber aspirations for autonomy and their desire for revenge against the rich masters. They had the sympathy of North Africa's growing Christian community, especially the Donatist heretics, who themselves led a revolt against official Christianity from their remote rural settlements in Numidia.

Before the end of the first century, Christianity had spread into Egypt, to the Greek-speaking educated urban population, who increasingly were moving toward a monotheistic belief. Important Church fathers, among them Clement and Origen, helped establish this initial Greek predominance, with Alexandria as the most significant theological center of the empire, vying with Rome for pre-eminence. When large numbers of Copts, as the indigenous Egyptians were known, converted in the last years of the third century, Church leaders produced a corpus of Coptic literature written in the Greek alphabet, helping to fuse Greek and Coptic elements of the population into a new unity. Hermits, who withdrew alone or in groups into the Egyptian desert, where the demons of temptation were believed to dwell, helped organize the first monasteries in Christendom. As monks, they spread the faith among most of the rural folk during the fourth century. Attempts were also made to convert the Nubians, but they had little effect before the sixth century when new Nubian states arose.

Christianity took root in the Maghreb during the second century among slaves, Berber agricultural laborers, and lower-class urbanites. By the third and fourth centuries, when the faith had spread throughout the country, the Maghreb, with its many towns, contained 600 bishops, more than Gaul and Egypt, combined, and produced such great Church fathers as Tertullian, Cyprian, and Augustine. Christian missionaries attempted to convert the Jewish minority, some of whom dated back to the Phoenician settlement and others to the destruction of the Temple in Jerusalem in CE 70.

Starting in the third century, North Africa, from Egypt to Morocco, became the scene of furious religious controversies, denunciations, and persecutions, which led to the establishment of local or national Christian churches such as those at the Monophysites in the Nile Valley and of the Donatists and Arians in Barbary. Doctrinal and partisan issues confused the illiterate, who often blindly followed their bishops in or out of the Orthodox Church.

The affinity for rebellion or rejection of submission and orthodoxy shielded the technologically weak, and therefore vulnerable, Berbers and other North African peoples from total assimilation and loss of identity despite centuries of alien rule. It eased North African integration into a wider ecumene, for by passing over the heretical road, segments of the population assimilated the basic ideas of their overlords without having to sacrifice their local heritages.

Donatism began as a simple heresy within a puritanical tradition; it emphasized martyrdom, unremitting faith, morality, and poverty. However, Donatism became the vehicle of a great social revolt of agricultural laborers whose situation had deteriorated by the fourth century. The Donatist heresy centered on the issue of whether or not members of the clergy who had yielded to Rome during its persecution of North African Christians should be restored to communion with the Church. Besides making Christianity palatable to the population of the central Maghreb, it acted as a convenient substitute for armed rebellion. It reached extremes by equating martyrdom with suicide and in allying itself with violent bands of migrant workers, the Circumcellions, who refused to be tied to the land. Until the Donatist sect was outlawed in CE 412, and even afterward, it won many adherents, especially in Numidia, and split the Church into an orthodox wing loyal to Rome and a puritanical African branch supported by many Berbers.

The Monophysite movement developed out of complicated theological disputes over the nature of God (whether he had one or two natures as the Father and the Son), with the Egyptians, led by the Alexandrine patriarchs, championing a strict unitary position. Until CE 451, the Alexandrines prevailed in Church councils, and their views were considered orthodox, but at the Council of Chalcedon, the bishops, led by the Constantinople hierarchy, rejected the Monophysite creed and declared that Christ had two natures. Those who supported the council came to be known as Melchites, or royalist followers of Constantinople, whereas the others, the Monophysites, were branded as heretics.

The partisan roots of this controversy dated back to CE 381 when Constantinople was declared the second city in Christendom, thereby pre-empting Alexandria's position as a rival to Rome. Alexandrine leaders fought this decision and used the Monophysite doctrine as a vehicle to outmaneuver Constantinople and maintain their dominance in the Church. The issue became an Egyptian cause, and the doctrine served as an ideology of national unity. When the bishops of Alexandria lost their majority at the Council of Chalcedon, the Egyptians broke away from the Roman-Byzantine Church, though Egypt still remained part of the empire until 616, when the Persians conquered the country.

With the doctrinal split between the Orthodox and Coptic sects well defined, the two competed for converts in the region of the Upper Nile. By CE 540, there were three separate Nubian kingdoms: the northernmost, Nobatae, or Nobatia, between the First and Third Cataracts; Makuria, with its royal city at Dongola; and farther south, Alodia, with its capital at Soba. After CE 640, Nobatia and Makuria were united into a single kingdom, with its capital at Dongola, and Monophysite Christianity became the state religion. Sometime early in the seventh century, Alodia also converted to the same sect. Greek became the liturgical language of all Nubia and was later supplemented by Coptic and Nubian, including Greek loan-words and written in the Greek alphabet.

After CE 410, the Maghreb was the only part of the western Mediterranean not seriously disrupted by Germanic hordes. The relative prosperity of Barbary, even though in decline, certainly must have attracted their attention. By this time, the Roman army in Africa consisted mainly of Goth mercenaries who constantly fought desert marauders. In CE 429, cousins of the Goths, the Vandals, crossed over from Spain to North Africa in Roman ships, after their king Genseric received an invitation from Bonifacius, the Roman governor of Africa, to join his mercenary forces. Within the next ten years, the Vandals, numbering some 80,000 and including 15,000 soldiers, had become ambitious in their own behalf and in CE 439 went on unopposed to conquer Carthage, nominally held by Rome.

All of Morocco and most of Algeria were untouched by the Vandal conquerors, who concentrated their rule on Tunisia and a small part of Algeria. Most of the Tunisian laborers who worked the large Roman domains stood by and watched one landlord replace another. The wealthy fled when they could to the Italian peninsula or Constantinople. Vandal governors won the support of non-Romanized pagan Berbers, and with their aid, Genseric formed a powerful fleet, which he used for piracy.

The conquest allowed independent Berber mountain republics to develop, and mountaineers raided Numidia and Mauretania. These desert invasions further hastened the disintegration of urban life. The Vandals respected the Roman civilization that they found there and did not ruin the country through "vandalism" - a term first coined in eighteenth-century France. They returned most of it to nomads and mountaineers, who brought to a standstill the slow assimilation processes that had characterized Carthaginian and Roman rule for a millennium.

The Vandal army, weakened by constant struggles against marauding Berbers and, more significantly, against invading Tripolitanian nomads, crumbled when the Byzantines launched their seaborne invasion in CE 533. The eastern Roman army contained trained archers who had perfected their warlike skills in battles with the Persians. The Vandals, accustomed to fighting with swords and spears, were technologically overwhelmed. The conquerors shipped the majority of Vandal male captives to Constantinople, where they were integrated into the imperial army. A small number remained in Barbary as slaves or artisans, and Vandal women married Byzantine soldiers.

The Byzantines conquered Vandal territories

with the aid of Berber chiefs, to whom they promised autonomy after victory. Instead, eastern administrators and lawyers attempted to re-establish Barbary as it was prior to the coming of the Vandals. Vandal proprietors were dislodged, and land was returned to descendants of former owners or turned over to the Church, the imperial Crown, or the conquering officers. The Byzantines also disestablished Arianism, the Christian heresy adopted by the Vandals. Because the eastern Romans did not fulfill their part of the bargain, they had to fight off continual revolts. Although the Garamantes converted to Christianity after signing a treaty of alliance with the Byzantines in CE 569, such alliances hardly sufficed to prevent nomads from raiding up to the walls of Carthage.

The Vandals had appointed new Arian bishops, who championed yet another heresy to weaken Christianity as a whole in Africa. People became confused even further when the Byzantines attempted to re-establish orthodoxy after ejecting the descendants of Genseric from Barbary and the Persians from Egypt in CE 626. In addition to the general corruption of the Eastern Empire and Church, the newcomers persecuted Arians, Donatists, Monophysites, pagans, and Jews alike, and succeeded in alienating the population that they had hoped to win over. A general atmosphere of disillusionment prevailed. Social solidarity, already strained by late Roman and Vandal times, was taxed even further, and resistance to foreign conquest crumbled. The way was opened to a syncretic religion like Islam, which in one prodigious sweep would render doctrinal controversies meaningless.

The new followers of Islam, invading from the East, took Egypt and Cyrenaica from CE 641 to 642. Tripolitania fell in 643, setting the stage for the first raids to the west, which began in 647. Although the new invaders faced little opposition from the Byzantine army, their initial conquests proved superficial. The real battles of establishing political control over the North Africans and winning them over first to Islam and then to Arabic culture still lay ahead. They accomplished these tasks in the Maghreb over centuries filled with rebellion, mass migrations, new heresies, and much political bargaining, and only, finally, on terms acceptable to the North Africans.

4

THE SPREAD OF ISLAM
JOHN RALPH WILLIS

The millennium between CE 500 and 1500 witnessed significant changes in the historical evolution of Abyssinia (Ethiopia), Arabia, and the East African littoral. At the commencement of this epoch, the Christian civilization of Axum was at its apogee. In the fourth century, somewhere between CE 320 and 350, Axumite warriors had successfully overthrown the power of Kush, invading its once-celebrated capital at Meroë. The final collapse of Meroë, which seems already to have been in decline, shifted the focal point of Nile Valley culture from ancient Kush to its successor states, the Christian kingdoms of Nubia. The prosperity of Axum derived from the strategic location of its chief port, Adulis, a favorite emporium for

Greek ships frequenting the Red Sea routes and other vessels participating in the east-west trade between the Yemen and the Nile Valley.

With the rise of Islam and the development of Arab power, however, came the disruption of the lucrative Red Sea trade and the eclipse of Abyssinian influence in this region. Henceforth, until the appearance of the Portuguese toward the end of the millennium, Arab culture and influence became the dominating force in the trading communities that sprang up along the East African coast. The rise of Arab power brought forth a rapid and wide-ranging diffusion of Islam into significant portions of East Africa (including parts of Abyssinia itself), and as far as North and northwest Africa, where it took root among Berber and Sudanic peoples. The chapter begins with a discussion of relations between Abyssinia and Arabia at the dawn of the Islamic period. Later sections trace the development of Arab culture on the East African coast and in the region of northwest and West Africa, where Islam emerged the dominant religion.

The sixth century seems to mark the apogee of Abyssinian influence in the Red Sea region. In CE 531, the Abyssinians succeeded in establishing their authority in southern Arabia. Subsequently, however, Abyssinians who had ruled in south Arabia at the pleasure of the Christian Negus broke away from Abyssinian control and set up an independent regime in the Yemen. The leader of this new state was a Christian Abyssinian called Abraha, formerly the slave of a Byzantine merchant of Adulis. The creation of a government in south Arabia, which fell outside the sphere of Abyssinia, caused difficulties for the latter as well as Byzantium, which together were at that time attempting to counteract Persian influence in the Red Sea zone. It was also in CE 530-531 that Justinian entered into negotiations with the Abyssinians, proposing that they attempt to purchase silk from the Indians and resell it to the Romans, thus circumventing their common competitor, the Persians, This scheme proved untenable, however, because Persian merchants had succeeded in taking control of the key harbors frequented by Indian ships and, in addition, had occupied the adjoining areas. By purchasing the entire cargoes of these ships, the Persians were able to monopolize Indian trade in the Red Sea region.

Toward the end of the sixth century, the Christian Yemenite leader Abraha is said to have launched an attack on Mecca, which was to result in the unification of the Arabs and the sealing off of their country against Abyssinian influence for all time. This was the beginning of the so-called War of the Elephant, romanticized in Arab history and mentioned in Qur'an (Koran).

Legend recalls that Abraha wished to undermine the attraction of the Kaaba, the ancient pagan shrine in Mecca to which pilgrims flocked from all over Arabia. According to Muslim tradition, Abraha set out to destroy the Kaaba, accompanied by a large number of troops and one (some sources say more than one) elephant. But upon entering the vicinity of the Meccan territory, the elephant is said to have kneeled down and refused to advance farther toward the city of Mecca, though when his head was turned in any other direction, his movement went unrestricted. Flights of birds are said to have dropped stones upon the invading troops, as mentioned in the Qur'an, who all died. A rationalizing explanation of this phenomenon held that the invading troops were in actuality smitten with smallpox. Abraha himself, it is claimed, was afflicted with the loathsome disease and repatriated to the Yemen, where he soon died.

Some authorities contend, however, that the legendary story of Abraha the Christian Yemenite is in reality a conflation of two records of south Arabian attacks on Mecca: that by Abraha and a much earlier one led by the Axumite king Afilas, whom numismatic evidence places at about CE 300. It was during this period that the kingdom of Axum exercised a brief hegemony over south Arabia, and it is thought that a military enterprise farther north was not an impossibility. According to these authorities, the word "Afilas," the Abyssinian, and *al-fil,* the "elephant" in Arabic, became confused as the two legends merged into one. A modern interpretation hazards that if Abraha had actually undertaken such an expedition, a more likely explanation of his aims is that the rapprochement between Abraha and his former Abyssinian superiors against Persian intrusions allowed Abraha to adopt a more aggressive policy toward Persia. According to this interpretation, the expedition was the first move in a projected attack on Persian dominions. In Islamic history, the main relevance of the episode of the "Elephant" was that tradition ascribes the birth of the Prophet Muhammad to this period, known historically as the Year of the Elephant (about CE 570).

In the Muslim view, the Islamic Dispensation constitutes the last in a series of Covenants between Allah and His people. Muslims readily recognize that other peoples, notably Jews and Christians, have entered into Covenants with the Almighty. Indeed, the Islamic revelations continue the Judaic and Christian traditions insofar as Islam accepts the authenticity of previous prophets and messengers through whom Allah communicated His Will. But the Qur'an is seen as the ultimate communication of the Divine Will, and Muhammad is looked upon as the final prophet of Allah. The followers of Muhammad are called Muslims because by embracing the message that Allah revealed to Muhammad, as contained in the Qur'an, they thereby "submit" themselves to the Divine Will. Hence, the words "Islam" and "Muslim," derived from the same root, both stress the necessity of "submission to what Allah commanded Muhammad to "recite" (the meaning of "Qur' an") to his people.

It was the genius of Muhammad that over a remarkably short period, he was able to transform the basis of Arab society - to mold out of the anonymity of collective life a place for the individual. The ties of Islam and the community of faith were to supersede the bonds of kinship. The inauguration of the Islamic Dispensation was to herald a new relationship between men. "The white man was not to be above the black nor the black above the yellow," said the tradition, "all men were to be equal before their Maker," and equal before the Law. Among believers, superiority was to be marked only by priority in the faith or by stricter observance of its precepts.

The Islamic religion came to be premised upon five pillars. Believers were required to accept the Muslim faith, professed in the words, "there is no Deity but Allah, and Muhammad is the Prophet of Allah." Belief in the "oneness" of Allah remains a fundamental tenet in Islam. Second, Muslims were required to pray at five prescribed times of the day. A third duty obliged all believers to give alms to the needy, and a collection was taken up for this purpose at certain times of the year. Muslims were further under obligation to endure a thirty-day fast, called Ramadan, during which they could neither eat nor drink between sunrise and sunset. A fifth duty prescribed that all Muslims undertake the pilgrimage to Mecca and Medina, the cherished cities of Islam, at least once in their lifetime, provided they had the means.

When Muhammad died in CE 632, he bequeathed a legacy of unity within his religious community. Four successors, who continued his work but did not inherit his gift of prophecy, were elected by the community, though not without opposition. Muhammad had been accepted by his people both as prophet and political leader. The Meccan and Medinan peoples through their *shaykhs,* or leaders, entered into a compact with Muhammad and recognized his authority. It became the task of his successors to maintain those treaties, and often they found it necessary to resort to force in order to secure the unity for which he had strived. Efforts to subdue opposition to the new leaders of Islam generated a movement that reached beyond Arabia and culminated in the expansion of Islam in many lands. The ancient provinces of the Roman Empire, including Egypt and Syria, as well as the once-powerful Persian dominions, all fell within the sphere of the rising Crescent.

But the expansion of Islam can be attributed to

another factor. Islam spread from the Arabian Peninsula by virtue of the jihad Muhammad's followers declared upon his enemies. Despite its popular conception, the jihad, another fundamental duty in Islam, involves much more than "holy war" waged to expand Islamic frontiers or to defend the faith against foreign intrusion. For the believer, jihad is a form of effort - "a struggle in the path of Allah" - that can be undertaken by peaceful or military means. In short, the diffusion of Islam was viewed by Muslims as a serious effort to be undertaken for Allah's sake, as indeed the Crusades were launched by Christians "for the glory of God" and the protection of His Church.

If the Persian intrusion had served to disrupt the sea and trade routes in the Red Sea to the detriment of Abyssinian interests, the expansion of Islam, which soon enveloped the whole of Arabia, had an equally damaging effect of severing Abyssinia, at least temporarily, from its spiritual source, the patriarchate of Alexandria. This was indeed the beginning of many centuries of isolation for Abyssinia, whose peoples retired within their impregnable mountain fastnesses. Moreover, the penetration of Islam led to the Islamization of the Abyssinian lowlands, as Muslim powers were able to establish sovereignty over the African Red Sea littoral. As the pace of conversion accelerated in Abyssinia, Islam reached as far as eastern Shoa and the Sidama country.

For Abyssinia, the period from the tenth century to the twelfth was a time of great internal weakness, as well as one that witnessed the continued penetration of Islam over a wide area. Early in the tenth century, a people called Falasha, Hamitic-speaking peoples who practiced the Jewish religion, were able to dislodge the "Solomonian" dynasty of Abyssinia (so called because of the attempts of Abyssinian rulers to link themselves genealogically with King Solomon of biblical times) and establish their own power. The result of this change of dynasty was that the preservers of "Solomonian" claims took refuge in Shoa to the south, and Axum (the ancient capital) ceased to be the political capital, though it remained the principal religious center and the place where subsequent kings of the "Solomonian" line were installed.

Muslim traders and men of religion were instrumental in the spread of Islam throughout parts of Abyssinia and the adjoining regions. Islam took root in the Dahlak archipelago, the Danakil and Somali coasts, among the Bedja (Beja) in the north, in the Ifat imamate of eastern Shoa, at Harar in the east, and near Lake Zway in the west. The religion also made converts of the Sidama peoples in the south, whose ruling classes, through trading relations, are said to have adopted the new persuasion.

Moreover, the slave trade proved a powerful stimulant to the Islamization of the coastal plains.

This was because trading in slaves, largely controlled by Muslim merchants, brought about a link with the Arab world and resulted in the creation and sustenance of such Muslim-controlled centers as Zeila and Mogadishu, which became linked with the Danakil and Somali hinterlands. It is further believed that slave raiding greatly aided in the diffusion of Islam among pagan peoples of the East African coast, as conversion would have been an expedient means of avoiding the difficulties of a slave existence. Islamic law forbade the enslavement of free Muslims but tolerated the continued enslavement of peoples who converted after their capture. Finally, it is known that the slave-raiding activity itself generated a process of state-building, which culminated in the establishment of Muslim power in Harar, Arussi, and the lake district in the southwest. Powerful slave merchants used their slaves as a source of influence and military power, and ultimately, as a basis for the establishment of independent states.

The beginnings of the Muslim state in eastern Shoa date most probably from the late ninth century CE. In 1285, however, the Shoan imamate was overthrown and absorbed into that of Ifat, the predominant Muslim state of Abyssinia and the *foyer* of Muslim expansion throughout that region. From the fourteenth until the sixteenth century, a war of attrition ensued between the highlands of Christian Abyssinia and the swiftly developing Muslim imamates or communities that became entrenched all along the eastern and southern fringes of the Abyssinian plateau. It was during this period that the walled city of Harar to the south of Zeila became a Muslim city-state and a powerful center of Islamic commerce and cultural propagation.

Shortly after the rise of Islam, Muslim Arabs and Persians created a series of coastal settlements in the region that came to be called Somalia. In these towns, Arab and Persian merchants settled as local aristocracies, initiated a process of Islamization, and by intermarrying with local women formed a mixed Somali-Arab culture - the Somali counterpart to the more extensive Swahili society of the East African coast to the south. The Somali traditionally set much store on alleged descent from noble Arab lineages and, indeed, from the family of Muhammad himself. Such claims commemorate the prolonged period of contact between the Somali and the civilization of the Arabian coasts - a contact that has brought Islam and many other elements of Muslim-Arab culture to Somaliland. Such cultural borrowings betray themselves in the Somali language, which contains numerous Arabic loan-words, and again are manifest in the widespread use of Arabic as a second language. Conversely, however, the Somali language retains its unique character as a separate and vigorous tongue possessing an unusually rich oral literature. Poetry among the Somali is not merely the private medium of the author, but frequently the collective tongue of a clan or other group.

Typical of those centers of Arab influence in northern Somalia were the seaports of Zeila and Berbera. The walled city of Zeila, after the decline of Axum in the sixth century CE, became the most important port for the coffee trade of the Abyssinian highlands; it was described by Ibn al-Wardi (about 1340) as the "emporium of the Habash," or Abyssinians. It emerged also as one of the largest ports for the slave trade with Arabia. In ancient times, goat skins were the chief export that the Yemen market absorbed in great quantities during the course of a rapid development of the leather industry under Persian rule. In the fourteenth century, Zeila was visited by the celebrated Arab traveler Ibn Battuta, who died in 1377. While conceding its importance as a commercial center, Ibn Battuta described the town as "vile and evil-smelling." The infamous stench of Zeila rose from the great quantity of fish that was brought there, as well as from the blood of camels customarily slain in the streets. In the fifteenth century, Zeila was occupied by the Turks, but in 1516, they gave way to the Portuguese, who burned the town.

Berbera, southeast of Zeila and opposite Aden, was identified by the *Periplus,* Ptolemy, and Cosmas Indicopleustes as the Land of Frankincense - a designation more properly ascribed to the Arabian region of Mahra, the most productive source of aromatic plants. Situated in the state of Ifat, Berbera formed part of the Muslim province of Adal, whose amir, or commander, was apparently strong enough to rule Ifat in the fifteenth century. Founded in the ninth or tenth century, Adal frequently served as a refuge for Muslims farther to the south, who sought to flee Abyssinian jurisdiction. Its rulers belonged to the ruling house of Zeila, and the history of the two areas was often linked. Adal reached its zenith in the fourteenth century but declined precipitously during the Muslim struggles to conquer Abyssinia in the sixteenth century.

In later times, when the Somali began to expand, their relationship with the Arab cities of the Banadir coast - Mogadishu, Merca, and Brava - developed from that of a trading partnership to one of political domination. The Arab cities of the Banadir were commercial towns largely dependent for their prosperity upon the trade between Abyssinia, Arabia, and the markets of the East.

The foundation of Mogadishu (Maqdishu) as an Arabian colony is ascribed to the tenth century CE. Evidence from certain inscriptions points as well to a Persian settlement, which took place at about the same time. João de Barros, writing in the sixteenth century, noted that the first people to export gold from Sofala were the merchants of Mogadishu. By the end of the twelfth century, however, the gold trade had passed into the hands of Kilwa traders. The original commercial treaty was made between Mogadishu and Sofala, but later this most favored treatment was acquired by Kilwa, and with it, the gold trade of *Sofala*. The merchants of this Indian Ocean entrepôt were constrained at times to band together against the Somali threat, which seemed to be constant, and against other invaders who came by sea. They organized themselves into a confederation of thirty-nine clans. One of these clans, the *Muqri*, acquired a religious supremacy over the others who agreed that the *qadi,* or jurisconsul, in religious matters should be appointed from within its ranks. In the sixteenth century, Mogadishu declined in commercial prosperity due to continued Somali intrusions. Archeological remains uncovered at Mogadishu reveal it as larger than and culturally superior to Kilwa, though the latter was more important as a commercial center.

Brava (Barawa), directly south of Mogadishu, was known to the Arab geographer Yaqut al-Rumi, who died in CE 1229, as an amber-exporting area. Tradition holds that it was founded shortly after Mogadishu, and the commercial fate of the two cities was always closely linked. The Bantu language "Chimbelazi" survives in the town of Brava and is probably derived from the common speech of the coastal cities in Somalia.

In the earlier period of its history, African traders frequented the coast with slaves and ivory, which were conveniently stored in centers near the mouth of a river or on some offshore island until they could be gathered by dhows, which came south before the beginning of the monsoon season. Gold and ivory were brought from the region of what is today Rhodesia and exchanged at Sofala for Indian beads. The trade route down to Sofala and by sea along the coast of Kilwa was of crucial importance to the economic prosperity of East Africa. Other commodities that drew merchants to the coast were leopard skins, palm oil, copper and iron, tortoise shells, rhinoceros horns, and the more prosaic hides. In addition to beads, foreign traders used spears, knives, axes, and porcelain as items of exchange.

By the tenth century, a striking change in the commercial character of the coast had taken place. No longer were the participants traders from the Yemen, as the East African trade was now separated from that of the Aden Gulf coast. In place of the Yemenites, we find merchants from the Persian Gulf and Oman. And by this period, the trade had extended itself as far as the Comoro Islands, the lands of the Zambezi, and the great island of Madagascar. The trade in ivory was probably the most important at this period. According to al-Masudi, who died in CE 956, ivory was seldom employed for indigenous use owing to its value as an export item. Although the slave trade is not specifically mentioned by this author, it doubtless continued to be of considerable importance.

Kilwa served as an entrepôt for gold traded from Mutapa (Mwenemutapa or Monomotapa) through Sofala. Its domains are said to have included the settlements that developed along the coast as far as Kilwa Kivinje, and possibly to the Rufiji River, the island of Mafia, and in the south, to the region of Mozambique and Sofala. It was probably at its apogee in the twelfth and thirteenth centuries, but regained some distinction after the rebuilding of the Great Mosque, the finest surviving monument in East Africa. It struck a copper coinage of a single denomination from the commencement of the thirteenth century, but it is conjectured that this might have been more a matter of prestige than of commercial convenience.

Vasco da Gama, who visited Kilwa (Quiloa) on his second voyage, left a detailed description of the town and its inhabitants (about 1502). He described the city as large, and being of "good buildings of stone and mortar with terraces, and . . . much wood works. The city comes down to the shore, and is entirely surrounded by a wall and towers, within which there may be 12,000 inhabitants. The country all round is very luxuriant with many trees and gardens of all sorts of vegetables, citrons, lemons, and the best sweet oranges that were ever seen, sugarcanes, figs, pomegranates, and a great abundance of flocks, especially sheep, which have fat in the tail, which is almost the size of the body, and very savory. The streets of the city are very narrow as the houses are very high, of three and four stories, and one can run along the tops of them upon the terraces, as the houses are very close together: and in the port there were many ships."

There is some evidence of an Umayyad-Abbasid tradition of architecture at Kilwa. According to the *Kitab al-Zanuj* (the Chronicle of the Zanj) and other late sources, all of which are difficult to assess as to their reliability, immigrants came to East Africa from Arab lands during the chronological period spanned by the Umayyad and Abbasid dynasties (CE 661-1258). One is tempted to associate this architectural tradition with these early immigrants, although there is an alternative hypothesis. The Kilwa Chronicle speaks of immigrants arriving from the Persian city of Shiraz and settling at Kilwa in about the tenth century CE. Some authorities have suggested that these immigrants might have been responsible for the distinctly Umayyad- Abbasid type architecture at Kilwa. Recent archeological findings in the region, however, point toward a much later immigration of the Shiraz newcomers. These investigations indicate that the Shiraz settlement took place some two hundred years later than the date in the latter part of the tenth century, which has hitherto been accepted. The arrival of the Shirazi, as they are called, is related to the appearance of coins of Ali b. al-Hasan, who is identified with the first ruler of the so-called Shirazi dynasty at Kilwa (about CE 1200). From this change of dynasty is interpreted a marked cultural break in the latter part of the thirteenth or early fourteenth century. Subsequent to this event came a fresh settlement of immigrants and the seizure of Sofala and its gold trade. Finally, it is contended that the Shiraz settlement consisted not of a migration of people from the Persian Gulf directly to Kilwa and other places, as was formerly held, but rather a movement of settlers from the Banadir coast.

The legendary Sofala, situated in the southern region of Mozambique, was often called Sofala or Zanj or Golden Sofala in order to differentiate it from another port by the same name near Bombay in India. This medieval emporium was known to al-Masudi as a rich gold-producing area possessing an agreeable climate and a fertile land. It was also al-Masudi who pointed to Sofala as the place wherein the Zanj built their capital—important evidence that may lend support to the contention that the Bantu (if we read "Bantu" for "Zanj") had already inhabited the coast of Africa south of the equator by the tenth century. (A full discussion of the Bantu migrations appears in Chapter Seven.) The Bantu are known to have arrived from the interior, and at their farthest northern extension, they are said to have reached the Webbe Shebeli

River, which flows through Somalia, curving southward parallel to Mogadishu and Brava.

Subsequently, however (probably about the eleventh century), these Bantu speakers were driven south by the Somali to the valley of the Juba River in southern Somaliland. Here they remained for another 500 years. The Bantu, however, cannot be considered a significant factor in molding the culture of the East African coast during the period under discussion. Their impact was farther south and in the interior, though they are known to have forged important trading links with the Arab settlements on the coast. Export to Kilwa from various Bantu-dominated areas can be presumed for an earlier period, while more regular trade developed after the establishment of Sofala by the Arabs in the tenth century.

According to al-Idrisi, who died in CE 1166, Sofala was famous for its iron mines as well as its gold. Yaqut perpetuated Sofala's reputation as a land of gold; he mentions that commercial transactions were effected by means of "dumb barter" (that is, the participants made no actual contact with each other during the trade). During the time of the Arab geographer Ibn al-Wardi (about 1340), Sofala gained some distinction for its iron deposits. Iron from Sofala mines was considered purer and more malleable than that found in India. The Indians smelted the iron and made steel, from which tools and weapons with fine cutting edges were fashioned. De Barros spoke of a "tower" at Sofala over twelve stories high, as well as similar erections of stone, all of which the Zanj called *Zimbabwe* (literally "stone house") in referring to the official residences of their leaders. Modern archeology has revealed the Zanj as a hunting and fishing people of the Bushman type - at least this designation would apply to those who inhabited the Azanian coast. The implements of these autochthonous inhabitants of the coast have been found in many places, and it is from their discovery that archeologists have been able to reconstruct something of their cultural characteristics.

In the sixteenth century, the commerce of Sofala shifted to Quelimane in the region north of the Zambezi, and by the seventeenth century, Sofala's exports were insignificant. When the Portuguese upset the balance of power and the pattern of trade in the Indian Ocean, Arab trading settlements such as Sofala were at their zenith. The results of the Portuguese intrusion were manifest in the interruption of the gold trade between the coast and India. The Portuguese sought to redirect this trade to their own advantage, and in the course of doing so, wrought much destruction upon the wealth of Arab trading cities, which had so long monopolized commercial transactions on the coast.

Islam and Arab civilization also took root in many parts of North and West Africa. In East Africa, Islam failed to develop significantly in the hinterland, although Arabs were able to evolve a prosperous series of settlements along the coast. In contrast, Islam in North and West Africa was accepted by urban dwellers along the coast and in the interior, as well as by nomadic groups who inhabited the vast Saharan regions. The Islamization of North and West Africa, however, was a long and uneven process. Although Islam made its first appearance in this area in the seventh century (as early as CE 639), the initial Arab venture was more a reconnaissance mission than a settling migration. The first Arabs in North Africa came for the purpose of establishing a foothold. The military contingents used for this purpose were not extensive, and the soldiers were compelled to leave their families behind and bring only that which was necessary to accomplish a limited military objective. Hence, it is highly unlikely that substantial conversions to Islam could have taken place much before the beginning of the eighth century on the coast and the tenth century in the interior. The diffusion of Islam before the eighth century would have taken a veritable army of specialized religious teachers to preach Islamic doctrines appropriately. Moreover, these teachers would have had to speak Berber, the language of the dominant group on the coast, and further, would have had to establish the necessary rapport among the people conducive to the spread of a new religion.

In North Africa as in East Africa, Muslim proselytizers achieved more rapid success along the coast. Urban centers were created or revived by the Arab occupiers, and because of a larger Arab presence, the Islam that developed in metropolitan areas came to differ quite markedly from that which took root in the hinterland. Qairawan (Kairouan), the first Muslim military outpost (established in what is today Tunisia) also became an important religious center, with an important mosque and several places of religious instruction. Other cities, however, were slow to develop, a factor that seriously restricted the intensity of Islamic diffusion. Indeed, until the creation of Fez (CE 808), one can hardly speak of cities in Morocco, except for Tangier and Ceuta, which were quite atypical. Between Tlemcen and Constantine was a barren area almost totally devoid of settlement. It would not be until the second half of the tenth century that such cities as Ashir, Medea, Miliana, and Algiers would make their appearance or reappearance. Only Ifriqiya (Tunis) could demonstrate a relatively substantial urban density.

Qairawan, the capital of Ifriqiya, was built by Uqba b. Nafi, the Arab commander who led the initial reconnaissance expedition to North Africa. The city was established in CE 670 as a base of operations, supply depot, and a means of keeping in awe the numerous Berber groups that inhabited adjacent areas. "I intend," the historian al-Nuwairi makes him say, "to build a town which can serve as a depot of arms [Qairawan| for Islam to the end of time." The site of the new town, two days' journey from the shore, had been chosen to put the Muslims beyond the danger of an attack from the Byzantines, who still held the towns on the coast. The earlier part of its existence, to the mid-eleventh century, is commonly held to have been one of great economic prosperity, especially remarkable for its agriculture. A political, economic, and cultural metropolis, Qairawan seems also to have been a major commercial and industrial center.

Until recently, it was thought that the prosperity of Qairawan declined sharply as a result of the eleventh-century invasion of Ifriqiya by the nomadic Hilali Arabs. Unlike the first Arab intrusion in this region, described above as a reconnaissance mission, the Hilalian invasion was a veritable settling migration involving nomadic Arabs as well as their women and children. It differed further from the initial mission in that the Hilalians settled in the interior among the Berber peoples, who carried on a similar nomadic existence. The Hilalian appearance in this region was likened to a swarm of locusts swooping down upon the unattended agricultural plains of Ifriqiya and wreaking havoc and destruction in its wake. The Hilalians were further made responsible for a cessation of gold trade from the Sudanic lands of the deep interior to Qairawan on the coast.

Such traditional interpretations, which make the Hilalians the cause of Ifriqiya's woes, have fallen into disfavor. Recent research reasons that the effect of the Hilalis was perhaps more to precipitate a development already well advanced, to wit, the gradual weening away of Qairawan's satellite regions from the metropole. A final and crucial distinction that must be made between the initial reconnaissance mission and the Hilalian settling migration is that the latter was of great quantitative significance. Although figures advanced to reckon Hilalis in the millions are doubtlessly a gross exaggeration, one may conservatively hazard that their numbers must have been in the thousands, whereas the initial wave of the Arab quest numbered no more than a few hundred fighting men. In short, for the first time, Arabs arrived in sufficient numbers to make a lasting impact on the culture and civilization of the North African hinterland and beyond.

In the thirteenth and fourteenth centuries, Arab nomads arrived in the Maghreb in ever-increasing numbers, settling not so much along the coast, but rather in the interior, among Berber nomads. These series of nomadic Arab settlements culminated in the Arabization and Islamization of Berber peoples throughout the region. Arabic became a principal language among these people, and through its use, they began to acquire the basic rudiments of Arab culture. At least initially, Islamic doctrine was poorly understood by those Berbers, as indeed it had been superficially held by their nomadic Arab counterparts. What is important to remember, however, is that despite its unlearned character, rural Islam developed within a decidedly Muslim framework and attained a certain vigor that was to give rise to the two great Islamic revivalist movements of the period under discussion. The Almoravid and Almohad revolutions, as they were called, were generated from the rural hinterland by militant Berber groups seeking to diffuse Islam among unconverted pagan peoples. The Almoravid movement gained numerous adherents among the Sanhaja Berbers of the Western Sahara. It began as a movement to implement stricter Islamic practices among various Berber groups that later formed the Sanhaja confederation. Its leader, Abd Allah b. Yasin, attempted to impose a rigid adherence to Islamic law upon those Berbers who were constrained to follow closely classical legal texts that interpreted Qur'anic dictates for the believers. The Almohad movement rose partly as a reaction to such rigidity, and its leader, Ibn Tumart, a Berber of the Masmuda clan, sought to allow a more direct access to Qur'anic teachings without total reliance upon classical Muslim exegetists. The Almoravid movement, begun in the middle of the eleventh century, was carried to Morocco, as far as Algiers, and then to Spain, where the ideology of the Muslim West and a part of Christian Europe merged in a new synthesis. Similarly, however, the Almohad efforts at Muslim revival were not restricted to the Maghreb, as the followers of the Ibn Tumart's teachings subjected much of Spain after CE 1145.

In the thirteenth century, after its temporary unification under the Almohads, the Maghreb was divided into three independent states: the Marinid regime prevailing at Fez, the Abd al-Wadid state with its capital at Tilimsan (Tlemcen), and the Hafsid state of Ifriqiya. The last was to become the most formidable of these states, ultimately bringing the others under its control. Hafsid power spread as far as Morocco and Spain, which fell under a token submission. The Hafsids entered into treaties with Provence, Languedoc, and the Italian republics, and from 1239 onward, relations with Sicily became more intimate. At about the same time, bonds of friendship were forged between the Hafsids and Aragon, and Christian merchant communities (notably Spanish, Provençal, and Italian) settled in the ports of Ifriqiya, each with its own consul. Moreover, during this period, many Spanish Muslims, craftsmen, and men of letters emigrated to Hafsid domains, and before long constituted a powerful Andalusian political force. Hafsid rulers continued relations with Christian nations, especially with the kingdom of Aragon, which came to the assistance of the Hafsids during several internal crises.

Tunis under the Hafsids developed into a thriving commercial state. Many markets were established under the direction of merchants trading in cereals (during times of good harvest), dates, wax, olive oil, salted fish, fabrics, tapestries, coral, armaments, items of leather, and above all, wool. In exchange for these export commodities, the Hafsids imported cereals, wild fowl, items made from wood, armaments, jewels, ironmongery, cotton, silk, flax, hemp, and various metals, perfumes, medicinal plants, and spices.

During the period from the thirteenth to the sixteenth centuries, Islamic culture attained maturity in North Africa. By the middle of the thirteenth century, the Hafsids had already adopted the madrasa, a kind of religious boarding school, as a center of learning. The institution of the madrasa in Islam grew out of the older form of education associated with the mosque, which was at once a place of worship and religious study. In Muslim education, students were encouraged to commit the Qur'an to memory and to master the corpus of Hadith, consisting of all the actions and sayings of Muhammad, which formed the basis of proper conduct for the believer. Within 150 years, some ten major madrasas were founded, one of the more famous being al-Zaytuna, which is still extant in Tunis. From the beginning, the madrasa was a state institution, enjoying the patronage of the sovereign. One of its functions was to defend

Islamic orthodoxy against heretical doctrines, though it emerged also as a principal center for the exposition of legal texts.

Sufism, or Islamic mysticism, developed rapidly in the Maghreb from the thirteenth century onward. Originally, it was the expression of the devotional feeling of the townsmen - grinding a channel of its own that burst the bonds of orthodox discipline and found a new freedom in the ranges of mysticism. As early as the eleventh century, Sufism enlisted in its service a large proportion of the vital spiritual energies of the Muslim community and created within Islam a fount of self-renewal, which maintained its spiritual vigor throughout the later period of political and economic decay.

The movement in its early stages was personal and individual, but late in the eleventh century, it became organized and confronted the opposition of the official Islamic clerisy and sometimes the leading political figures of the state. Simultaneously, however, the movement swelled beyond the ranks of the faithful and appealed to the popular imagination, supplying a spiritual satisfaction and vitality that militated against the rigidity of the law and its teachings - in short, it emphasized the inwardly felt spiritual needs of the believer, whereas the law, made somewhat sterile by the strict interpretations that prevailed, stressed the external or formal requirements of Islam. The earliest religious confraternity to rise from North African soil was the Shadhiliyya, based on the teachings of Nur al-Din al-Shadhili (1196-1258). Tunis provided a rich recruiting ground for the new order, but al-Shadhili later encountered hostility from political authorities and was forced to flee to Alexandria, where he was instantly successful in his teaching.

In the Maghreb, Islam had been, down to the end of the fourteenth century, a religion of towns and cities. Late in this century and early in the following, this situation radically changed. Islam became primarily a rural phenomenon. The *zawiya*, the Sufi religious center, replaced the mosque and the madrasa as the chief center of learning, and the Sufis displaced the traditional clerisy as guardians and expounders of the faith.

The Islamization of the Sanhaja Berbers, which culminated in the Almoravid movement, meant the ultimate defeat and displacement of the Sarakholle (a Mande-speaking group also known as the Soninke) living in the Adrar in the early part of the ninth century. According to tradition, the desert (before the outbreak of the Almoravid movement) was inhabited by black peoples who led a sedentary existence. At the end of the eighth century, the Lamtuna, part of the large Sanhaja confederation, adopted the militant creed of the Almoravids, which espoused a purified version of Islam - to be spread by force if necessary. The result of their efforts was the partial Islamization of the Sarakholle, some of whom went on to take their place among the most avid agents of Islamic diffusion. Sarakholle proselytizing activity took place in Diara (a region of Nioro in the Sahel) and in some of their colonies in Massina (in Mali), notably Dia (Diakha). The cultivation of Islam by the Sarakholle also occurred in Galam (near Bakel in Senegal) and in Takrur (Futa Toro, Senegal) - an area which itself became synonymous in the eyes of Arab geographers and historians with West African Islam. Countless Takruris (or Sudanis, to cite another common term) made pilgrimage to the Muslim holy cities of Mecca and Medina.

Similarly, the Mande-Diula traders (who, according to their traditions, also emanated from Massina and merged with the Sarakholle of Dia) were greatly responsible for the diffusion of Islam around the Niger Bend as far as the limits of the dense forest region at Begho on the Black Volta. Near the end of the fourteenth century and the beginning of the fifteenth, the Muslim cities of Bonduku and Kong in present-day Ivory Coast were founded.

What was the impact of Islam on the western Sudan at this early date? Islam has been made responsible for far more than its implantation in this region would seem to warrant. Many authors have held that Islamic conversion brought with it a "higher culture" and the development of a unique trading system that arose along the trans-Saharan caravan trails. Such vigorous assertions must be regarded with considerable caution. The role of Islam in the development of the so-called Sudanese Empires is still a subject of heated debate. There is good reason to believe that Islam acted more as a stimulant than a catalyst in the evolution of these states. It is undeniable that the early Sudanese states of Ghana, Mali, and Songhai had already achieved a high degree of development before the adoption of Islam by their ruling aristocracies. What seems also irrefutable, however, is that Islam fertilized anew the more ancient culture of the Sudan and stimulated new growth and new forms of government and institutions. But what is often lost sight of is that the old institutions formed the basis of these developments; that they were rarely completely abolished or overthrown; and that when change did take place, it was more in the guise of syncretistic developments, which owed their origin to the old as well as the new.

There is little basis, for example, for crediting Islam with the creation of a commercial network in the western Sudan. When Muslim merchants first entered the Sudan, they encountered a well-arranged system of commerce established everywhere and conducted along roads well suited to their purpose. This is not to deprive the Muslims of specific innovations that brought about change within the network - it is simply to emphasize that such creations took place within an ancient framework.

The implantation of Islam among the common people was slow to take effect. To understand the reasons for this slow, albeit steady, development, it is necessary to say something of the nature of African society. To early authorities such as Maurice Delafosse and Jules Brévié, Islam had appeared in Black Africa as a religion of travelers and Berber nomads, whereas the indigenous population (largely composed of sedentary cultivators) remained animist or "naturalist." "Naturalism" was a direct outgrowth of the communal needs and temperament of animist hunters and cultivators, whereas Islam corresponded more closely to the requirements of wandering nomads. The Arab, observed Brévié, condemned to travel eternally in solitude at the head of his flock, would not take easily to a *religion du foyer* - a faith that would attach him to the tomb of his ancestors. The nomad's conception of the deity was one of a "unique, omnipresent God, in whom the believer is immersed at every hour, and in every place, who will not abandon the believer during the course of his errancy, who may be invoked at each hour of the five daily prayers without recourse to priests, nor need of temples, and whose eyes are forever watchful over him." Hence, when the nomad perished in the wilderness, his comrades commended his spirit to Allah and his body to the desert, and departed.

The religious life of the "naturalist," however, was seen as a successive link in a sequence of transformations: The "naturalist" was not his own master, he was but an element of the clan. While living, he dwelled beside his ancestors (interred at his bedside) and communed with them constantly for his sustenance. At death, he entered the familial burial ground, where he awaited the moment of incarnation. As a consequence, neither peasants who pained over the soil nor artisans wedded to ancient methods of exploiting iron to whom the land was the source of all their requirements could conceive of a religion in which the earth, the rain, the rivers, and the stones were not the focal point of veneration.

In contrast to this rural majority was a minority of individuals who did not live off the land, either because they had left tillage to inferiors or because they had taken to a commercial existence of an itinerant nature. These town dwellers had lost contact with the land, and they had gained in the interim an important intangible: leisure. And it was precisely this sector among the African populace that emerged the most susceptible to Islamic conversion. Islam seemed to satisfy their pietist sentiments derived from preoccupation with an agrarian cult; it responded to their philistine instincts to differentiate themselves from their rural counterparts; it flattered their urge to instruct themselves and to occupy their leisure with theological and canonical discussions, the reading of sacred texts and famous secular works. They were to constitute the Islamic elite in Black Africa, and there would fall to them the task of convincing their ethnic counterparts of the superiority of this new dispensation.

5

KINGDOMS OF
WEST AFRICA
A. ADU BOAHEN

In West Africa, the area bounded to the north by the Sahara desert, to the south by the Atlantic Ocean, and to the east by Lake Chad and modern Cameroon, a number of independent states and empires evolved in the period between CE 500 and 1470. Among them were Ghana, Mali, Songhai, Kanem-Bornu, and the Hausa states, which were clustered along the southern frontier of the Sahara. Still farther south, between these states and the forest region, arose the Mole-Dagbane states and the Mossi states. Finally, in the forest and coastal zones of Guinea emerged the states of Takrur and Wolof in the region of the Senegal and Gambia rivers, or Senegambia; the Akan, Fante, arid Ga states in the area of modern Ghana; and the states of Ife, Oyo, and Benin in Nigeria.

When did these states and empires crystallize and when did each attain its peak of greatness? How and why were they formed, and how were they governed? And what cultures and civilizations did they develop before the arrival of the Portuguese?

It is significant that the earliest of these states to grow into large kingdoms and empires were those in the savanna immediately to the south of the Sahara. Of these three, namely Ghana, Mali, and Songhai, the first to reach maturity was Ghana, peopled by the Soninke. It is not known for certain when it took form as a state. However, if there were as many as twenty-two kings before the rise of Islam in CE 622, as the oral traditions of Ghana tells, and if by the time the Persian geographer Al-Fazari was writing in CE 773-774 Ghana was already well known to North African and Middle Eastern traders as the Land of Gold, it is not unreasonable to suppose that it emerged as a full-fledged state in the fifth or sixth century CE.

There is no doubt that by CE 1000, Ghana had attained the peak of its power, an empire ruling over a number of smaller tribute-paying states and monopolizing West Africa's enormous and valuable gold trade to North Africa and Europe. This meant that Ghana and its formidable armies also dominated the roads of the Sahara and the savanna. Ibn Hawqal, the first known Arab explorer of the western Sudan, offers in his tenth-century

Book of Ways and Provinces his impression of the Ghanaian sovereign: "the wealthiest of all kings on the face of the earth on account of the riches he owns and the hoards of gold acquired by him and inherited from his predecessors since ancient times." He based his estimate on the quantity of goods he saw being shipped through the Moroccan entrepôt of Sijilmasa.

Ghana's capital city was then Kumbi Saleh, which the Arab writer Al-Bakri described in 1067 as consisting of "two towns situated on a plain, one principally inhabited by Muslim traders, the other settled by the emperor and the local populace." The Muslim town was "large and possessed twelve mosques; in one of these mosques they assembled for the prayers on Fridays. There were imams and muezzins as well as jurists and scholars."

Ghana, however, began to decline during the second half of the eleventh century. Saharan Berbers, driven by territorial ambitions and inspired by Almoravid zeal, succeeded in disorganizing trade and stirring up rebellion among Ghana's tributaries. The empire was overthrown in 1235 by one of its former vassal states, the Susu kingdom, under its ruler Sumanguru Kante.

Mali, which succeeded Ghana, had emerged as a rather small principality by the end of the ninth century CE. Between the eleventh and the thirteenth centuries, it was dominated first by Ghana and then by the Susu kingdom, and it was not until the reign of Sundiata (1230-1255) that Mali embarked on its career of conquest. Building upon the administrative model of Ghana, it extended its trading empire over large parts of the western Sudan, and through the leadership of Mansa Kankan Musa, who reigned from 1312 to 1337, it absorbed such centers as Timbuktu, Gao, and Walata. Ibn Battuta, visiting Mali two decades after Mansa Musa's death, was astounded by the peace, order, and racial tolerance that prevailed in the empire: "They are seldom unjust and have a greater abhorrence of injustice than any other people. Their Sultan shows no mercy to any one guilty of the least act of it. There is complete security in their country. Neither traveler nor inhabitant in it has anything to fear from robbers or men of violence. They do not confiscate the property of any white man who dies in their country, even if it be uncounted wealth. On the contrary, they give it into the charge of some trust-worthy person among the whites, until the rightful heir takes possession of it."

Although the Portuguese, when they first came ashore in 1441, found that most of the states on the coast as well as in the immediate hinterland were still under the control of Mali, the state was already in a period of decline and Songhai was on the rise.

The Songhai people, with the city-state of Gao, or Al-Kawkaw, as their political center, had become active in the trans-Saharan trade by the end of the ninth century. Al-Yaqubi described Gao in 871 as "the greatest of the realms of the as-Sudan, the most important and most powerful, and all the other kingdoms obey its rulers." However, until the last quarter of the fourteenth century, it was controlled first by Ghana and then by Mali. Ibn Battuta, visiting Gao during the era of its vassalage to Mali, described it as "one of the finest towns . . . also one of their biggest and best provisioned towns with rice in plenty, milk and fish. . . ."

In 1375, however, Gao broke away from Mali, though it did not grow into an empire until the reign of Sunni Ali, the celebrated politician, soldier, and administrator who reigned from 1464 until 1492. The empire was consolidated and its frontiers further extended by the second of its most famous rulers, Askia Muhammad the Great. It was during his reign, which lasted from 1493 to 1528, that Songhai attained its peak, controlling the entire central region of the western Sudan.

Leo Africanus, a Christianized Arab geographer who visited Songhai in about 1510, has left some vivid accounts of its intellectual and commercial life. For example, Gao was a town full of "exceeding rich merchants . . . cloth here brought out of Barbarie and Europe. . . . It is a woonder to see what plentie of Merchandize is dayly brought hither, and how costly and sumptuous all things be."

However, during the last decade of that very

century, this sprawling and famous empire completely disintegrated. Its rulers were forced to retreat south along the Niger into their ancestral home in the region of Dendi.

In conformity with the Hamitic hypothesis, scholars of the 1930s and 1940s attributed the foundation of these three states, as well as that of Kanem-Bornu and the Hausa states, simply to some white-skinned invaders from the north. More recently, the introduction of the use of iron has been emphasized as the determining factor. To the present writer, their ascendance was the result of several major developments. The first was the rapid growth of population in the area immediately to the south of the Sahara and especially in the regions of the Niger Bend and the Senegambia. The second was the development of the caravan trade and the subsequent activities of wealthy and therefore powerful and ambitious families. The third was the spread of Islam.

The steady increase of the savanna's population between 1000 BCE and CE 300 or 400 was caused, in part, by the Neolithic revolution (that is, the change from the hunting of wild animals and the collection of wild fruits to the cultivation of food crops and domestication of animals). Historians and ethnobotanists are still hotly debating whether or not there was an independent Neolithic revolution among the Mande peoples in the region of the Niger

Bend in about 5000 BCE. But even if this revolution was introduced into Africa from Asia via Egypt, there is no doubt that the area between the Niger Bend and the middle Senegal River as well as the areas around Lake Chad proved a superior environment for the cereal crops, especially sorghum and millet, which were among the first crops to be cultivated. The Mande and the Kanuri peoples of those areas must, therefore, have obtained an early lead over all the others. Since they could also supplement their diet through fishing, these peoples must have been able to produce food in such quantities that their numbers multiplied. As the contemporary British Africanist J. D. Fage has pointed out, this Neolithic revolution must have also led to "the beginnings of urbanization and of organized government and administration, and, even, perhaps, the flourishing of the idea of a king as a god-like being supreme over all his subjects."

This increase in population must have been further accelerated by the steady desiccation of the Sahara from about 3000 BCE onward. As the Sahara slowly assumed its barren look, a process that was complete by 1500 BCE, some of its inhabitants began to drift into the savanna belt.

The use of iron tools must also have had its effect on population growth in that it facilitated agriculture, but surely it was not, as some scholars have argued, the principal factor in the rise of the western Sudanese states. If this were so, it would follow that the states would have emerged much earlier - nearer 300 BCE, when iron technology is thought to have reached the Nok culture on the lower Niger - and first in the east rather than in the west as, in fact, happened.

It would seem then that by about the last century BCE or the first century CE, the whole of the savanna in general, and the regions of Lake Chad, the Niger Bend, and Nok in particular, must have been occupied by large populations living in family, lineage, or clan groups, in villages bound together by kinship ties or even in city-states and small kingdoms ruled possibly by "divine" kings. Something else must have been needed to stimulate one or more of these nuclei to develop into larger kingdoms and, eventually, empires, and this stimulus must have been provided by the caravan trade. From rock paintings of two-wheeled horse-drawn war chariots and from other archeological data, it is clear that by 1000 BCE, the caravan trade was well established along two main routes. These were a western route through Morocco to the Niger Bend and a central route through the Fezzan, Ghat, and Adrar des Iforas, possibly to the region of Gao on the Niger. The main beasts of burden were bullocks and, after 1200 BCE, horses. It is equally clear from the fifth-century BCE accounts of Herodotus and from other ancient Greek and Roman sources that both the Carthaginians and the Romans were trading with the people of the savanna belt through Berber intermediaries settled in the Fezzan and the Western Sahara.

However, this trade could not have been extensive until the introduction of the camel. The use of this singularly endowed beast of burden spread westward and then southward into the Sahara, and as a result, a complicated network of caravan routes across the Sahara was developed between about CE 200 and 500. To the Morocco-Niger route and the old Garamantes' route from Tripoli to Chad and to Gao was added a caravan route from Egypt to Gao by way of the Saharan oases, including Ghat and the future site of Agadès.

As trade expanded with the use of the camel, not only did more and more people grow wealthy, but handicrafts, mining, and agriculture were stimulated. So, too, urban centers grew in size and influence. Wealth, of course, generates among individuals and families still greater ambition and the desire to control more and more trading activities and trade routes. It is the activities of the talented members of these families (especially of such men as Sundiata and Mansa Musa of Mali and Sunni Ali and Askia Muhammad of Songhai) and not the mere use of iron that brought about the creation of large states and empires.

The people who would be the first beneficiaries of this increasing trade would naturally be those living in the border zone between the Sahara and the savanna, an ideal position from which to play the lucrative role of the middleman. The Soninke of Ghana and the Kanuri of the old state of Kanem were the peoples at the crossroads of the Sahara and the savanna, and they were among the first to develop kingdoms and then empires. The fact that no large kingdoms emerged in Hausaland until the fourteenth century, when the north-south trade began there, provides a further indication of the importance of caravan trade in state-building.

The final factor, which did not cause, but rather accelerated or facilitated to some extent the growth of the empires of Mali and Songhai, as well as Kanem-Bornu and the Hausa states, must have been the introduction of Islam. This religion penetrated the Sahara via the caravan routes and reached the savanna in the ninth and tenth centuries.

Islam is not just a body of doctrines, but a complete way of life, having its own laws, its own system of taxation and administration of justice, its own statecraft, and its own language and traditions of scholarship. Islam's adoption by the rulers of Gao in the tenth century and of Mali and Kanem in the eleventh century must have given them access to all these sciences as well as the means by which to create an educated bureaucracy. A more intense exposure to Islam was gained by those who took the hadj, or pilgrimage, to the Islamic civilization of the Middle East.

It is known, for instance, that on Mansa Musa's celebrated pilgrimage to Mecca in 1324–1325, he met the Spanish scholar, poet, and architect As-Sahili, whom he successfully persuaded to go with him to Mali. It is also known that not only did As-Sahili insist on a strict observance of Islam, but he revolutionalized the architecture of Mali and of the western Sudan in general by introducing brick as the building material for mosques and palaces. Similarly, during his equally famous hadj to Mecca in 1497, Askia Muhammad the Great also met and befriended great scholars such as Abd ar-Rahman as-Suyuti and Muhammad al-Majhili, with whom he began a lifelong correspondence. The latter actually visited him in Songhai and gave him as well as the king of Kano a great deal of advice on religion and politics.

Nevertheless, the governments of all these early Sudanese Empires were of the divine-kingship type, a typically African conception, indicating that these states did not derive their political institutions from Islam, but possibly from ancient Ghana or, in any case, from indigenous Mande institutions. At the head of each was a hereditary monarch. He was assisted by a council of ministers, whose members, following the introduction of Islam, were mostly literate Muslims. Al-Bakri, writing in 1067, tells us that even though the king of Ghana held animistic beliefs, the official in charge of his treasury and the majority of his ministers were Muslims. Unfortunately, we do not have the titles of the ministers of Ghana, but they were probably similar to those of Songhai, whose cabinet included the *hi-koy* (the commander of the navy), *dyina-koy* (commander in chief of the army), *hari-farma* (minister in charge of navigation and fishing), *fari- mundyo* (minister of taxation), *waney-farma* (minister in charge of property), *korey-farma* (minister in charge of foreigners), and *sao-koy* (minister in charge of forests).

The divine-kingship nature of the government is further borne out by descriptions that we have of their court protocol and ceremonial. According to Al-Bakri: "The king [of Ghana] adorns himself like a woman wearing necklaces round his neck and bracelets on his forearms, and when he sits before the people he puts on a high cap decorated with gold and wrapped in a turban of fine cloth. The court of Appeal is held in a domed pavilion around which stand ten horses covered with gold-embroidered materials. Behind the king stand ten pages holding shields and swords decorated with gold and on his right are the sons of the vassal kings of his country wearing splendid garments and their hair plaited with gold. The governor of the city sits on the ground before the king and around are ministers seated likewise. At the door of the pavilion are dogs of excellent pedigree who hardly ever leave the place where the king is, guarding him. Round their necks, they wear collars of gold and silver studded with a number of balls of the same metal. The audience is announced by the beating of a drum which they call daba, made from a long hollow log. When the people who profess the same religion as the king approach him, they fail on their knees and sprinkle dust on their heads for this is their way of showing respect for him. As for the Muslims, they greet him only by clapping their hands."

Ibn Battuta, who visited and had an audience with Mansa Sulaiman, the brother and successor of Mansa Musa, describes another court ritual: "On certain days the Sultan holds audience in the palace yard . . . The Sultan comes out of a door in a corner of the palace, carrying a bow in his hand and a quiver on his back. On his head he has a golden skullcap . . . [he] is preceded by his musicians. . . . As he takes his seat the drums, trumpets and bugles are sounded. . . . Two saddled and bridled horses are brought, along with two goats which they hold to serve as a protection against the evil eye . . . If any one addresses the king and receives a reply from him, he uncovers his back and throws dust over his head and back for all the world like a bather splashing himself with water. I used to wonder how it was they did not blind themselves."

And finally, from Leo Africanus's eyewitness

account of the court of Songhai at Timbuktu: "The rich king of Tombuto hath many plates and scepters of gold, some whereof weigh 1300 poundes . . . and he keepes a magnificent and well furnished court. When he travelleth any whither he rideth upon a camell, which is led by some of his noblemen; and so he doth likewise when hee goeth to warfar, and all his souldiers ride upon horses. Whosoever will speake unto this king must first fall downe before his feete, & then taking up earth must sprinkle it upon his owne head & shoulders: which custom is ordinarily observed by them that never saluted the king before, or come as ambassadors from other princes."

The drums, the linguists, the praise singers, the gold swords and caps, the prostrations and the removal of sandals in the presence of the king are closely observed to this day in some courts of African kings (for example, among the Akan of modern Ghana). It is true that both Mali and Songhai added such Muslim trappings as banquets and Turkish and Egyptian bodyguards to their courts, while some of their symbols of investiture - the tunic, turban, and sword - were certainly Islamic. But the basic court ceremonial and protocol, and the position of the king in both Mali and Songhai, were definitely pre-Islamic and African in origin, most probably deriving from those of ancient Ghana.

However, some differences appear in the system of

royal succession. It is clear from Al-Bakri's account that like the present practice among the Akan people, royal succession in Ghana was matrilineal, whereas in the later Mali and Songhai Empires it was patrilineal. Al-Bakri was informed that Tunka Manin succeeded not his father but his maternal uncle. And as if to dispel any doubts, he added: "This is their custom and their habit, that the kingdom is inherited only by the son of the king's sister." He goes on to give an explanation of what appeared to him to be a most odd and non-Muslim practice: "He the king has no doubt that his successor is a son of his sister, while he is not certain that his son is in fact his own, and he does not rely on the genuineness of this relationship."

Although the fourteenth-century Tunisian historian Ibn Khaldun did report that one of the kings of Mali, Abu Bakr, was the son of a daughter of Sundiata, and although it has been inferred from this that royal succession in Mali at times went through the female line, a recent authority has shown that this was an exception to the rule. It would appear then that royal succession in both Mali and Songhai generally followed the patrilineal rather than the matrilineal rule. This difference might well be due to the impact of Islam.

The systems of provincial government in these Sudanese Empires show some differences, but in degree rather than in kind. In all three cases, the kings were directly responsible for the administration of the core, or metropolitan part, of the empire, which they divided into provinces ruled by governors. In the case of both Mali and Songhai, these governors either were members of the royal family or former generals. The governors, in turn, appointed district chiefs to administer a number of villages, each of which was ruled by a village chief.

The other parts of the empire, consisting of states conquered and reduced to vassal or tributary status, were governed in a variety of ways. In Ghana, it would appear that the states remained under their own rulers and that their main obligations were to pay annual tribute and to supply contingents to the king's army when called upon to do so. Sons of vassal rulers were occasionally kept at the king's court to ensure their fathers' continued allegiance. In Mali, the same system prevailed, with some minor improvements: The sovereigns of the conquered states retained their right to rule, but only after being invested by the Mansa and given a Mande title; the swearing of allegiance and the payment of tribute were seen as proofs of loyalty.

The kings of Songhai, especially Askia Muhammad, made still greater improvements toward centralizing the administration of government. Askia Muhammad ruled metropolitan Gao directly, but he reduced the status of the conquered rulers further by placing governors and minor governors over them. As was the case in Mali, these were court favorites or members of the royal family. Above this structure, he created four viceroyalties, or regions, each under a viceroy, or commissioner, who was in charge of a cluster of provinces. These viceroyalties were Dendi, Bal, Benga, and Kurmina. Since most of these administrative posts were appointive rather than hereditary, Songhai must have had a much more tightly controlled and more effective system of provincial administration than the other two.

Arabic sources do not throw much light on the system of justice in these states. For the most part, the kings were directly responsible for its administration. We are told by Al-Bakri that the kings of Ghana went out on horses every day to summon those people who had been wronged or had suffered any injustice to come and lodge a complaint. Trial by wood was also practiced in ancient Ghana. According to Al-Bakri, "When a man is accused of denying a debt or having shed blood or some other crime, a headman takes a thin piece of wood, which is sour and bitter to taste, and pours upon it some water which he then gives to the defendant to drink. If the man vomits, his innocence is recognized and he is congratulated. If he does not vomit and the drink remains in his stomach, the accusation is accepted as justified." The kings held what seem to have been courts of appeal in their palaces. Cases were initially heard, especially in the towns, by *qadis*, who obviously administered justice in accordance with the Koran and the Sharia (Muslim law). These judges also wielded great influence at the court of the kings. Ibn Battuta's main contact with the king of Mali was a *qadi*. The chroniclers of the Timbuktu *Tarikh* indicate that the *qadis* of that town were all from the Aqit family and wielded considerable influence over the Askias. One of them, Al-Aqib, who died in 1583, was noted for his frankness. "He was of stout heart," wrote one of the chroniclers, "bold in the mighty affairs that others hesitate before, courageous in dealing with the ruler and those beneath him. He had many conflicts with them and they used to be submissive and obedient to him in every matter. It he saw something he thought reprehensible, he would suspend his activities as *qadi* and keep himself aloof. Then they would conciliate him until he returned."

These high-ranking officials appear to have been rewarded for their services. Most of them, certainly those of Mali and Songhai, were given fiefs, or serf domains, as well as valuable goods. According to Al-Umari, some of the provincial governors of Mali received as much as "1500 mithqals [a unitary measure equal to one-eighth of an ounce] of gold every year besides which he the king keeps them in horses and clothes." To encourage civil servants and military men, the kings of Mali instituted various decorations, such as the award of golden bracelets, collars, and anklets. The highest of all the awards, presumably given to soldiers, was the Honor of the Trousers. An eyewitness told the fourteenth-century writer Al-Umari: "Whenever a hero adds to the list of his exploits, the King gives him a pair of wide trousers, and the greater the number of a knight's exploits the bigger the size of his trousers. These trousers are characterised by narrowness in the leg and ampleness in the seat."

It is interesting to note that the Scottish explorer Alexander Gordon Laing, who visited among the Mandingos of Solimana in 1822, observed: "The width of the trousers is a great mark of distinction." This is true of the Dagomba and Mamprusi of northern Ghana to this day.

For the maintenance of law and order, and for defensive as well as offensive purposes, each of these west Sudanese Empires had an army. Mali and Ghana had no standing armies; they, like many African kingdoms, depended on contingents contributed upon demand by vassal states. According to Al-Bakri, the kings of Ghana could raise an army of 200,000, of whom 40,000 were archers; and Mansa Musa of Mali could call up 100,000, a tenth of whom were cavalrymen. Songhai also relied on levies until the reign of Askia Muhammad, who instituted a professional army. It was this new army that enabled him not only to ensure stability and order but to extend the boundaries of the empire he had inherited from Sunni Ali. The armies of all these empires used the same weapons and were organized in the same way: divided into cavalry and infantry, their main weapons being spears, swords, javelins, and bows and arrows. Firearms were completely unknown until the Moroccan invasion late in the sixteenth century.

It would appear that both Mali and Songhai established diplomatic relations with the Maghreb and Egypt and kept up regular contacts with the sultan of Morocco. Mansa Sulaiman, Mansa Musa's brother and successor as king of the Mali, exchanged deputations with Morocco's Marinid sultans, and on the occasion of a new sultan's enthronement, sent an embassy to do him honor. Sulaiman's successor is also known to have sent gifts to the new sultan of Morocco. Among them was a giraffe, which the Moroccans talked about for a long time "because of the various adornments and markings which it combined in its body and attributes."

The complex administrative machineries of these states must have been expensive to run. Three main sources filled the royal treasury: tribute from vassal states, import and export duties, and imperial domains. Details of the annual levies have not been preserved, but of the duties collected in Ghana, Al-Bakri writes, "for every donkey loaded with salt that enters the country, the king takes a duty of one gold dinar, and two dinars from every one that leaves. From a load of copper the king's due is five mithqals and from a load of other goods ten mithqals." We are also told that in Ghana, any gold nugget found by anybody had to be surrendered to the king. Both Mali and Songhai imposed similar duties on goods coming to and fro. In fact, Songhai had a minister solely concerned with taxation.

The third, and probably the greatest, source of revenue was from the royal estates. Ghana's records are quite silent on this, but it is clear from the accounts of Mali and Songhai that the kings had royal domains - some hereditary and some acquired by war - in different parts of the empire. After his victory over Mali, Askia Muhammad is said to have added twenty-four fiefs to his holdings. These were occupied and worked by slaves whose overseers, or *fanfa*, were charged with raising a fixed quantity of produce every year for the kings.

"Some of these *fanfa*," says the chronicler of the Askia dynasty, "had under them 100 slaves employed in cultivation, whilst others had 60, 50, 40, or 20." Each estate had a special function: Some had to provide such commodities as yams, grain, or fish; others had to manufacture such goods as bows and arrows. Before the reign of Askia Muhammad the Great, the quantity of articles or provisions to be produced by each fief was not fixed, but Askia the Great set rigid quotas. Thus, the Abda estate in the province of Dendi had to produce 1,000 sunhas

(6,500 bushels) of rice annually. A chronicler reported: "This was fixed, which could neither be increased nor reduced." The Dyam Tene and Dya Wali estates had to supply 100 iron spears and 100 arrows per family per year. As the personal property of the kings, the estates were often given away as presents to trusted courtiers and friends.

The principal exports of Ghana, Mali, and Songhai were gold, ivory, slaves, and later, from the thirteenth century onward, kola nuts, a stimulant highly prized among Muslims. Most of these commodities, especially gold and kola nuts, came from the forest regions along trade routes controlled mainly by the Diula, a Mande people. The chief imports from the north were salt, horses, textiles, linen, books, writing paper, swords, and knives.

Ghana, situated as it was in the borderlands between the Sahara and the savanna, was most dependent upon the caravan trade; its people played the leading role as middlemen between producers and merchants. Al-Yaqut says of thirteenth-century Ghana: "From here, one enters the arid waste when going to the land of gold, and without the town of Ghana, this journey would be impossible."

Elsewhere Al-Yaqut adds that merchants from the north took with them Ghanaians as interpreters and go-betweens in negotiating with gold miners to the south. (It would appear that only small amounts of gold were mined in Ghana itself.)

Ghana was also able to control the crucial and lucrative trade in salt imported from the Taghaza mines of the Western Sahara, "the source of an enormous income," according to Al-Bakri.

Since both Mali and Songhai successively gained direct control over some of the southern gold-producing regions, Wangara in particular, and since they were able to establish peace and order along the caravan routes, they must have derived even more income from trade than had Ghana. It is quite clear from Maghrebin, Egyptian, and Sudanese sources that from the thirteenth to the fifteenth centuries, when Europe and the Muslim world were facing an acute shortage of precious metals, the western Sudan was their chief source of gold. The enormous quantities of gold that both Mansa Musa and Askia Muhammad took with them on their pilgrimages to Mecca, in 1324 and 1497 respectively, leaves no doubt about the wealth their states possessed in gold.

However, other commodities also contributed to the income of Mali and Songhai. Both were favorably situated to practice agriculture, cattle breeding, and fishing. Ibn Battuta and Leo Africanus indicate that a certain amount of rice and millet was exported great distances. Fishing was quite important among the Sorko clans of Songhai, and some of the royal estates had their quota of fish to catch. Numerous craftsmen, tailors, blacksmiths, and cloth weavers attracted traders, too. Leo Africanus reports that Timbuktu had "many shops of artificers and merchants and especially such as weave linen and cotton cloth." Another chronicler wrote that there were as many as twenty-six tailors' workshops in the crossroads city, each with between fifty and 100 apprentices.

Society in the Sudanese states was highly stratified. At the top was the ruling aristocracy, consisting of the royal families, officials, and Muslim scholars. The second and major part of the population consisted of merchants, farmers, fishermen, and cattle breeders. At the bottom were the slaves, who constituted only a small percentage of the population. It should be emphasized that the status of a slave in these early states, as indeed in almost all African societies, was fundamentally different from that which would prevail in the Americas. Not only was the number relatively small, but slaves were treated as human beings rather than as chattel.

Although Islam had remained essentially the religion of foreigners in ancient Ghana, superficial changes reflecting the influence of the new faith began to appear in Mali and Songhai. The administration of justice and the system of taxation in those states were based on the Koran. The architecture of the principal buildings, the mosques, and the palaces was Islamic, as was the attire of the town dwellers. Al-Umari wrote that "they wear turbans with ends tied under their chin like the Arabs, their cloth is white and made of cotton which they cultivate and weave in a most excellent fashion." Ibn Battuta was also impressed by the attention paid to religious worship. "They are careful to observe the hours of prayer," he noted, "and assiduous in attending them in congregations, and in bringing up their children to them."

By the late fifteenth century, Timbuktu had developed into the educational and commercial metropolis of the western Sudan, or rather, as one writer called it, the Queen of the Sudan. Its university, in the Sankore district of the city, produced such scholars and historians as Mahmud al-Kati, author of the *Kitab al-Fattash,* a chronicle of Songhai's Askia dynasty, and Abd al-Rahman as-Sadi, author of the *Tarikh as-Sudan,* a chronicle of the Sudan. Even the West African historian J. Spencer Trimingham, who is rather skeptical about Sankore as a university, admits that there were as many as 150 Koranic schools in Timbuktu alone. Leo Africanus also talks of "the great store of doctors, judges, priests, and other learned men that are bountifully maintained at the King's cost and charges. And hither are brought diverse manuscripts or written books out of Barbarie which are sold for more money than any other merchandise."

Mahmud al-Kati pays tribute in the *Kitab al-Fattash* to his colleagues: "The scholars of this period were the most respected among the believers for their generosity, their force of character, and their discretion." We also have the names of scholars who went on lecture tours and set up schools in different parts of the western Sudan, and especially in Hausaland. Mahmud Ibn Umar, for instance, lectured in Kano in 1485 to large and reverent crowds of people. Indeed, the Timbuktu tradition of learning dominated the cities of the western and central Sudan until the beginning of the nineteenth century.

But if the towns in Mali and Songhai assumed an Islamic hue, it would appear that the rural areas of both empires stuck to their traditional ways. They maintained their animistic beliefs, their traditional cults and indigenous African way of life, their initiation rites, their sorcerers, and their family and clan heads and chiefs, who administered justice in accordance with customary law.

In spite of the skepticisms of certain European writers, the early empires of the western Sudan were true states, with all the fundamental attributes of government that statehood implies. They had paid bureaucracies, strong economies based on trade, mining, agriculture, and political machinery capable of ensuring law, order, security, and diplomatic exchange.

The fall of all these states was due to both internal and external factors. The internal factors were usually the rivalries among members of the royal family. The external factors were, for the most part, foreign attacks. With the possible exception of Songhai, none of these empires had a really durable provincial administrative structure. As pointed out earlier, the conquered states and kingdoms within each empire were governed by their own rulers and were held to the central authority mainly by military might. Moreover, each empire was composed of different ethnic and linguistic groups; hence, it lacked cultural and ethnic homogeneity. Some of the rulers of both Mali and Songhai did attempt to use Islam to provide cohesion, but only with limited success. Both Ghana's central authority and its army were weakened as a result of the defeats they suffered between 1054 and 1076 by the adherents of the Almoravid movement. This was an Islamic movement that arose in the eleventh century among the Sanhaja Berbers who occupied the Western Sahara. Although Ghana did reconquer its capital from the Almoravids after 1087, it never really recovered from those earlier blows, and its vassal states broke away. The coup de grâce, however, was delivered in 1203 by an external force, the rulers of the Susu kingdom to the south.

Mali fell victim principally to the internal breakdown of the central government, as a result of the inordinate ambition and frivolity of its royal family. The trouble began at the end of the reign of Mansa Sulaiman in 1359-1360. The history of the kings of Mali for the next several decades was a sordid record of regicides, civil wars, contested successions, and coups d'état. Indeed, within the brief period from 1360 to 1390 as many as seven people were enthroned, four of them between 1387 and 1390. Central authority collapsed, anarchy and instability came in its wake, and as in Ghana, the vassal states began to break away. The demise of the empire came after Mali had been attacked from three sides: the Tuareg attacked from the north, the Mossi from the south, and the Songhai from the east. By 1433, the Tuareg had captured Arawan, Walata, and Timbuktu, and in the 1460s and the 1470s, the Mossi took arms against the southern and even the central regions of Mali. The rulers of Mali appealed to Portugal for assistance in the 1490s and again in the 1530s. The Portuguese could do nothing but send words of encouragement. The Songhai attacks delivered the final blow, and by the fourth decade of the sixteenth century, Mali had shrunk again into the tiny Mande principality of Kangaba.

Songhai's glory lasted little more than a century after its victories over Mali. The establishment of the Askia dynasty in Songhai in 1493, a result of the military coup organized and led by Askia Muhammad, was the beginning of the internal division of the country. Being of the Soninke rather than the Songhai people, he tried to replace the animistic beliefs of the Songhai with Islam, as indeed Sunni Ali, his predecessor, had done in an effort to unify the empire. Though Askia Muhammad's attempts only alienated the Songhai people, he was shrewd and strong enough to contain these internal differences. His successors could not. As had been the case in Mali, a series of disputed successions, revolts, and usurpations broke out among members of his family. In the sixty years after his deposition as many as eight people mounted the throne. However, it would appear that at least one of the rulers, Askia Daud, was quite competent, and during his long reign from 1549 to 1582, the fortunes of Songhai improved. Although disputed successions broke out again after Daud, and as many as three rulers came to the throne between 1582 and 1591, the central authority would appear to have remained intact.

It was the decisive defeat inflicted by the forces of Sultan Al-Mansur of Morocco that precipitated the disintegration of the empire. Led by Judar Pasha, a young Spanish eunuch, the sultan's army crushed the Songhai army at the battle of Tondibi in 1591 and marched south in search of Songhai's fabled riches. The Songhai army was estimated by Al-Kati to have been a huge one consisting of 18,000 cavalry and 9,700 infantry, while the Moroccans are said to have numbered only 4,000. The Moroccan victory was in some measure due to the fact that the Songhai fought with spears, swords, and bows and arrows, whereas the Moroccan army was equipped with harquebuses and cannons. When the advisers of Al-Mansur tried to dissuade him from undertaking what they considered to be a crazy enterprise, the sultan is said to have replied: "You talk of the dangerous desert we have to cross, of the fatal solitudes, barren of water and pasture, but you forget the defenseless and ill-equipped merchants who, mounted or on foot, regularly cross these wastes which caravans have never ceased to traverse. I, who am so much better equipped than they, can surely do the same with an army which inspires terror wherever it goes. . . . Moreover, our predecessors would have found great difficulty if they had tried to do what I now propose, for their armies were composed only of horsemen armed with spears and of bowmen; gunpowder was unknown to them, and so were firearms and their terrifying effect. Today, the Sudanese have only spears and swords, weapons which will be useless against modern arms. It will therefore be easy for us to wage a successful war against these people and prevail over them."

Following Al-Mansur's military success, however, anarchy broke out in the area of the Niger Bend, and it would continue intermittently until the late nineteenth century.

And what was happening in the regions to the south of the empires of Ghana, Mali, and Songhai? As has been already pointed out, a simultaneous process of state formation was at work. Arising just to the west in the regions of the Senegambia was the kingdom of Wolof; to the south emerged the Mole-Dagbane states and the Mossi kingdoms. Still farther south arose a number of forest and coastal states: Ife, Oyo, and Benin in Nigeria; the Ga kingdom and Akan states in modern Ghana. Their emergence was due to factors similar to those that gave birth to Ghana, Mali, and Songhai. Of first importance was the extension of the caravan trade routes southward into the savanna, the forest, and the coastal regions; of second was the development within the region of trade among the coastal peoples; and of third were the activities of the wealthy and ambitious families or clan groups who were stimulated by those commercial activities.

As has already been pointed out, the mainstays of the caravan trade - gold, kola nuts, ivory, and slaves - could all be obtained in the regions of the southern savanna and forest. From evidence rapidly accumulating today, it is certain that by the end of the fourteenth century, at the height of Mali's power, the trade routes from the Sahara, which had earlier stopped at the savanna cities of Walata, Timbuktu, Jenne, and Gao, had now been extended westward and southward.

The people who were responsible for the development of this trade between the forest regions and the states of Mali and Songhai were certainly the Diula group of the Mande people.

They founded a number of caravan posts, including Bobo-Dioulasso (in modern Upper Volta), Kong and Bouna (in modern Ivory Coast), and Wa and Begho (in modern Ghana). Begho, the last of them, was established just north of the forest zone in about 1400. From Begho, routes radiated directly south to the coastal regions of Axim (in southwest Ghana) and southeastward through Asante to the coastal region of modern Cape Coast and Elmina.

Proof of the extension of northern trade routes to the coast can be taken from the fact that two items of clothing, *lanbens* (shawls) and *aljaravais* (dressing gowns) that were manufactured in Morocco and Tunis were in great demand on the coast of modern Ghana before the arrival of the Portuguese. Describing that trade in 1500, the Portuguese agent Pacheco Pereira also mentions peoples from the interior: "Boroes, Mandingoes, Cacres, Andeses, or Souzos." Here again, the "Boroes" are obviously the Bono of northern Asante, the "Cacres" are possibly the Kasena-Grusi of northern Ghana, and the "Mandingoes" and "Souzos" are readily identifiable as the Mandingos and the Susu of the larger family of Mande peoples.

The Portuguese and later the Dutch traders found the coastal peoples enjoying lucrative salt and fish trade with the inland peoples. The Dutchman Pieter de Marees, writing in 1601 about one of the Akan settlements, states that "the inhabitants of the sea-side, come also to the markets with their . . . fish, which their husbands have gotten in the sea, whereof the women buy much and carrie them to other townes within the land, to get some profit by them, so that the fish which is taken in the sea, is carried at least one hundred or two hundred miles up into the land, for a great present." William Bosman, an official of the Dutch West India Company who came to the coast during the second half of the seventeenth century, made a similar observation. There is no reason to think that trade in salt and fish was not going on prior to the arrival of the Portuguese. Salt has always been an indispensable commodity and has generated contact between people who produce it and those who do not, and we know that salt is not found in the forest region and can be produced only in small quantities in the savanna regions to the north.

It also seems clear that the Mande were responsible for the extension of the routes eastward from Timbuktu and Gao into the Hausa states, probably in the fourteenth century. From these Hausa states, trade routes radiated southwestward across the Niger and through the Mole-Dagbane areas into the gold- and kola-producing areas of Asante in modern Ghana. The Kano Chronicle states that kola nuts reached Hausaland from northern Ghana during the first half of the fifteenth century. Other routes also led southward through the regions surrounding the confluence of the Benue and

Niger rivers and into the Yoruba and Benin areas to the southwest. Ibn Battuta talks of copper from the Takedda mines being exported southward into Nigeria, and judging from the bronze works of Ife and Benin, it is not unlikely, as the British ethnographer Frank Willett has suggested that "some of this Takedda ore eventually found its way even farther south."

Pre-European trade also existed between east and west via the sea, especially between the coasts of modern Ghana and Nigeria. Evidence for this conclusion is found in the oral tradition, widely held among the Ga and the people of Asebu (one of the Akan states), that they migrated from Benin by sea into the coastal regions of modern Ghana and that the Ga kingdom was, in fact, a part of the empire of Benin. However, on the basis of linguistic and other ethnological data, it is exceedingly unlikely that the Ga and the Asebu originated from Benin. Rather, the oral tradition seems to be an echo of the old trading contacts between the people of Benin and those of the coast of modern Ghana. The fifteenth- and early sixteenth-century accounts of the Portuguese traders suggest that they merely exploited a pre-existing pattern of trade to their own advantage. Pacheco Pereira, who was there in the 1500s, says that they bought slaves at the port of Benin for "twelve or fifteen brass bracelets each, or for copper bracelets which they prize more; from there the slaves are brought to the castle of

S. Jorze da Mina [the extant fortress of São Jorge at Elmina on the Ghana coast] where they are sold for gold." He also says that they traded on the Niger near the coast of the Bight of Benin, "principally in slaves, in cotton stuff, some leopard skins, palm oil, and blue beads with red stripes which they call 'coris' - and other things which we are accustomed to buy here for brass and copper bracelets. All these commodities have value at the castle of S. Jorze da Mina. The Factor of our prince sells them . . . in exchange for gold."

Pereira goes on to describe the local people's manner of travel: "At the mouth of the River Real [the Bonny River] . . . there is a very large village, consisting of about 2,000 souls. Much salt is made here, and in this country are to be found the largest canoes, made of a single trunk, that are known in the whole of Ethiopia of Guinea; some are so large that they hold 80 men. They travel distances of a hundred leagues and more down the river, and bring many yams, which are very good here and make a tolerable diet, many slaves, cows, goats, and sheep."

Writing early in the next century, Pieter de Marees also describes the canoes in use on the coast of Ghana. He notes that the people of Accra had large canoes "to fish or go to sea withall," and that he saw one "cut out of a tree which was five and thirty foot long and five foot broad and three foot high, which was as big as a shallop, so that it would have held thirty men." In the same century, Jean Barbot, agent general of the French Royal Africa Company, also saw canoes on the coast of Ghana of sizes ranging from fourteen to forty feet long, and he added that the largest of them could "carry above ten tons of goods with eighteen or twenty blacks to paddle them." He stated further that the best canoe men were the Elmina blacks, who "drive a great trade along the Gold Coast, and at Wida by Sea [Ovidah, a seaport in the area of modern Dahomey], and are the fittest and the most experienc'd men to manage and paddle the canoes over the bars and breakings, which render this coast, and that of Wida so perilous and toilsome to land either men, goods or provisions." One may conclude from these descriptions that going to sea in large canoes was already well established on the eve of the Portuguese arrival. Indeed, it probably dated as far back as the first millennium CE, when the coastal areas began to be occupied by peoples from the interior, and commercial and cultural contacts were initiated.

As was the case farther north, the West African peoples who were geographically situated to play the role of middlemen would be those who could develop large states and kingdoms. To the south of Ghana and Mali, the first states to become sizable kingdoms were the Wolof kingdom to the west, the Mole-Dagbane and Mossi states to the south in the Volta River Basin, and the Ife, Oyo, and Benin kingdoms to the southeast. All except Benin were situated in the southern savanna belt. The Wolof people could control not only the lucrative salt trade from the sea, but could share in the gold trade with Morocco. The Mole-Dagbane states and the closely related Mossi states - all of which were founded during the first half of the fifteenth century - expanded mainly to establish a firm control over the trade routes linking the Niger Bend and Hausaland with the Akan's gold fields and kola-tree groves.

The oral traditions of the Akan peoples indicate that the first Akan states to emerge early in the fifteenth century were Bono-Manso in the region between the savanna and the forest and Adansi and Assin in the region where gold was obtained. Later on, different groups migrated northward to establish city-states, which were all within a few miles of where the routes that led from the Niger Bend terminated. It was these states that would later form the nucleus of the famous Asante Empire.

The other Akan states of Aguafo, Fetu, Asebu, Fante, Agona, and the Ga kingdom - the so-called Gold Coast states - were created mainly in response to the demands of the transoceanic as well as the overland north-south trade. Their failure to develop into powerful kingdoms prior to the arrival of the Portuguese can be explained by the fact that they were one step further removed from the source of gold, trading through the intermediary of their sister Akan states in the interior. The Gold Coast states were also hampered by being crowded into a relatively short stretch of coast - the five Akan states occupied no more than 100 miles.

Primarily by virtue of its geographical position, Benin became a center of both overland and sea trade, the latter by way of Ghana. Of the Yoruba states that later developed to the northwest of Benin, between 1380 and 1420, the first to develop into a sizable kingdom was Oyo. This northernmost Yoruba state was situated in the savanna region just below the Niger and, by the end of the fifteenth century, was able to claim the dominant share of trade between Hausaland and the Niger Bend and the other Yoruba states to the south. However, since Oyo had as rivals other centralized states to the south and west, its expansion could not be as rapid as that of Benin. Indeed, it was not until the seventeenth and eighteenth centuries that, using guns, Oyo's army extended its frontiers to the Guinea coast.

What then were these kingdoms like when the Portuguese first established contact with them? Pacheco Pereira reported in 1505: "Here at the Senegal you find the first black people. This is the kingdom of Wolof, a hundred leagues long and eight broad. The kingdom of Wolof can put into the field an army of about 10,000 cavalry and 100,000 infantry." It would appear from the early sixteenth-century accounts of Alvise da Cadamosto, a Venetian explorer in the service of Prince Henry of Portugal, that the kingdom consisted of five polities, all under a single ruler. Valentine Fernandes, a Lisbon printer of Moravian origin, writing in the same period, furnishes us with further details. He says the king had many subjects under him and administered his state with the aid of Muslim "dignitaries after the fashion of dukes and counts" and "white bischerigs who are priests and preachers of Mahomet, and can read and write." He adds that some of the ordinary people had embraced Islam, though the majority of them were sticking to their animistic beliefs. It is not surprising that some of the people should be Muslims since the kingdom was situated to the south of Takrur, into which Islam had penetrated as early as CE 1000.

The Portuguese found the 1,500-mile-long stretch from Gambia to the borders of modern Ghana only sparsely settled; it appears that no state of any size emerged along that coast before the end of the fifteenth century. But in the area of modern Ghana, between the Pra and Volta rivers, the explorers-traders came upon the cluster of Akan states described earlier.

The three contiguous Akan states of Aguafo, Fetu, and Asebu were similar in organization: At the head of each state was a king (he lived in a capital a few miles from the coast), who was assisted by a council of elders. Eustace de la Fosse, writing in 1479, reports taking security from the "Mansa and Caramansa," who, he adds, "are the king and viceroy of Aguafo," and it was with the viceroy that Don Diego de Azambuja negotiated for the plot at Elmina, on which the castle São Jorge was built in 1482. Each of these states had trading villages or outlets, some of which became European settlements.

In contrast, the Fante state seems to have been composed of a series of inland townships, or quarters, within about three to five miles of one another. Collectively, they made up the capital district of Mankessim (alternatively Fantyn), and each quarter was under a chief, or *braffo,* who was advised by the family or clan heads. One *braffo* was recognized as overall leader, though his authority was limited, and he had to consult the others before he could declare war or make peace. It is also evident from the oral traditions and from a shrine that has survived near Mankessim that all the Fante recognized one national god, whom they called Nanaam. Orders emanating from the chief priest of Nanaam were binding on all the Fante. Thus, the government of the Fante was a sort of theocracy with political power being controlled by the chief ruler and the chief priests. Like the other states, the Fante also had some coastal outlets; these were Anomabu, Little Fantyn, and Kormantin.

The Fante remained in Mankessim until the last three decades of the seventeenth century when, probably as a result of population pressure, they began to move out of the townships to establish kingdoms within a twenty- or thirty- mile radius of the capital.

No sizable states had emerged in the area between the mouth of the Volta River and Yorubaland by the middle of the fifteenth century, but in the western and midwestern regions of Nigeria, the Portuguese found the Yoruba and Edo peoples living in what were probably the most advanced and certainly the most interesting states of the Guinea coast: Ife, Benin, and Oyo. The oldest of these was Ife. Indeed, the Yoruba-speaking peoples regard Ife as the center of the world and the cradle of their civilization. According to one of their traditional accounts, it was there that God's children landed and set about to create the world. The most senior of these children was Oduduwa, whom they regarded as the first ruler, or *oni,* of Ife. He is said to have had sixteen children, whom he sent out to found the Yoruba states.

From a careful analysis of these oral traditions and the terra-cotta art of Ife, Willett has concluded that these oral traditions represent the arrival of "a small, but influential group of people," probably from the east or northeast. He postulates further that these people found the indigenous Yoruba and

Igbo peoples already working in terra cotta, and that they introduced the art of bronze casting and the ideas of divine kingship, and that these new arrivals founded Ife, from which place the other Yoruba kingdoms would be created. Whether founded by the Yoruba or by invaders from the east, Ife never developed into a kingdom, for reasons that are still not apparent. It remained throughout essentially a city-state ruled by a "divine" king, who, as a Portuguese observer put it, was held "in great reveration as is the Supreme Pontiff with us." Nevertheless, Ife is of vital interest because it has remained from its foundation the religious center of all the Yoruba peoples and because it was there that the Yoruba's world-acclaimed sculpture in bronze, wood, and terra cotta was first developed.

From there, this unique art spread to the whole of West Africa. The bronze sculptures, their supreme achievement, were made by the lost-wax process. The best of these were created in the classical period of Ife art, which conventionally has been said to have lasted from the beginning of the thirteenth to the middle of the fourteenth century. However, in view of the bronze sculptures recently discovered at Igbo-Ukwu, which have been dated by the radiocarbon process to the ninth century CE, many scholars are beginning to accept an earlier date for Ife's classical period, probably before our millennium, bringing it closer to the Nok culture.

To the southeast of Ife, in the forest area, Benin emerged. Whereas Ife remained a city-state, Benin had developed into a sizable kingdom by the middle of the fifteenth century. Pereira, who visited Benin four times, wrote in 1505: "A league up this river on the left two tributaries enter the main stream: if you ascend the second of these for twelve leagues you find a town called Huguatoo [Gwato], of some 2,000 souls: this is the harbor of a great city of Beny [Benin], which lies nine leagues in the interior with a good road between them. Small ships of fifty tons can go as far as Huguatoo. This city is about a league long from gate to gate; it has no wall but is surrounded by a large moat, very wide and deep, which suffices for its defense . . . Its houses are made of mud walls covered with palm leaves. The Kingdom of Beny is about eighty leagues long and forty wide; it is usually at war with its neighbors. . . ."

It seems clear from the traditional accounts of Benin that there are at least two periods of Benin history. All that can be pieced together is that during the first period, Benin was a city-state under the rule of the Ogiso dynasty and that this family was replaced by the Oba dynasty sometime before 1300. Establishing themselves among the Edo-speaking peoples, who were organized only into clans, lineages, and village groups, the new Oba kings claimed supernatural powers. They soon succeeded in converting the city-state into the sizable and thriving kingdom that the Portuguese found on their arrival in the 1470s.

The oral traditions of Benin, Ife, and Oyo shed some light on how the Oba dynasty came to power. The histories of all three kingdoms agree that after a period of anarchy, the people of Benin beseeched the *oni* of Ife, Oduduwa himself, for a ruler, and he sent his son Oranmiyan. But believing that it would be better for a native of Benin to rule there, Oranmiyan married a daughter of one of the local chiefs and shortly thereafter had a son, Eweka, to whom he gave the throne. Oranmiyan then returned to Ife and from there went on to establish the kingdom of Oyo. Eweka thus became the first *oba* of Benin, but he had to obtain his insignia of office from the *oni* of Ife. It seems obvious from this account that the founders of the Oba dynasty of Benin, like the founders of Oyo, came from Ife.

To govern this kingdom, it would appear that the Oba kings developed certain political institutions that were an amalgam of Ife traditions and local political and social ideas. At the head of the kingdom was the *oba*, who, like the rulers of the early Sudanese states and those of Ife, was a "divine" king. As the English explorer Thomas Wyndham observed in 1553: "And here to speak of the great reverence they give to their king, it is such, that if we would give as much to our Saviour Christ, we should remove from our heads many plagues which we daily deserve. . . ."

The king was assisted by three ranking classes. The first class was the *uzama,* or king makers, whose position dates from Benin's early dynastic era. They had to perform certain important state rituals, including the installation of the *oba.* The second group was the *eghaevbo n'ogbe,* or palace chiefs, who were responsible not only for the *oba*'s regalia, his wives and children, his personal relations, and his doctors and divine men but also for the administration of the provinces, or fiefs. The third estate was the *eghaevbo n'ore,* or town chiefs, whose leader was the *iyase,* the prime minister and commander in chief of the army, and from whom other war leaders, as well as other governors of provinces, were chosen. Since most of these officials were appointed by the *oba* himself, he enjoyed considerable powers, though he still had to ensure his position by playing one group against another.

Provincial Benin, that is, the conquered territories, was divided into three administrative units. At the base was the village under a village head; at the intermediate level was the chiefdom made up of a number of villages, each administered by a chief appointed by the king; at a higher level were the fiefs, or provinces, each consisting of a number of chiefdoms and directed by either a town or palace chief. This system of administration remained without any fundamental changes until the late nineteenth century.

Regarding Benin's achievements in art, the local oral tradition admits to learning the art of bronze casting from Ife. It is related that Oguola, the fifth *oba* of the second dynasty, who reigned during the end of the fourteenth century, sent to the *oni* of Ife for a bronzesmith to teach his people. The *oni* is said to have agreed and sent Iguegha, who is worshiped to this day in Benin as the patron of bronze-smiths. In fact, the style of the early Benin bronzes is quite similar to that of Ife, but by the sixteenth century, using the same lost-wax process known in Ife, Benin artists had evolved a distinctive style of their own, which was less naturalistic and more formal. As in Ife, the people of Benin also worked in wood, ivory, and raffia.

Despite the widespread tradition that attributes the founding of both Benin and Oyo to Oranmiyan, it is now generally agreed that Oyo's founding occurred nearly a century later, between the last two decades of the fourteenth and the first three decades of the fifteenth centuries. That it had grown into a fairly large kingdom by the end of the fifteenth century through expansion northward must have been due partly to the ability of Oyo's founding kings and partly, as we have seen, to its position in an area best suited for the domination of the trade routes from the north. Their art was derived from Ife, but as Frank Willett has pointed out, it shows "gradually declining naturalism, as if the social pressures which produced the naturalism of Classical Ife have gradually weakened."

Oyo's political institutions were based, as in the other kingdoms of West Africa, upon a "divine" king. The *alafin* ruled the kingdom with the advice of a council composed of seven notables known as the oyo mesi under the leadership of the *bashorun,* or prime minister. The *oyo mesi* was not only responsible for the election of the *alafin,* but according to a historian of Yoruba tradition, Samuel Johnson, its members "represent the voice of the nation, on them developed the chief duty of protecting the interests of the kingdom." The *alafin* could not declare war or peace without their consent. Moreover, should the *bashorun* ever declare three times, "the gods reject you, the people reject you, the earth rejects you," the *alafin* was obliged to commit suicide. However, some safeguards were instituted against the abuse of this power. Firstly, one of the members of the *oyo mesi,* known as "the *alafin's* friend," had to die with the *alafin.* Secondly, both the *alafin* and the council were controlled by the *ogboni,* a secret earth cult consisting of all members of the *oyo mesi,* heads of the other cults, rich traders, and prominent diviners. This society had to ratify certain decisions of the *oyo mesi,* among them the rejection of *the alafin* by the *bashorun.* It seems clear that the people of Oyo devised a system that had checks and balances built into it to eliminate arbitrary or dictatorial exercise of power.

In summation, the people of West Africa, stimulated by trade and ruled and inspired by talented leaders, did form states and develop political institutions that were truly unique and truly African between 500 and 1450. Some of them also developed artistic skills, which in their aesthetic sensitivities were comparable, if not superior, to those of contemporary Europe.

6

THE NIGER TO
THE NILE

BASIL DAVIDSON

E astward from the western Sudan the states of the upper and middle Niger, from the lands of ancient Ghana and Mali and Songhai, the same broad plains of grass and sifting soil flow for 2,000 miles until they reach and overleap the waters of the Nile. These plains of the central Sudan traverse Hausaland and Bornu, their populous heart and center, encircle the marsh-trimmed mirrors of Lake Chad, and lead on thirstily through the solitudes of Kanem and Zaghawa and Wadai, lands where the world is altogether flat but for the slow deception of long-dry riverbeds.

Then, as though reflecting the drama of this great region's history, the plains confront the sudden glacis of Darfur, where green peaks rise into the mists of Jebel Marra's 10,100-foot summit. But at once, the land falls away to plains again. They flow on now into the hard cattle country of little water and infrequent pasture that is Kordofan. Beyond Kordofan, they come to the oases lands of Nubia and the White Nile. They cross these and continue to the Blue Nile and the highlands of Ethiopia. And that, at last, is their frontier.

The peoples of the central Sudan, like their neighbors in the western Sudan, have an interrelated history much the same in kind and content. Its dominant themes are those of political adventure and ambition; of swift conquest and defeat among peoples to whom good horsemanship and fine horses have always mattered much; of ceaseless movement and migration brought to rest and stability only where long-distance trade routes crossed and became knit together within the defensive walls of market towns or royal capitals. Its poets and scholars, Muslim, but rooted in African tradition, have told similar stories of empires and warriors, of battles and booty, of the joys of home.

"The clash of spears had long been doubtful, yet it ended in glory . . . These were our deeds: they lived in the memory of all. Oh, triumphant expedition! But the greatest joy is still to tell, joy most precious, the recovery of my lost love, a part of myself! Silks from India are less soft than is her skin, her noble form is timid as a fawn. . . ." It was thus that a

Bornu ruler returning from a fight set down his praise poem in due and proper verse. The poem is from the nineteenth century, but could have been written any time back to about CE 1000.

In contrast with the oral traditions and written records of many parts of Africa, the histories of the central Sudan are for the most part dynastic. They are principally concerned with powerful monarchs and their rise to power, with the enclosure of broad areas of trade and tribute within systems of centralized rule, with the impact of Islam upon methods of government or upon social and moral attitudes and customs. The characteristic note of these chronicles is epic. "On the next day, all the soldiers mounted their horses after equipping themselves and their horses with armor, with breastplates, shields and their best clothing," wrote a courtier of the great Idris Alooma (1570-1602), who was *mai*, or ruler, of Kanem-Bornu at the same time that Queen Elizabeth I was reigning over England. "When we had all ridden a short distance we met the messengers of the lord of Stambul, the Sultan of Turkey. . . . Our troops charged toward them, and they galloped their horses toward us. This continued for a long time until the infantry were tired of standing still. . . ."

Nearly two centuries later, passing far eastward through the Sudanic sultanate of Sennar on the Blue Nile, the Scottish traveler James Bruce described the cavalry of the Funj people as though he were speaking of the same scene. Each lancer possessed a shirt of mail and a helmet of beaten copper, and their horses were "all above sixteen hands high, of the breed of the old Saracen horses, all finely made and as strong as our coach horses, but exceedingly nimble in their motion."

This sort of history may read agreeably, but it has the disadvantage of telling little about everyday life. In countries pestered by royal ambition, whether in Africa or not, peaceful or productive citizens figure little in the records. Yet, the deeper truths, revealed by archeological discoveries, are reasonably clear in their general shape and outline.

From early times, the Niger-Nile region formed a zone of migration and slow settlement, where indigenous Stone Age peoples were joined by groups from the southern Sahara and other neighboring regions. This mingling gave rise in remote antiquity to new peoples, ancestors of the peoples who inhabit the region today. By CE 500, they had begun to acquire their characteristic cultures, modes of speech, religious beliefs, political systems, and notions about themselves. By CE 1000, they had assumed patterns of community life that would give rise to all subsequent development, even now marking these peoples with a distinctive quality.

Central to the history of much of the region is the record of the Kanuri and their 1,000-year predominance in the Lake Chad region. The Kanuri played the same role here, in the sense of being the "core" people of a masterful centralizing polity, that the Soninke played in Ghana, the Mandinka (or Mandingo, as they are frequently known) in Mali, and the Songhai in the middle Niger area.

Peripherally, there were many other peoples. There were nomads of the southern Sahara, seminomads of the grasslands, and sedentary farmers in the forest zone to the west and south, some of the last group being culturally linked to the peoples of the northern Congo Basin. Several of these smaller societies early acquired small centralizing polities of their own, opposed the Kanuri in their bid for mastery, and fought them in many wars and raids. Others, somewhat farther away, stayed altogether free of Kanuri overlordship. Even then, the Kanuri influence continued.

Prominent among these more distant neighbors were the Hausa-speaking groups to the west; the Nupe and Jukun astride the Benue valley to the south; the Berber raiders and traders of Air and Bilma, the little kingships of the central-southern Sahara. And woven into their midst, at least from the middle of the fifteenth century, there were groups of Fulbe, or Fulani, as their Hausa neighbors and subsequent historians have called them; their origins were far in the west. These Fulani were sometimes to play a vigorous role in religion and politics.

All these peoples belong to the "Country of the Blacks," as the region is commonly known; however, there is considerable variation in skin pigmentation of its inhabitants, ranging from the relative pallor of the Fulani to the luminous "black" of the Hausa. Despite these apparent differences, they shared a common pastoralist culture, which continues much the same even today. The people of the central Sudan early took advantage of grasslands, which were largely free of the menace of tsetse flies, to raise sizable herds of cattle, and many were farmers whose skills in growing millet and other crops were developed 2,000 years ago and more. Some of them acquired the techniques of ironworking not much later than that.

Two factors influenced the development of those among them who formed kingdoms and organized under some type of governmental rule: long-distance trade and Islam. As in the western Sudan, these elements are fundamental to West African history as a whole; but the roots of the Niger-Nile region have supported a distinctively different cultural flowering from that in the western Sudan. So far as the first of these shaping factors is concerned, this difference is explained by the fact that the north-south routes of the trans-Saharan commerce were supplemented in the central Sudan by an important system of lateral communications from the region of Wadai through Darfur to such crossroads towns as Sennar, which linked the region with routes running to Egypt, the Red Sea, and the Horn of Africa.

At any rate, since the rise of the post-Meroitic Christian kingdoms of Nubia after CE 540, and probably much earlier during Meroitic times, there was trade and travel along well-known routes reaching between Lake Chad and the Nile. Little or nothing is known of those who may have passed that way, if only because detailed histories of Meroë and the Nubian kingdoms are almost entirely lost; today, there remains just a scattering of potsherds to indicate the connection. Sherds of probable Meroitic origin have been picked up in long-dry wadis east of Lake Chad, but at present the sole sure fragmentary evidence of a Christian presence (or of links with Christian Nubia) is a single piece of pottery, found in the ruins of one of the old Kanuri capitals east of the lake. According to A.D.H. Bivar, a noted British Africanist, it bears the characteristic cream slip of the pottery from the Nubian state of Makuria, which flourished between about CE 600 and 1300. That so little material evidence has survived is disappointing, especially in view of the known trading enterprise of the Nubian kingdoms. Yet, the hint of influence from the Nile remains curiously insistent in central Sudanese civilization, not least of all in the old Kanuri skills of building in brick, such as the Meroites and Nubians possessed.

Of early north-south connections, there are far more

sure indicators, though these, too, are tantalizingly rare and often imprecise. During Carthaginian and Roman times in North Africa, the Garamantes of the central Fezzan seem mainly to have used a trail going southwestward from their country through the Ahaggar massif to the Adrar des Iforas mountains and probably onward to the middle Niger. But to the east, the central-southern Sahara also offered valuable commodities and oases to lure and sustain the trader (for example, the salt deposits of the Bilma oasis in the modern Niger Republic). The existence of many later links between the Fezzan and the Chad area makes it probable that the Garamantes had also come this way.

Writing soon after 450 BCE, the Greek historian Herodotus says that the Garamantes "hunt the Ethiopian [among classical writers the generic term for "African"] hole-men, or troglodytes, in four-horse chariots, for these troglodytes are exceedingly swift of foot - more so than any people of whom we have any information. They eat snakes and lizards and other reptiles." These cave dwellers were possibly the Tebu people, between whose homeland in the Tibesti Mountains and the Fezzan there are at least two sites where ancient wall paintings of horse chariots are found. If the Garamantes themselves had left any written records, they would no doubt have revealed much more information on the subject. Roman records are almost as silent. An expedition led by one Julius

Maternus of Leptis Magna reached the "land of Agisymba." Judging by the report that they found rhinoceroses in abundance there, the adventurers must have been somewhere in the Sudan, whatever else they may have learned about this land, aside from its being a country where black people lived, remains unknown.

Yet early north-south links seem probable. Though lacking gold, the Lake Chad region could provide elephant ivory, and it probably did. There had once been great numbers of elephants in North Africa as well as in the Sudan, but Mediterranean demand for ivory may well have depleted the local supply. (So honored was the creature in Leptis Magna that the authorities erected a statue of an elephant in one of their streets.) Accordingly, behind the history of the Niger-to-the-Nile region there hangs a shadowy backdrop painted with the symbols of ancient trade and contact with North Africa and the Nile, and possibly, though on this the records are entirely silent, with the Congo Basin and southern Nigeria.

If the central Sudan was a trading crossroads from ancient times, it was little used for a long time, and its indigenous peoples were left to evolve their own early structures of self- rule and development. How and when they did this remains a matter for conjecture. All that can be affirmed is that toward the ninth century, four or five protostates can be discerned in the region around Lake Chad. These began to be dominated by the Kanuri people, operating under powerful chiefs of the Saifuwa lineage. The Saifuwa were able to rise to power over their neighbors for reasons far from certain, though a good central position commanding trade routes west and east and a relatively fertile land were no doubt high on the list.

Their manner of organization also played a determining role. Like the early kings of Ghana, and afterward of Mali and Songhai, the Saifuwa must have drawn their initial strength among the Kanuri from a ritual authority. Saifuwa seniority came, in other words, from their standing in the line of divinely sanctioned ancestors, who were, in turn, the "owners" of the land.

The Saifuwa were thus the intermediaries between the spiritual power and the people, or so they succeeded in presenting themselves; and from that position of strength, evidently reached late in the ninth century, they were able to accumulate the consequential powers of secular rule, both political and military. The traditions are vague or silent on the ways in which they did this. But it may be inferred from later African examples, which are far better known, that they became kings because the Kanuri (or at least their clan leaders) were agreed on the need for stronger, and hence more unified, means of getting tribute and controlling trade: in short, for assuring themselves of all those desiderata that gave rise to regular governments in Africa and elsewhere. The Kanuri chose to achieve these ends by putting government into the hands of kings.

Stronger than their neighbors, the Kanuri under their early Saifuwa kings embarked on conquest and began the building of an empire, at this time mainly in the region of Kanem to the east of Lake Chad. By the eleventh century, however, Islam was beginning to be a major factor in West African history. The expansion of that faith, which had followed the Muslim conquests in North Africa, profoundly influenced all it touched, including the trans-Saharan commerce and, eventually, the rise of the larger Kanem-Bornu Empire.

Kharijite Berbers, dissenters from Abbasid religio-political rule, led the way in opening up the Sahara and, ultimately, the Sudan beyond. They gathered in states greatly given to trading enterprise. Sijilmasa and Tahert became crossroad city-states in the western and central Maghreb, while in the Fezzan, two small Kharijite states in the neighborhood of Jebel al-Nafusa and Zawila, only a short distance from the ancient but long-since-abandoned homeland of the Garamantes, took shape toward the end of the eighth century.

Closely linked to one another by religious ties and

trading interests, these little states rapidly assumed command of the middle Saharan trade routes. In the steps of the Garamantes, they revived the old route southwestward to the Niger, and they pioneered a new route, though perhaps following the trace of one far older, south through the oases of Kawar and Bilma to the borders of Chad and the central Sudan.

This Kharijite primacy in trans-Saharan trade - a trade now to become far greater than before - was due, in part, to Egypt's abandonment of the Nile-to-the-Niger transversal Saharan route. During the late ninth century, caravans appear to have ceased making regular use of this road, which had led from the northern Nile through the Kufra oasis and then on to Gao on the middle Niger, mainly because its perils were considerably greater than those of the alternate routes being opened up throughout the Fezzan and the Maghreb. Partly, too, the Kharijite states owed their success to stubborn enterprise, itself the product of their zealot culture.

One scrap of evidence that seems to affirm their central position in the whole great trading system, now in the course of growth, is the fact that a ninth-century governor of Nafusa could speak "the language of Kanem," presumably Kanuri, in addition to Arabic and his native Berber. Another indication of Saharan contacts with the Mediterranean coast is the fact that Cairo's east gate during the high days of that city's prosperity under the Fatimids was called the Bab al-Zawila, the "Gate of Zawila."

Thus Nafusa and Zawila, like Tahert and Sijilmasa, put the peoples of the western and central Sudan in touch with a worldwide system of trade. For Sudanese kings and traders, business partnership with Muslims meant a growing acquaintance with the manners and attitudes of Islam, and they became attuned to techniques of commercial credit and contract, such as were now becoming indispensable to a trade conducted over distances as great as these were and in volume ever larger than before. As with later incursions of Christianity in Africa, early Islam traveled in the trader's knapsack.

There was, of course, much more significance to these outside contacts than that. At least by the tenth century, Islam could teach Sudanese potentates a good deal about new techniques of centralizing government, whether in respect to law or administration. Beyond that, it could offer them membership into a wider world of power and prestige than any they had known before, thus broadening the horizons of their provincial obscurity. It could bring them the services of scribes and scholars, and it could lend a sometimes dazzling glint to their majesty and pomp. In other words, Islam could provide a new and necessary cultural framework in which to construct a stronger, more centralized system of government and a more autonomous basis for royal rule. This is not to derogate from the spiritual attractions of Islam. Yet, however real these attractions were, they could not have prevailed without their more secular attendants.

The first Kanuri king to accept Islam for himself and his court was Umme Jilma; Saifuwa traditions award him a reign in the late eleventh century. Thenceforward, the Saifuwa kings were all Muslims. They made the pilgrimage to Mecca, some of them more than once. They introduced Muslim laws and customs, being careful (like their contemporaries in the western Sudan) not grossly to offend the sensibilities of their non-Muslim subjects, who would remain a large majority until recent times. They welcomed scholars from the great schools of Cairo and the Maghreb, and probably from Spain. They encouraged the founding of their own Koranic schools. Gradually, through this cautious spread of Islam in court and marketplace, they undercut the power of rival nobles who relied upon the religious loyalties of Kanuri tradition. More and more, they gathered to themselves the attributes of supreme monarchs rather than the more limited privileges and powers of leaders of councils of lineage peers. And they tied themselves ever more successfully into the trans-Saharan trade.

At least from the eleventh century, these kings

had regular contact with the Fatimid rulers of Ifriqiya. Fatimid records tell of presents received from the "Malik al-Sudan," which in this context undoubtedly refers to the *mai,* or king, of the Kanuri. Such presents were mostly *'abid,* a word that may be loosely translated as "slaves," so long as modern implications are not read into the word. These *'abid* were mainly men who had forfeited their civic rights and status for one reason or other, commonly by capture in raiding warfare, and who were used as royal bodyguards. Relatively few in number, they were selected for good health and strength, and were expensive to buy and maintain. Yet, Ifriqiya's Fatimid governors, always anxious to re-ensure themselves against uncertain local loyalties, were able to assemble enough *'abid* from the Sudan to maintain a regular company of troops.

These small but successful attempts at diplomacy encouraged the Kanuri kings to extend their hegemony across the northern desert. Late in the twelfth century, the Fatimid rulers of Cairo were overthrown by the forces of the Syrian Saladin (Salah al-Din). Not long afterward, these voracious, predominately Asian, mercenaries began looting the Kharijite states of the Fezzan. Evidently they continued in this way for a long time. They "set the country ablaze," in the words of a thirteenth-century writer, and greatly disturbed the desert trade. Reacting at last in 1258, the king of Kanem "sent emissaries to kill [one of these mercenaries], and [so] delivered the land from strife. His head was sent to Kanem and exhibited to the people," a detail that suggests "the people," or at least the traders, had by this time lost a lot of sleep over the plundering of their trans-Saharan commerce. After that, Zawila is said to have come under Kanuri control, while the Kanuri kings of this blossoming empire of Kanem-Bornu saw to it that they continued to enjoy fruitful relations with the Hafsid rulers of Tunisia.

Such was the formative framework, so far as external factors were concerned, affecting the Hausa to the west of the Kanuri, as well as many peoples to the east of them. Potent even in early times, the influence of long-distance communications grew in later centuries. Even if the written records are mainly lost, the remaining ones still give strong evidence of these connections. Thus, the earliest attested example of diplomatic correspondence in the central and western Sudan is a letter from a Kanuri king to the Sultan Barquq, of the Mameluk dynasty of Egypt, written sometime around CE 1391; it would not have been unique. And when, much later, Mai Idris Alooma's court scribe celebrates a meeting with messengers from the Ottoman sultan in Istambul, he is speaking for a tradition of far-ranging correspondence, which is already very old.

Yet the cultures that took shape in Kanem, as

elsewhere in the central Sudan, were far more than copies of their prestigious examples beyond the desert. Although increasingly marked by Islam after the twelfth century, these cultures were no more Arab or Berber than were those of Mali and Songhai. On the contrary, they were the expression of local and indigenous factors of development that have never ceased to mark them with a depth and resonance that is all their own. This was the originality, the power of local beliefs and skills, which explains their long endurance through the years. Islam might show the way to a wider world, whether spiritual or social: all these peoples continued nonetheless to stand, and stand firmly, on their own sense of identity and purpose. Their history shows this clearly.

Like its neighbors to the east and west, the Kanuri state used Islam to modify and strengthen structures already firmly in place. It was a transformation that took place slowly. King Umme might accept Islam. His successor, Dunama I, might twice make the pilgrimage, and according to tradition, suffer drowning in the Red Sea while on a third trip to Mecca. Those who followed might reinforce their links with the Fezzan and Tunisia or with Libya and Egypt. Yet, they continued to owe their power to local concepts of authority and its use. For then and long afterward, the king was little more than *primus inter pares*, or prime minister, of a ruling council of lineage peers. This council numbered twelve, and something is known of its organization. Under the *mai,* they formed a government that Ives Urvoy, the first twentieth-century historian to concern himself with these matters, aptly called "the administrative council of the Saifuwa family firm."

As the early empire crystallized, these councilors acquired regular titles and "departments," governorships of provinces, and commands of armed forces. Among such titled offices were the *kaigama,* "lord of the south," who was commander of the kingdom's army; the *galadima,* "governor of the west," who administered the country west of the lake that was later called Bornu; and the *chiroma,* who, in some sense, was the king's deputy and also nominated heir to the throne. Some of these titles have survived to this day. A modern visitor to the palace of the emir of Kano in northern Nigeria will be asked to obtain a pass from the office of the *madaki,* a Hausa corruption of the Bornu title *mat dawaki,* "the lord of the cavalry"; once inside, he may find not only the emir but also the emir's *chiroma.* In Bornu, the survivals are stilt more numerous.

In early times the Saifuwa made their *main* capital - for they had several, like all such states resting upon a network of tributary power over long distances at N'jimi, whose exact location is unknown, but was undoubtedly near the eastern borders of Lake Chad. Here they developed a court at which the *magira,* or queen mother, had much authority, as did also the *gumsa*, the king's senior wife, and where the Saifuwa "family council" met. Here, too, as Islam grew in influence, *'ulama*, or learned men, wrestled with the growing problems of juridical and economic development. From time to time, the court shifted its residence, following the king to one or other of the regional capitals, whose imposing brick ruins may still be seen by anyone who can take the time to go there - though it seems that the builders of a new Africa are fast making away with the bricks.

This pattern of government expanded greatly in the thirteenth century, when Kanuri power ranged far to the east of Lake Chad, as well as some way to the west, and had its northern outposts as distant as the Fezzan. Kings numbered eighteen to twenty-one in lists established by Ronald Cohen, an American cultural anthropologist, were all entitled *Dunama*, "the Great," and were the leaders of a large imperial enterprise. Their reign dates were probably between about CE 1150 and the beginning of the next century. They were succeeded by others - down to about number thirty in Cohen's lists - who enjoyed a similarly wide-ranging power.

But what proved good for the Kanuri proved also good for some of their neighbors. Even before CE 1400, there were several vassal peoples, among them the Bulala, who were east of Chad and who had grown strong enough to contest Kanuri overlordship; coupled with dynastic strife, this challenge led to a major shift in the fortunes of the Saifuwa and their dependents. Driven out of that portion of Kanem east of Chad, they took refuge in the territory governed by the *galadima* west of the lake. Here in Bornu, they developed a new capital at Birni N'gazaragamu, which is today situated near the border between Nigeria and the Republic of Niger. From this place, surrounded by a tough brick wall, the Kanuri successors were to rule until well into the nineteenth century. Having recuperated their dynastic and military strength, their kings were able to embark on fresh imperial adventures not long before CE 1500. Again, they thrust their armies east of Chad, subduing the Bulala and possibly pushing on as far as Darfur. And once more, they mastered the southerly terminals of the Saharan trails to the Fezzan and Libya.

This new Kanuri Empire reached its zenith under the sixtieth king in Cohen's lists. This was the memorable Mai Idris Alooma, who reigned in the last quarter of the Sixteenth century, and whose power possibly reached as far east as Kordofan. The empire largely remained at this pinnacle of power until about CE 1750, when Al-Hajj Ali Dunama saw the outset of a new time of troubles. The last ruler of the Saifuwa dynasty, the seventy-fifth king, died shortly after 1846, ending more than 1,000 years of royal succession.

More telling than the events of this dynastic history are the changes in structure that enabled these Bornu kings to reassert the primacy of their forebears in Kanem. From about 1450, there came the same political evolution that, a little later, was to characterize Songhai under Askia Muhammad I. This is the gradual and cautious development of administrative power by appointment rather than by right of birth. In ways that remain to be understood in detail, the grand council of Saifuwa peers begins to lose its authority to a king, who is still a constitutional monarch in that he is bound by law and custom, as well as by the balance of internal power within the structure, but is no longer merely *primus inter pares*. While continuing to uphold Kanuri religion, if only because it is Kanuri religion that lies at the root of his power, he relies increasingly on Islam for the shaping of new forms of delegated power, which stand outside the customary lineage network.

Adapting Muslim examples in Egypt and elsewhere, commoners and "slaves," who are sometimes eunuchs, begin to form an administrative corps of "king's men," whose loyalty is not to any lineage but to the person of the king himself. The *kaigama*, for example, was almost certainly considered to be of noble lineage in early times. A Kanuri praise song composed shortly before 1700 celebrates him as "the chief slave" of the king: "star of the morning, holder of the principal of the king's offices, less than the king certainly, yet greater than all the prosperous men . . ."

Having such men at his command, the king can begin to offset the authority of his princely rivals and nobles, and even displace them in their governorships and commands. Building on the same method, he selects captives for a troop of "king's soldiers," and so provides himself with an armed force whose loyalties are likewise outside the lineage structure. Mai Idris Alooma even imported Turkish musketry instructors and formed a little corps of musketeers.

With all this increase in prestige and power, royal expenses multiply. Long-service soldiers prove expensive, and so do their armaments and horses. A growing administration drains the royal purse, while heightened prestige calls for still larger palaces and still higher walls of clay and timber. Royal hospitality has to be lavish if it is not to seem ridiculous. Somehow there has to be ever more revenue from taxation and tributes, and so the imperial process acquires a momentum of its own. Only the corresponding growth and rivalry of neighboring peoples will bring it to a halt. This did not happen to the Kanuri Empire until the eighteenth century.

Important among neighboring state systems, which developed by much the same constellation of local and intrusive factors of growth, were those of the Hausa, lying west and southwest of Bornu. Although the early formative factors in Hausaland were similar to those of the Kanuri, the results were markedly different.

Like the Kanuri, the Hausa emerged around or soon after the middle of the first millennium CE from a mingling of ancestral stocks; some of their ancestors may have come from Bornu or Kanem or possibly farther east. Like them, the early Hausa were pastoralists and farmers, workers in iron, and traders, who took a lead among other ethnic groups in the localities where they had settled and proved able to dominate large areas. Unlike the Kanuri, however, the Hausa evolved no single unifying system. Their independent cities, each governing lands extending a long way from its walled center, were rivals rather than allies, and this rivalry, thanks to the competition fostered by long-distance trade, grew stronger with time. Enterprising in commerce, skilled in handicrafts, shrewd in their handling of community affairs, these city-states were to become a most notable element in the whole West African scene.

At the beginning, according to Hausa traditions, there were seven true states: Biram, Gobir, Daura, Kano, Katsina, Rano, and Zaria. Their rulers were all grandsons of a "founding-hero" called Bayagidda, also said to have been the son of a princess of Bornu, an early pointer to the influence of Bornu that recurs throughout their history. Then, at some later time, there likewise appeared seven "illegitimate" Hausa states: Kebbi, Kamfara, Gwari, Jukun, Nupe, Yauri and Ilorin (referring here to Yoruba, north of the forest). Their founders had not been among the progeny of Bayagidda but had adopted Hausa ideas and institutions. These traditions manifestly point to an early period of population movements and cultural interchange.

From the first, it seems, these emergent Hausa communities acquired their separate identities in stockaded villages, or *birni*, where initially villagers and nearby farmers took shelter in times of trouble. About 1,000 years ago, these *birni* appear to have grown into towns governed by kings. Here they developed their language and their customs, their beliefs and political structures. This is indicated by detailed Kano traditions, which now begin to be supported by new archeological research. By 1300, in any case, these towns had become the centers of states with frontiers between them. If such frontiers for a long time marked out little more than claims to spheres of interest, they were already well enough defined to set the pattern of possession and rivalry between power systems whose institutions remained closely similar.

Although the legitimate states of Kano, Katsina, and Zaria took the lead sometime before the fifteenth century, all the Hausa city-states manifested a dominant interest in local and long-distance trade, at which their men excelled, and they served both as emporiums and as centers of handicraft manufacture in textiles, leather, metals, and other goods. After 1400, with Islam becoming increasingly more influential, they were also centers of learning, and the level of intellectual discourse there was high enough to attract noted scholars from distant places. Except for a time in the sixteenth century when western Hausaland and even Kano came under the influence and partial control of the Songhai emperor Askia Muhammad I, the Hausa states looked generally to Bornu and its rulers for new ideas about government and for solutions to new problems. Some of the states even came under official Bornu overlordship.

Here, as elsewhere, society was becoming more deeply stratified; kings were acquiring more power; new forms of servitude were beginning to appear. Of King Abdullahi Burja, who ruled in Kano between about 1438 and 1452 and who was probably under strong Bornu influence, the traditions say that he set up "slave settlements" by regularly raiding their non-Muslim enemies for captives who could be put to productive work. This was clearly an innovation that reflected the growth of deeper social divisions, just as it did in Bornu. But it would be wrong to see in this the transformation of Kano's economy to one based on slavery. The actual status of slaves probably differed little in practice from that of neighboring free villagers, and nothing like a plantation economy ever developed.

A few decades later, King Muhammad Rumfa of Kano established a nine-man council of state that was possibly modeled on Saifuwa practice. No doubt to emphasize his power, he built himself a new palace, which appeared grand and glorious to his courtiers and was to be the model of other and later palaces in Hausaland. More important in the long run, Rumfa also gave a strong thrust to that process of appointing "king's men" - whether commoners, eunuchs, or other "slaves" - who stood outside the aristocratic establishment and enabled Kano and other Hausa states to evolve the intricate checks and balances of their monarchial systems.

Such innovations, and the socioeconomic reasons that provoked them, called for the introduction of new laws and customs. Learned men were expected to show how this could best be done. Intellectuals at court might have been ornamental, but they were looked to for practical advice as well. According to the Kano Chronicle, soon after 1450, a number of Fulani priests "came to Hausaland from Mali, bringing with them books of divinity and etymology"; they initiated a period of Fulani intellectual leadership that persists to this day.

But the scholar best remembered as an influence on the remodeling of Hausa institutions was, as it happened, neither from the western Sudan nor from Bornu. He was Muhammad al-Majhili, a renowned jurist of Tlemcen in western Algeria, who sojourned in Kano at the end of the fifteenth century; he wrote for Muhammad Rumfa a book whose title is reasonably translated as *The Obligations of Princes*. A little later, Al-Majhili went to Gao and gave advice to Askia Muhammad I.

Evolving in this way, the stronger of these states flourished by trade and tribute. They became vital components in the whole long-distance commerce of West Africa. Although they often quarreled with each other, their wars stopped short of large-scale destruction. Menaced from time to time by Songhai or Bornu, they managed for the most part to retain their independence. Much can be guessed from their traditions.

Happily for history, however, there appeared in 1550 the celebrated eyewitness description of Leo Africanus. It is unlikely to have been a reliable description, as it was written many years after Leo's visit to Hausaland and for a European audience with no means of critical judgment, as Leo must well have known; but it was and is the only one of its kind and therefore the best. Published in Venice nearly a quarter of a century after the writing was finished, this work startled mercantile Europe with a vision of distant power and wealth in much the same way as Columbus's reports on the Americas had done fifty years earlier.

Leo Africanus, whose given name was Al-Hasan ibn Muhammad al-Wazzan az-Zayyati, had visited Timbuktu at the age of seventeen with an uncle who was a Moroccan ambassador. Soon after 1500 (the date remains uncertain), he made another journey to the Sudan, at which time he passed through Hausaland. By now he was about thirty and in the diplomatic service of the king of Fez in Morocco.

While sailing westward from Tripoli in 1518, he was captured by a Christian pirate named Pietro Bovadiglia. Realizing that he had an important prisoner on his hands, Bovadiglia turned the future Leo over to Pope Leo x, who imprisoned him for a year in Rome's Castel Sant' Angelo on the banks of the Tiber. There, the young captive was instructed in Christianity by three bishops; in 1518, he was baptized as Giovanni Leo de' Medici, after the pope. Soon afterward, he began making notes for a book about his African travels. This he completed in 1526; the notes are lost, but what appears to be the finished manuscript came to light in 1931. The manuscript had been edited sometime before 1550 by a leading Venetian administrator, Giovanni Ramusio, who brushed up the author's faulty Italian (Ramusio also gave Leo the name by which he is remembered) and published the result.

Ramusio's volume had an instant and widespread success and was subsequently translated into numerous European languages, including an

English version by John Pory, whose 1600 edition is quoted throughout this text. Considering the history of its production, the story is a lively one and may still be read with pleasure. In it, the Hausa states of the early sixteenth century are vividly depicted. Gobir, Leo Africanus found, was rich in cattle and people, many of them living in thriving towns. "Heere are also great store of artificers and linnen weavers: and heere are such shooes made ...the greatest part whereof be carried to Tombuto [Timbuktu] and Gago [Gao]."

Leo described another state later absorbed by Katsina as "very populous, and having a king raigning over it, which maintaineth a garison of seven thousand archers, and five hundred horsemen . . .," or cavalry, that is, hired as mercenaries from some other state. "The inhabitants are very rich, and have continuall traffique with the nations adjoining. Southward thereof lieth a region greatly abounding with gold," is a reference to Hausa trade with the gold-producing country of the Akan in present-day Ghana.

Kano appeared to Leo as a great capital whose "walles and houses whereof are built for the most part of a kind of chalke [baked clay]." (These structures can be seen today.) "The inhabitants are rich merchants and most civill people," just as the German explorer Heinrich Barth would find them more than three centuries later, and just as they are now. Of Zaria he writes: "The inhabitants are rich and have great traffique unto other nations." Bornu has "a most puissant prince . . . Horsemen he hath in continuall readines to the number of three thousand, & an huge number of footmen; for all his subjects are so serviceable and obedient unto him, that whensoever he commandeth them, they will . . . follow him. . . ."

The little that is known of Hausa rule before CE 1600 suggests that its cost continued to grow, as pomp and majesty kept pace with military reinforcement. Later evidence supports that analysis. For example, under Muhammad Sharifa, king of Kano from 1703 to 1731, tradition says that taxes and tribute had increased to such a point that "the Arabs left the town and went to Katsina, and most of the poorer people fled the country." No doubt this exaggerates the situation. But the fact that many Hausa freemen did indeed become acutely discontented with their lot is strongly suggested by the relative ease with which the Fulani jihad, launched in 1804, would succeed.

Yet, if taxes and tribute continued to grow heavier, such evidence as there is indicates that the constraining power of Hausa checks and balances within the governing system itself did also. These checks and balances turned upon a shrewdly managed structure of offices, whether filled by appointment or inheritance, whereby the king could maneuver in favor of his own decisions, but could seldom or never act as an autocrat. On one side were the leaders of traditional Hausa lineages - the kingmakers of the past - whereas on the other were slave officials, eunuchs, and similar courtiers, whose privileges depended only upon royal power. Thus, Dr. Michael G. Smith, a British anthropologist, concluded from his study of the evidence that, "in the seventeenth and eighteenth century, a Hausa ruler concentrated his attention on rival chiefdoms [within his state], and on his senior kinsmen or free officials. The ruler took such steps as he could to deprive lineage rivals of power and to reduce powerful officials," playing the one off against the other as opportunity might allow.

Much the same was undoubtedly true of Bornu, just as it was of Songhai after the reforms of Askia Muhammad I. Here, as in contemporary Europe, kings might wish to be dictators, but found in practice that they had to maneuver and mollify the ruling oligarchies, whether free or slave, upon whom they always depended. In so far as the term is valid for monarchies of that period, these were of a constitutional type: they depended upon an institutional structure within which the kings, though always having the last word, could act only by a systematized consent.

In other, lesser polities, east of Lake Chad and the old lands of Kanem, it was probably much the same, though little is as yet known about them.

The state of Darfur appears to have emerged in distant times as a relay intermediary in the Nile-Niger trade. Darfur traditions speak of a dynasty called the Daju, identified only in vague and contradictory legend, which was followed by the slightly better-documented Tunjur dynasty, based in the hills to the north of Darfur's Jebel Marra. Some of these early kings were probably in contact, and perhaps in partnership, with the later rulers of Meroë. In addition, a fine brick complex erected on one of the hills in the Jebel Dar Furnung north of Jebel Marra seems to have been built as a Christian monastery, an indication that the Christian kingdom of Makuria had established a far-western mission settlement there.

Islam evidently came to power in Darfur during the sixteenth century, perhaps under one of Mai Idris Alooma's ancestors or under Idris himself; and there emerged at Jebel Marra a new dynasty known as the Keira, which was undoubtedly ruled with a Muslim constitution similar to that of Bornu. The earliest of these Keira kings, to whom tradition gives the name of Sulaiman Solong, appears to have ruled in the middle of the seventeenth century. He or his successors took over an earlier tradition of building in brick that may have started in Meroë, but in any case had long since passed westward to Kanem and Bornu. By the reign of the seventh Keira monarch, Muhammad Teirab, the kingdom had acquired enough centralized power and wealth to erect imposing, fortified stone structures.

The evidence is inconclusive as to whether or not the kings of Bornu were able during the sixteenth century to bring Darfur, even briefly, within their sphere of influence and tribute, but there is no doubt about one major point. From sometime before CE 1500, the history of the peoples of the grasslands east of Darfur, and of Darfur itself, belongs to the tragic afterglow of Christian Nubian civilization.

Already seven centuries old when the kingdom of Makuria collapsed at the end of the fourteenth century, Nubia's kingdoms stood for a remarkable African achievement. Internal written records have never been recovered, but surviving Arabic memoirs tell a little of what they were like. Writing in CE 1208, Abu Salih the Armenian claimed that Alodia, the southernmost of the three kingdoms, had 400 churches as well as many monasteries, and praised the wealth and comfort of its capital. Archeological finds during the 1960s have added greatly to the list of its noble church buildings and saved at Faras in the north a large number of superb religious frescoes.

Of the final decades of Christian Nubia, almost nothing is known. The Ethiopians, barricaded behind high mountain passes, were able to survive the Muslim onslaught and upheaval and, eventually, to turn the tables on their rivals, notably the sultanate of Adel, located in what is northern Somalia today. But the Nubians had no such natural defenses. Invaded by Mameluk armies from the north, infiltrated by Muslim migrants moving down the Blue Nile in the south, Christian Nubian civilization disappeared during the fifteenth century into a historical mist that no research has managed to penetrate. When at last the mist begins to clear late in the fifteenth century, the scene has altogether changed, and the Islamization of Nubia is far advanced. Nomad peoples dominate Makuria. Control southward from the riverain frontier of Alodia is held by the Funj, a people of uncertain but possibly southern Nilotic origins who had also accepted Islam. In 1503–1504, their first listed ruler, Amara Dunqas, founded his capital at Sennar. Here the Funj kings would rule until the nineteenth century.

These disturbances meant little to the western peoples. Although the ancient trading route from the Nile through Darfur to Chad ceased to feed their commerce, they continued to thrive upon the north-south Saharan routes. By 1600, they were just reaching the apogee of cultures formed 1,000 years earlier. Beginning in the seventeenth century, they would come slowly to grips with the challenge of a wider western world from which they were still separated by the vast distances of inner Africa. With modern reassessment of written and oral records, and the aids of archeology, historians can now set forth these cultures not only in outline but also in considerable detail. Here, as Ahmad ibn Fartua, Idris Alooma's chronicler, remarked nearly four centuries ago about his own written history of Bornu, "we have mentioned very little, passing over much from fear of being lengthy and verbose. But the thoughtful reader will understand that beyond the river lies the sea."

If one were to embark on that sea, however, there would be interesting things to speculate about as well as to say. King Idris Alooma and England's Queen Elizabeth I certainly spoke different languages, but were their basic administrative and political problems so dissimilar? Both, after all, were much concerned with the overweening power of nobles and the need for loyal servants; both had a great deal of trouble with each.

In a different direction, southward into the far interior of Africa, other comparisons with Kanem-Bornu's social order might be found. For there, too, south of the Congo forests in geophysical circumstances not markedly different from those of the Sudan, the sixteenth and seventeenth centuries saw the emergence of another cluster of kingdoms much concerned with trade. Undoubtedly, at least two great differences divided them: in the Sudan there was the formative influence of Islam, reaching into every field of organized life, whereas in the south there was the ever-destructive tsetse fly. Yet, the basic nature of the problems of centralizing rule might have been much the same, and the solutions - superficialities aside - of the same order.

The story of the kingdoms and lesser polities of the far interior belong rightly to another chapter. Yet, that of the Nile-Niger region, as of the remainder of West Africa, can undoubtedly help to illuminate it.

7

INNER AFRICA

JAN VANSINA

I nner Africa enters history on the tide of a huge migration that covered a subcontinent - all of Africa south of a line from the Bight of Benin to southern Somalia. This invasion of Bantu-speaking people was one of the great upheavals of all time because of the area affected, the time span covered, and above all, because of the linguistic and cultural tradition it left.

Among the results of the migrations was the formation of 400 or so different languages, all as closely related to each other as are the Romance languages. Just as the peoples speaking Romance languages inherited many features of Rome's civilization, shaping it by their indigenous cultures and their subsequent history, so the Bantu speakers inherited the civilization of their common ancestors and diversified the common inheritance in similar ways.

The original people are called the Bantu, and in recognition of the great cultural and physical mixing that has since occurred, their descendants are most properly known as Bantu speakers. The word *bantu* means "the people," plural of *muntu*, "a person." It is still found in this form in all the Bantu languages and comes from the ancestral speech, the proto-Bantu language. Much of the vocabulary of proto-Bantu has thus survived, and from this as well as from the geographical distribution of languages scholars can tell how the original Bantu lived, where they came from, and how they migrated; but they cannot date with any exactitude their coming.

The original home of the Bantu was territory south of the middle Benue River valley in eastern Nigeria, an area well watered, fertile, rich in fauna and flora because it lay on the fringes of forest and savanna. The people were principally fishermen. They used dug-out canoes, nets, lines, and fishhooks in their business. They also hunted big and small game, and cultivated African yams and palm trees as well as some millet and sorghum. They made pottery, used bark cloth, and perhaps already wove fibers of the raffia tree on wide looms. They bred goats, perhaps sheep, and some cattle. (But the last could not thrive near the forest, so they would leave them behind during the migration.) Iron was not worked; rather, tools were fashioned out of wood or stone.

These fishermen were sedentary and lived in compact villages of unknown size. Their communities were organized, in part, on a basis of kinship. The leaders were the older men, and all others obeyed them because the elders were their grandfathers, fathers, uncles, and granduncles. The right to exercise authority was legitimized by common ties of blood, and in matters of succession and inheritance, kinship among them was matrilineal. Thus, a man's estate went to the son of his sister, not to his own son. Polygyny was common. Because of the nature of the descent system and the fact that women left their villages to follow their husbands, the descent groups, or lineages, were dispersed over different villages. As a result, village organization could not be based entirely on kinship; rather, the settlement may have been governed by a council. Certainly, chiefs were recognized and had territorial power, but we do not know if they ruled over one or several villages.

The Bantu also had religious specialists, acting as both medicine men and diviners, though the roles were often performed by the same person. The Bantu believed that witchcraft was a major cause of misfortune. They may have believed as well in the influence on the lives of men of nature spirits or ancestors. Nothing is known about their arts, and no archeological sites traceable to them have yet been found. They must, however, have been excellent wood-carvers, and they may have produced terra-cotta sculpture.

The Bantu expansion was triggered probably by a great influx of population in Nigeria, which itself was the result of the arrival of many people who had gradually been driven out of the increasingly arid Sahara after 2500 BCE. At first, the population pressure found an exit eastward by expanding along the forest fringes as far as the present border of the Republic of Sudan. The invaders were farmers of the savanna; they spoke a language belonging to the Adamawa Eastern group that spoke a Central Sudanese language and had lived in those areas before them. The older inhabitants were scattered north, east, and south until an equilibrium of forces was reached.

Then the pressure in Nigeria built up once again. It was relieved this time by the Bantu southward migrations, which were made easier because of their ability to adapt successfully to life in the forest near the rivers. The forest became their home, and it was a good home. It furnished as much timber as was needed for housing and canoes, and the people could fell trees without woodsmen's tools, by burning them at the base of the trunk.

The forest was rich in game, and the marshes and rivers were well stocked with fish. It was more pleasant than the savanna because it was cool, provided a more temperate climate, and was never dusty. It also contained scattered huge patches of savanna called the *esobe,* where flora and fauna typical of the savanna could be found. Within the forest, the Bantu could find all the advantages they had known in the mixed environment of the forest fringe.

As for the Bantu's means and manner of migration, being fishermen, they were able to load themselves, their goods, and livestock aboard canoes. The larger boats could take as much as a ton and a half, and the Bantu were carried along rivers and thence along the Atlantic coast, settling the island of Fernando Po early on. They knew where to go because scouting comes naturally to fishermen, whose quests take them many miles from home.

The migration was not a single mass movement, but a gradual process. People packed and went farther on when they felt they had too many neighbors or when there had been quarrels or when they feared witchcraft at work in their village. Because the waterways made travel relatively easy, a village might, in a single move, migrate a substantial distance. Reckoned in centuries, the rate of Bantu dispersion was relatively rapid, and thus at the end of the first phase, the people had come to occupy most of the equatorial forest, mixing with the indigenous peoples, including Pygmies and black hunters of a larger stature, about whom nothing more is known.

The movement slowed down for a time when the Bantu encountered new environments on the far sides of the forest and were forced to adapt their economies accordingly. To the east, a different sort of forest - more tropical in its vegetation and providing no *esobe*, or clearings - was reached. There the tropical forest covered the great mountain range west of the Great Rift Valley, and the society based on fishing had to transform itself into a hunting and agricultural community. Similarly, where open savanna was reached again in the south, the cultivation of cereals became more important.

Another consequence of these adaptations was a differentiation in the Bantu language as it was spoken among the increasingly dispersed migrants. Thus, one can later distinguish between western and eastern subgroups of Bantu speech, the more marked innovations appearing in the east, where other aspects of the Bantu culture would also undergo considerable changes through the influence of a substantial autochthonous population there. But no certain trace of these aborigines has remained to give a clue to their racial identities.

Once the adaptation to the savanna had been made, the southern migrations gained momentum again. The Bantu speakers still stuck to the rivers where possible, not only for the fish found there but also because something approaching the ideal conditions of the savanna-forest fringe could be found in the less dense gallery forests that grew along the river banks. One migratory route seems to have gone downriver on the Congo and then eastward and southward on the Kasai River and other Congo affluents. Following a network of lesser rivers and occasionally traveling overland, this group reached the headwaters of the Zambezi River, from whence they could float downriver to the Indian Ocean and the island of Zanzibar, and then paddle north along the coast as far as Somalia.

At the same time, the mass of Bantu migrators that had initially taken a more direct route eastward toward the Great Rift Valley and the interlacustrine area was making much slower headway. The terrain of the Great Lakes area was difficult, and the eastern Bantu had adapted to the social organization of the indigenous population living in relatively dense, well-defined societies. So these Bantu, traveling along their more obstructed route, may have reached Lake Victoria at about the same time the southern wave reached Zanzibar.

During the later part of this second period of expansion, some remarkable technological changes percolated throughout the whole Bantu world. First, they learned how to smelt and work iron. The new technology came to them from several sources. This author concludes that the art had spread south from Meroë after 500 BCE, reaching East Africa shortly after the beginning of the Christian era. It reached northern Nigeria around 300 BCE, perhaps from North Africa. So the northwestern Bantu - those who joined the later waves of migrations - acquired the knowledge from Nigeria; the Bantu who moved through the interlacustrine area received it from pre-existing populations in East Africa; and those who moved southeastward and then up the coast were introduced to ironworking by sailors from southern Arabia, perhaps in the first century CE or earlier. From all these sources the knowledge spread to other Bantu speakers. In the equatorial forest, excellent charcoal could be manufactured, and soon the metal produced there, probably from ore bought in trade for other goods, surpassed what was made anywhere else in inner Africa. It is a sign of the cohesion of the Bantu world that the terminology for working iron developed homogeneously over the whole area occupied by Bantu speakers.

Other innovations at first produced more dramatic results than the knowledge of iron smelting. Banana and taro, crops of Southeast Asian origin, had been introduced in East Africa late in the first millennium BCE. By way of the Zambezi valley and the Great Rift regions, the new crops spread all over Central Africa, becoming the staples for the forest populations as well as for the peoples of the interlacustrine area. If it was the Bantu peoples who picked up these crops along the coast and transported them inland, they must have migrated there before the birth of Christ.

Lastly, the eastern and southeastern Bantu reacquired cattle. (Their ancestors had lost their incidental herds to the ravages of the tsetse fly when they first entered the forests.) They met with cattle-keeping people in East Africa and perhaps Zambia, and learned the art of husbandry from them. So at the end of this phase, the Bantu peoples had acquired a totally new mode of life. They were now farmers and herdsmen rather than fishermen, grew banana and taro as well as cereals, and smelted iron - with consequent changes in social organization. The lapse of time required to change the old way of life must have lasted well over a century and probably much longer.

And then the expansion began once again. Between the first and the fifth century CE, the Bantu speakers, with their cattle, went from the Zambezi valley all the way to the Transvaal (in the northeastern region of what is now the Republic of South Africa) and continued southward. By the thirteenth century CE at the latest, they were in the

Transkei (a territory within South Africa's Cape Province), but there is evidence that they may have completed their move much earlier. During this last period, they also moved into the regions of southern Angola and South West Africa (known to its indigenous inhabitants as Namibia).

In East Africa, further gains of territory were slow, even though Bantu speakers advanced from the west, south, and east into the interior of Kenya and Tanzania. Progress was slow because the Eastern Rift of Kenya and Tanzania and large parts of northern Kenya and Uganda were not sufficiently fertile to support sedentary farmers, but were well suited to support pastoral nomads; peoples engaged in herding were already occupying these lands. So the Bantu farmers could not deeply penetrate those areas. Then there were places in the region of Tanzania with a fairly dense population and established cultural patterns, which did not allow for Bantu speech or customs to assert themselves.

However, as a general rule, the Bantu immigrants assimilated the native peoples they encountered, transmitting not only speech but often their whole civilization; the Bantu and successive autochthones often merged, becoming one population. How did this happen?

The Bantu civilization was generally not much more complex or appealing than the civilizations of the local peoples. This was not comparable to the spread of Rome's Superior civilization over much of barbaric Europe. Rather, the process of Bantuization seems to have been similar to that of urbanization. The immigrants lived in compact settlements that acted as centers or "towns" for the more dispersed nomadic camps of the non-Bantu peoples around them. The aboriginal hunters and/or farmers came to these centers to exchange produce with the Bantu, married with them, took gradually to their speech, and through it, adopted the Bantu civilization. And, to a lesser extent, the Bantu took on features of the aboriginal peoples as well.

Since the Bantu villages were small, the difference between "town" and "country" was slight, and the process of assimilation went on slowly. Still slower was the Bantuization of indigenous hunters, whose nomadic life brought only intermittent contacts with the villagers. Examples in Zambia show that Bantu farmers and autochthonous hunters lived side by side without amalgamating until the thirteenth or perhaps even the fifteenth century.

Bantuization, then, did not take just a few centuries but covered almost two millenniums. The process was completed only in the western and central equatorial forests and in the savanna as far south as southern Angola and Rhodesia. Pockets of hunters surviving in the forest in southern Africa and even in parts of East Africa represent specialized populations that have adopted Bantu speech and live in a symbiotic economic relationship with the Bantu. But among others assimilation never happened (for example, the Pygmy hunters living in the oriental parts of the great equatorial forest).

And so the Bantu civilizations evolved from a mixture of proto-Bantu culture and of features produced after the migrations by internal invention and even more by contact with neighboring groups. The Bantu languages cannot be classified in clearly recognizable genetic subgroups. Languages grow only in relative isolation from each other. A particular language first develops dialects, and these become daughter languages of the ancestral mother language after the passage of some centuries. But if the communities that speak those dialects are not sufficiently isolated, as happened among the English in Great Britain, it then becomes impossible to find out in what way the daughter languages descended from the ancestral tongue. This is obviously what happened with the Bantu languages. One can recognize that the original Bantu divided into two languages called Proto-Bantu A and Proto-Bantu B. One can also see that the 400-odd languages that are spoken now stem from eighty to ninety mother languages. But the relations between them cannot be determined with precision, which proves that at all times since the original expansion, Bantu speakers have kept up a great deal of communication with each other all over the huge subcontinent they occupied.

The relatively constant communication between these people must be attributed above all to the development of trade. Everywhere fishing folk exchanged pottery, fish, game, and vegetal and cereal foods. Areas blessed with the required raw materials exported such goods as ironware, copper, salt, basketry, mats, and sometimes even canoes and wooden tools. Trade was fueled not only by the needs of people but by their tastes. Thus, a householder in the southern Congo might add imported woven ware to his store of locally made baskets and mats simply because the designs or shapes appealed to him.

If trade was of great importance in opening avenues of contact between near and distant neighbors, the accompanying spread of technological skills was also of major significance in the Bantuization process. The effects are visible both from linguistic evidence and the diffusion of items found. Among the objects and techniques that came into use over wide parts of the Bantu-speaking area, perhaps the most important set of items is the shaft furnace and its associated technology, which between CE 700 and 1200 ushered in the later Iron Age for inner Africa. These had been developed in the forests of the Congo, mainly because the hardwoods growing there produced a charcoal that allowed iron to be treated at much higher temperatures. This area remained foremost in the quality of its iron and steel products well into the twentieth century. Other, lesser centers of metallurgical skills were in Katanga, where evidence of the later Iron Age is attested as early as the eighth century and somewhat later in central Angola. This new technology allowed men to fashion large iron tools, both for peace and war. These broad-bladed hoes, heavy axes, and large spears enabled people to carry out their tasks much more effectively than did the brittle and clumsy small iron tools they had used before this time.

Also, archeological evidence tells us that by CE 1200 the Bantu civilizations had reached the point at which one finds in each region a set of different but related cultures, and no further differentiation occurred. Even though the major proof for this development stems from an examination of pottery, it is sufficiently established that the regional Bantu cultures of 1200 are the direct forerunners of those ethnic cultures that began to be identifiable by 1800. From this time on, the history of the continent is best told by geographical areas: the savanna north of the equatorial forest, the forest itself, the southern savanna, Africa south of the Zambezi River, and East Africa.

The peoples of the northern savanna, both the autochthonous Central Sudanese speakers and the Adamawa Eastern speakers who had invaded the area, never lost touch completely with the culture of the Sahel (between Lake Chad and the Nile), and the Bantu never made any imprint here. The early evolution of this area is still shrouded in mystery. A complicated set of population movements resulted in the present crazy quilt of language groups, but a fairly uniform culture pattern was preserved over most of the area now occupied by the Central African Republic, the northern Congo, southern Sudan, and parts of Cameroon. The people were skilled farmers, living in dispersed homesteads that were organized into tiny kinship groups, and they recognized leaders only in time of war.

On the upper Ubangi River, one group of people began to organize a kinship system that included many hundreds of relatives or supposed relatives and brought them under the control of a tribal patriarch. By 1600, the concept of territorial kingship had been introduced, and a fairly small kingdom was born. The first tiny states were led by members of the Bandia clan, whose kinsmen, the Avongara, also developed a micro-kingdom. By 1750, one of these proto-states began a career of conquest, pushing farther eastward with each generation. (This was to become the Zande nation in the nineteenth century.) The result of the expansion was the adoption by the new inhabitants of an incredible range of objects, techniques, behavior, and values, producing in their fusion an extraordinarily complex new civilization. They took over every indigenous crop cultivated by the people they subjugated, adding them to their own repertoire. This could only be accomplished by altering the rotation of crops, and it ultimately produced a wholly new type of agriculture that relied on the growing of perhaps forty crops rather than two or three staples.

Trade between this northern savanna and other areas may have remained negligible before the eighteenth century, though the existence of ancient underground iron mines not far from the Ubangi Bend indicates a brisk trade in iron. Traders from Darfur and even distant Egypt reached the Mbomu by traveling directly south. From then on, the relative isolation of the area was completely shattered. The mystery is why influences from the Sahel had not percolated much sooner all over these great grasslands, especially along the 1,400-mile-long Chari River, whose many tributaries linked parts of Central Africa with the Lake Chad region.

As stated earlier, a major consequence of the Bantu migrations was a change in their way of life as they entered new vegetation zones. Following their arrival in the forest zone, the Bantu began to specialize. Some groups turned to farming and hunting, while others remained fishermen. In the Congo Bend area, where the specialization was most marked, the fishermen, owing to their greater mobility, took on additional roles as traders. The local trading networks grew bigger and bigger with the passage of time as one group of fishermen made contact with other groups, and markets arose among them.

There was no lack of products to trade. People outside the forest needed ironware, red camwood for ornamentation and medicine, copal (a kind of resin obtained from trees), canoes, and later even such particularized items as sugarcane wine, certain types of knives, and certain kinds of caterpillars to eat. In exchange, people in the forest sought such goods as copper and copperware, coastal salt or salt from Katanga, iron ore (probably from the Ubangi region), and later, raffia cloth, ornaments, and certain types of seashells used in monetary exchange. In a general sense, the same situation prevailed all along the coast, from the Niger delta to the mouth of the Congo and up the estuaries of the rivers there. The trade can be attested by such traces as the strong similarities found in polychrome sculpture from Yorubaland to the Congo. Just before 1700, a European trader even claimed that African sailors from the Gold Coast traveled all along the coast southward, reaching as far as Loango, near the mouth of the Congo.

But in the area roughly equivalent to the mountainous parts of southern Cameroon, Gabon, and eastern Congo there was no such specialization between Bantu fishermen-traders and farmers. There, especially in the northeastern Congo, the intermixture with autochthonous hunting bands became pronounced. By the thirteenth century CE, new Bantu-speaking immigrants from the area of the Great Lakes arrived in the hospitable country. In some cases, their superior social and political structures enabled them to wrest the leadership from the autochthones. In most cases, however, the newcomers lost their own cultural background almost totally and blended with the cultures they found. In the northeastern Congo, the process was less complex and happened on a much smaller scale, but still many Bantu groups there began to take on Pygmy physical features. But the effect was rendered less distinct when the mighty nineteenth-century invasion of the Bantu-speaking Fang overran the area, adding still another element to the culture.

In the central portions of the forest, all along the affluents of the Congo, an institution of ritual chieftainship arose between perhaps the thirteenth and the seventeenth centuries. This was an important change in the whole way of life because it replaced the notion of authority by virtue of superior age in the kinship system with the notion of authority based on territory. The new system also led to a great flowering of rituals, all of which are related in their oral tradition.

Thus the spread of ideas, intense trade, and local migrations brought about a remarkable uniformity of civilization over equatorial Africa. The influence of the forest environment is particularly noticeable in the realm of religion. For the Pygmies, there was only one god: the forest. The Bantu speakers observed a more complex set of beliefs, wherein the banks of pools and the thickets were the abode of nature spirits whose whims controlled life; but ancestors and forms of magic also had a place in the system.

In other aspects of their cultural life as well, the Bantu speakers achieved a high degree of sophistication. The popular image of tiny settlements lost in the awesome majesty of unending depths of foliage could not be more wrong. The people were neither lost nor barbarous, and some of the most original monuments of African civilization originate with the forest peoples. From the lake regions of the Great Rift Valley to Cameroon, the forest was the home of great epics, literary masterpieces of a scope and length unequaled elsewhere in Africa. In the eastern Congo and Gabon, a rich and delicate tradition of sculpture existed, and in the central forest, the arts of dancing and polyphonic song achieved great distinction.

By the eighteenth century, the increase in trade and the linkage of more and more local networks into large commercial systems led to the fusion of all into one far-reaching system for the purpose of exporting slaves and ivory to the coast. By 1800, the network that fed into Stanley Pool (a lake-like expansion of the Congo some 350 miles from its mouth), and thence to the Atlantic, spanned 1,000 miles, reaching to the Central African Republic, the Adamawa plateau in Cameroon, and to the Stanley Falls in the Democratic Republic of the Congo. Indeed, the northern affluents of the Congo connected with Darfur and Egypt.

In the southern savanna, two areas stand out as centers of Bantu evolution: northern Katanga and the lower Congo. Archeological finds from the former area show that by the eighth or ninth century, a complex culture existed there. Several earlier cultures had fused together, as evidenced from pottery, and both potters' art and metalwork had reached amazing virtuosity. The distribution of the population was dense; there can be no doubt that a political structure based on the occupation of common territory had evolved and that a form of chieftainship had developed. By the twelfth century, long-distance trade in copper was under way, differences in wealth between poor and rich had increased, and chiefs or kings ruled over larger areas than earlier. The territorial structure had expanded so that certain chiefs had authority over headmen of villages, but themselves became subjected to overlords, whom we can call kings. With the development of this type of kingship came an increase in the complexity of the ideology of kingship, the etiquette connected with it, the quality and number of regalia that expressed it.

Descendants of these twelfth-century chiefs arose to lead great kingdoms, perhaps in the sixteenth century, if not somewhat earlier. The renowned Luba kingdom was created by Kalala Ilunga, whose deeds are recorded in Luba oral history. Kalala Ilunga introduced the notion of *bulopwe*, a form of sacred kingship. All the descendants of his line were supposed to have a special sort of blood, and its virtues were such that anyone endowed with this blood had a right to rule. Only people with *bulopwe* could mystically protect the country against harm and promote the fertility of crops and of women or ensure the success of the hunt - the central concerns of all Luba.

Well before 1600, but after the foundation of the Luba kingdom, a prince from that realm introduced the Luba concept of *bulopwe* to the Lunda people to the west. Tradition has it that the Lunda were then governed by a young queen, Rweej. She met the handsome Kibinda Ilunga, a Luba hunter, at a camp near an idyllic brook, married him, and let him rule. Her twin brothers, dissatisfied with the arrangement, left for the interior of Angola to carve out new chiefdoms for themselves.

The Luba kingdom proper did not expand beyond the plains of the upper Lomami River before the eighteenth century, and even then, the territories added were lost again by 1850. The kingdom was a collection of hereditary chiefdoms of all sizes, joined by a common allegiance to the sovereign. Despite the theory of *bulopwe,* or rather beyond it, the kings in practice enforced their government by the use of a small bureaucracy of titled officers and the threat of force against recalcitrant chiefs, who were never fully welcomed into the system of Luba kinship.

The Lunda adopted a modified form of this, blending it with a political institution of their own. Their earlier form of government had fused in an original way the idea of ties by blood with territorial authority and structure. Everyone in the family was supposed to obey senior members and also to collaborate with junior members (that is, men of equal status). From this, it evolved that chiefs were considered to be members of a family headed by the Lunda king or queen. So chiefs were related to one another as brothers, cousins, nephews, and the like, at least fictionally. To preserve the fiction, it became practice that a successor took over the name of the deceased chief and his whole personality so that he, too, now was the brother, nephew, cousin, and so on, of other chiefs. Even the wives of the deceased became his wives; so much did the successor "become" the dead man.

It was easy to adapt this principle to the titled bureaucracy introduced by the Luba. It allowed the whole political system to function, whatever the social structure of a people might be, since it could be adapted to any system of political succession. The Luba system, by contrast, could not. The Luba were patrilineal, and offices were inherited either by the brothers of the deceased or by their male children. This hampered the diffusion of the Luba model of government whenever societies were organized matrilineally (for example, whenever their practice was to have nephews rather than sons as heirs). In addition, the Luba system meant that with the passing of each generation, the ties between chiefs weakened, and attempts at breaking away from the realm or wars between chiefdoms in the kingdom became more and more probable as time passed.

The difference between the Lunda and Luba systems explains why large numbers of peoples actually subjected themselves to the rule of Lunda chiefs. These chiefs still remained in touch with the Lunda emperor. By 1750, the Lunda had created an empire stretching from the Kwango River in the west to the Luapula River and Lake Mweru in the east, ruling over a million inhabitants or more.

The net effect of the Luba and Lunda expansion was to establish transcontinental long-distance trading routes from Angola to Mozambique and to leave a powerful imprint upon the civilizations of all the peoples living in the southern savanna east of the Kwango. The commodities traded were mainly slaves, but also included ivory, copper, salt, European goods, as well as items of local produce. Ramifications of the trade routes covered the whole savanna and linked up with the forest peoples' network.

As for the cultural influence, all sorts of institutions were diffused - from initiation rituals for girls to veneration of a special tree in ancestor worship. The most remarkable facet of this was perhaps the extraordinary efflorescence of a system of common symbols. Using these symbols, the southern savanna peoples elaborated a complex philosophy applicable both to an investigation of reality and to the ordering of societal relationships. But the diffusion was not total; in some fields there was none. For instance, the Luba homeland and central Angola were two centers where distinct styles of sculpture developed before 1600. Not only did these two styles not influence one another, but the Lunda, who lived between the centers, did not take to sculpture at all. The example of sculpture brings home the point that diffusion is not an automatic process. The societies that are exposed to new objects, behavior, or ideas are selective, taking only those things that complement their own traditions well.

North of the lower Congo River chiefdoms began to form primitive states perhaps as early as the twelfth century. Continuing growth led to the establishment of three major kingdoms, Congo, Loango, and Tio - all by the fifteenth century at the latest. Of these, Congo became the most famous. Congo civilization encompassed the kingdoms of Congo and Loango and stretched from there through northern Angola to the Kwanza River and beyond; east of the Kwango River, Congo influence mingled with Lunda features. The Tio type of civilization asserted itself on all the high and drier plateaus around the Stanley Pool and toward the lower Kasai River.

By 1480, Congo was a flourishing state. Initially, the staple crops were millet and banana, superseded in the sixteenth century by maize and 100 years later by cassava. A rich and highly accomplished technology flourished. Pottery making, weaving, smithing, and other crafts were fully established, and a brisk trade brought products from all parts of the kingdom and beyond to its major markets. The arts were well developed, especially sculpture. Stone statues of chiefs, dating to the seventeenth century, have survived.

There was state-controlled currency, based on the exchange of a small seashell found only near the coastal town of Luanda, and it was controlled by the state's treasurer. Government was somewhat more centralized than elsewhere in Central Africa partly because the king could depose any chief and hereditary succession was not recognized except for kingship. All lesser officers served at the pleasure of the rulers, at least in theory. In practice, the relations between a territorial chief and a king were determined by power politics, and there are many instances in which the sovereign could not oust some of his lesser officers. Despite the fact then that Congo was perhaps the most centralized of the Central African kingdoms, the structure of the state was still unimpressive when compared with the West African states.

Conflicts developed between the aristocracy and the farmers, and the system of royal succession worked poorly. Finally, contact with the Portuguese brought about the state's downfall after 1665. The increased slave trade that followed in the whole area, unhampered by political checks and balances, allowed individual entrepreneurs to become wealthy and powerful men. They invested their profit in guns and armed guards, made up of slaves and poorer kinsmen. Thus, the fact that power could be achieved by anyone who was successful in trade undermined the belief that only the nobility should or could rule and indirectly undermined the basis for any royal authority itself. For the authority of a monarchy was based ultimately on the belief that the king ruled because it was preordained by his birth into a royal lineage, and the royal lineage ruled as if preordained by natural law. The emergence of powerful merchants changed all this. The monarchies survived, but after 1800, the major states had either fallen apart or had become hollow shells, mere shadows of a former structure.

Two other influential Bantu-speaking civilizations were those of the Lozi and the Ovimbundu. Lunda migrants to the upper Zambezi blended with the locals to form the Lozi kingdom, in which a new, unique culture arose. The Ovimbundu civilization grew out of a mixture of Lunda and Congo elements, with some southwestern cattle-keeping Bantu intermingled in the Angolan highlands. Cattle raids by the Ovimbundu chiefdoms kept them perennially at war until their restlessness was turned toward the acquisition of wealth through trade after 1750. The Ovimbundu became, especially in the nineteenth century, the most successful long-distance traders in the interior.

In southern Africa, even before 1200, the development of localized cultures resulted in the establishment of the main distinct civilizations that have since dominated there: the *bantu botatue,* or "the three-people group" in Zambia; the Malawi, living in what is now the Republic of Malawi; the Shona in Rhodesia; and the Sotho and perhaps the Nguni speakers (including the Xhosa, Zulu, and Swazi) of South Africa. All of these are set apart from the civilizations discussed so far by their emphasis on cattle: possession meant wealth and power. The transfer of cattle regulated all inter-group relations: Tribute to the king was paid in cattle; bridewealth was paid in cattle to the father of the prospective bride by the father of the groom; important sacrifices required the slaughtering of cattle.

Africa: A History

The great importance cattle assumed in these societies is called the cattle complex. Historically, the complex originated in East Africa. Cattle were not sacred animals as in India, but there was an intimate bond between cattle and people. Men had their favorite single steer or ox and identified with the animal even more than some Western people do with their pets. Cattle were considered the most beautiful creations of nature, and much of the poetry in East Africa and also in southern Africa describes the beauty of the hides, horns, and behavior of herds or individual beasts. Cattle were also the intermediaries between man and the spirits. When an ox was sacrificed, one often told the animal before it was killed what to say to the ancestors in the next world. Cattle produced wealth for their owners by producing offspring or by being hired out. In addition, men could be made vassals of a lord simply because they were entrusted with his herd. There is no aspect of life in which cattle did not figure prominently.

The civilizations south of the Zambezi did not only absorb features from East and Central Africa, they interacted daily and for a full millennium with non-Bantu peoples: the Khoikhoi (Hottentots) and San (Bushmen). The former were nomadic pastoralists; the latter hunters and gatherers. The farther one goes from the Zambezi to the south or to the west, the more one finds the imprint of Khoi or San ways of life on the cultures of the

Bantu speakers. Thus, in the region of South West Africa, the black and Bantu-speaking Herer are culturally pastoralists like the Khoikhoi, whereas the black and Khoi-speaking Bergdama took over a Bushman way of life. Thus, one can show that language, culture, and race do not necessarily go together at all. The Herero took over only a Khoi way of life, but kept their language; the Bergdama took over a Khoi language and a San way of life. Both Herero and Bergdama are black, and different from the yellowish Khoi or San.

After 1300, the influence of the Luba civilization began to affect the technology and political organization of the area. Luba emigrants founded a large kingdom in Malawi, while the Shona, new settlers in Rhodesia, founded the states that were to fuse into the empire of Monomotapa by 1450. Even before the Luba's arrival, however, trade had developed with ports along the Indian Ocean. Gold had been mined in Rhodesia perhaps as early as the fifth century CE. The precious ore became a major export around CE 1100, being sought after by Arab and Portuguese traders, and it rapidly turned into the keystone of the prosperity of all the Swahili cities on the east coast. The gold trade brought through the harbor of Sofala such imports as cloth, beads, and porcelain. The presence of foreign traders also stimulated the export of other commodities along the Zambezi, mainly ivory, leading to the creation of a dense network of local exchange in all manner of minerals, household goods, and luxury items. With the arrival of the Portuguese in Mozambique, the patterns and volume of trade did not change much, but the routes did. A steady expansion continued until the eighteenth century when even north Transvaal had become a major trading area. By the end of the eighteenth century, the goods, including many slaves now, went from Lake Malawi to the Portuguese coastal settlements at Kilwa, the Zambezi estuary, and Algoa Bay.

The Malawi kingdom did not long outlast the arrival of the Portuguese. It was a loose confederation, and the power of the monarch was linked directly to the control of trade. The state reached its zenith in the seventeenth century with Portuguese help and then fell apart when the Yao, a Bantu-speaking people dwelling in Mozambique and southern Tanzania, managed to wrest the commerce in ivory and slaves.

Meanwhile, the Monomotapa Empire had gradually grown from a set of chiefdoms into a large state. But after fifty-odd years, in about 1475, its southern half broke away and became the kingdom of the Rozwi, a Shona clan. The Shona people are responsible for some spectacular stone ruins in Rhodesia; but these do not include the ruins at Zimbabwe, a site that antedated the empire of Monomotapa. The size of the walls, the wealth in gold, stone sculpture, and oriental porcelain, led to wild speculations as to when the site was founded. Some even held that this was the land of the Queen of Sheba! Now it is evident that the place was occupied over a long period by Bantu speakers and that it developed along with the growth of local states.

The Rozwi were skilled builders in stone, and their art was passed on to peoples in South Africa, where builders copied the forms in wattle and daub as well as wood. Their empty villages are still found from the Zambezi River to the Orange Free State.

Beyond statecraft and architecture, the Shona were remarkable for their spiritual beliefs and organization. There was an official religion invoking royal and lordly ancestors by oracle, in the person of a chief priest, who transmitted to kings and commoners the wishes of Mwari, the creator-god. The oracle's authority extended throughout the kingdom, and lower priests were linked to him in a loose hierarchy.

Of the peoples living in what is now South Africa, little is yet known of the period before colonial rule was established. The stone ruins probably belonged to the Sotho; traces of Nguni settlement have not yet been found, even though the Nguni were presumed to have reached Natal by the eleventh century and are known to have developed chiefdoms there by the fourteenth. All evidence indicates that there was a slow growth of territorial chiefdoms over a long period of time. These political units were not welded into kingdoms, perhaps because there always was room for further expansion in unoccupied or sparsely settled territory, a situation to which political practice among the Nguni had adapted itself. Whenever a quarrel for the succession to a chieftainship broke out among two contenders, one could always move out of settled territory with his followers and set up a brand-new chiefdom. When no further expansion was possible, however, weaker chiefdoms were incorporated into bigger states, and the process culminated with the creation of the Zulu nation in what is now the South African province of Natal.

Meanwhile, the San and Khoikhoi lived on in western South Africa, where desert conditions made farming impossible. The Bantu who arrived in this environment adapted to it and were unable to Bantuize the original inhabitants, who kept their traditional ways. These civilizations have been remarkable not only for the skills exhibited by Bushmen rock painters and engravers but especially for the mythology and religious beliefs that they developed. The myths are richer, more varied, and infinitely more poetic than those of the agricultural peoples, and the mythology influenced deeply the oral literature of both the southwestern and southeastern Bantu peoples.

In East Africa, the evolution of the societies turned out to be more complex than in any other part of inner Africa. The great variety of environments in the area, including the exceptionally arid Great Rift Valley of central Kenya and Tanzania, can be held responsible, in part, for the complexity. The pattern of immigration further complicated matters.

Sometime before 1500 BCE, the indigenous Khoikhoi and San hunters encountered migrations of peoples of Ethiopian origin, who made pots and owned cattle. These farmers occupied the fringes of the Rift Valley and dispersed over southern Tanzania. Next, there appeared a group of truly nomadic pastoralists, speaking kindred tongues known technically as the Nilotic languages. These people originated in the area between the White Nile and the Ethiopian highlands well over 2,000 years ago. By the time of the birth of Christ, their languages had split into three branches: Western, Eastern, and Southern Nilotic. The speakers of Western Nilotic migrated toward the White Nile, while the speakers of Eastern Nilotic stayed in the area of their collective origin. Southern Nilotic speakers moved toward the Great Rift Valley of East Africa, where they became the first people to perfect a pastoral economy suitable to the arid environment of the Rift Valley. There they were able to maintain a social organization that allowed nomadic life and yet provided an orderly society on a fairly large scale.

The basis of the specific institutions by which this feat was achieved were systems of age grades, which guided the males of a society as they passed, with other males of their generation, through a succession of duties and roles within the community. Each age set, recognizing leaders within its number, entered the system as boys, when they underwent initiation. After a fixed number of years, the young men moved from one grade to the next. The most junior grade was that of the warriors. At the next level, the men founded households; at the next, they formed councils and directed the group; and at the most senior level, the old men were advisers to the leaders. On this pattern, each society embroidered its own arabesques to make the system even more effective. Most of the Southern Nilotic speakers remained in Kenya, the exception being the Tatog, who occupied the fertile plains south of Lake Victoria. This, therefore, was the mixture of people the Bantu found on their arrival in the area.

The Bantu first absorbed the Ethiopian farmers of southern Tanzania and chased the Tatog away from the fertile parts of the eastern Tanzanian plateau. Near the Great Rift Valley, however, both the hunters and the Ethiopian farmers stood their ground, and a complicated interaction with the Bantu followed. Some of the farmers began to take over Bantu speech, as happened perhaps with the Gogo and Iramba, while in other cases, the Bantu speakers lost the speech of their ancestors and for a time adopted that of the farmers of Ethiopian origin, as was evidently the case with the Iraqw. The way of life of the incoming Bantu speakers and that of the aboriginal farmers was equally well adapted to the environment and equally complex, which explains this pattern of mutual interaction. By 1500, however, the whole of eastern and southern Tanzania was Bantu-speaking, and the highlands of Kenya east of the Great Rift were also occupied by Bantu speakers. On the coast itself, where the Bantu had arrived sometime earlier, they accepted many features of the Persian and Arab ways of life, and by CE 800, Swahili civilization was already formed there. A major influence is evident in the language; nearly half the vocabulary is borrowed from these foreign sources. Such observances as Nauruz, the New Year's festival, are also of Middle Eastern origin.

After Bantu settlement, development in southern and eastern Tanzania came about much more slowly than in the southern Congo, yet on the same lines. Internal trade in salt, pottery, basketry, and iron developed locally. The dominant form of government was the chiefdom; but as in South Africa, chiefdoms did not amalgamate into kingdoms. Whenever they attained a certain size, they split, and by 1750, there were hundreds of these microstates on the plains. True, clusters could be recognized among them wherever people followed the same customs or spoke similar dialects or where their chiefs claimed descent from a common ancestor. But growth into bigger states would not come here until the nineteenth century. Only in parts of northeastern Tanzania did kingdoms form before 1880 - near the Kenya-Tanzania border part of the Pare Mountains, people were united under one dynasty as early as the sixteenth century, and the neighboring Shambaa were welded into one monarchy around 1700. In eastern Kenya, the Bantu adopted age-grade organizations, similar to those recognized by the Southern Nilotic speakers, and thus remained on the whole loosely structured.

All this stands in sharp contrast to the interlacustrine area, where the population was growing fast because of the great fertility of the soil, for which banana and beans, as well as millet, were well suited. Around CE 1000, pastoralists of unknown cultural affiliation from northern Kenya or southern Ethiopia arrived in the area, occupying the less fertile and consequently almost unpopulated land that they prized for their cattle.

Being more mobile and better able to call up greater numbers of men at a shorter notice than the Bantu-speaking chiefdoms they encountered, they finally became lords over most of the Bantu speakers, adopting Bantu rituals and sacred kingships. In Uganda, the large state of Kitara grew and survives in legend. Founded perhaps before 1300, it was overrun around 1450 by Western Nilotic speakers, who moved upstream from the White Nile. The Chwezi, rulers of Kitara, were defeated; they were replaced by invaders, the Kitara Bunyoro, who also gave dynasties to two tiny states in the vicinity, one of which was to become Buganda.

The defeated Chwezi, or at least a group of them, went south and founded a host of smaller states on the western shore of Lake Victoria. Among these, Ankole and Karagwe were to become the biggest. From 1500 to 1800, the two major developments in the area were the unending struggles between Buganda and Bunyoro, in which the former gradually took the lead, and the emergence of Rwanda as the leading state in the south. After 1800, Burundi was to become as powerful as Rwanda, and these two kingdoms are the only ones that survived the colonial period to become independent nations.

Every one of the four major states was organized in a somewhat different manner. For most of the period, Bunyoro was the greatest in territory, but its population, principally millet farmers, was small. A significant part of the aristocracy was seminomadic, and consequently, royal control remained limited. In Buganda, agriculture was based on the cultivation of bananas, which are land-intensive but labor-extensive crops, thus freeing relatively more men to perform other duties such as warfare. Buganda saw the power of its king grow all during this period, and by the end of the nineteenth century, its bureaucracy was the tightest and most centralized of all kingdoms, with its state encompassing about 1 million inhabitants. The Rwanda monarchy followed the example of Buganda in strengthening the powers of the king. However, the internal caste structure of the country meant that the nobility remained much more dominant than in Buganda, and the bureaucracy was less well developed, even though Rwanda controlled perhaps 2 million inhabitants. As for Burundi, it was a major power only for a relatively short time, and its kings never succeeded in asserting their power over that of their own relatives in most of the country. It, too, controlled over 2 million inhabitants.

The contrasting civilizations that existed and the caste systems that have developed out of them are reflections of this history. The three major castes are: Pygmy hunters, Bantu-speaking agriculturalists, and Nilotic or other pastoral rulers. The complicated set of values linked with the cattle complex was the main ingredient brought by the pastoralists, whereas the complex rites of kingship were a Bantu inheritance. A peculiar effect of the downfall of the Chwezi was their transformation in the memory of their former subjects into glorious heroes around whom a religious cult arose. This spread over the whole interlacustrine area and even into eastern Tanzania. Despite a great many local variations, there remains everywhere a common core of myth and ritual as well as an ideology of equality that clashes violently with the fundamental inequality inherent in the caste system. In time, each of the civilizations developed further by internal growth. Thus, the political structures, especially the particular forms of landholding and rights over cattle, evolved in different ways.

The invaders of Kitara had only been a fraction of the Western Nilotic speakers. The others continued their trek in northern Uganda and then along the eastern shore of Lake Victoria. They settled in all these lands and turned to a mixed economy. In some places, Bantu speech ousted Nilotic, whereas in others, Nilotic dominated. But the cultures were quite comparable blends of Bantu, Western Nilotic, and some Southern and Eastern Nilotic features. This process of settlement lasted from 1450 to the end of the nineteenth century. The Eastern Nilotic speakers moved southward from the cradle lands of all Nilotic speakers into what is now Kenya and adjacent parts of Uganda, probably before 1000 and certainly before 1450.

Meanwhile, the Nandi, another southern Nilotic group, occupied the whole Rift Valley from 1500 to 1650. Their pastoral way of life was much better adapted to local conditions than any of the other peoples living there. Yet, they, too, were swept away from the Great Rift by an Eastern Nilotic group, the Masai. The Masai had improved on the military and the political organization of the

Nandi. In less than a full century, they occupied the Great Rift. After that, stiff resistance from Bantu groups on the edges of the Rift Valley and the sedentarization of the Kwavi, an offshoot of the Masai, blocked further advances and produced an armed stalemate, which was to last throughout most of the nineteenth century.

Northern Kenya, that part of the Rift Valley and the highlands to the west of the Rift, remained home for different groups of Nilotic nomads. The tragedy of all the nomads in East Africa was to be the success of their adaptation to the environment in which they lived. For their nomadic ways were to become a major handicap to modernization in our times.

The history of inner Africa is the story of how large numbers of original civilizations grew from Late Stone Age cultures and the common inheritance of the original Bantu civilization. Further growth and development stemmed from internal developments and also from mutual borrowing; these were facilitated by the increase in trade, political growth, conquest, and the more modest practice of intermarriage between groups. These processes led to increasing cultural elaboration, both in the direction of a better adaptation to each particular environment and in the direction of an intellectually more satisfying way of life. Personalities must have played substantial roles in these developments, but the nature of our sources is such that little is known about their impact. Only the fruits of their works are still visible.

As these civilizations emerged, they left a unique legacy for all mankind. Inner Africa has been less affected by the world outside than most of the other civilizations elsewhere on the earth. At the same time, the complexity of these ways of life takes them out of the range of the simple societies; there is nothing primitive about them. As Leo Frobenius, the German ethnologist and explorer, said: "They are civilized to the marrow of their bones." Because they grew in relative isolation, the flowering of human ingenuity and creativity that these civilizations and their history represents is a unique thread in the cloth that is the achievement of mankind. And so inner Africa's history teaches man more about himself everywhere.

8
THE COMING OF THE EUROPEANS
A. ADU BOAHEN

Africa south of the Saraha has been known to Europeans since Greco-Roman times, but it was not until the fourth decade of the fifteenth century that they began to arrive in numbers on its shores. The first to come were the Portuguese. They were followed in the 1450s by the Spaniards, who soon after abandoned Africa to explore the Americas; toward the end of the century, some English and French adventurers and traders arrived. However, their governments were not to give official backing to such enterprises until the sixteenth and seventeenth centuries. The Dutch were the next to appear on the African scene, and during the last decade of the sixteenth century, they effectively challenged the lead enjoyed by the Portuguese. The Danes dropped anchor in 1642, the Swedes in 1647, and the Brandenburgers in 1682.

The reasons for this sudden surge of interest were partly political, partly economic, partly technological. In the first place, no overseas activities could succeed without the patronage and direction of a strong nation-state enjoying stable and peaceful conditions at home, and no such nation-states emerged in Europe until after the end of the fourteenth century; and these continued to be wracked by foreign and civil wars for another 100 years or more.

Portugal was the first European state where conditions were favorable for overseas expansion. It had expelled the Moors in 1262, and a new dynasty, the house of Aviz, had emerged in 1385. The new ruling family drew its support mainly from the towns, and the first of its rulers, John and his wife Philippa, the daughter of John of Gaunt of England, raised a new aristocracy rooted "not in blood and landed estates, but in commercial enterprise." Therefore, unlike most of their contemporaries, the kings of Portugal could count on the support of the aristocracy in any overseas activities. Furthermore, John had five sons, all of whom were anxious to win laurels on the battlefield. The third of them, Henry, later to be called the Navigator, was ready to provide patronage, inspiration, and direction for overseas exploration, especially after 1415, when the

Portuguese conquered Ceuta, a Muslim stronghold on the Moroccan side of the Strait of Gibraltar.

It was during this campaign that Prince Henry is said to have had "a vision and a purpose to which he would remain faithful to his death." According to Gomes Eannes de Azurara, the chronicler of his activities, Henry's vision and purpose were to find out what lay beyond the Canary Islands and Cape Bojador, to capture the trans-Saharan trade, to investigate the extent of Muslim power, to convert people to Christianity, and to form an anti-Muslim alliance with any Christian ruler who might be found, especially with Prester John, the legendary ruler of a Christian kingdom thought to be located in the heart of Africa. With the financial and moral support of the Crown, Prince Henry provided the essential impetus to the commencement of overseas adventures, namely patronage, inspiration, and direction.

On his return from Ceuta, Henry settled at Sagres on the southwestern tip of Portugal. There he founded a school of navigation, gathering around him map makers, astronomers, sailors, and shipbuilders, and began the systematic exploration and study of the coast of Africa. Thenceforth, until the seventeenth century, the young and united kingdom of Portugal - under the rule of a new and energetic dynasty, free from attacks from its neighbors as well as from internal struggles, and full of crusading ardor - held the lead in overseas adventuring.

Besides these political conditions, there were also economic and technological reasons for the sudden interest of Europeans in western and southern Africa. Until the fifteenth century, Europe did not have much difficulty in obtaining prized commodities from the Orient. Chinese and Persian silks, Indian cloth and emeralds, rubies from Burma, sapphires from Ceylon, and above all, spices, came by sea, mostly in Venetian, Genoese, and Florentine ships. However, with the occupation of much of the Middle East by the Ottoman Turks in the fifteenth century, not only did the volume of trade decrease but prices of Oriental goods in Europe soared, owing to the prohibitive duties imposed on them. Therefore, European consumers began to look for alternative supplies or alternative routes to the East. According to Azurara, Prince Henry was aware of the commercial possibilities of a sea route to the East, and the Spanish Crown certainly had as one of its cardinal aims the discovery of an overseas route to India and beyond.

Equally strong was the pull exerted by gold. With the steady emergence of nation-states had come the growth of international banking, with many nations beginning to mint gold instead of silver coins. As Europe did not supply any goods to the East in exchange, Europe's reserves of the precious metal were diminishing faster than Hungary and the other continental suppliers could replenish them. It had long been known that the gold that was imported into Europe from Barbary originated in the regions south of the Sahara; but, however strong the economic motivation, Europeans could not have sailed to western and southern Africa until the fifteenth century for the simple reason that it was not technologically feasible.

The types of ships used in Western Europe from Roman times until the fourteenth century were the oar-driven galley and the cog. While both were suitable for the calm seas of the Mediterranean, they were helpless in heavy seas and totally unsuitable for long ocean voyages. It was not until the first half of the fifteenth century that, borrowing from the superior technology of Arab sailors, the Portuguese and other Western Europeans were able to devise ships capable of undertaking long-distance voyages. The caravel, which had both square sails and fore-and-aft-rigged triangular sails, was able to sail into the wind without the help of oars. This revolutionary development in ship design made possible the great voyages that characterized the fifteenth century.

Furthermore, it was in that same century that most of the problems of navigation were finally solved. By the fifteenth century, an experienced navigator could find his latitude and had a good compass and charts to plot his course. It is not surprising that Portugal was the first to begin the systematic exploration of the coast of western and southern Africa, for it was technologically superior and politically more stable than any other European state.

The voyages, under the auspices of the Portuguese kings and Prince Henry the Navigator, began in 1417, and Portuguese explorers reached Madeira in 1418. Cape Bojador was rounded by Gil Eanes in 1434, and in 1441 Nuno Tristão and Antão Gonçalves reached Cape Blanco on the coast of present-day Mauritania; three years later, Dinis Dias explored the mouth of the Senegal River and Cape Verde. The mouth of the Gambia River was reached in 1446, and the coast of Sierra Leone was explored in 1460, the year in which the prince died. After a break from 1462 to 1469, due mainly to the fact that King Affonso v of Portugal was engaged in a crusade against Morocco, the voyages were resumed. The coast of modern Ghana was reached in 1471, the Bights of Benin and Biafra between 1471 and 1474, and the mouth of the Congo in 1483; in December 1487, Bartolomeu Dias rounded the Cape of Good Hope and sailed as far up the east coast as the Fish River in South Africa. After another pause of ten years, an expedition under the command of Vasco da Gama retraced Dias's course, continuing onward along the East African coast as far as Malindi in modern-day Kenya, from which he set sail for India. Thus, by the end of the fifteenth century, the Portuguese had greatly expanded Europe's geographical knowledge of the world beyond its shores, though it is important to note that with the exception of the interior regions of Angola and Mozambique, this knowledge was to be confined to the coast of Africa until the second half of the eighteenth century.

It is quite evident from the accounts of the Portuguese explorers, particularly those of Alvise Cadamosto, Duarte Pacheco Pereira, Ruy de Pina, and above all, Vasco da Gama, that they were astounded and elated by the complex, even sophisticated, character of the African civilizations they came across, by the extent of political development, and by the wealth and splendor of the courts. They particularly admired the city-states of the East African coast, where a lucrative trade with other Indian Ocean markets had long existed, and the gold and silver mines in the area of modern Ghana, Angola, and Mozambique.

Finally, accounts of the legendary Prester John and his Christian Utopia, as related by Vasco da Gama, must also have filled the hearts of the Church fathers with hope. To quote the explorer: "We were told . . . that Prester John . . . held many cities along the coast, and that the inhabitants of those cities were great merchants and owned big ships. . . . This information, and many other things which we heard, rendered us so happy that we cried with joy, and prayed to God to grant us health, so that we might behold what we so much desired."

Up until 1518, a date that marks the end of the first period of European contact with Africa, the Portuguese were the only Europeans effectively operating in Africa south of the Sahara. Politically, the Portuguese showed interest in colonization, though this interest was confined exclusively to the Atlantic islands off the coast of Africa the Canaries, Madeira, the Azores, the Cape Verde Islands, São Tomé, and Fernando Po - where they established sugar plantations and vineyards.

On the continent of Africa itself, however, the Portuguese did not attempt any extensive settlement, partly for reasons of climate, but mainly because of the opposition of the Africans themselves. Instead, they erected a number of forts and posts to protect themselves against the African kingdoms as well as other European nations and to serve as collecting centers and depots.

The first and the most impressive of these forts was São Jorge, built in 1482 at Elmina on the coast of modern Ghana; on the same coast were erected during this period forts at Axim, Shama, and Accra. In 1487, farther north of the Senegal River, the Portuguese established an inland post at the caravan center of Wadan to tap the gold trade across the Sahara; it was abandoned in 1513. They also erected a fort (later named Freetown) on the coast of modern Sierra Leone and another at Gwato, the port of Benin, but soon abandoned both, the latter in 1516.

The limited nature of the Portuguese colonizing activities in West Africa makes the title "Lord of Guinea," which their king John II assumed in 1486, a particularly empty one. They did not at this time rule any Africans, but engaged in commerce with them. During this first period, they also acted as proselytizers. In spite of what some historians say, there is absolutely no doubt that during this first period, the Portuguese took the work of converting Africans to the Christian religion seriously, indeed, and with the full support and blessing of the pope of the Catholic Church.

The effort began in earnest as soon as the first West African islands were explored; indeed, there were some Franciscan monks aboard the Portuguese ships that anchored at Madeira in 1420 and Cape Verde in 1446. In 1441, when the first shipload of black people was brought to Portugal, Prince Henry, as grand master of the Order of Christ, had them baptized. He also selected the most talented man among them to be trained as a missionary, but the African died before repatriation. Again, when in 1458, Henry received reports of the favorable disposition of the rulers of the Wolof kingdom toward Christianity, he promptly dispatched the abbot of Soto de Casa; unfortunately, we do not know the outcome of this mission. By the time of Henry's death in 1460, Christianity had been firmly established on the Portuguese-held islands. Interest in evangelical work continued, and in 1462, Father Alphonsus Bolano was appointed as the missionary, or prefect apostolic, for the whole of Guinea.

Subsequently, when the Portuguese built their castle at Elmina, they also dedicated a church to Saint Anthony; according to the Portuguese chronicler João de Barros, some Africans were converted. It is also recorded that when King John II of Portugal received news of the *oba* of Benin's request for missionaries, he was quick to comply. Not only did the *oba* welcome them and grant permission for a church to be built in Benin but he also "gave his own son and some of his noblemen, the greatest in his kingdom - so that they might become Christians."

Even more spectacular and surprisingly successful were the early Portuguese missionary activities that began in 1484 or 1485, a year or more after the first visit of Diogo Cão. During Cão's second visit, the king of the Congo (Kongo), Nzinga Nkuwu, accepted the Christian religion and sent some of his people to Portugal to be educated. He also asked King John for assistance, to which the Portuguese king responded in 1490 by sending three ships with a group of priests, masons, carpenters, and other skilled artisans. This mission was successful, and Nzinga Nkuwu, most of the members of the Congolese royal family, and some of the king's subordinate chiefs were baptized. Nzinga Mvemba, one of the royal family to embrace the religion, was baptized as Afonso and succeeded to the Congo throne in 1507.

During his long reign, from 1507 to 1543, Afonso remained a sincere Christian and did initially receive assistance from the Portuguese in his effort to convert his kingdom into a Christian and modernized state. He learned to read and write Portuguese, and he gave every encouragement to the missionaries in their work. He himself supervised the building of a cathedral and other state churches in his capital at Mbanzakongo and saw to the building of schools and churches throughout the kingdom.

In 1513, two members of Afonso's family, who were educated in Portugal, headed a Portuguese embassy to the pope. One of them had been baptized with the name of Dom Henrique and was later consecrated as bishop of Utica in Tunis. He returned to the Congo in 1521 as vicar apostolic, and with the assistance of several Congolese who had been ordained priests, he continued the evangelical work in progress. Dom Afonso also established a new court modeled on that of Lisbon, bestowing Portuguese titles of marquis, duke, count, et cetera, on his courtiers and ministers. It looked as if Christianity was taking firm root in the Congo, and that all was set for the conversion of the Congo into the first Christian and Westernized kingdom in western Africa.

Besides their colonizing and missionary activities, the Portuguese also paid a great deal of attention to commerce. And in this field, too, their achievements were not inconsiderable. Portuguese traders literally followed the explorers. The first commodity to be shipped was dried fish, which was obtained from the valuable fishing grounds between Cape Bojador and Rio de Oro, and along various parts of the Guinea coast. Sugar produced from cane grown on the Cape Verde Islands as well as on São Tomé and Fernando Po was the next export, and the output steadily increased throughout the fifteenth century. The traffic in pepper from what became known as the Grain Coast as well as from Benin was also sought. Ivory was another prized commodity obtained along the West African coast - especially in Ghana, the region of Little Popo, and the area that was to become known as the Ivory Coast. Other minor exports were wax, hides, amber, and indigo.

By the end of the fifteenth century, however, gold and slaves had superseded all other exports. The first quantity of Ghana coast gold was brought to Portugal by Gonçalves in 1441, and subsequently, so much gold was found in the area that the Portuguese dubbed it the Gold Coast. (This name was later applied to the whole of the British colony, and it was not changed to Ghana until March 1957, when that colony won its independence from Britain.) By the sixteenth century, the monetary value of this export was about £100,000 per year (reckoned by the British historian J. D. Fage to be one-tenth of the world's supply of gold at the time).

The first batch of slaves consisted of twelve men, who were captured in raids conducted by the explorers Gonçalves and Tristão and brought to Portugal in 1441. At the time of Prince Henry's death in 1460, 500 slaves were being exported annually to Portugal and its Atlantic island colonies. By 1500, the slave trade had increased to about 670 a year, according to historian Philip Curtin's recent figures. These slaves were obtained mainly from the Senegambia region, the Slave Coast, and the area of the Congo. It was not until 1518 that the first shipment of slaves was sent directly to the New World; an event that can be seen as opening the second phase of Afro-European contact.

At this juncture, the Portuguese Crown took complete control of the lucrative commercial contacts that its subjects had developed, making it a capital offense for any Portuguese to go to Guinea without a license. In exchange for gold, fish, sugar, pepper, ivory, and slaves, agents of the king exported to states of western Africa horses, silk items of clothing (imported mainly from the Barbary States and Benin), brassware, beads, handkerchiefs, and wine.

One other accidental but useful and lasting by-product of the first phase of the European contact with West Africa was the introduction of a number of food plants from the Americas and the East Indies. From the former, the Portuguese brought maize, tobacco, cassava, the sweet potato, the pineapple, and the tomato. From the Indies were introduced oranges, lemons, limes, rice, and sugar cane. The cultivation of these food items, especially maize, the tomato, and rice, spread rapidly throughout western Africa, and there is no doubt that these food crops greatly accelerated the population growth in the coastal regions.

What was the reaction of the Africans to the Europeans during this first phase of their confrontation? Naturally, the Africans found the new arrivals, with their white skin, long hair, and funny-looking ships, profoundly strange. In the beginning, trade between the two took the form of dumb barter, or silent trade. However, after a period of fear and distrust, mutual confidence developed, and the Africans began to meet the European ships, and the Europeans to go ashore. It would appear that genuine trouble began only when the Portuguese asked for permission from the

African kings to erect permanent fortified posts. João de Barros has left us a detailed account of the negotiations that took place in 1482 between Diogo de Azambuja and the representative of the king of Fetu for permission to build a castle on the coast of modern Ghana. Azambuja and his men attended the palaver "smartly dressed but with hidden arms in case of need," while the *caramansa,* the king of Fetu's representative, who was also the chief of that coastal village, turned up with his men in full battle array, "armed after their manner, some with spears and buckles, others with bows and quivers of arrows." After the initial exchange of courtesies, Diogo de Azambuja asked for permission to build a storehouse where merchandise could be kept and in which the traders could be housed. He emphasized that that castle could be of advantage to the king "since that same house, and the power of the King [of Portugal] would be there to defend him." Azambuja also expressed the anxiousness of his ruler to convert the chief and his people to Christianity. To this request, the caramansa replied in words that should be written in letters of gold. Responding courteously to the Portuguese envoy's remark, the *caramansa* is reported to have said: "During that time nothing had astonished him as much as the captain's arrival; on the other ships he had seen ill-dressed and ragged men only, who were content with whatever he gave them in exchange for their goods. This was the aim of their voyages to those parts; all they asked was to be dealt with immediately, since they preferred to return to their country rather than to live abroad. But with him, the captain, it was otherwise. He came with many people, and with much more gold and jewels than there were in these parts where they were found, and moreover with a new request - that he might establish a residence in that land. From this he conjectured . . . that a man as important as he was surely came on great affairs, such as those of God, who made the day and night, about whom he had heard so much, and whose servant his King was. But considering the nature of so important a man as the captain, and also of the gallant people who accompanied him, he perceived that men of such quality must always require things on a lavish scale; and, because the spirit of such a noble people would scarcely endure the poverty and simplicity of that savage land of Guinea, quarrels and passions might arise between them all; he asked him, therefore, to be pleased to depart, and to allow the ships to come in future as they had come in the past, so that there would always be peace and concord between them. Friends who met occasionally remained better friends than if they were neighbors, on account of the nature of the human heart. . . . He did not speak thus to disobey the commands of the king of Portugal, but for the benefit of peace and the trade he desired to have with those who might come to that port; and also because, with peace between them, his people would be more ready to hear of God, whom he wished them to know. Therefore, since time would reveal these inconveniences, he asked the captain to avoid them by allowing the traffic to continue as it had before."

What words of tact, wisdom, and above all, prophecy! Had the Portuguese listened to them or, alternatively, had they not been allowed to settle or build forts, but carried on their trade from their ships, the course of the European-African confrontation would most probably have been different. However, the *caramansa* and his king allowed themselves to be persuaded by Azambuja to grant permission for the fort on condition that the Portuguese pay rent for the land on which it was built. And as the *caramansa* had predicted, time did reveal the "inconveniences." In fact, shortly after the completion of the fort, Diogo de Azambuja burned down the village as punishment for "so many thefts and evil deeds" that the subjects of the *caramansa* were alleged to have committed. However, during this first phase, such "reprisals" were infrequent. The Portuguese by and large remained on good relations with the people of the west coast and treated the African kings as equals and allies rather than subordinates or vassals.

The reception given the first ambassadors from Benin and Wolof, and the early letters exchanged between the kings of Portugal and those of the

Congo, bear eloquent testimony of the respect they were accorded. De Barros reported that Prince Bemoym of Wolof, who went to Portugal in 1488, was "treated in every respect as a Sovereign Lord, accustomed to our civilization and not as a barbarous Prince outside the law." In the letters exchanged between the king of the Congo and the king of Portugal between 1512 and 1540, the former referred to the latter as "Most high and powerful prince and king my brother," while the king of Portugal addressed his Congolese counterpart as "Most powerful and excellent king of Manikongo," and as his "friend and brother."

Finally, throughout this period, it was the Africans themselves who dictated the terms of trade, and without their cooperation nothing could be done. It is not surprising that in the 1590s Richard Eden would give the following advice to his English compatriots: "They are a very wary people in their bargaining, and will not lose one sparke of golde of any value. They use weights and measures, and are very circumspect in occupying the same. They that shall have to doe with them, must use them gently; for they will not trafique or bring in any wares, if they be evill used."

There is no doubt that the first phase of European contact with Africa was, from the point of view of the peoples of western Africa and the Congo, both beneficial and promising. Although the trade in slaves had begun, it was relatively small in volume, for the demand was still confined to São Tomé, the Atlantic islands, and the Iberian Peninsula, where it would soon have reached a saturation point. The new food crops that were introduced caught on rapidly, and two of them, grain and rice, soon became the principal diet of most coastal peoples. The seeds of Christianity were also being sown, and there was every indication that Western education and techniques would soon be firmly established in the Congo and possibly on the coast of Ghana, whence they would spread to other parts of the continent. And throughout, there was an attitude of mutual respect. The first period must have ended, then, on a note of great hope.

Meanwhile, Portuguese policies and activities in Central, South, and East Africa during the first period were quite different from those they pursued in West Africa and the Congo. From the beginning, the Portuguese officially ignored the area of western Africa that is modern Angola, though both the Congo kings and the Portuguese living in São Tomé obtained some of their slaves from there. It was not until 1520 that the first official expedition was dispatched to Angola in search of souls and silver. The Portuguese ignored southern Africa. The reports of the explorers made it clear that there were no prospects there for trade in minerals, spices, and ivory, the commodities then of primary interest to the Portuguese. In fact, it was not until after 1650 that those areas were of any strategic interest to either Portugal or the rest of Europe.

However, along the east coast of central Africa, precisely for strategic considerations - wresting control of the Indian Ocean trade from the Arabs and their Swahili allies - and also because of the great hopes raised by stories of the fabulous gold and silver mines in the African hinterland, the Portuguese Crown did commence activities. As early as 1502, Vasco da Gama returned to East Africa, this time as an invader, compelling the ruler of Kilwa to pay tribute to the Portuguese Crown. He was followed in 1503 by Ruy Ravasco, who sailed along the coast, pillaging and raiding and finally besieging Zanzibar.

Most of the well-established and wealthy states in the region successfully resisted these early attacks, but in 1505, a carefully prepared expedition under the command of Francisco de Almeida was dispatched to subdue the entire East African and Mozambique coast. Sofala yielded after little resistance, and a fort was erected there. Kilwa and Mombasa resisted, but both were captured; a fort was built at Kilwa. Only Malindi, in the north, was friendly to the invaders, and it became one of the two administrative centers from which Portugal controlled the entire coast of Mozambique and East Africa. The other center was the island town of Mozambique in the south, where in 1507, the Portuguese built a fort, a hospital, and administrative buildings. It soon replaced Sofala as the main depot for the Zambezi region and as a revictualing and refitting center for ships bound for India, and the fort at Sofala was abandoned in 1512.

However, apart from isolated journeys, mainly by António Fernandes, the interior parts of the whole of Africa and even some of the coastal areas had still not directly felt the presence of the Europeans. This and every other aspect of the Afro-European confrontation were to undergo revolutionary changes during the second phase from 1518 to 1700, and these changes were by and large to be disastrous to the Africans.

The first and probably the most conspicuous of these changes was the great increase in the number of European nations operating in Africa. The English were the first to encroach on the hitherto exclusive Portuguese preserve. The first English trading voyage to Guinea during this period was undertaken by William Hawkins III 1530. He was followed by Thomas Wyndham in 1553, who traded in Benin late in 1554, and by William Towerson, who made three voyages to West Africa between 1555 and 1557. It is important to note that all these early English traders did not deal in slaves but in gold, ivory, camwood, wax, and pepper. It was not until 1562 that, with the full support and blessings of the queen of England, John Hawkins (the son of William Hawkins) set off on the first English slave trading voyage. He made two more voyages; in 1564 and in 1567, selling his captives to planters in the Caribbean.

The French also entered the Guinea trade in 1530, and within a few years, their trading and piratic activities had extended as far as the Bight of Benin. It was the Dutch who were the first to successfully challenge the Portuguese monopoly. Entering the Guinea trade for the first time in 1593, soon after their struggle for independence, the Dutch launched systematic attacks on the Portuguese, both in Africa and in the Indian Ocean. Although their attack on Mozambique in 1607 was unsuccessful, by 1610, they had completely destroyed Portuguese naval power in the Indian Ocean. From there, they turned their attention to the west coast of Africa and they soon gained a footing on the coveted golden coast of Ghana. They built a fort at Mouri in 1612, and five years later, they also built two forts on Gorée Island and established a trading post on the opposite mainland at Rufisque. Finally, between 1637 and 1642, they captured the Portuguese strongholds of Elmina and Axim in Ghana as well as São Tomé and the port of Angola, and they even took Brazil. Although the Portuguese were able to reconquer Angola, São Tomé, and Brazil between 1648 and 1654, they never regained their position on the coast of Ghana. Likewise, the Danes, Swedes, and the Brandenburgers, all focused their attention on coastal Ghana.

The appearance of so many European nations on the African coast touched off a cutthroat rivalry among them. The Dutch, having replaced the Portuguese in the interior regions of Ghana and the Gambia, lost to the English and the French. They then concentrated on the coast of Ghana and on South Africa, which they occupied in 1652. Soon after, the Swedes were eliminated altogether from Africa's shores. It was partly because of this rivalry and partly because of the political divisions on the coast of Africa, and especially that of Ghana, that a great number of European-manned forts and castles were built on the west coast of Africa

On the east coast, the position of the Portuguese was first challenged from the hinterland when the Zimba invaders, a Central Bantu people, captured Kilwa in 1587 and attacked Mombasa. In the following century, the Portuguese also had to face seaborne challenges from the Dutch, the Turks, and the Arabs of Oman on the Arabian Peninsula. At the invitation of the indigenous peoples of the coast, the Oman Arabs invaded Portuguese enclaves in 1652, 1660, 1667, and 1679, and by 1700 had succeeded in expelling them from the area of the East African coast north of the Ruvuma River.

Despite the intensity with which grabs for trade hegemony were pursued, no European showed any interest in inland exploration. Traders remained blatantly ignorant of these regions, as dramatically illustrated by the fact that they did not know the direction of the flow of the Niger River until the 1790s or of the location of its mouth until 1830. Scientific curiosity, which had been one of the motives behind Prince Henry and his countrymen, completely lost its thrust during the second period of expansion. Nor did the Europeans show any interest in colonization - not the British, nor the Dutch, nor the Danes, nor the Brandenburgers. Only the French attempted to establish a colony at the mouth of the Senegal River in 1687, but this failed mainly because of the opposition of the king of Cayor. Thus, the record of the Europeans in the field of colonization in the second period was nil.

The attempts to introduce Christianity, Western education, and Western technology were also gradually abandoned. The Portuguese did continue their missionary efforts in the sixteenth century but haphazardly and half-heartedly. They gave up all interest in missionary work in Benin after 1538. When evangelical activities were resumed in 1657 by the Capuchin Order, they were under the auspices of the *Sacra Congregazione di Propaganda Fide,* founded by the papacy; but the missionaries were soon expelled from Benin for interfering with religious festivals involving human sacrifice. Although the Capuchins sent missions to Benin and Warn in 1663, 1684, 1687, 1691, and 1695, no success attended their efforts, and in 1713, they, too, finally abandoned the attempt.

Christianization was impressed with a similar lack of fervor in the Congo. Whereas both the Portuguese and Afonso, the king of the Congo, had initially taken the work of converting the kingdom into a Westernized Christian state seriously, the Portuguese seem later to lose interest in this aspect of their activities. For instance, in 1526, Afonso, in a moving and sincere letter, appealed for "two physicians and two apothecaries and one surgeon, so that they may come with their drug-stores and all the necessary things to stay in our kingdoms." In the same year, he wrote to the king, asking him to send neither "merchants nor wares," only "priests and people to teach in schools, and no other goods but wine and flour for the holy sacrament." The Portuguese paid no heed. In 1540, missionary work was resumed with the arrival of three Jesuit priests and a teacher. About 2,000 people were baptized within the first four months, three churches were built at Mbanzakongo, which was now renamed São Salvador, and schools were also established. But these successes were short-lived. In 1552, mainly because of the opposition of the Manikongo people and the resident Portuguese community, but partly because even some of the priests took to slave trading, the mission abandoned the Congo. A second mission followed in 1553, but that also failed for the same reason and withdrew in 1555.

It would appear that no serious efforts were made again in this field, and by 1700, there was hardly a trace of western education or Christian life in the Congo, excepting the deserted city of São Salvador with its twelve ruined churches.

The English, the Dutch, and the French also made some efforts in the missionary and educational fields, but these initiatives were sporadic, evanescent, and unproductive. For instance, chaplains who were supposed to administer to the whites, as well as the blacks, were attached to Dutch stations on the west coast. In 1634, the Dutch actually opened a school for the education of African children at Mouri, but it was soon abandoned. In 1644, they also mooted the idea of establishing a school at the port of Accra, but the scheme was never carried out. Nothing more was heard of Dutch schooling throughout the second half of the century. In 1694, an English mission set up a school at Ghana's Cape Coast, but it was abandoned two years later when its only teacher died. In 1705, a similar attempt failed.

The French also made some efforts in the seventeenth century. In 1637, they sent five Capuchins to Assini, another West African port. Subsequently, two young men of the place, Lewis Aniaba (Hannibal) and a man named Roanga, were selected for further training and sent to France in 1687 to be educated. We do not know what happened to Roanga, but Aniaba returned home in 1701 and, upon his arrival, is reported to have done away with his French clothes, his foreign manners, and his Christian faith. The Capuchins, who like the Jesuits lacked the financial resources and manpower to sustain their efforts and were doubtless ill-adjusted to the coastal climate, soon withdrew from Assini, and with this vanished all traces of missionary activities in that area. Although Christianity was flourishing on the Atlantic islands and São Tomé, it had gained no permanent footing anywhere on the mainland.

However, in spite of the many setbacks in the fields of science, missionary work, colonization, and exploration, in this second phase of Afro-European contact (between 1518 and 1700), the Europeans not only stayed on in West Africa but increased their numbers. This was due to one main activity that occupied their attention: trade. Unfortunately for Africa, in this activity, they found increasing profit. Indeed, the goods traded became vital to the growing capitalist and industrial economy of Western Europe, and the plantation economy of the New World.

During the first four or even five decades of this second phase of expansion, the principal interest of all the European nations involved was in articles such as pepper, gum, wax, ivory, and above all, gold. Had trade been confined to these natural products there is absolutely no doubt that all would have been well; but in the coastal areas of the Congo, and in areas included in the modern states of Nigeria, Dahomey, Togo, Ghana, the Gambia, and Senegal, human beings constituted the main export commodity by the end of the sixteenth century. From the end of the seventeenth century to the first four decades of the nineteenth century, the slave trade would completely eclipse all other trade on the entire coast of West Africa and the Congo.

Although the overseas slave trade began as early as 1441, it still had not become the principal objective of the Portuguese even 100 years later. It was the exploration of the Americas and the West Indies between 1492 and 1504, and the subsequent commencement of mining activities and the establishment of tobacco and sugar plantations there that brought the slave trade to its full growth. The Europeans, confronted with an acute labor shortage in their attempts to exploit the natural resources of the New World, at first tried to use Indians to work the mines and plantations, but they proved unequal to the task. As one Spaniard reported in 1518: "When Hispaniola [modern Haiti and the Dominican Republic] was discovered, it contained 1,130,000 Indians. Today, their number does not exceed 11,000. And judging by what had happened, there will be none left in three or four years' time unless some remedy is applied."

The remedy was indeed found in Africa, and the first cargo of black slaves was transported from Spain to the Americas in 1501; the second shipment of seventeen slaves followed in 1505. In 1510, the Spanish Crown legalized the sale of white as well as black slaves in the New World. In 1515, the first slave-grown sugar from the Caribbean entered Spain. It was, however, not until 1518 that the first cargo of slaves was shipped directly to the Americas from the west coast of Africa in a Spanish ship. The Portuguese joined in November 1532, when the *Santo Antonio* transported 201 slaves from the island of São Tomé to Santo Domingo and San Juan. In 1562, the English, represented by John Hawkins, also sent their first cargo of slaves directly to the West Indies. In 1619, a Dutch frigate landed the first twenty black slaves on the mainland of North America at Jamestown in Virginia. The Atlantic slave trade had well and truly been inaugurated.

According to Philip Curtin's calculations, the number of slaves that landed in the New World increased from 125,000 between 1501 and 1600 to 1,280,000 between 1601 and 1700 (greatly accelerated in the last quarter of that century by the stepped-up demand for slaves on the North American mainland), and to 6,265,000 between 1701 and 1810. Assuming that about 16 percent of them died during the "middle passage," or sea voyage, Curtin reckons that a total of 11,300,000 slaves were exported from Africa to the New World before slavery ended. (Earlier writers such as W. E. D. Du Bois, Robert R. Kuczynski, Roland Oliver, J. D. Fage, and Robert Rotberg have offered estimates of as many as 15 million forcibly removed from Africa.)

Treated with extreme brutality and inhumanity, all these slaves were used in the New World mainly for the extraction of minerals such as silver and copper and for the raising of sugar, cotton, tobacco, and indigo. It was the ready supply of these commodities that, as Eric Williams has shown in his brilliant study *Capitalism and Slavery,* gave birth to the textile, distilling, sugar-refining, metallurgical, and indirectly, the shipbuilding industries - enterprises on which the economies of the countries of Western Europe so heavily depended. And it was some of the simple products of these industries that were exchanged at enormous profits in Africa for the slaves who were sold in the New World for even greater profits. With the rise of the Atlantic slave trade then, the European-African contact developed into a wider European-African-American contact, and as the sole producers of the manufactured goods involved, as the sole sellers of the slaves in the New World, and as owners of the plantations in the New World, the European nations were obviously the greatest beneficiaries. It is not surprising therefore that all of Europe's leading traders and financiers had interests in one or more sides of the triangle. As the great nineteenth-century British historian L. B.

Namier has concluded: "There were comparatively few big merchants in Great Britain in 1761, who in one connection or another, did not trade with the West Indies, and a considerable number of the gentry families had interests in the Sugar Islands, just as vast numbers of Englishmen now hold shares in Asiatic rubber or tea plantations or oil fields." And this was also true of France and Holland; as the French historian G. Gaston-Martin has written: "The founding of industries, private fortunes, public opulence, the rebuilding of towns, the social glories of a new class: great merchants eager for public office that should reflect their economic importance and impatient to be rid of what they called, with careless exaggeration, 'the shame of servitude'; such were the sum of the essential consequences for eighteenth-century France of the African slave trade."

What was the role of the African in all these activities? In West Africa and to some extent in the Congo, during this period of expansion as in the former period, the Africans themselves were responsible for the production and the supply of all the commodities as well as the slaves involved in the trade. As the Dutch merchant William Bosman correctly pointed out in a letter to his uncle in 1701: "There is no small number of Men in Europe who believe that the Gold Mines are in our Power; that we, like the Spaniards in the West-Indies, have no more to do but to work them by our Slaves. Though you perfectly know we have no manner of access to these Treasures. . . ." Indeed, attempts made by the Dutch themselves in the 1650s and 1690s to prospect for gold along the Ankolora River and in Komenda in modern Ghana were met with stout local resistance and had to be abandoned.

In the case of the slaves, early forays made by the Portuguese were soon abandoned as a method of acquisition. From about 1500 onward, apart from a few kidnapping attempts made by unscrupulous captains or an occasional adventurer like John Hawkins, it was the Africans themselves who delivered slaves to the Europeans for sale. These slaves were obtained in four principal ways: criminals sold as punishment by their rulers; domestic slaves who were resold; persons obtained from raids upon neighboring states; and prisoners of full-scale wars. It is evident from a recent study of some 179 freed slaves in Freetown, Sierra Leone, that the principal sources of the slave trade were raids and wars. Similarly, most of the slaves from Ghana, Ouidah, Yorubaland, and Benin were products of war.

However, some coastal areas were also ravaged by slave raiders. Likewise in the Congo, the slaves were obtained either as a result of wars or were brought from the inland regions by the *pombeiros,* Afro-Portuguese subtraders who traveled "a hundred and fifty or two hundred leagues up the country to buy or raid for slaves." But throughout West Africa and the Congo, it was the ruling aristocracy - the kings and their nobles - who were ultimately responsible for supplying these slaves, for they waged the wars organized the raids, tried the criminals and debtors and passed the judgments. The French commercial agent Jean Barbot was correct when he wrote that "the trade in slaves is the business of kings, rich men, and prime merchants."

Why then did African rulers cooperate with the Europeans in this hideous traffic? Before answering this question, it must be pointed out first that some of these rulers did try to stop the slave trade when they realized its disastrous effects. A typical example was Afonso, the king of the Congo. In one of his letters to the king of Portugal in 1526, he complained bitterly: ". . . we cannot reckon how great the damage is, since the mentioned merchants are taking everyday our natives, sons of the land and the sons of our noblemen and vassals and our relatives, because the thieves and men of bad conscience grab them wishing to have the things and wares of this Kingdom which they are ambitious of; they grab them and get them sold; and so great, Sir, is the corruption and licentiousness that our country is being completely depopulated, and Your Highness should not agree with this or accept it as in Your service. . . . It is our will that in these kingdoms there should not be any trade of slaves nor outlet for them . . ."

But no heed was paid to his appeal, and the trade received increasing support from subsequent Congolese kings and the Portuguese authorities. As the Nigerian historian I. A. Akinjogbin has recently shown, another unsuccessful attempt to put a stop to the trade was made by the kings of Dahomey, who extended their sway from the inland town of Abomey to the coast and conquered Ouidah and Ardra. But they also failed and were compelled to join a devil they could not beat.

Alan Ryder, an authority on Benin's history, has also emphasized the *oba*'s "general indifference to the demands and opportunities of the European slave trade" in the early decades of the sixteenth century. Indeed, until the close of the seventeenth century, the kings of Benin enforced a total embargo on the export of male slaves.

As European commerce had become increasingly limited to the acquisition of slaves, and as most of the African kings and the members of the aristocracy had by then become addicted to the European goods, especially to spirits, tobacco, guns, and gunpowder, they had no choice but to sell their fellow men to obtain them. From about the middle of the seventeenth century in most areas of West Africa and the Congo, the European traders demanded only slaves. C. B. Wadström, who toured many parts of western Africa in the 1780s and made a special study of the slave trade, told England's

Privy Council Committee of 1789 that "the Kings of Africa . . . incited by the merchandise shown them, which consists principally of strong liquors, give orders to their military to attack their own villages in the night. . . ." James Watt, who visited Timbo in Sierra Leone around the same time reported that he was told by the *almani*'s deputy "with a shocking degree of openness, that the sole object of their wars was to produce slaves, as they could not obtain European goods without slaves, and they could not get slaves without fighting for them."

Cooperation in this shameful business must also, in this author's opinion, have been made easier by the African rulers' ignorance regarding the treatment of slaves on the other side of the Atlantic. Slavery and the slave trade were not European introductions to Africa. Both had existed from time immemorial in many areas in Africa, but a slave in any African society was treated as a human being who could own property, marry, and have children. He lived and was treated as a full member of the household and often occupied offices of responsibility. Slavery was a relatively humane institution in Africa and in the Muslim world. It was this humane institution that the African suppliers of slaves must have assumed they were dealing with in the New World. It is this author's feeling that had the kings and chiefs been aware of the enormity of the difference in the status of a slave in their own society and in the society of the New World, they probably would have put up greater and more sustained resistance.

Besides controlling the production and supply of the commodities, the Africans of the coast of West Africa also had a decisive say in the conduct of that trade. Without the permission of the rulers, no European nation could build any fort or trading post, and land rental had to be paid in all cases. In some areas such as Ouidah, Ardra, and later Dahomey, the kings even specified the material that was to be used in the construction of the forts. If the rent was not paid, trade could be stopped. In 1723, the London officials of the Royal African Company wrote to the agent in Sierra Leone: "We are sorry to find there are misunderstandings between you and the Africans. We find it arose from the not paying them the small rent due to them." Furthermore, the Europeans had to pay duties on all imports or give presents before they were allowed to trade. In Ouidah, as Bosman reported: "The first business of one of our Factors . . . is to satisfie the Customs of the King and the great Men, which amount to about 100 Pounds in Guinea value, as the Goods must yield there. After which we have free License to Trade, which is published throughout the whole Land by the Cryer." As the kings and chiefs were traders themselves in many areas, their products and slaves had to be bought first before those of their subjects. Bosman added that "before we can deal with any Person, we are obliged to buy the

King's whole stock of Slaves at a set price; which is commonly one third or one fourth higher than ordinary: After which we obtain free leave to deal with all his Subjects of what Rank soever." This was true also in Benin and Bonny. Lastly, the chiefs and leading merchants had a decisive say in fixing the basis of exchange and the prices of commodities, especially of slaves, and this was done after a series of palavers that often dragged on for days, much to the disgust and discomfort of the European traders. Some Africans even set up their own trading concerns and came to gain almost monopolistic control over the trade in their own towns or regions. Typical examples of such merchant-princes of the seventeenth century were John Claessen and Jan Hennequa of Fetu, John Cabes of Komenda, John Currantee of Anomabo, and John Konny of Ahanta, all in modern Ghana.

With a view to gaining control of trade, the Europeans encouraged Africans to live around the forts and castles they built. The Europeans furthermore sought treaties giving them exclusive trading rights. However, though many such treaties were exacted, especially by the Dutch and the English, the Africans paid absolutely no heed to their terms and throughout traded with everyone as they chose. Finally, the Europeans resorted to the practice of interfering in local politics, especially in succession disputes, with a view to putting their own nominees on the throne and in other influential positions. The English and the Dutch constantly did this in Komenda, Eguafo, and Fetu; the Dutch, the French, and the English in Ardra and Ouidah; and the Portuguese in the Congo and Angola. But these methods proved ineffective. Hence, during the second period as in the first, the Africans on the west coast, and to some extent in the Congo, maintained their predominant position and rigidly controlled the trading activities of the Europeans while their states enjoyed complete autonomy.

In Angola, Mozambique, and South Africa, however, the situation was different. Although the people of the Congo and the Portuguese settlers on São Tomé had been unofficially trading for slaves in the region now called Angola in the late fifteenth and the beginning of the sixteenth centuries, it was not until 1520 that the Portuguese dispatched the first official trading mission there. Its leader, Balthasar de Castro, met with failure. Arriving in the kingdom of Ndongo, then a vassal state of the kingdom of the Congo, he was imprisoned by the ruling *ngola,* or king, the title from which the Portuguese formulated the name Angola. Nothing more was done to formalize relations for another forty years, though trade between São Tomé and the Angola region continued, and it was with the assistance of some of these Portuguese traders that the ngola was able to defeat a punitive expedition sent against him by the king of Congo in 1556 and to declare himself independent. Four years later, the *ngola* appealed for a Portuguese political, religious, and commercial mission, obviously to prove that he was the equal of his former Congo overlord. Under strong pressure from the Jesuits, who were anxious to start missionary work in that region, the Portuguese Crown dispatched Paulo Dias de Novais and four missionaries; they were to convert the king and his people to Christianity. The 1560 mission was a total failure. They arrived to find that the ngola who had issued the invitation was dead, and his successor promptly imprisoned Dias de Novais and one of his Jesuit companions, Father Francisco Gouveia. Novais was released five years later, but Gouveia was kept prisoner until his death in 1575. Partly because of the continued imprisonment of the missionary and partly because of the hope of exploiting the silver and copper mines rumored to be in existence in the interior, in 1571, the king of Portugal granted Paulo Dias de Novais a charter for the conquest of Angola and its conversion into a Christian Portuguese colony.

The expedition landed in 1575, and the conquest of Angola and the search for the mines began in 1579. In the following 100 years and through intermittent wars, the Portuguese completed the conquest of Ndongo, or Angola, founded the coastal towns of São Paulo de Luanda and Benguela in 1576 and 1617 respectively, and established a number of fortresses and towns inland. An administrative machinery was also established. The colony was divided into military districts, or *presidios,* ruled by captains who were responsible to the governor of the colony. Each *presidio* was made up of a number of chiefdoms under traditional rulers, on whom the administration imposed a head tax, or *Peca da India,* paid in slaves.

Jesuit missionaries operated in Angola from the time of their first appearance with the 1560 mission. But their number was insignificant, and some of the few soon took on so much trading and political activities that few converts were won. As late as 1694, according to Irish publisher James Duffy, there were only thirty-six priests actively operating in the whole of the interior, and most of the churches and schools had by then fallen into ruins.

The Portuguese also paid some attention initially to locating the reported silver and copper mines of Angola. In 1604, however, Cambambe, the reputed center of silver mining, was finally reached by Manuel Cerveira Pereira, and a second market at Tete, another 150 miles farther upriver. But the Portuguese did not make any move to colonize or conquer the reputed gold mines of the interior until 1569, when a huge and well-equipped expedition under the command of Francisco Barreto was sent out. This expedition pushed on to Sena in 1571, and with the approval of the *monomotapa*, as the king of the Shona was known, Barreto launched a series of attacks on one of its rebellious vassal chiefs.

(*Monomotapa* came to be applied to the Shona kingdom as well as its capital.) These attacks failed, and Barreto had to retreat to Sena, where he died shortly thereafter. His successor, Vasco Fernandes Homem, and a small party pushed on to the gold mines but found them disappointing. Because of Homem's discouraging report, coupled with the high rate of mortality, no government expeditions were sent inland again until the first decade of the seventeenth century.

However, it would appear that during the second half of the sixteenth century, independent Portuguese traders and adventurers pushed inland in search of gold and trade, and by 1600, a number of them had acquired large land and mining concessions from the local chiefs. After the turn of the century, the *monomotapa,* who was facing a series of revolts, again invited the Portuguese government to render aid. In return, he made generous concessions of land, and trading and mining rights. In 1629, however, the new *monomotapa,* Kapararidze, embarked on a policy of driving out all the Portuguese from his empire, and by 1630, only five agents were surviving in the Shona territory and only seven in Manicoland to the south. In retaliation, the Portuguese dispatched a huge army under the command of Diogo da Meneses. This army inflicted a decisive defeat on Kapararidze, who was then executed. A new king, reportedly a Christian, was appointed by the

Portuguese, and he was forced to sign a humiliating treaty with them on May 24, 1629. Under its terms, the *monomotapa* was to consider himself a vassal of the Portuguese; he was to "make his lands free to the Portuguese" and was to allow complete freedom to Portuguese traders, miners, and missionaries; he was to expel the Arabs, and within a year, he was expected to recognize a Portuguese envoy as "Captain of the Gates" at Masapa, the principal Shona market. From then on, more and more Portuguese and Indians living on the coast moved inland to acquire estates, or *prazos*. Many trading posts were also established throughout the gold-bearing regions of Mashonaland. The most important of these were Luanze, Ongoe, Dambarare, and the aforementioned Masapa.

By the 1650s, it has been estimated that at Tete there were about forty Portuguese residents and about 600 Christian Africans and half-castes living in the district. The power of the Portuguese representatives at Masapa had also grown with the years, as is evident from the following account of João Dos Santos, who visited that region at the beginning of the seventeenth century: "The Captain at Masapa has jurisdiction . . . over all the Kaffirs who come to Masapa, and those who live on his lands or within his borders. He has power to give verbal sentence in all cases, and can even comdemn the guilty to be hanged. This authority has been given him by Monomotapa. He serves as agent in all matters between the Portuguese and Monomotapa . . . . . . [and receives] all the duties paid to him by the merchant, Christian or Arab, which are one piece of cloth for every twenty brought into these lands to be sold."

It would appear then that by the middle of the seventeenth century, the Portuguese had succeeded in establishing their control over the hinterland of Sofala and Mozambique and the territory of the *monomotapa*. They governed the areas directly under their control through the *prazo* system. The colony was made up of *prazos*, or estates, owned by individual Portuguese. Each *prazo*-holder was ultimately responsible for the people, or *colonos* (freemen), living within his district; but local rule was maintained by headmen, or chiefs, known as *fumos*. The *prazo*-holder appointed and dismissed *the fumos,* dispensed justice, collected tribute, and could use his *colonos* as guides, carriers, and even soldiers. The armed might of each *prazo*-holder was based on a private force of his own, consisting usually of slaves. The *prazo* system was not abolished until 1832.

In Mozambique, the primary interest of the Portuguese was not in slaves, but in gold and ivory. However, as historian A. J. Willis has pointed out, "it is doubtful whether the government gained more from the gold trade than sufficed to balance the expenditure on forts and warehouses and on official salaries at Sofala and elsewhere." Some missionary efforts were also made in Mozambique in the sixteenth and seventeenth centuries, especially by the Dominican friars; but as late as 1700, as in other parts of mainland Africa, there was hardly a trace of Christian influence anywhere among the Africans, and it can be said that the Portuguese efforts in Mozambique were almost a total failure.

As was the case in Angola, the rulers and people of the eastern interior did not remain indifferent to the encroachment of the Portuguese. The Shona kings of the sixteenth and early seventeenth centuries welcomed them because they needed their help to suppress the numerous revolts with which they were confronted. But as soon as they felt secure, they took up arms against the Portuguese. A trader who visited the interior in 1634 reported that he found the position of the Europeans rather insecure. "The Portuguese," he noted, "have many forts in the empire of Monomotapa . . . They have to depend chiefly on their flintlocks, which each person keeps ready; for in Kaffir country where trading goes on, rebellions often break out, and then each one's best defense is his gun. . . . The power of the natives is vastly greater than that of the Portuguese in this country." He also noticed the relatively strong position of the Arabs. "Many Arabs," he wrote, "dwell in the empire of Monomotapa. They are opposed to us always and everywhere." As the years rolled on, and as the Portuguese *prazo-*holders grew more arrogant and oppressive, the *monomotapas* and their subjects became more restive. In their helplessness, the *monomotapas* appealed to the Changamire rulers of the Rozwi kingdom for help against the Portuguese. In 1693, the Changamire attacked the Portuguese fair at Dambarare and wiped out its residents. Then, after seizing the other posts, they turned against the ruling *monomotapa* and overthrew his kingdom. Thus, by 1700, the Portuguese were confined to the Zambezi valley and the immediate hinterland of the coastal areas, the area more or less of modern Mozambique. Politically, economically, and religiously, their adventure in east Central Africa had brought no gains.

On the southern tip of Africa, the Portuguese had shown little interest after the late fifteenth-century exploratory visits of Bartolomeu Dias and Vasco da Gama. Meanwhile, by 1610, the Dutch had wrested control of the East Indies from the Portuguese. Failing to capture Mozambique, traditionally the jumping-off point for eastern voyages, they found a more convenient and direct route to the Indies in 1611. This route placed the Cape midway between Europe and the Indies, thus making it of strategic importance in controlling trade. As Dutch, English, and French ships began to stop there, it was obvious that one of these nations would establish a station sooner or later; eventually the

Dutch East India Company did so. In April 1652, it dispatched an expedition of about ninety men under Jan van Riebeeck to the Cape. Van Riebeeck and his men landed at Table Bay in May 1652, and soon, a fort, a hospital, workshops, a mill, houses, and fruit gardens were established. By 1659, the station was flourishing, and each Dutch ship was leaving there victualed with at least a twelve- or fourteen-day supply of carrots, beets, parsnips, turnips, and other sturdy vegetables, plus numbers of live sheep.

The Dutch had no intention of establishing a colony at the Cape. Their decision to found that settlement was precipitated by their need for a refreshment station and by the fear that their deadly enemies, the Portuguese and Spaniards, might otherwise use the Cape as a base for attack. Indeed, Van Riebeeck was given strict instructions to keep the station as small as possible, not to colonize inland, and not to interfere in the affairs of the local people. Lest too much land be acquired, Van Riebeeck ordered a hedge planted to enclose the approximately 6,000 acres that he deemed adequate for the task. Less than a decade later, the need to raise more cattle as well as crops, and the continued fear of French or English attack, compelled the Dutch East India Company to permit free farmers, or burghers, to migrate there. As a consequence, slaves from Angola and West Africa began to be imported in 1658. By 1679, the number of burghers had increased to 259, and by 1680, settlements had been founded as far inland as Stellenbosch. The number of whites at the Cape was further increased after 1688 by the arrival of 200 Huguenots, who left France following the revocation of the Edict of Nantes. At the close of our second period then, the Dutch revictualing station had developed into a thriving settlement, producing far more grain, cattle, sheep, and provisions than was demanded by Cape Town and passing ships.

Socially, four groups had emerged. The first consisted of black slaves from West Africa and Angola, who by 1700 numbered about 17,000. The second was made up of the company's European employees, who were regarded as temporary residents. The third consisted of the Dutch Boers, or farmers, and Huguenots, who made the Cape as their permanent home. The fourth was the mixed group, who were a product of the miscegenation between the whites and the blacks.

The Boers, numbering about 1,600 by 1700, were fanatical adherents of the Calvinist faith. They identified themselves as the chosen people of the Old Testament and regarded the slaves and the blacks as the damned. Thus were formed the racist attitudes that would harden in the eighteenth and nineteenth centuries into the hideous philosophy of apartheid that governed the relations between the Boers and the blacks of South Africa until 1994.

What sort of people did the Europeans find in the region of South Africa on their arrival there in the 1480s and 1490s? Contrary to the contentions of some misguided Boer historians, South Africa was not unoccupied when the Portuguese and the Dutch arrived there. It is clear from archeological and ethnological evidence as well as from the early accounts of Portuguese sailors that the area was occupied by two principal peoples: the Khoisan-speaking peoples and the Bantu-speaking peoples. The Khoisan group was made up of two principal peoples: the Bushmen and the Hottentots. Both of them had a tawny-yellow skin color, were rather short in stature, and spoke languages with the unique clicking sounds. Although they shared common religious beliefs and practices, they differed in many other respects.

The Bushmen neither practiced agriculture nor kept cattle, but lived in small units of 100 or so, hunting and gathering wild fruits and tubers. Although they led a wandering life, each unit had a specific territory, which it guarded jealously. The Bushmen had been living in southern and central Africa for thousands of years, though by the time of the Portuguese arrival, they had been forced into the interior part of southern Africa.

Their fellow Khoisan speakers, the Hottentots, were cattle breeders, and though they, too, were nomadic, each group had to have its own home area. They were organized into much larger units than the Bushmen, with each unit made up of a number of related clans under a chief. As cattle owners, the Hottentots recognized wealth and private property. Less widely distributed than the Bushmen, at the time of the Portuguese arrival, they occupied southwest Africa, the coastal areas around the Cape of Good Hope, and the eastern coastal strip as far north as Transkei.

The Bantu speakers, consisting of three principal subgroups, were living in the areas mainly to the north of the Orange and Vaal rivers and on the east coast. They were mixed farmers, rearing cattle and cultivating the land. The most numerous of them were the Nguni-speaking peoples - Zulu, Pondo, Tembu, Xhosa - who lived in the fertile and well-watered regions of the east coast. To the west of them were the Central Bantu, or the Sotho-Tswana, peoples, who occupied most of the central plateaus west of the Drakensberg Mountains. Farther to the west were the Western Bantu - the Herero and the Ambo. All these Bantu peoples were organized into relatively small kingdoms ruled by chiefs, who were assisted by officials often called *indunas,* or military leaders.

The Bushmen and the Hottentots were the first to come into contact with the Europeans in the 1480s and 1490s. Not until 1702 did the Bantu and the Europeans confront each other near the present-day South African town of Somerset East. The Hottentots consistently met the Portuguese with great hostility. They fought with the men of both Bartolomeu Dias and Vasco da Gama. In 1503, the Hottentots attacked and wounded António de Saldanha and his men when they landed at Table Bay. In 1510, they attacked a party led by Francisco de Almeida, the Portuguese viceroy at Gao, and killed sixty of them, including the leader. As a result, the Hottentots earned a reputation as a really fierce and dangerous people, and reports that they were cannibals gained currency in Europe. Indeed, it was not until the favorable reports brought back to Holland by the crew of the *Haarlem,* who lived in Table Bay for a year after having been shipwrecked there in 1647, that the Hottentots' unsavory reputation was perhaps neutralized, thus preparing the way for the establishment of the victualing stations.

It would appear that the Hottentots took more kindly to the Dutch settlers, and they were the main suppliers of meat to the Dutch ships. However, as soon as the Dutch settlers began to expand inland and to occupy the land for farming purposes, both the Hottentots and Bushmen reacted sharply, and the first war between the Hottentots and the Boers broke out in 1658 and lasted two years. Van Riebeeck, having interviewed a Hottentot prisoner, summarized their grievances. They made war on the Dutch, he said, "for no other reason than that they saw that we kept in possession the best lands, and grazed our cattle where they used to do so, and that everywhere with houses and plantations we endeavored to establish ourselves so permanently as if we intended never to leave again, but take permanent possession of this Cape land (which had belonged to them during all the centuries) for our sole use; yea to such an extent that their cattle could not come and drink at this fresh water without going over the corn lands, which we did not like them to do." The Dutch, of course, were not prepared to leave, and a second war broke out in 1673 and continued till 1677. Induced by European commodities, especially tobacco and brandy, and decimated by the white's man's diseases such as smallpox, the remaining Hottentots gave up resistance and began to take on jobs as servants and laborers of the Boers.

The Bushmen, however, proved less susceptible. Unused to the concept of wealth and unattracted by the baubles and liquor introduced by the Europeans, they continued their resistance. They constantly attacked the burghers and killed, maimed, or drove off their cattle, all in defense of their hunting grounds and water holes. With a view to breaking this resistance, the Boers developed the commando system. Organizing themselves into mounted groups and equipped with three days' rations, firearms, and ammunition, which were supplied by the government, they went on periodic hunts for the Bushmen. In this way, they steadily exterminated the indigenous population, driving them farther and farther inland to the semi-desert areas of the northwest Cape and beyond the Orange River, where they are found to this day. By the middle of the eighteenth century, the resistance of the Bushmen had been completely broken.

The Dutch had yet to subdue the third and largest group, the Bantu, and it was not until the last quarter of the eighteenth century that the Boers, steadily moving eastward, confronted the main body of the Eastern Bantu across the Great Fish River. The result was the Kaffir Wars, which raged throughout the eighteenth and the nineteenth centuries and which in some sense have continued among their descendants to this day.

By the end of the period under review, there was hardly a coastal region of Africa in which the European nations were not operating. In the case of Angola, South Africa, and Mozambique, they did not confine themselves to trading from their forts and castles as they did in West Africa, but had become colonizers and administrators, thus provoking deadly conflicts with the Africans. It is to the lasting shame of these European nations in general, and to the Portuguese in particular, that they abandoned almost all the activities that would have benefited and improved the lot of the African, at least materially if not spiritually, to concentrate on the most inhuman, the most destructive - sale of man by man.

Politically, Europe's impact on Africa was at best a mixed blessing. In the Congo, Angola, and on the East African coast, it led to the weakening and total disintegration of almost all kingdoms that were in existence on their arrival: the kingdom of the Manikongo in the Congo, the Mbundu kingdom in Angola, nearly all the city-states on the east coast of Africa, and above all, the remarkable kingdom of Monomotapa. All these states were the victims of active foreign interference in their internal affairs, coupled with military attack on them by the Portuguese, or by other African invaders, or by both - the Portuguese in Angola, the Rozwi in Monomotapa, the Zimba in Mombasa and Kilwa, and both the Portuguese and the Jaga in the Congo.

The west coast, on the other hand, experienced the rise or rapid expansion of a number of city-states, especially in the Niger delta area, and of no less than four empires - Asante, Dahomey, Oyo, and Benin - which were to dominate West Africa in the eighteenth and the nineteenth centuries. Indeed, many historians are of the opinion that these empires were the product specifically of the Atlantic slave trade, built upon the desire of their rulers to capture slaves for sale. It seems clear to this writer, however, that such an explanation is true only of the states that emerged in the area of the

Niger delta, such as Bonny, Opobo, Brass, Cross, and Creek Town, all of which started as trading corporations organized to supply slaves either by war or raids. Significantly, however, not one of them grew into a large kingdom. The empires of Benin, Oyo, Asante, and Dahomey, on the other hand, were not creations of the Atlantic slave trade. The rise of both Benin and Oyo began long before any European set foot on the coast of Guinea. And though both Asante and Dahomey did commence their development during the second half of the seventeenth century, other motivating factors are indicated. Dahomey's drive toward the coast was initiated with a view to stopping the slave trade. Asante's rise, as is evident from recent research, was inspired first and foremost by a desire to throw off the tyrannical rule of the kingdom of Denkyira to the south and second to gain control of the trade routes running not only southward to the coast but also northward to Hausaland and the Niger Bend.

It is nevertheless true that the presence of Europeans did affect the growth or expansion of all these empires. Most important, the Europeans brought guns and gunpowder to West Africa, especially after 1640, and there is no doubt that the growth of the four inland states of Oyo, Benin, Asante, and Dahomey was greatly accelerated by the use of these weapons. Additionally, the presence of the Europeans on the coast provided these inland states with a motive to extend their sway down to the coast, thereby trading directly with the Europeans and eliminating the middlemen and their sharp practices. Although these states expanded mostly by waging wars against their weaker neighbors and although most of the captives they took were sold as slaves, it is wrong to see these wars as motivated primarily by the desire to profit from the slave trade. Slaves were only accidental by-products.

The economic effects of the impact of Europe on Africa were even more profound. With the exception of the east coast, the centers of wealth and economic opportunity prior to the arrival of the Europeans were inland. Now trade began to be diverted more and more toward the coastal regions, with the inland states extending themselves to meet the challenge. However, West Africa's ancient trade with the north and the Saharan regions continued, though its volume decreased as the greater part of it, especially the trade in gold, was diverted southward.

The second principal economic effect was that in western and west-central Africa, agricultural, hence peaceful, pursuits were neglected, and orderly economic development was ruled out as the slave trade became the principal occupation of the area's rulers. Some historians, including J. D. Fage, have argued to the contrary, saying that the slave trade must "have been a considerable stimulus to the internal economic development in Guinea." But this view is untenable. The sale of slaves simply could not have brought about any internal economic development. On the contrary, by taking away Africans mainly between the ages of fifteen and thirty who could have worked and produced wealth at home, by carting away craftsmen and traditional industrialists, by killing local industries such as the textile industry through the importation of cheap wares and copies, by retarding agricultural development, and by giving to Africans in return for their products only baubles and barrels of liquor, the European trade with Africa in general and the Atlantic slave trade in particular definitely delayed economic development in Africa for well over 300 years.

It was in the social sphere, however, that the European impact was virtually an unmitigated disaster - in fact, a crime against Africa. The first and obvious effect was the depopulation of Africa. Historians are still arguing about the number of slaves that were actually taken out of Africa, from 15 million to Curtin's most recent figure of 9.4 million. Of course, neither figure includes the uncounted numbers of Africans who must have been killed during the raids or in the wars or who died during the march from the inland regions to the coast. But it can be asserted that the total loss of population to Africa as a result of the Atlantic slave trade was something close to 20 million. Some European historians have contended that not only did Africa not suffer far-reaching depopulation, but as J. D. Fage argues, "it may have been preferable for some parts of this area to have exported the equivalent of its natural growth of population rather than to have kept it at home." These views are highly objectionable. Firstly, depopulation in the magnitude of 20 million people - people in the prime of manhood - is serious and far-reaching. Secondly, it is nonsensical to talk of overpopulation in sub-Saharan Africa even today, let alone 200 years ago. And, in any case, given a choice between dying in Africa of hunger or being reduced to chattel and being humiliated, flogged, or worked to death in the New World, this writer, as an African, would have chosen the former.

Beyond the matter of decimating the population, the perpetual raids and wars for slaves must have created an atmosphere of social insecurity, fear, and chaos. The English observer John Atkins wrote in 1721 that on the west coast "they never care to walk even a mile from home without fire arms." Such an atmosphere could not help but impede all orderly social development and retard cultural activities. Indeed, by 1700, the great art and sculpture of the people of Ife, Benin, and Oyo had virtually disappeared. Missionary and educational activities were also halted, partly because of the insecurity and anarchy caused by the inhuman traffic and partly because of the fact that even some of the priests, missionaries, and teachers turned to that traffic themselves. Significantly, it was only after the steady suppression of the slave trade that missionary activities began to take root in Africa.

Furthermore, the slave trade brutalized everyone involved, white as well as black, but especially the traditional African rulers. In their anxiety to obtain people for sale, these rulers abused customary law and practice, fabricated charges of adultery, theft, or treason, and even imposed slavery instead of fines as punishment for petty offenses. In his travels in the northern districts of Sierra Leone in 1822, Alexander Gordon Laing noted that following an investigation into the death of a young girl in a village he visited, the authorities were not able to place blame on anyone. "Had the slave trade existed," he commented, "some unfortunate individual might have been accused and sold into captivity." African religious leaders also abused their offices by turning them into instruments of enslavement. For instance, the Aro people of Iboland, in present-day Nigeria, used their famous oracle Chukwu to enslave thousands of Ibo from the inland regions. There is no doubt that the European presence in general and the slave trade in particular brought about the moral degeneration of many members of the ruling aristocracy.

Another deplorable effect of the trade was the change in the attitude of Europeans toward Africans, or the black race. Once the white man began to buy blacks and to treat them as chattel and beasts of burden, he naturally began to develop an attitude of contempt toward his victims. The feeling of equality and mutual respect that had characterized the first period of Afro-European contact was steadily replaced by one of superiority on the part of the Europeans, an attitude that has not entirely disappeared to this day.

The social impact was not confined to Africa alone, but could be seen in the New World. It was in the United States, South America, and the Caribbean islands that the feeling of white superiority and black inferiority reached extreme proportions, becoming the basis of the present, highly explosive confrontation between blacks and whites.

On balance then, politically, economically, and socially, the European presence and activities in Africa during the second period were virtually an unmitigated disaster for the Africans. By 1700, all the great hopes that had been conjured up during the earlier phase of exploration had turned sour. To borrow historian Basil Davidson's term, Africa had by then been turned into the "Black Mother," producing slaves solely in the interest of the growing capitalist system in Europe and the New World, and it was to do this for another 150 years. At the beginning of their contact, sub-Saharan Africa was politically, culturally, and artistically comparable to Europe. By 1700, Europe had leaped forward technologically and socially, but Africa and its black peoples had become paralyzed and impoverished, a tragedy from which they still have not recovered.

9
TIME OF TROUBLES
JOHN HENRIK CLAKRE

Africa's time of tragedy and decline started in Europe and Africa itself. For more than 1,000 years, Africans had been bringing into being empire after empire. But the opening of Europe's era of exploration, Africa's own internal strife, and the slave trade turned what had been Africa's golden age into a time of troubles.

The Crusades may be called the beginning of Europe's reawakening. A religious fervor, not unrelated to politics, had stirred Europeans out of their lethargy and their indifference to the larger world. The First Crusade, begun in 1095, was precipitated by the Seljuk Turks, whose persecution of Christians had placed even Constantinople in jeopardy. The Eastern heads of the Church appealed to Pope Urban II for help. At a great Church council in France, the pope pointed out that if Constantinople fell to the Turks, Western Europe would soon be overrun. He made an eloquent plea to the kings and princes gathered, and to all Western European Christendom, to rally to the aid of the Christians in the East and to drive the "infidels" from the Holy Land.

This religious crisis gave Europe a semblance of unity, and although it can be said that the Crusades were military and religious failures, they did provide the opportunity to bring new information to Europe. The religious wars also had a profound effect on the political development of Europe. The Western monarchs were able to strengthen their authority and develop a strong central government while many members of their turbulent aristocracies were fighting in the Holy Land.

Contact with the East had a deep and lasting effect on the Crusaders, who belonged to a civilization where culture and learning had almost vanished during the Dark Ages. The princes in their castles and the peasants in their huts were equally ignorant and uneducated. When they arrived in the East, they soon realized how backward the people of the West were. They marveled at the beautiful cities, the thriving commerce, the busy industries, the art, and the learning. The impetus for exploration was fueled by what the Crusaders met along the way. Ships built to ferry the Crusaders to the Holy Land returned laden with the products of the East. The cargoes of spices, fruits, rich silks, satins, velvets, and other luxury goods had found a ready market. Thus, the Crusades brought into being the first attempts to open fresh trade routes to the East. Early in the fifteenth century, Europeans, in search of new worlds to conquer and of a food supply to feed the continent's hungry population, began to venture across the seas.

• NORTH AFRICA: By 1492, North Africa was confronted with the painful fact of its waning influence in Mediterranean Europe. Spain and Portugal, which had broken the yoke of North African domination, were asserting themselves as powerful, independent nations with colonial aspirations in the lands of their former conquerors. Islam, a great religious and military force in North Africa and the Middle East since the latter part of the seventh century, was now torn apart by internal strife and bickering. The relationship of North Africa to the people of the western Sudan was deteriorating. For hundreds of years, this relationship had been good. Africans from the western Sudan had participated in large numbers in the conquest of Spain in the year CE 711. These Africans made up the major military force that kept Spain under North African domination, and they participated in that country's intellectual life, as is still reflected in Spain's art, culture, and literature.

In order to understand this neglected aspect of history - the role of Africans in the conquering and ruling of Spain - it is necessary to go back in time to retell, at least briefly, the part that black Africans played in the rise of Islam and in the spread of Islamic influence to Mediterranean Europe.

Hazrat Bilal ibn Rabah (more often referred to simply as Bilal) was the first high priest of Islam. After Muhammad himself, it may be said that this great religion began with Bilal, who was an Ethiopian. Bilal is considered to be the Prophet's first African convert. Zayd ibn Harithah, another convert to Muhammad's faith, later became one of the Prophet's foremost generals. Muhammad adopted him as his son and later made him governor of his people, the proud Koreish who lived in what is today Saudi Arabia. Like Bilal, Zayd ibn Harithah was also an Ethiopian. He eventually married into the Prophet's family, the highest honor possible. Zayd ibn Harithah was killed in battle while leading his men against the armies of the Byzantine Empire. The authoritative *Encyclopedia of Islam* has hailed him as one of the first great heroes of Islam.

By the early part of the eighth century, the followers of Islam had swept across North Africa and were moving into the western Sudan. Among the Africans' military chiefs who converted to the Islamic faith during the Arab invasion of Morocco was a great general known as Tarik ibn Ziyad. Tarik held the rank of general in the Arab-Moorish armies of Musa ibn Nusayr, the governor of North Africa. Tarik entered into friendly relations with Count Julian, the Christian governor of Ceuta, who was on bad terms with his master, Roderick, the king of Spain. Count Julian urged Tarik to invade Spain. In the meantime, Musa ibn Nusayr learned that the Spanish king was busy in the north of his country in a campaign to put down an uprising of the Basques. Musa decided that time was ripe for an invasion of the Visigothic realm. An African army was recruited and placed under the leadership of Tarik. In 711, the army landed on a Spanish promontory just thirteen miles across the Mediterranean from Ceuta. The place was later named Gebel Tarik, meaning the "Hill of Tarik," or as we now call it, Gibraltar.

Tarik's army captured several Spanish towns near Gibraltar, among them Heraclea. Then he advanced toward Andalusia. King Roderick learned of the invasion and raised an army for defense. The two armies met in battle at a place called Jerez, not far from the Guadalete River. In this battle, King Roderick was defeated. Tarik sent for reinforcements from Africa, and with them conquered most of the Iberian Peninsula. Thus began the African domination of Spain. The Gothic kingdom of Spain was laid low by Africans who had been converted to the Islamic faith, not by Arabs.

After consolidating their position in Spain, the Muslims began to establish institutions of research and learning, whose brilliance was felt far beyond Spain's borders. This was an achievement not of the Arabs alone. It was brought into being by a combination of Africans and Arabs, collectively referred to by Europeans as Moors. (The word "Moor" entered the vocabulary of the Europeans meaning "blacks," as in "blackamoor.") The Moors built magnificent cities in Spain. Córdoba in the ninth century was much like a modern city, with streets paved and illuminated at night, and sidewalks for pedestrians.

The intellectual achievement of the Africans in Spain outweighs all other things that can be credited to them. These Islamic Africans re-examined the moral foundations supporting Western civilization. They found that it had been the legacy of the Greeks that had enabled the West to make intellectual progress. This answer created a question: What had gone wrong in Europe - spiritually and intellectually - before and after the decline of the Roman Empire? The inquiry led in essence to the following conclusion: By the time Europe's Christian foundation was firmly set, the intellectual means and moral fiber of the people were exceedingly weak, and there existed a deep gulf between faith and reason.

These Muslim Africans in Spain came to this

conclusion while trying to bridge a similar gap in relation to their own religion and culture. While Europe was largely ignorant of its Greek legacy, these Africans rediscovered and preserved it. Their assimilation and distribution of that treasure forms one of the most fascinating chapters in the history of man's quest for knowledge.

In the course of their labors, the African conquerors of Spain did far more than mere translation. They commented upon and explained the Greeks, gradually erecting upon the Greek foundation an intellectual edifice of their own. While the initial work was done in the Near East, it was greatly elaborated upon by other scholars, mainly in Sicily, Spain, and Morocco.

In the meantime, Islam had moved deeper into Africa. The Arabs' language and religion brought together a large number of peoples and cultures that had not previously related to one another. When the second wave of North African merchants reached the western Sudan about the year CE 1000, they found flourishing kingdoms that had already been influenced by Islam. The commercial relations they established there lasted for more than 500 years despite continuing conflict. The Africans south of the Sahara made a rallying cry around Islam and in large numbers began to prey on the nations in West Africa and the Niger River area, accusing the people of not properly observing the faith - Islam.

Often the spread of Islam and trade with North Africa came at the same time. Therefore in the western Sudan, the defenders of this religion had both a commercial and a religious motive.

This gave rise to the dynasty of the Almoravids, who derived their name from the Arabic *al-Murabitin,* meaning "members of the ribat" a kind of militarized convent. The Almoravids were started by Abdallah ibn Yasin, head of a tough, warlike family from Senegal, across the desert. Puritanical in their approach to Islam, they sought to impose their own interpretation of the faith. After establishing a series of ribats where the disciples devoted themselves to strict religious practices and military exercises, the Almoravids swept north across the Mauritanian deserts and gained possession of the mountainous regions of Morocco. Ibn Yasin's successor, Yusuf ibn Tashfin, founded the capital at Marrakesh in 1062 and laid siege to Fez in the following year.

The Almoravids succeeded in reuniting Morocco, parts of West Africa, and Islamic Spain. By 1076, they had conquered the ancient empire of Ghana. After ruling this fallen country for ten years, they pulled most of their armies out of Ghana in order to give more support to their coreligionists in Spain. There they were successful in stemming the Christian tide that threatened to engulf all Islamic Spain after the fall of Toledo in 1085.

In the middle of the thirteenth century (about CE 1240), another dynasty rose up within the framework of Islam and challenged the rule of the Almoravids in Spain and in Morocco. Its followers are known as Almohads, a Spanish corruption of an Arab word meaning "unitarians." They, too, were a religious and military movement, offering another puritanical interpretation. The conflicts between the Almoravids and the Almohads weakened the Africans' control over Spain. The eventual decline of both dynasties affected all North Africa, the western Sudan, and Mediterranean Europe.

The Almohads did not yield their power easily. They called upon other followers of Islam for support. A vigorous people from the Sahara, known as the Marinids, came to their assistance and eventually usurped the waning power of the Almohads. This dynasty consisted mainly of soldiers and administrators. Abu Yahya (1248–1258) established the Marinid capital at Fez and prepared the ground for another leader, Yaqub al-Mansur, who extended their religious empire into what is now Algeria. The Marinids left their stamp both on Spain and North Africa, where they proved to be some of the greatest builders and patrons of the arts that Morocco had known.

By the end of the fourteenth century, southern Europe had gained enough strength - military and otherwise - to challenge their African masters. The constant pressure from Christians in Spain and from the new waves of Arab immigrants from the East created a situation that the Marinids found difficult to handle. By the end of the fifteenth century, the Moors had lost all of Spain except the kingdom of Granada. The Christians, although they also had their internal disputes, were finally united. The marriage of Ferdinand and Isabella joined the formerly hostile royal houses of Aragon and Castile, and together their forces blockaded the city of Granada. After eight months, the Moorish governor finally surrendered.

This marked the end of an era. Europe had literally been reborn. The Africans who had planted the seeds of progress in southern Europe had not made the best use of the harvest that followed. The progress and excitement that had inspired Europe during the fifteenth century and had carried medieval Europe over into the modern world had brought no progressive changes to North Africa, now rocked with conflict.

In the countries of North Africa, especially in Morocco, political stagnation seemed to be the general rule, and strong men with selfish intent found their opportunity to seize power. They no longer protected the poets and scholars; they left no monuments to embellish the conquered cities. To North Africans, the fifteenth century was a time in which Spain was a lost and hated land, a century in which Portugal robbed North Africa of a large part of its western seacoast.

The news in 1492 of Christopher Columbus's discovery of the New World came swiftly to the courts of Fez, Marrakesh, and Cairo, and was no cause for rejoicing. To the marabouts (holy men), who were the interpreters of the Islamic world of that day, this event was grave indeed. That same year, Granada fell, and Moorish exiles returned to their homes in Morocco without the customary heroes' welcome.

During the early part of the sixteenth century, the forces in North Africa were turning two ways. Attempts were made to settle internal differences, and plans to take over the still-rich nations in the western Sudan were formalized. The nations of the western Sudan were comparatively stable, due, in part, to their lack of firearms and the conflicts that would have resulted.

Portugal's growing control of the northern coast now began to impede commercial progress. This came at a time when the vassals and allies that the Portuguese had among the North African people began to desert them in favor of reawakened nationalism. Most Muslims regarded the Christian Portuguese with hostility and were determined that they should be driven into the sea. To accomplish this, the Muslims needed a leader. The search led them to Abu Abdullah, sheik of the Beni Saadi, a people of Arabian descent who had established themselves in the Draa River region of southern Morocco. Under the leadership of Abu Abdullah, the people of the Souss valley moved against the Portuguese, who had established a port on the Atlantic coast of Morocco at Agadir. Abdullah's power increased, although not all of his wars were successful. In the coastal strip west of the Atlas Mountains of Morocco, he and his two sons established a capital and fought the Portuguese. When Abu Abdullah died in 1518, his sons, as expected, carried on his work. The years of nationalist feeling in North Africa had produced a number of leaders who were able men determined to drive the Portuguese from their land. In 1541, Portuguese power in North Africa began to decline. They lost their stronghold at Agadir, and subsequently, as they became more involved in their Asian colonies, they abandoned other North African territories under their domination.

Meanwhile, in 1549, the Saadian dynasty came to power in Morocco and showed itself to be equal to the job of nation building. The greatest of the Saadian kings was Ahmad al-Mansur, who ruled from 1578 to 1603, He not only defended Morocco from Turkish invasion, strengthening the strategic fortifications of the country and reorganizing it on the Turkish model, but also developed the agriculture of the Sus and Haouz regions and won a favored position for Morocco in the markets of Western Europe.

While the reign of Ahmad al-Mansur brought a high degree of security and prosperity to Morocco, it brought tragedy and decline to the nations of the western Sudan, for the Saadians lusted after the gold of the Niger River nations and tried to seize it by force. They were by no means the first Moroccan dynasty to make this national policy; in the eleventh century, the Almoravids had financed their northward movement with gold from this region.

After the death of Askia Muhammad in 1528, his great Songhai Empire showed signs of having seen its last days of power and glory. Ahmad al-Mansur systematically planned the conquest of the western Sudan, giving his profound attention to this military and administrative heart of West Africa. In the year 1591, an army of some 4,000 musketeers under the leadership of a Spanish mercenary officer, Judar Pasha, crossed the Sahara and was on the borders of Songhai before any serious attention was paid to the danger. Songhai's ruler, Askia Ishak II, called up an army that was superior in numbers but armed with traditional weapons. The two armies met on April 12, 1591, at a small town called Tondibi, about fifty miles from the capital city of Gao. In spite of the brave stand made by the army of Songhai, the Moroccan soldiers moved into the country, and the wrack and ruin began.

Ahmad al-Mansur expected great treasures in gold to be sent back to Morocco soon after the conquest. When these treasures were not forthcoming, Ahmad dismissed Judar Pasha and sent another general, Mahmud ibn Zergun, to Songhai. His orders were to take charge of the army and press onward until he had driven Askia Ishak out of the Sudan and discovered the place where the people were hiding the gold.

The Moroccan invasion of Songhai and other nations of the western Sudan was made all the more tragic because in most cases, it was Muslim against Muslim. The invaders from North Africa and their European mercenary troops did not spare anyone - not man, woman, or child. They pitilessly slew the now demoralized citizens who cried out to them: "We are Muslims; we are your brothers in religion." The war brought no honor to either side, and in the years that followed, an appreciation of their intellectual and material contribution to Spain and the other nations of the Mediterranean sphere was lost from the respectful commentary of human history.

While the drama of Morocco and the western Sudan was unfolding, Egypt and other North African nations were encountering a new force. Like the Mameluks before them, this new force came from

Turkey, where its dreams of empire had begun to take shape with the conquest of Constantinople in 1453. By 1516, the eastern Mediterranean from Greece through Asia Minor and Syria was under Ottoman rule. By 1517, the reigning Mameluk sultan of Cairo had been publicly executed and replaced by an Ottoman ruler. Algeria was taken in 1518 by Khayr al-Din Barbarossa, who went on to make his reputation as the admiral of Turkey's dreaded corsair fleet. The Barbary Coast states of Tripolitania and Tunis became semi-independent tributaries of the Ottoman Empire in the 1550s.

Cultural ties with the Islamic world of northwest Africa and the Middle East continued as before. The Ottoman Turks were content to rule through military oligarchies and to collect taxes, holding the land under a feudal system that invited a steady decline in the prosperity of the people and the fertility of the land. No fresh ideas came in; all business was operated in the interest of the Turks.

It was not until the end of the eighteenth century that a number of influences were combined to rescue Egypt from the decadence of Ottoman rule. First, in 1798, came Napoleon's abortive expedition immediately designed to cut Great Britain's route to the Indian subcontinent. (The French had been considering the idea of seizing Egypt since 1769 when annexation was proposed as compensation for the loss of its American territories.) Napoleon's invasion fleet arrived off Alexandria on July 1. Three weeks later, he met the Ottoman forces at Embaba on the left bank of the Nile, just north of Giza. Winning a dramatic victory in the Battle of the Pyramids, Napoleon seemed to have laid France's claim to Egypt. But ten days later, Admiral Horatio Nelson located Napoleon's fleet in Abukir Bay, and in the brief Battle of the Nile that followed, gave Napoleon's Egyptian campaign a major setback. (Napoleon would remain in Egypt for another year, his decimated forces suffering further defeats from a variety of diseases and from the Turkish army.) Napoleon returned to France in 1799, leaving Jean-Baptiste Kléber and his lieutenants to oversee the province. They, too, were forced to leave in 1801 when a British expedition of some 17,000 men and a Turkish army combined to deliver the final blow.

Short-lived though the occupation was, the awakening of European interest in the cultural and scientific achievements of ancient Egypt was to have a permanent effect. Napoleon's occupation had included a scientific commission, the Institute of Egypt, which applied itself to studying zoological and botanical curiosities, surveying the land, and exploring the archeological ruins of the ancient Egyptian kingdoms. (At the Delta town of Rashid, called Rosetta by the French, a French engineer stumbled upon a stone showing the multilingual inscription that would lead to the deciphering of Egyptian hieroglyphs.)

Next, Muhammad Ali, an enlightened Turkish soldier who had come to Egypt to expel the French, initiated the modernization of Egypt. Named the Turkish viceroy in Egypt in 1806, he gradually strengthened his power base until, in 1811, he was able to break with the Ottoman Empire. The way to Egypt's renaissance was thus opened. Having observed the technological achievements of the French occupation, Muhammad Ali undertook to revolutionize Egypt's agriculture, industry, and army along Western lines. To supply an ever-growing demand for Egyptian cotton, he invited European hydraulic engineers to work with indigenous specialists to revive and improve the land's use of irrigation, and within a few years, the Nile Valley was producing two crops per year where one had been the rule. As a further aid to productivity, he nationalized the land, making the peasants all but owners of their fields so long as they paid taxes. The considerable profits realized from these reforms were invested in the military and economic development of the country, for it was one of the tenets of Muhammad Ali's rule that foreign investment capital should be kept out. His remarkable success proved so troublesome to British interests that outside pressures were eventually brought against him. The last years of Muhammad Ali's life showed a considerable slowing down of the modernization process.

• WESTERN AND CENTRAL SUDAN: The

collapse of the western Sudan after the Moroccan invasion of 1591 is one of the saddest events in African history. Security gave way to fear, and violence succeeded tranquillity.

After the fall of Songhai, many of their conquered provinces revolted, pillaging and destroying lands to the south and east. Half the kingdom fell prey to anarchy. By 1595, the Moroccans had brought the main parts of the once great empire of Songhai under control. The administrator of the colony, who was appointed by the king of Morocco and served as his representative, took the title of pasha, or governor.

One result of the Moroccan conquest of the western Sudan was the decline of the once-prosperous trans-Saharan trade. The city of Timbuktu, at one time the pride of the western Sudan, was now a ghost of its former self. The Songhai chronicler Abd al-Rahman as-Sadi had once called Timbuktu "an exquisite city, pure, delicious, blessed with luxury and full of life." He boasted that its people had "never been soiled by the worship of idols." Timbuktu, he went on to say, "gradually developed into a trade center. Its greatest days came during the time it was the meeting place for traders from Egypt, the Libyan Desert, the Oases of Tuat, Fez, and the gold lands."

One of the most shameful and far-reaching tragedies of the Moroccan occupation was the attempted destruction of the intellectual life of the nation. The attack on the University of Sankore at Timbuktu and the exiling of its black scholars was an act of inexcusable arrogance. Moroccan troops and their white mercenary leaders literally declared war on all institutions and intellectuals. In 1594, the great scholar Ahmad Baba was exiled to Morocco. He had been the last chancellor at Sankore. Ahmad Baba was the author of more than forty books in Arabic, ranging from Arabic grammar to astronomy. His life is a brilliant example of the range and depth of West African intellectual activity before the colonial era.

With the loss of all its scholars, businessmen, judges, and men of religion, the light of knowledge and education went out in the western Sudan. Moroccan soldiers robbed the houses of valuables, including maps and manuscripts containing the history of the western Sudan. Revolts against the invaders, and the further suppressions that followed, worsened matters, as did internal revolts among the subject people.

The royal family that the Moroccans found on the throne of Songhai was still trying to save the country from the worst aspects of the invaders' wrath. Ishak II had been banished because of his opposition. His brother, Muhammad Gao, became the next *askia*. He pledged allegiance to the sultan of Morocco, but the Moroccans did not completely trust him. Nevertheless, during the great famine of 1592, they were forced to rely heavily on him for their food supplies. Mahmud ibn Zergun, the governor, asked the new *askia* to prove his loyalty by sending the much-needed food to the Moroccan army. This Muhammad Gao did in good faith. He ordered all crops on the Hausa side of the river to be cut and brought to the Moorish camp. Then Pasha Mahmud ibn Zergun chose to test his loyalty again. He asked Muhammad Gao to call the local kings and men of affairs to swear obedience to the sultan of Morocco. This was done, and the assembled men were murdered without warning. Muhammad Gao now knew that none of the Moroccans could be trusted. He continued to go through the motions of being their puppet while passing information to his rebel brother, Askia Nuh.

Nuh had not accepted Moroccan rule. He was an astute leader and fighter. Some of the fragmented army of Songhai rallied around him and helped to keep up continued harassment of the enemy army. The people of Songhai, in defiance of their Moroccan overlords, declared him *askia* and said that they would obey no other ruler. He was wise enough to avoid giving his enemies a chance to open battle. The hills, swamps, and thick bush of Borgu, a region in northern Nigeria, became his encampment. He attacked the Moroccan outposts at night and withdrew to the forest and the hills. The people of Borgu did not particularly like the army of Songhai, which at a previous time had conquered them; but they united and fought with Askia Nuh because they hated the Moroccans still more, and like the people of Songhai, wanted to drive out the Moroccans.

The pressure and the harassment inflicted by Askia Nuh forced Mahmud ibn Zergun to turn once more to the sultan of Morocco for help. He complained that the tsetse fly was killing his horses and that disease and bad food and water were causing many deaths among his men. The sultan sent more soldiers and supplies and continued to wait for the treasures in gold that he had long expected. At the end of two years, Mahmud ibn Zergun had neither large amounts of gold nor news of great success to send to his sultan. He was forced to give up the fight with Askia Nuh for a while, and he returned to Timbuktu.

There he faced more disappointments. The people living in Timbuktu had rebelled against the Moorish guard left to hold the city. The troublesome Tuaregs were raiding the Niger valley again. Ibn Zergun, now an angry and frustrated man, suspected that the educated people were the cause of the rebellions, and he conceived a plan to punish them further.

An announcement was made that all the homes in the town would once again be searched for weapons, except the houses belonging to descendants of a revered local *qadi*, which meant, in effect, the houses of the educated class. Hearing this, the rest of the citizenry took their valuables to the exempted houses for safekeeping. Then the pasha ordered all the holy man's descendants to go to the Great Mosque of Sankore to swear obedience to the sultan of Morocco. Only after the group had gathered at the mosque did they discover the governor's cunning plan. These men, who had lived in comfort most of their lives, were put in chains and sent together with their wives and children across the desert to Morocco to be sold as slaves. Few of them survived the journey.

Mahmud ibn Zergun derived no benefit from this cruelty. Soon he was once again in trouble with the sultan of Morocco. Out of the vast riches that he had at last obtained from the rape of Timbuktu and other major cities in Songhai, he had sent the sultan only 100,000 mithqals of gold. Though this was a large amount, the sultan thought that it should be much larger. In his anger, he decided that he could no longer trust Ibn Zergun. After ordering that he be arrested and put to death, the sultan sent another governor.

The news reached Mahmud ibn Zergun before the new governor, Mansur Abdurrahman, arrived. He left Timbuktu and decided to risk a more honorable fate in the continued fight against his old enemy, Askia Nuh. Mahmud ibn Zergun met his death in the city of Zaria, located in present-day northern Nigeria.

Over the years, Moroccan pashas were either poisoned or forced to leave the Sudan after failing to bring the area under control. The first contingent of invaders from Morocco who were still in the Sudan chose to elect their own officers. Some had married into the local population and had local loyalties. Some had fought fiercely among themselves over the control of what was left of Songhai. (In certain ways, this condition would still prevail when the French arrived in this area during the latter part of the nineteenth century.)

Intermarriage between the local Africans and the Moroccan invaders produced, in another generation, a large number of Africans bent on the pursuit of power alone. Fights over who would inherit their fathers' land and power lasted for well over 100 years; they wrecked or retarded the progress of most of the nations in inner West Africa and the central Sudan. Still, old nations were reorganized, and new nations were born in the midst of this recurring conflict. We should look, at least briefly, at some of these nations and how they survived Africa's time of troubles.

A number of states began to emerge in the area that is present-day Nigeria. Some of the former colonies of Songhai began to consolidate their territories and form new states. In parts of the central Sudan, a degree of safety and security was re-established by people who moved away from the area of Moroccan domination. Some of the internal trade routes of the sub-Sahara not specifically connected with North Africa were reopened.

Among the new states that emerged before and during the Moroccan occupation of the western Sudan, Kanem-Bornu is outstanding. This state had the strength and leadership that was needed to preserve its independence from the Moroccans. Perhaps the greatest of the Bornu kings was Mai Idris Alooma, who reigned from 1570 to 1602 and was a contemporary of Queen Elizabeth of England. Although the slave trade had already started, the central Sudan would not feel its full effect until much later. The Hausa states had already reached a high level of prosperity and cultural development. The Yoruba, the Ibo, and the people of Nupe, Borgu, and Jukun were also developing powerful state structures.

At the close of the eighteenth century, the two most powerful states in Hausaland were Gobir in the northwest and Bornu in the northeast. The Jukun kingdom had ceased to be a menace, but Nupe retained its independence, though much weakened. Some of the Hausa states were nominally independent, but still under some strong influence from Bornu. This was the political situation on the eve of the nineteenth-century Fulani wars, which would resolve some of the old problems and create new ones.

Meanwhile, the effects of the coastal slave trade had reached the states of inner West Africa while the area was still trying to recover from the Moroccan invasions. With the aid of firearms, the Europeans and their corrupted African partners pushed the slave trade farther into the interior. When the conflicts between rival West African states did not produce enough prisoners of war to be sold into slavery, new conflicts were created. As a result, a number of states collapsed. This first occurred along the coast in such once-powerful states as Benin, Dahomey, and Asante; within 100 years, the pressure of the slave trade was felt in the interior, diverting energies from the development of politics, the arts, and culture to a preoccupation with slaving wars and wanton destruction. Africans who had lived in peace with their neighbors for hundreds of years now became suspicious and started wars to capture their neighbors, for fear their neighbors would capture them.

With the opening up of the New World, and the vast plantation systems that followed, often the slave-hungry Portuguese literally put a gun in an African's hand and pointed another one at his stomach, saying, in effect, "Either you capture a slave for me or you become one." And thus Africans were caught in one of the most tragic binds in history. Other Africans went into the slave trade because they were corrupt, having developed a liking for European liquor, clothes, guns, and other foreign goods.

Apart from the physical destructiveness and social dislocations that the Europeans inflicted on African societies, the absence of political unity exposed some of the small and poorly organized African communities to the ravages of their more powerful neighbors. Entire communities were fragmented and driven from their original homes. Those African people who did not have strong leadership attached themselves to one of the larger and stronger nation-states for protection. Sometimes the attached people were reduced to vassals; sometimes they were sold as slaves; sometimes they were totally integrated into the larger society, enjoying all benefits, responsibilities, and privileges of that society.

The slave trade had projected the Africans into a crossfire the like of which no one had ever before encountered. On the economic side, the slave trade had damaged the production of goods and the creation of wealth in Africa. The market towns in many cases went out of existence. The most valuable African resource, human labor, was forced into slavery and sent to the New World. Those African craftsmen who had escaped slavery could not compete economically with European manufacturers. As a result, African art and craftsmanship deteriorated and in some cases had to be abandoned.

The long period of slavery had completely undermined all elements of culture and growth in Africa. In some cases, the evidence of the achievements of medieval times had been destroyed. At Timbuktu, the once-great university of Sankore was now a fallen heap of bricks, stone, and mud. There was no one alive who could remember Ahmad Baba.

Near the end of the eighteenth century, when the era of slavery was drawing to a close, Islam reasserted itself in the western Sudan, and several jihads, or holy wars, were set in motion. The most noted of these was led by Usman Dan Fodio of northern Nigeria's Fulani. The real nature of Usman Dan Fodio's jihad is still in debate. To understand this war, it is necessary that we know more about the Fulani people and their evolving role in the Sudan.

At the time when England and other European powers were attempting to end the slave trade and start the colonial system, the Fulani movement burst upon northern Nigeria like a thunder clap, setting in motion a long chain of events that is still reverberating.

The Fulani were a pastoral people living in scattered clusters from the Atlantic margin of the Sudan in the Senegal valley to the Adamawa plateau in Cameroon. They generally lived without opposition on the fringes of agricultural societies, taking those lands that were relatively poor for crop cultivation. Their origins are usually traced to the Senegal valley, where, it is thought, they long ago mixed with Berber nomads who had been driven south from Morocco in the eleventh century. This theory would account for the remarkable physical diversity found among the Fulani, who range in complexion from the light skin of a large number of North Africans to the darker complexion and more black physical features of most of the people of western Africa. Prospering, the Fulani began to expand eastward from the Senegal basin, marrying with still other peoples along the way, leaving large settled populations in Futa Toro, Futa Jallon, Kita, Marina, Liptako, Sokoto, Bauchi, and Adamawa. Their search for new grazing land for their large herds of cattle was combined with a search for new areas to convert to Islam.

A careful examination of the events leading up to the jihad shows that the movement was purely religious at first, owing much to the inspiration of Islam. It would develop, according to some interpreters, into a national and political movement of the Fulani people seeking domination over peasants and traders. Usman Dan Fodio became the great national leader, taking the title of Sarkin Musulmi (meaning "commander of the faithful"), which is still borne by his descendants. He was born in the Hausa state of Gobir in 1754, and in his youth became known as a strict Muslim teacher, continually traveling to the countries of northern Nigeria to exhort the people to a more conscientious performance in their religious duties. This eventually brought him into conflict with the young *sarkin* of Gobir, one of his former pupils, who was also a leader of a northern Nigerian movement that did not strictly impose Islam upon all his subjects. Disciples and adherents flocked to both men. The younger man hoped to defeat Dan Fodio's movement before it could gain a foothold in the large cities. The *sarkin* of Gobir attacked the town of Degel, where Usman Dan Fodio was living. Not being prepared to fight at this time, Dan Fodio fled to the city of Gudu, where he was joined by others who believed in his cause. The *sarkin* of Gobir, who had pursued him, was defeated on June 21, 1804, at Tabkin Kwotto on the shores of Lake Tobin. This battle began the Fulani wars.

The Lake Tobin outbreak also stirred up other opponents of the Fulani. Some of the Hausa kings attacked the followers of Usman Dan Fodio and were met with a widespread Fulani uprising, led by the trusted generals of Dan Fodio. Each general had a flag personally given to him by his leader. These flag bearers took over most of northern Nigeria and claimed the land for their respective families. (The descendants of these generals are even today considered the rightful bearers of power in northern Nigeria.) They quickly swept through Hausaland. In 1804, the city of Zaria was taken, followed in 1805 by Katsina and Kano. Before the *shehu* met any formidable opposition, the great trading cities of northern Nigeria had fallen. Not until Dan Fodio's forces reached Bornu did a national leader, Al-Kanemi, successfully resist Fulani advances. The Fulani army was able to take only the border country. The rest of Bornu maintained its independence. By 1810, the jihad was almost over. Usman Dan Fodio had established his rule over more than 100,000 square miles and was recognized as sovereign by 5 million people. He died in 1817 and was buried in the city of Sokoto.

In many ways, the ground had been prepared for Usman Dan Fodio before he was born. The Niger River states had been torn with internal strife since the early part of the eighteenth century. The Oyo Empire had long been in decline before the jihad. The warning signs began to appear during the period of Bashorun Gaha (1754-1774). During this time, the Egba people revolted and were not brought back into the fold of the empire. As the Oyo army became a mere shadow of its former self, other peoples broke away from Oyo domination. Eight years before the jihad, the collapse of the empire was already noticeable; the jihad merely accentuated it.

This jihad was the last flowering of African military prowess in the central Sudan before the British and the French took over. It had its glorious aspect and its tragedy, too. Before the war was over, some Muslims were attacking other Muslims. By attacking Bornu, an ancient Islamic state with its roots in the tenth century, the men of the Fulani jihad made it apparent that political ambition as well as religious zeal drove them. The state of Bornu had scrupulously observed the tenets of Islam, and as its ruler Shaykh al-Amin protested, there was no justification for the Fulani to attack. But, as in all revolutions, separate resentments and grievances found their opportunity. In 1812, Dan Fodio retired in triumph, dividing his huge empire between his brother, Abdullah, who received the lands east of Sokoto, and his son, Muhammad Belo, who was given the capital at Sokoto and the remaining Hausa states. As the nineteenth century progressed, threats to Fulani power developed. Some of the original inspiration of the movement faded away, and no further conquests by the Fulani were attempted. The forest and the tsetse fly were obstacles to the kind of cavalry warfare that had made the Fulani warriors famous and feared. Yet, the kings and emirs retained their positions, ruling strongly until they were challenged at the end of the nineteenth century by another invading power: the British.

• THE WEST COAST: During the latter half of the fifteenth century, Spanish ships began to interfere with the Portuguese slave trade. This caused the Portuguese to build a cluster of forts along the west coast of Africa to protect their interests. The first and most famous of these forts was at Elmina, in what is present-day Ghana. Gold was the currency of the day, and this naturally attracted the Portuguese. They had landed in this part of Africa early in the year 1482. The leader of the expedition, Diogo de Azambuja, wasted no time in asking to see the country's reigning king, Nana Kwamena Ansa. The Portuguese offered friendship, but Nana Kwamena Ansa was slow in accepting their offers and in showing that he believed their promises. However, he still did not gain enough time to rally the support of his people and allies. Azambuja's expeditionary force set to work fortifying the area.

Europe's Reformation and the subsequent conversion of England and Holland to Protestantism in the sixteenth century also had repercussions in Africa. Protestant kings no longer felt bound to obey the authority of the pope. Owners of ships in these countries felt free to enter the slave trade in areas that the pope had assigned to the Portuguese and the Spaniards in 1493. Francis I of France voiced his celebrated protest: "The sun shines for me as for others. I should very much like to see the clause in Adam's will that excludes me from a share of the World." The king of Denmark refused to accept the pope's ruling as far as the East Indies was concerned. Sir William Cecil, the famous Elizabethan statesman, denied the pope's right to "give and take kingdoms to whomsoever he pleased."

The years of rivalry among European nations over their place in the African sun had started. At the close of the sixteenth century, France had no colonies. Henry IV wished to develop trade with the new lands in America and Africa, including, of course, the slave trade, but his minister of state, the Duc de Sully, who represented large groups of rural interests, did not share the expansionist desires of his monarch. It was not until after the noted Cardinal Richelieu came to power in 1624 that the French began to trade in slaves. Richelieu and Louis XIII approved of the early plans, and the Saint Christopher Company was founded in 1626 to exploit the tobacco and wood found on the Caribbean island of this name. The French also occupied Tortuga and parts of Saint Domingue. In Africa, they took over an area stretching from the mouth of the Senegal River to the Bight of Benin and started trading with peoples living along the Gambia River. By virtue of licenses issued on June 24, 1633, the French traders of Dieppe and Rouen obtained "permission to trade in Senegal, Cape Verde, and other places." In 1640, a stockade was constructed on an island at the mouth of the Senegal

River, marking the founding of the settlement of St. Louis. The concession for Cape Lopez was accorded the Maloe Company of Guinea, as it was called. This was the first French challenge to the power and territories of the Portuguese; the effort would soon peter out because of the lack of French resources or interest.

By the beginning of Louis XIV's reign in 1643, only a few private traders sustained the original effort poorly, taking no more than a few hundred slaves a year, as the demand was still small. There was no regular commercial traffic between France, its small West African holdings, and the developing colonies in the Caribbean islands. From Cape Verde to the Congo, the whole remaining coast of West Africa was in the hands of governments hostile to France or in competition with it commercially.

Of the European nations competing for a place in Africa, France had shown the least astuteness. This condition changed rapidly when it began to understand the importance of the slave trade in the intensive exploitation of their New World colonies. In 1664, Jean-Baptiste Colbert, Louis XIV's minister of finance, officially organized the trade for France. Soon the French caught up with the other European nations in West Africa, becoming at least their equal in competition.

The British, for their part, came late and furious into the slave trade. Captain John Hawkins and his "good ship Jesus" inaugurated the venture with the approval of Queen Elizabeth, who invested some of her personal fortune in underwriting it. The year of this first English slave-trading expedition was 1562. This was a buccaneering expedition that was meant to challenge the papal decree giving Portugal and Spain exclusive rights in Africa. After the establishment of the British colonies in the West Indies and the introduction of the sugar industry, the British participation in the slave trade became widespread and better organized, with various corporations being formed in England for that purpose. King Charles II and King James II held stock in some of these companies.

After the French and the British entered the slave trade, the Portuguese outposts were threatened. For 100 years, the Portuguese had been moving down the west coast of Africa, looking for new lands to conquer and new slave-trading areas. They made their first appearance in the Congo as early as 1482. The people of the Congo did not oppose the Portuguese at this time. The Congolese were a secure people, with years of well-organized government behind them.

Manikongo Nzinga (also known as a Nkuwu) welcomed them to his domain. Diogo Cão, the captain of this expedition, had broken the long isolation of the Congo, but the significance of this act eluded him. He sailed a little farther before going ashore. Months later, after returning to Lisbon, he told the king of Portugal about the Congo discovery. Thenceforth nothing was spared in the effort to make the Congo a Christian nation.

All the converts did not stay in the new religion. After having been converted to Catholicism and baptized in 1491, old King Nzinga gradually returned to the religion of his ancestors; but before his death in 1506, he designated as his successor his son, who had been converted under the name Afonso. Once on the throne, Afonso turned out to be a great king, and the kingdom of the Congo entered active international life. However, this good relationship between the kingdom of the Congo and the Portuguese did not last. By the end of the reign of Dom Afonso, extortion, alcoholism, and the slave trade were rampant in the Congo.

In 1590, another *manikongo* started a campaign to expel the Portuguese from the Congo. He made use of the known rivalry between European powers, pretending to put his country under the tutelage of the Holy See. Then he encouraged the arrival in the Congo of the Dutch, who were beginning at the time to acquire a foothold in Africa. The Portuguese were forced to abandon the Congo, and they turned their attention to the region of Angola, which offered them a more favorable field in which to further their commercial ambitions.

Early in the seventeenth century, other areas in the

Congo showed new life and new creative efforts in state building. One of the most remarkable of these states was the kingdom of Kuba of the Bantu-speaking Shongo people. Situated between the Kasai and Sankuru rivers, it is perhaps the most ancient of the Congolese kingdoms. Among the kingdoms in Central Africa only the Shongo culture kept its records and transmitted them almost intact to modern researchers. Oral tradition preserves what appears to be an accurate list of more than 120 Kuba kings, the earliest of whom lived in the fifth century CE.

Oral history relates that their greatest king was Shamba. The years of his reign, from 1600 to 1620, were really the golden age of the Kuba kingdom. He had the originality and humanity to abolish the use of weapons, especially the famous throwing of knives that had earned his people the epithet "the lightning people." It was also he who was the first to have a sculptor of his court execute his portrait statue. We also know from oral tradition that King Bo Kama Bomanchala saw an eclipse at noon on March 30, 1680, and that King Mbope Mobinji, who lived to be very old, saw the comet of 1843 and was the first Kuba to come in contact with Europeans in 1884, when Hermann von Wissmann's expedition passed through.

In the meantime, while this picture of order and culture was being revealed in one part of the

Congo, more troubles were developing wherever the Europeans were involved. The contest between the Netherlands and Portugal for control of the kingdom of the Congo continued throughout the entire seventeenth century. After the Dutch captured Luanda in 1641, thereby briefly supplanting the Portuguese on the western shore of Africa, a new diplomatic current was established between the Dutch and the king of the Congo. The latter sent ambassadors to Brazil and Amsterdam and asked the prince of Orange for help against the Portuguese. On the other hand, a Dutch delegation was received at the Congolese court with ceremonial splendor reportedly equal to anything that the visitors had seen in the courts of Europe.

The Dutch intrusion did not make the Portuguese give up their desire to re-enter the Congo. In a few years, the Portuguese recovered their lost positions and some of their military power. In the sixteenth century, they had been driven by greed for imaginary gold mines. This greed was now more rampant among them, though they still had no proof of the mines' existence. They embarked on open warfare against the king, Dom António, and defeated him in the battle of Mpila in 1665. A search of the country did not reveal any gold mines. After this, they left the Congo and devoted the next 100 years to completing the conquest of Angola.

In David Birmingham's book, *The Portuguese*

Conquest of Angola, we are told: "The first incentive to the Portuguese to conquer a colony in Angola was the hope of acquiring lands suitable for European settlement similar to those which were being settled in Brazil. Another reason was the Portuguese expectation of finding mineral wealth in Angola, which led them to conquer the site of supposed silver mines."

The failure to find the mineral wealth in Angola made the Portuguese double their efforts in the slave trade. Their most stubborn and colorful opposition as they entered the final phase of the conquest of Angola came from a queen who was a great head of state and a military leader. The important facts about her life have been extracted from a biography by the American historian Roy A. Glasgow.

Nzinga's story begins in 1583 when one of the most extraordinary and romantic figures in African history was born. She was the sister of the then-reigning king of Ndongo, Ngola Mbandi. Nzinga was one of a long line of African women freedom-fighters that dates back to the reign of Queen Hatshepsut in Egypt, 1,500 years before the birth of Christ. Nzinga belonged to the Jaga people. The Jaga were an extremely militant group and became more so when Queen Nzinga took over their leadership.

Nzinga's ancestry goes back to the end of the fifteenth century when her great-great-grandfather, the king of Matamba, conquered neighboring Ndongo and gave it to his son, Ngola Kiluanju, as an appendage to the other territory held by the Jaga. Nzinga stated that she was descended "from the kings who had reigned over the whole state before it was split into two parts." She based her claim to rule over the entire region upon her ancestral connections.

In 1623, at the age of forty-one, Nzinga became queen of Ndongo - even while her right to the throne was being questioned under the law. The supporters of her late brother had not wasted any time before stirring up dissension against her. She began at once to increase her position of power. One of her first acts was the strengthening of the traditional laws that ensured the cultural integrity of the Jaga people. She also forbade her subjects to call her queen, preferring to be called king; when she led her army in battle, she dressed in men's clothing.

Nzinga never accepted the Portuguese conquest of her country and was always on the military offensive. As part of her excellent strategy against the invaders, she formed an alliance with the Dutch, intending to use them to defeat the Portuguese slave trade. At her request, she was given a militia of Dutch soldiers. The officer commanding this detachment in 1646 described her as "a cunning and prudent virago so much addicted to the use of arms that she hardly uses other exercise, and withal so generously valiant that she never hurt a Portuguese after quarter was given and commanded all her slaves and soldiers the like."

She believed that after defeating the Portuguese, it would be easy to surprise the Dutch and expel them from her country. Consequently, she maintained a good relationship with the Dutch and waited for the appropriate time to move against them. Her ambition extended beyond the task of freeing her country from European control. In addition to being queen of Ndongo, she envisioned commanding a great Western Empire stretching from Matamba in the east to the Atlantic Ocean in the west. To this end, she was an astute agitator-propagandist, easily summoning large groups of her fellow countrymen to hear her. In convincing her people of the evil effects of the Portuguese, she would single out slaves and slave-soldiers who were under Portuguese control and direct intensive political and patriotic messages in their direction, appealing to their pride as Africans. She offered them land and freedom. This resulted in a serious security problem for the Portuguese, with thousands of these slave-soldiers deserting to join her forces. Politically far-sighted, competent, self-sacrificing, and devoted to the resistance movement, she attempted to draw many kings and heads of families to her cause in order that they, in turn, might recruit their people for her revolution against the Portuguese.

Nzinga's most enduring weapon was her personality. She was astute and successful in consolidating power. She was particularly good at preserving her position by ruthlessly dealing with her foes and graciously rewarding her friends. She possessed both masculine hardness and personal charm, depending on the need and the occasion.

The Portuguese now suspected that they were not going to win her over to their side by peaceful means. The priests were disappointed because they had seemingly lost the battle to convert her to Catholicism. However, in her campaign to drive the Portuguese out of Angola she suffered a series of setbacks in 1645 and 1646. Her sister was taken as a prisoner of war and thrown into the river. Nzinga began to weigh the merits of her own god, Tem-Bon-Dumba, against the god of the Portuguese. Was it possible, she asked, that the Catholic god was stronger? A number of other questions arose for which there was no satisfactory answer. She had heard the Jesuits say that the Christian god was a just person and an enemy of all suffering. Why then did he assist the invaders of her country? Why were the Portuguese building forts in her country without her consent? With these questions still unresolved, she decided to join this religion and test its strength in her favor. For the remainder of her life, she used Christianity or put it aside, depending on her needs.

In 1659, she signed a treaty with the Portuguese that brought her no feeling of triumph. However, time would reveal that her part of the treaty had been based upon political and military realities, for she was now faced with overwhelming odds and superior weaponry. She had fought the Portuguese for most of her adult life. She was more than seventy-five years old now, and some of her faithful assistants and followers were dead or had given up the long fight.

On December 17, 1663, this great African woman died, marking the end of one epoch and the beginning of another. With her passing, the planting of the Cross and the occupation of the interior of South West Africa had begun. The massive expansion of the Portuguese slave trade followed.

As stated earlier, the British opened the last phase of the slave trade in West Africa. When Captain John Hawkins organized the manpower and ships for this aspect of England's worldwide expansion, the structure and administration of this inhuman business were permanently changed. Spheres of influence were established among slave traders, guaranteeing one another's rights to conduct business in certain areas of West Africa without interference. In a word, the business was put on a business basis. Because of his success, Captain Hawkins is often referred to as "the man who stole a continent."

It took the British nearly 100 years to drive the Portuguese and other lesser powers out of West Africa. In 1701, the "Most Christian King of France," Louis XIV, and "His Catholic Majesty," Philip V of Spain, signed an agreement conceding to the Guinea Company a monopoly on the introduction of black slaves into the Spanish West Indies. This agreement lasted ten years, ending in 1712. Its objective was to procure reciprocal profits to both the Catholic king of Spain and the Christian sovereign of France, who derived considerable revenues from the trade through a head tax levied against the slave merchants for each captive delivered. The Guinea Company pledged to introduce an increased number of slaves from all parts of sub-Saharan Africa, with the exception of Elmina and Cape Verde, the latter still under Portuguese control.

The War of the Spanish Succession (1701-1714) radically changed this and other schemes for expansion in Africa. As a consequence of a protracted series of battles on the European continent, French domination of Europe was ended, parts of the Spanish Empire were parceled out to a number of claimants, and Britain's supremacy of the seas established. The Peace of Utrecht, which followed, was an attempt to set guidelines for the peaceful expansion of overseas empires, one of several European treaties that decided the destiny of Africa without African participation.

One of its acts, the infamous Asiento Treaty signed on March 26, 1713, granted the British government a monopoly on the importation of slaves to Spain's remaining American possessions for a term of thirty years (1713-1743). His British Majesty, no less illustrious than the French and Spanish majesties, pledged through the agency of the South Sea Company to introduce 144,000 slaves of both sexes at the rate of 4,800 annually. The conditions of the contract, with few exceptions, were the same as those previously made with France. In every possible way, the British got the best of the deal. The Anglo-Spanish contract was later altered to permit importation of a still larger number of slaves annually, and at a higher price per head than originally negotiated. For the rest of the eighteenth century, the British would maintain leadership in this hideous business.

By the end of the eighteenth century, however, the slave trade had run its course and was a declining institution. But the Africans had no cause for rejoicing. The British, who led the fight to abolish chattel slavery, became the major architects for the establishment of the colonial system, another form of slavery.

• EAST AFRICA: When the Portuguese explorers arrived along the east coast of Africa, they found the shore from Sofala (in present-day Mozambique) to Somalia occupied by a chain of

Arab-Swahili settlements, strongly Africanized by centuries of contact with the Bantu-speaking people. They traded with the Africans who brought gold and ivory from the hinterland. They were at first cautious about their interest in slaves. The Portuguese almost at once identified Sofala with the gold-rich biblical Land of Ophir. They built a fortress along this coast in 1505 with the intent of monopolizing trade. In order to accomplish this, the Portuguese first tried to bypass the Arabs and the large number of Swahili-speaking people and deal directly with the Africans. Fortunately for the Portuguese, their arrival in East Africa occurred during a time when intertribal rivalries prevailed. Some of the great city-states along the coast were in decline. A number of the powerful trading families were torn apart by internal disputes. Later, when the first strategy proved inadequate, the Portuguese took full advantage of this lack of unity to gain a greater measure of control. They supported the sultans of Malindi against the more powerful rulers of Mombasa in the sixteenth century, and in the next century they helped the princes of Faza, another of the coastal city-states, against their Pate (Patta) neighbors.

The main effect of the Portuguese on East Africa was destructive and negative. They built forts, churches, and homes for themselves, while literally declaring war on all local institutions. But they could not govern the coast after the East Africans had turned against them. The traditional rulers still controlled the city-states, and it was largely a matter of political expediency that some of them acknowledged the sovereignty of the Portuguese. The external Muslim powers such as the Turks and the Oman Arabs did not even go that far, as will be shown later.

What can be said of the Portuguese can also be said, with varying degree, of all East Africa's invaders. East Africa, more than any other part of Africa, was preyed upon by one invader after the other for well over 1,000 years. All these invaders took more from East Africa than they gave. The modern history of East Africa is the history of a people trying to recover from the aftereffects of invaders and build or rebuild indigenous institutions.

At the beginning of the eighteenth century, Portuguese pressure was lessened, but not out of any benevolence. The Portuguese were in serious trouble in other areas of the world, and they did not have the forces that were necessary to maintain their old power connections in East Africa. The divide-and-rule tactics that had worked so well for them in the early years of their expansion were no longer dependable. Some of their puppets now had power ambitions of their own. In Asia, their presence was being seriously challenged. In the New World, the original settlers of Brazil were questioning the authority of the mother country while still demanding more slaves. To the Portuguese, East Africa was only one part of their global design. They extracted both gold and slaves from the coastal states and did not try to occupy all of them. For a number of years, Mombasa Island, off the coast of modern-day Kenya, was their major stronghold in East Africa, along with neighboring Fort Jesus.

The relative security the Portuguese had known along the east coast was first upset in 1649 by the emergence of the Oman leader, Nasir bin Murshid, who had a navy strong enough to challenge the Portuguese at sea. *The Mombasa Chronicle* records that the inhabitants of that city made an appeal to Sultan bin Saif, who became ruler of Oman in 1649. In 1652, vessels from the sultan's fleet raided Zanzibar, 150 miles south; a number of Portuguese settlers, including several Augustinian Fathers, were killed. As a result of a poorly planned expedition, the following year the queen of Zanzibar was driven off the island by the sultan's forces, who joined with dissident locals. A Portuguese official who was responsible for the defense of the island claimed that he rescued 400 Christians and saved them from being captured by the Arabs.

For the next forty years, the revolts against Portuguese rule continued, mainly in the city-states. The city of Pate was in a state of perpetual revolt. In the punitive expeditions against this city, the Portuguese had the assistance of some East African communities that felt threatened by the strength and military prowess of a small and powerful trading city-state like Pate. The king of Faza, who ruled another micro-kingdom on the island, considered the ruling family of Pate to be his hereditary foe. In 1687, a former king of Pate crossed the Indian Ocean to the Portuguese colony of Goa and offered many concessions in exchange for assistance in his attempt to regain his throne. His most attractive offer was to allow the Portuguese to erect a church at Pate and convert Muslims and pagans without hindrance.

When this king returned to Pate, escorted by a squadron of Portuguese ships, he found that an Arab fleet from the Persian seaport of Muscat had anticipated his action and was ready to forestall him and his allies. The greater damage to the king's pride was in the discovery that his former subjects had turned against him. The Portuguese were not strong enough to fight the Arabs nor could they protect the king. There was no choice for them but to take refuge in Mombasa. For the remainder of the seventeenth century, the Portuguese in East Africa would have no rest from conflict; their African allies would fare no better.

On the island of Pemba, a state of rebellion kept the Portuguese from making strategic use of the land and the people. In about 1679, a distant faction of the royal family drove out the reigning queen. Like the king of Pate, she took refuge in 1687 in the Portuguese colony of Goa. While there, she became a Christian, an act that destroyed the chance that she would effectively be restored to power in her island kingdom. Nevertheless, the exiled queen continued to speak for the people of Pemba, and the Portuguese listened and indulged themselves. They were slow to realize that the aging queen no longer had power. In an act of desperation, partly in gratitude for refuge she had received, she willed her kingdom to the Portuguese. They were never able to claim this inheritance. In 1694, the island was still in a state of rebellion. The viceroy of India reported the matter to Lisbon, where the decision was made to give up the plan to reduce the Pemba people to submission.

Two years later, in 1696, the Arabs took full advantage of this and other conflicts along the east coast. A fleet from Oman arrived in Kilindini, the chief port of Mombasa, and wasted no time in laying siege to Fort Jesus, where a large number of local inhabitants, including many who were unfriendly to the Arabs, had taken refuge. Among the refugees was Bwana Daud bin Bwana Shaykh, whose father had been driven from power by the people of Pate in 1686. The struggle lasted nearly three years. The Portuguese sent ships from Goa and Mozambique in support of the Africans but were not able to lift the siege. Plague and disease reduced the defending forces until they could no longer continue the resistance. Before the Portuguese conceded defeat, the queen of Zanzibar made one last unsuccessful attempt to run the blockade and send supplies to the fort. The garrison became so weak that African women were taking their turn as sentries. With the fall of Mombasa, the Portuguese had lost all of their holding stations north of Cape Delgado. Faza had been abandoned in 1688 when the Arabs of Muscat took possession of Pate Island. Zanzibar had also been taken by the Arabs. Zanzibar's queen, Fatima, who had been loyal to the Portuguese, was deported to Muscat, but she was allowed to return after ten years of exile. Sometime before 1710, the Arabs, in search of material with which to build a small fort, had partly dismantled the Augustinian church on the island. All evidence of the once-obvious Portuguese presence was destroyed.

The Africans now were trapped in a bind between the Arabs and the Portuguese. They would not extricate themselves for another 100 years. When the Portuguese retreated from Mombasa, some of them went to their Indian colony at Goa, and others went to their southeast African colony at Mozambique. The Arabs at Mombasa acted unwisely, as if the Portuguese threat was over forever. Large numbers of Africans who disliked both Portuguese and Arab rule would attempt to get rid of the Arabs at Mombasa now that the

Portuguese had been driven out. The opportunity came quite unexpectedly.

In 1727, Ahmad bin Said, the Oman governor of Mombasa, set out on a pilgrimage to Mecca and left his deputy, Nasser bin Abdullah al-Mazrui, in charge. He then began to treat the garrison of soldiers at Mombasa with severity. Grievance over this matter developed into open revolt. The rebels made Abdullah al-Mazrui a prisoner and took over Fort Jesus. Immediately they began to seek support from the local inhabitants. They, like the mutineers, feared the governor, Ahmad bin Said, and knew that he could get support from the Arab states. The rebels hoped to organize the local inhabitants in their favor before the governor returned. But a member of the Malindi family persuaded the people not to support this rebellion. They, in turn, demanded that the rebels surrender the fort. This demand was rejected. The conflict that followed is called a war, but it was really an internal dispute. Without a large supply of arms, the rebels were limited in what they could do. Knowing that Fort Jesus was more or less impregnable, they made no attempt to attack it. They found targets within their limitations and took possession of several walled towns and some outlying forts at Kilindini. The local population had grown accustomed to conflicts and reverses in power struggles but was somewhat confused over this turn of events. For the rebels, fortune turned temporarily in their favor. The rulers of Oman became involved in civil disorders at home on the Arabian Peninsula and could not send support to the Arabs at Mombasa. The rebels now had the opportunity to set up an independent state, and would have, except for the intervention of the Portuguese, who had partly recovered from their defeat on the island.

The Portuguese found their opportunity when a special emissary was sent by the king of Pace to Goa to obtain Portuguese help in expelling the Oman Arabs from Pate. An agreement was drawn up between the emissary and the Portuguese viceroy at Goa. The main parts of this treaty were: No Portuguese subject, Christian or otherwise, could be compelled to become a Muslim; all previous Christians who had been compelled to become Muslims should have the right to return to the Roman Catholic Church if they desired to do so. On the other hand, the Inquisition was not to function in the land.

When the Portuguese reached Pate early in 1728, some resistance was offered from one faction, but they eventually surrendered, knowing that they could expect no support from Oman at this time. The Portuguese took full advantage of the unrest at Mombasa and similar dissensions in the island of Pate farther to the north. Both Pate and Mombasa were regained with little fighting. At Mombasa, Shaykh ibn Ahmad al-Malindi at once disclaimed all relations with the rebels. The Arab governor, having little stomach for warfare, quickly surrendered. The Portuguese had promised that he and his men would be given ships to return to Oman.

In celebration of this event, the Portuguese entered what was still left of the church of the Augustinian convent and conducted High Mass before a roughly made wooden cross. An Augustinian Father preached on this occasion from the text in Isaiah lxvi: 10: "Rejoice ye with Jerusalem, and be glad with her, all ye that love her: rejoice for joy with her, all ye that mourn for her." Inside the church, the Fathers found a chest containing church ornaments; it had been left unharmed for more than thirty years. The chapel of the Misericordia was also found undamaged.

The Portuguese became more confident when the king of Zanzibar came to Mombasa to make submission to the governor. A party of Portuguese soldiers and civil servants was sent to Zanzibar to establish a "factory," or in more precise language, the slave trade.

In their short-lived triumph, the Portuguese had overlooked issues relating to their return. They had not been invited back by the populace at large, nor did a large number welcome them. They had been asked back as arbitrators of an internal dispute, mainly involving the rulers of Mombasa, Pate, Zanzibar, and related territories.

In spite of the comparative ease with which the Portuguese seemed to have regained their lost possession, trouble between the Portuguese and the inhabitants was soon to develop. Treaties were barely signed before they were broken. On August 29, 1728, a new treaty was made with Pate. The Portuguese, with unwarranted confidence, made new demands and tried to revise some old ones. They insisted on the payment of tribute and took for themselves a large share of the island's revenue. The African faction that had invited the Portuguese to help them against the Arabs was now having second thoughts. Friction developed between the king of Pate and the Portuguese commander. Eventually, the Portuguese garrison found itself in a state of siege with no local allies. After being reduced to the verge of starvation, the Portuguese were willing to forgo all previous agreements and return to Goa. Also, the Portuguese garrison at Mombasa was expelled, and their flag lowered at Fort Jesus for the last time.

Portuguese conduct had destroyed whatever good will had been previously built up among the people in East Africa. The Portuguese were completely intolerant of the Muslims. According to the Mombasa Chronicle: "They flung stones at the people while they were at their prayers; and they used to turn the people out of their houses and take possession of them; and take their wives to themselves."

The loss of Fort Jesus and other Portuguese settlements left the Oman Arabs militarily in charge of the cast coast of Africa and the large slave-trading island of Zanzibar. Fort Jesus was handed over to an Oman garrison, and Muhammad ibn Said al-Maamri was installed as governor. After the final withdrawal of the Portuguese from Mombasa, we hear no more of Christianity and Christians in East Africa for a century. An uneasy partnership developed between the Portuguese and the Arabs. The big Portuguese colony of Brazil was calling for more slaves than the Portuguese could furnish, and the Arabs filled the breach as suppliers.

The East African trade, in a formal sense, can trace its roots no further than the first half of the eighteenth century, and the early Portuguese chronicles make only passing mention of the slave trade. Much more important were the gold and ivory traded to Arabia and India. It was in search of these products that the Portuguese invaders had come in the sixteenth and seventeenth centuries. But the Arabs had dealt in human chattel since the twelfth century. Not only along the coast of Kenya and Tanzania but also in Mozambique and Zimbabwe did they deal in slaves. The great trading center at Zanzibar had about 100 years of active commercial slave trading before the European powers entered the area.

Near the end of the eighteenth century, other

European powers, principally Great Britain, began to make themselves felt along the east coast of Africa. They would in the next fifty years wage a successful war on the East African slave trade and, subsequently, install the European colonial system.

• SOUTH AND SOUTHWEST AFRICA In the year 1652, when Oliver Cromwell was proclaiming his creed of "liberty and conscience," and American seekers of religious freedom were cautiously penetrating the American continent in search of new lands, a band of thirty white settlers (employees of the powerful Dutch East India Company under the leadership of Jan van Riebeeck) came ashore below the 3,500-foot shadow of Table Mountain to establish the Cape Colony at the southernmost tip of the horn of Africa. Although this did not mark the first appearance of European people in southern Africa, it was the first sustained attempt to form a permanent white settlement. This was the beginning of South Africa's "Troubled Years." Contestants for control of the area would soon be the Dutch, the British, the Hottentots, the Bushmen, and the Bantu-speaking peoples.

Although the Portuguese had landed on the Cape before the arrival of the Dutch, they had not established a trading station. There were many reasons for this. The coast was a stormy one, and there were no settled tribes with whom they could barter for slaves. Almost 150 years elapsed before the Dutch decided to set up a station, and only after they had wrested a large part of Europe's Indian Ocean shipping business from the Portuguese.

The stated intent of Van Riebeeck was to start a refueling station for the ships of the Dutch East India Company on their way to and from the East. His band of settlers absorbed a handful of Huguenot refugees who had arrived ahead of them, and after 1667 started importing slaves from Malaya and other Asian countries. The first African people they encountered were the Hottentots, or more properly, the Khoikhoi people. (The term Khoisan is anthropologists' construct, meant to include both the Khoikhoi and the San, or Bushmen.) A king of the Hottentots, Autshumayo, led them in the first futile attempt in 1659 to stop Van Riebeeck and his company from seizing the best pasture lands in the Cape Peninsula. Thus, the nationalist struggle in South Africa had its beginning in this little-known rebellion. King Autshumayo's people were enslaved and deprived of their cattle. The Bushmen were hunted like game. To keep from being destroyed, they retreated into the Kalahari Desert, where they still live. The basic historic conflict in South Africa - the struggle between different national entities to control the land - had been set in motion.

The first European settlers took on some of the habits and traits of the Africans that they had practically destroyed. These Boers, or farmers, acquired large herds of cattle, mainly from Africans whom they had defeated. They became nomadic, land-hungry "white Africans," hunters without human regard for the indigenous people of South Africa.

The settlement grew with infusions of slaves from the east, Mozambique, Angola, and the addition of still more Huguenots and Dutchmen. While the women of the Khoikhoi and the San were sexually used and abused by the white settlers, the Dutch East India Company for a number of years countenanced, and even encouraged, legal marriages between the white settlers and their Asian slaves. They were building the ethnic buffer between themselves and the blacks; this group was to become known as the "Cape Coloreds." In present-day South Africa, they number more than 1 million. The dangerous doctrine of white superiority had already been developed by the Boers (later called Afrikaners), but they did not at this time see that the sanctioned marriages between themselves and their Asian slaves were in contradiction to this concept.

Many of the Boers who made up the first large white settlement in southern Africa were political and religious malcontents before leaving their homes in the Netherlands. Their outlook on life was based on strict Lutheranism and Calvinism, the aftermath of the bitter struggle to preserve the newly established Protestant faith against the powerful attacks of the resurgent Catholic Church.

The Boers had neither security nor peace during their first 100 years in South Africa. The Khoikhoi people, who were friendly to them when they first arrived, soon began to look upon them as invaders and land grabbers. They saw their land being fenced off and white men with guns protecting the land that the whites had claimed for settlements. The Khoikhoi considered the land to be inalienable and sacred, a part of nature for common use. Continued encroachment on their land caused this friendly and peaceful people to take up arms.

The Khoikhoi fought three major wars to regain the vast grazing lands of South Africa. Between 1786 and 1795, over 2,500 Hottentots were killed and 600 captured. Those taken prisoner, mainly women and children, were enslaved by the farmers. None of the adult males submitted to the enemy; they fought to the bitter end. Their courage, even in the face of overwhelming odds, was phenomenal. These early wars of resistance have in most cases been lost from the official history of southern Africa.

The lack of labor to tend the vegetables and fruit gardens of the Dutch hampered the work of European settlement. The Khoikhoi could not see the necessity of exchanging their freedom for money when they had the land. The importation of slaves to do the hard work became the next logical step. As for the Boers, the status of being Christian and master was becoming confused in their minds with their being white. Color consciousness helped them to erase the knowledge that all men were human.

The real dynamics of the black-white struggle in South Africa did not reach profound and tragic proportions until after the British occupation of the Cape in 1795. The British pushed the Boers; the Boers pushed the Zulu, and the Zulu pushed back. But this is, of course, an oversimplification. The story of this clashing of powerful forces and the struggle to control South Africa is complicated and protracted. In the meantime, other forces, issues, peoples, and nations were evolving in southern Africa.

South West Africa is a little known, though important, part of southern Africa. This country and its people were late in coming into the mainstream of southern African history. In some ways, this was fortunate. During the early period of European expansion, South West Africa was not an area desired for large-scale European settlement or slave trade. A number of ethnic groups, but chiefly the Herero, a pastoral people, and the Ambo (Ovamba), an agricultural people, developed small nations within the region.

The Portuguese, led by Diogo Cão, made a brief appearance in South West Africa in 1484, leaving a lonely cross to mark the occasion. John II of Portugal had sent them to explore that area of the coast which until that time had remained for the

Europeans a land of fable and mystery. This was eight years before Christopher Columbus and his sailors set foot on the islands of the New World. The landscape that the Portuguese beheld was not encouraging and did not cause them to prolong their stay. There were seemingly endless high sand dunes along the dreary desert coastline, known to later seamen as the Coast of Dead Ships. Two years later, Bartolomeu Dias, a Portuguese adventurer, brought an expedition to these shores aboard a little fifty-ton ship. He landed at a narrow southwest bay, which he named Angra Pequeña (today, Lüderitz).

In the next few centuries, this part of Africa remained free of any conflict relating to European expansion. The few Europeans who ventured into this large and thinly populated land did not at first make any claim. In 1738, a secret overland expedition was organized by William Van Wyk and other Boer farmers in an attempt to establish trade with the people in this area. The leader of the expedition was surprised to find that another white man, Pieter de Bruyn, had arrived ahead of his party. Bruyn was probably the first white man to set foot in the interior of South West Africa. In 1762, Jacobus Coetsee, an elephant hunter, crossed the Orange River and heard reports of great herds of cattle possessed by the Herero people. Rumors of copper in the interior drew several expeditions to South West Africa during the middle of the eighteenth century. The governor of the Cape,

Simon van der Stel, sent an expedition to find the mouth of the Orange River. Men returned from South West Africa with wild stories about long-haired blacks who wore linen clothes. A later expedition, in 1762, also sent out by a Cape governor, found none of these mythical people.

In 1795, the British proclaimed ownership of the South West African coast and declared that only British ships were permitted to hunt whales and seals offshore. This was an empty claim because the British did not have the manpower to patrol this vast area. The full weight and reality of European colonial oppression did not reach South West Africa until the latter part of the nineteenth century. During the period of the partition of Africa in the 1880s, the heavy hand of German colonialism would take over this part of Africa.

Meanwhile, in South Africa, the Zulu began to be a force to reckon with. In his book *The Bantu Past and Present* (1920), the South African writer S. M. Molema argues that these Bantu-speaking people have been migrating in and out of southern Africa for more than 10,000 years. South African archeologists discovered in 1970 a mining complex in Swaziland that is reportedly 43,000 years old. This opens up still other matters for further investigation (for example, what has been considered to be the youngest part of Africa for human habitation may yet prove to be one of the oldest parts).

In the Nigerian magazine *Tarikh,* November 1965, J. D. Omer-Cooper presents one of the numerous new appraisals of the Zulu people and the impact of Chaka (Shaka) on South Africa. He tells us, in essence, that the eastern coastland of South Africa, known as Zululand and Natal, is one of the most attractive places for human settlement in all Africa. This is the area where the Zulu people first settled after migrating to southern Africa.

The Zulu were mixed farmers, with cattle as their chief possession. They did not begin to make their mark on the history of South Africa until early in the nineteenth century. Before this time, they gave allegiance to the king of the Mtetwa people. Then in 1786, a son was born to the reigning king of the Zulu, Senzangakhona. The child's name was Chaka. In his lifetime, his impact on southern Africa would be profound, dramatic, and to a degree, tragic. This warrior-nationalist was literally the father of the Zulu nation. He fought to consolidate the blacks of South Africa in order to save them from white enslavement. He was not understood then, and he is not completely understood now. Chaka and his people stood astride the history of South Africa for the entire nineteenth century. For this period, the history of this troubled land is essentially the story of the rise and fall of the Zulu people.

Chaka's early years were not easy, and he had to

fight for a place among his people. Except for his mother, Nandi, the favorite wife of King Senzangakhona, Chaka might have been lost from Zulu history. Nandi was the daughter of the king of the Langeni people and a woman of great influence among the Zulu.

When Chaka was a year old, Nandi took him to her parents' house to be weaned, as was the custom among the Zulu. Chaka was a restless boy who did not get along well with anyone except his mother. It is said that when his father offered him the lion-skin covering that is worn by older Zulu boys to symbolize their future status as warriors, he refused it and behaved disgracefully. This angered his father because he had high hopes for Chaka, his first-born son, and he naturally expected Chaka to grow up and become king after him.

At last Chaka found a friend, probably through the efforts of his mother. Dingiswayo of the Mtetwa people saw that this troublesome young man had fine qualities. He presented him with the young warrior's lion skin that he had refused to accept from his father years before. Chaka became a soldier in Dingiswayo's army and soon earned the name "Dingiswayo's Hero."

Who was this man whom Chaka was willing to follow? He, too, had had trouble at home with his father. As he grew toward manhood, the Mtetwa prince found that his father, the great King Jobe, suspected him of treachery. The chief thought his elder son was going to rebel and usurp his power. The bitter feud caused the son to be driven into exile, where he remained until his father died. His years of his journeying away from his people earned him the name "Dingiswayo," meaning "The Wanderer."

When the news reached him that Jobe was dead, he sent word that he was coming back to be king. He at once began to teach the Mtetwa to fight a new way. He had lived in the Cape Colony and learned much about European methods of training men for warfare. He had seen firearms and had learned how to use them. Chaka had his first taste of success in battle in Dingiswayo's army.

Chaka had outgrown his brooding and rebellious disposition. In 1816, Senzangakhona died, and Dingiswayo helped Chaka become king of the Zulu. The two men - one king of the populous Mtetwa people, the other king of the smaller Zulu people - were friends, and their warriors fought together. But about two years later, Dingiswayo was captured by one of his rivals and was put to death. Then the Mtetwa people, who already knew Chaka as one of their leaders in battle, placed themselves and their great army under the Zulu king and took the Zulu name. This was the beginning of the greatness of the Zulu Empire, the foundation of their war machine, and the real power of Chaka.

The famous king Moshoeshoe, then trying to build up the Basuto nation, kept Chaka out of his country only by sending the warrior a message declaring that he recognized no other king but Chaka. Mzilikazi, who had been one of Chaka's best commanders, grew sick of the slaughter of other Bantu-speaking people and deserted the Zulu army, taking over 15,000 men with him. He went across the Drakensberg Mountains and established a new nation called Matabeleland.

Still, Chaka's war machine rolled on. He united by conquest the scattered thrones of numerous smaller kingdoms and incorporated their survivors into the Zulu nation. Four years after he started his first campaign, Chaka had conquered a territory larger than France. The loot and indemnities of war had made his people wealthy. He was at the peak of his military prowess, and all his known enemies had been killed or conquered. His magnificent army, 100,000 strong, was still ready and restless for more battle, and there were no battles to be fought. Chaka's rigid methods of army training had made the Zulu among the finest soldiers in the world. The whites in South Africa at that time thought it best to be on friendly terms with him.

Chaka's military movement was called the *mfecane*, meaning "the crushing." It was a process of social, political, and military organization and change that was largely internal to African society. In southern

Africa, this movement was created mainly out of the efforts of several Bantu-speaking peoples who were attempting to establish their status and their salvation. The Zulu were fighting their way up from vassalage. Once this was accomplished, they began to bring other people under their rule. In some respects, this movement can be compared to the jihad in northern Nigeria during the early part of the nineteenth century, though it was not a religious movement.

The power of Chaka began to decline in 1827, after the death of his mother. He led the Zulu in mourning for her and seemed not to be able to come out of mourning and lead them again in battle. Chaka became melancholy, constantly pinching his hands in self-reproach. Anyone who did not show grief became repugnant to him. He seemed to have lost all interest in governing his people and his empire. Many self-seekers were quick to take advantage of this. Those Zulu who had silently hated Chaka's terror for years grew openly rebellious.

In 1828, a year after the death of Chaka's mother, his two half-brothers, Dingane and Mhlangana, crept into his hut and stabbed him to death. This event shook the Zulu, but the empire did not fall until many years later.

During the last moments of Chaka's life, he is reported to have said to Dingane, who was to succeed him: "It is your hope that by killing me you will become kings when I am dead. But you are deluded; it will not be so, for the white man will come and you will be his slave. What have I done to you? Oh, children of my father."

After Chaka's death, the Boers began their trek into the hinterland, looking for more land away from the English, who had taxed and restricted them severely. This inland push of the Boers once more set the Zulu in motion. Dingane, now king, led the fight against the encroachment on Zululand. This phase of the struggle for control of South Africa would continue until Dingane was defeated in the Battle of Blood River in December 1839.

10
WARS OF RESISTANCE
STANLAKE SAMKANGE

By 1800, opposition to the slave trade had gained numerous spokesmen in Africa, Europe, America, and other parts of the world. It will be remembered that in 1526 Afonso, king of the Bakongo along the Congo, told King John III of Portugal: "It is our will that in these kingdoms there should not be any trade in slaves nor market for slaves." In 1724, King Agaja of Dahomey informed the British government that he wanted to stop the export of people from his country. A Swedish traveler visiting Africa in 1789 reported that the *almany*, or ruler, of Futa Toro in northern Senegal, had passed a law forbidding the transportation of slaves through his territories and declared that all the riches in the world would not make him change his mind.

In Europe, Frenchmen could cite a royal declaration of 1571, forbidding the importation of slaves into France, and a legal dictum of 1607, not only confirming the freedom of all people in the kingdom but also declaring all slaves to be free as soon as they set foot on French soil and became baptized. In England, the reform movement began with Lord Mansfield's judgment of 1772, which declared that common law did not recognize the status of slave; in the United States, as many as 60,000 black men had managed to gain their freedom, and many more had taken up arms for freedom in the Caribbean.

There were several reasons for this attitude. Decent men everywhere had become surfeited with the bestial cruelties perpetrated in the interests of the slave trade. Furthermore, the Industrial Revolution was creating a need for a different kind of labor. Slave traders found themselves less and less influential in political circles because of an organized movement for the abolition of the slave trade.

A strong argument for a new policy was that legitimate trade with Africa in manufactured goods and other merchandise could profitably take the place of slave trade. European industrialists also began to look to Africa for primary products in their own manufacturing enterprises (for example, palm oil used in making soap). Thus, Africa became an important potential market and source of raw materials. Before long, there was bitter rivalry among European powers for this market and its primary products. So taken were Europeans by this idea that they supported three schemes to repatriate freed slaves to Africa in order that they would become a nucleus for such trade.

Following Justice Mansfield's decision, 15,000 destitute black people were set free in England. Abolitionists, among whom was an African and former slave, Olaudah Equiano, later renamed Gustavus Vassa, supported a scheme to repatriate these "Black Poor," as they were called. The Black Poor from England were joined by other black people from Canada, where promises of land made to black soldiers had not been fulfilled, and by blacks - the Maroons - from the West Indies. This movement resulted in the founding of Sierra Leone in 1787.

Another scheme originated in the United States, where the Back-to-Africa movement was supported by wealthy Afro-Americans like Paul Cuffee, who on his own financed voyages of black people returning to Africa. Other prominent white and black Americans sponsored the American Society for Colonizing the Free People of Color (more commonly the American Colonization Society), which led to the founding of Liberia in 1822. A third such settlement was Libreville in

Gabon, founded in 1849 under French auspices as a settlement for former slaves.

Europe's contact with Africa through the slave trade resulted in its becoming richer from the wealth generated by the slave labor of the millions upon millions of Africans who crossed the seas in chains. Africa, on the other hand, was impoverished by the loss of its manpower and material wealth. Internecine warfare, engendered by the slave trade, weakened or destroyed its once-proud armies. Its village industries disappeared. Only weakness and disunity remained.

European powers needed to know more about Africa - its geography, natural resources, and people - to trade effectively or stake their claims with any degree of accuracy. So, travelers and explorers, backed by organizations of varied interests and motives, went into the interior of Africa to augment the scanty and sketchy knowledge of the coast that had been provided by sailors and traders. Mungo Park, David Livingstone, Henry M. Stanley, Richard Burton, Heinrich Barth, John Speke, René Caillié, Paul Soleillet, and many others made remarkable journeys and "discoveries." As feats of endurance, these journeys *are* truly remarkable; but perhaps even more remarkable are their inflated claims, for how does one discover, as Livingstone is said to have done, something like the Victoria Falls, which millions and millions of other people have known for generations by the name Mosi-Oa-Tunya, meaning "smoke that thunders?"

The journeys had another merit to Europeans. They portrayed Africa as virgin land for the planting of Christianity (and some would give the word "planting" the meaning it has in detective stories). So, European missionaries went to Africa to preach the gospel. They wore out soles saving souls and found themselves not only agents of life through death but of peace through war, accord through discord, education through Westernization, civilization through dehumanization, construction through destruction. Europeans were soon persuaded that only by waging ruthless wars of conquest or pacification (as such wars are euphemistically called) could peace reign in Africa. Only through discord - inherent in the injection of Christianity and rejection of traditional African ideas of god - could accord be achieved. Only through keeping Africans ignorant of the good in their culture and of the greatness in their history by teaching them Western values and the superiority of Europeans could they be educated. Only through the abandonment of a culture based on humanistic family and tribal ties, responsibilities, and sanctions, and the imposition of a dehumanizing, individualistic, and materialistic culture, could Africans be civilized. Only through the total destruction of African ideas, values, and mores could a new Africa be built.

The possession of colonies in Africa was regarded by European powers as a means of acquiring national prestige, mollifying wounded national pride, and keeping the balance of power in Europe even. Indeed, it is essential to study European politics of this period in order to understand why certain countries in Africa became colonies of certain powers in Europe and why boundary lines were often drawn in such an arbitrary manner as to put people of identical ethnic backgrounds into different states or lump together people who had no natural political affinity in one state. Some of these boundaries, drawn in the nineteenth century and dictated primarily by events in Europe, are a source of friction today; indeed, many of Africa's present major problems can be traced to decisions made in Europe at this time.

Actual colonization was, as a rule, undertaken not by governments but by syndicates and chartered companies because they were better suited for the task. The legal fiction under which such companies operated was that they were not representatives of the governments from whom they derived their charters. Their actions therefore did not necessarily have the agreement and sanction of their governments. This fiction enabled chartered companies to rush in where governments feared to tread. They were financed privately, at no cost to the taxpayer; so, according to the fiction, governments could not scrutinize and control minute details of the companies' operations. In actual fact, governments could and did interfere with chartered companies. It suited governments, however, to appear powerless against them because chartered companies were useful tools. They could conveniently be repudiated when they failed to pull off a particularly audacious and reckless plot like the 1895 Jameson Raid, by which British fortune hunters sought to displace the Boer government of the Transvaal in South Africa. On the other hand, territory in which a company operated was invariably taken over by a European power and turned into a protectorate, colony, or overseas province, when convenient.

Often protectorates were proclaimed and colonies carved on the map of Africa on the basis of fraudulent treaties and bogus purchases of land from unsuspecting African rulers. There were also poorly demarcated spheres of influence in which a single European power sought to exercise exclusive trading rights. The cupidity, intrigue, cutthroat competition, and rivalry that characterized the activities of some unscrupulous agents of syndicates and chartered companies generated much friction, hatred, and animosity not only among Africans but also among the nations that licensed them. To bring about some sort of order, the Berlin West African Conference of 1884–1885 was called to lay down ground rules governing the staking of claims and carving of colonies in Africa.

Conferees, which included all the major powers in Europe, plus the USA and the Ottoman Empire, decided that any power wishing to claim a colony or protectorate in any part of Africa should formally notify the other signatories and back its claim with demonstrable effective authority in the area concerned. Contrary to British wishes, there was to be freedom of navigation along the Niger and Congo rivers. In spite of the conference's decision requiring the effective occupation of an area before a claim could be recognized, most claims to colonies in Africa continued to be, in fact, based on concessions and treaties of doubtful and questionable validity. The impressive point, however, is that European powers agreed to base their partition of Africa on a set of rules acceptable to them all, and thus avoided coming to blows.

With this accord in Europe, the age of colonialism began in Africa. Europeans no longer took Africans into slavery in far-off places, but took possession of the land itself. Whereas in 1880, more than 90 percent of the continent of Africa was ruled by Africans, by 1900, a mere twenty years later, only a tiny fraction - Ethiopia and Liberia - was ruled by Africans.

What was Africa's response to the Berlin conspiracy of 1884–1885? Was there also concerted action to meet the European threat to Africa? It is safe to say that Africans in general knew little about

Europe and even less about Berlin. The days when radio, television, and jumbo jets would facilitate the formation of an Organization of African Unity were still far away. Yet, in spite of the social dislocations, in spite of the weakness of African armies, in spite of the inability of African rulers to consult, plan, and agree on a common strategy, the Africans continued to resist. They stood up and fought. Uncoordinated and inadequately armed though they were, Africans took up arms all over the continent. Let us look at these wars more closely. Let us scrutinize, one by one, the attempts of each European power to colonize Africa and see how Africans reacted.

Portugal was the first European power that tried to colonize Africa. It was the first to be resisted. When in 1556, a vassal of the king of the Congo, the *ngola* of Ndongo (or Angola), expected to be attacked by his overlord, he appealed to the Portuguese king for help. The Portuguese king responded by sending an expedition under the command of Paulo Dias de Novais, a grandson of the explorer Bartolomeu Dias. By the time the expedition arrived in Ndongo, however, the people had already fought and defeated the Congo army sent against them and declared their independence. Furthermore, the *ngola* who had requested Portugal's help had died. Succeeding him on the throne was Ngola Mbandi, who received Dias with great politeness, but compelled him to assist the Ndongo army in several local wars in which the Portuguese were not interested.

Paulo Dias was eventually allowed to return to Portugal, after which Sebastião, the king of Portugal, decided to undertake the military conquest of the Ndongo kingdom. Ndongo was divided into two colonies: One part, bounded on the west by the Atlantic, on the north by the Congo, and on the south by the Cuanza River, was to belong to the king; the other area, south of the Cuanza, was to belong to Paulo Dias and his descendants. Dias was to govern the king's as well as his own portion.

Dias returned to Angola in 1574 with the title "Conqueror, Colonizer, and Governor General of Angola." He took with him seven ships carrying 700 men. It was four years before the first skirmish with Africans took place. By that time, Africans no doubt knew what the Portuguese were up to. In 1578, they engaged a detachment of eighty Portuguese soldiers, killed twenty, took the rest prisoner, and freed them only after they had been ransomed. Having been warned that Dias was advancing with a strong army to fight him, Ngola Mbandi condemned to death the Portuguese traders at his court, confiscated their goods, and enticed the Portuguese soldiers into combat in the interior. There he massacred 500 of them and then attacked their fort at Nzele, thirty miles from their principal port at Luanda.

It was not until 1580 that Dias was able to march against Ngola Mbandi once more. This time, he first raided several independent African kingdoms, recruiting their men to fight on his side against the army of the *ngola*. Meanwhile, another Congo force was marching against Mbandi. The *ngola* was able to drive off this second threat, but when he met Dias at Massangano, his fatigued army was defeated. However, the Portuguese had not yet won conclusively. One of their detachments, comprising at least 100 men, was not long after completely routed by another African chief. At his death in 1589, fifteen years after he had set out as "Conquerer, Colonizer, and Governor General of Angola," Paulo Dias had not conquered, colonized, or governed the people of Angola.

Portuguese activity as slavers and would-be colonizers appears to have solidified African resistance, for in 1590, the *ngola* entered into an alliance with his former enemy, the king of the Congo, and with other neighboring kingdoms. That year, the African alliance defeated a Portuguese expedition, forcing it to retreat with heavy losses to Massangano. In 1594, another African force, under the command of chief Kafuche Kambara, ambushed and massacred a Portuguese force at Kissama. As long as the alliance held, the Portuguese made no progress toward colonizing Angola. But the alliance broke up about 1600, and the Portuguese gained the advantage.

In 1612, the *ngola* of Ndongo sent his sister Nzinga Mbandi to Luanda to negotiate a peace treaty with the Portuguese. When the Portuguese governor of Luanda would not give her a chair, she called forth one of her attendants, instructed him to get down on his hands and knees, and sat on him. Although the Portuguese agreed to recognize Ndongo as an independent kingdom, they reneged on other agreements. When sometime later the *ngola* died and was succeeded by Nzinga, who immediately renounced Christianity, the Portuguese sought to depose her and install a puppet. War broke out. Nzinga organized another African alliance, and for over thirty years, until her death in 1663, she valiantly warred against the Portuguese.

When the Dutch captured Luanda in 1641, the Portuguese found themselves fighting on two fronts. In 1643, 200 of their soldiers were captured by an African force, and an army sent to retrieve them was routed. Before his death, Ngola Kanini of Matamba defeated a Portuguese army at Katole. Long after, in 1872, another war of resistance to the Portuguese broke out in the Dembo region northwest of Luanda.

Farther south, a similar history unfolded. The Mbundu kingdoms of Huambo, Tchiyaka, Bailundo, Ndulu, Bié, and Kakonda resisted Portuguese slavers and colonizers. As early as 1660, Kapango, king of Tchiyaka, prevented the advance of a Portuguese expedition into the interior. In 1718, an African alliance inspired by Kapango's example attacked a Portuguese fortress at Kakonda, forcing them to withdraw from that area. In 1896, Numa, king of Bailundo, died while leading an attack on a Portuguese fort, and in 1902, his successor, Mutu-ya-Kevela, led another attack in an attempt to recover land occupied by Europeans.

In the kingdom of Huíla, Africans launched a series of ten wars, the Nano Wars, resisting Portuguese rule throughout the greater part of the nineteenth century. In the Humbe kingdom, there was an uprising against the Portuguese in 1858 that resulted in a temporary withdrawal of the Portuguese from that kingdom. Resistance continued intermittently until the turn of the century when a Portuguese army was massacred. In 1904, another Portuguese army was ambushed, and 300 of its soldiers were killed. Resistance in Humbe continued until 1915. Between 1874 and 1916, the Congo region in the north fought eight wars against the Portuguese. In the 1950s, resistance to Portuguese colonialism in Angola broke out again, and in 1975, it finally became an independent country.

Along the Atlantic coast of West Africa, in the region now known as Guinea-Bisseau, the indigenous peoples also challenged the foreign presence as early as 1679. In that year, the African chiefs of Mata and Mompataz unsuccessfully resisted Portuguese domination of the region around the Cacheu estuary. In 1697, the Papel people under Chief Incinhate and the Mandingos again took up arms against Portuguese rule and tried to expel them from the settlement at Farim. These wars persisted throughout the eighteenth century, compelling the Portuguese to maintain a military force for the protection of the European population. In 1753, the people, led by Chief Palance, interfered with Portuguese attempts to rebuild their fort in Bissau, killing nine men.

In 1824, 1842, 1844, and 1846 there were further Papel uprisings against Portuguese rule in Bissau. The last one was supported by the Mandingos, who again attacked Farim. Africans attacked Geba in 1865, assassinated the governor of Bissau in 1871, and massacred a Portuguese military force near the Bolor River in 1879.

That same year, the Portuguese separated the governance of Guinea from the Cape Verde Islands, creating two colonies. This new policy was aimed at undermining African resistance to its rule through the encouragement of intertribal rivalry. This time-honored colonialist device paid dividends when in 1880, one of the Fulani peoples under Mamadu Pate attacked a Portuguese military post at Buba. Their example was followed a year later by Chief Bacar Guidali of Forrea. One hundred Portuguese soldiers, supported by hundreds of

Mandingos, Fula-Preto (another Fulani group), and Beafada marched against the insurgents in 1881. The Portuguese failed to subdue Bacar Guidali but succeeded in turning Mamadu Pate against him, with the result that Bacar Guidali was defeated by his former ally on behalf of the Portuguese.

In 1882, the Portuguese fought the Beafada at Jabada, and in the following year, they attacked the Balanta. In 1884, a Portuguese military force that had been sent to Kakonda was ambushed by Felupe, and its gunboat seized. Two years later, another Portuguese army was forced to retreat to Bijante after suffering heavy casualties. The policy of divide and rule stood the Portuguese in good stead, however, when they were challenged in 1886 by Musa Molo. Leading the Fula-Preto, this Fulani chieftain succeeded in taking large areas around Buba and south of the Gambia River. He harassed the Portuguese at Geba and cut communications between that settlement and Bissau by attacking river boats and supply trains. However, the Fula-Preto were forced to desist and retreat when 4,000 Fulani and hundreds of Mandingos and Beafada came to Portugal's assistance.

In 1889, the Portuguese were compelled once more to take the field against the Fula-Preto, Mandingos, and Beafada, and the following year, they devastated many villages in a four-month campaign against Moli Boia, while Mamadu Pate and Musa Molo resumed their attacks on Buba and Farim. Throughout 1891 and 1892, the Portuguese in Bissau were in a state of siege. In April 1891, Africans destroyed a Portuguese force at Intim and killed forty-seven Portuguese officers and men near Bissau in May 1891.

In December 1893, over 3,000 Papel and Balanta tribesmen attacked a Portuguese fortress at Pijiguiti. Later, they attacked Bissau. In response, the Portuguese conducted two military operations: one against the Manjaco and the other against the Balanta and Mandingos. The Portuguese had as allies more than 3,000 Africans under the combined command of Mamadu Pate and the Beafada chief of Cuor, Infali Sonco. But these allies later turned against the Portuguese, causing them to retreat with heavy casualties.

By 1901, the Portuguese were in a position to resume military operations. In 1904, an expedition against the Manjaco in the Farim district met with disaster when more than 400 Portuguese soldiers were killed. Infali Sonco harassed the Portuguese on the Geba River, successfully preventing any commercial intercourse between Bissau on the estuary and Bafatá upriver. The Felupe at Varela, the Balanta at Gole, and the Papel people near Bissau continued their resistance. In 1907, the Portuguese were compelled to mount a major military campaign against African resistance to their rule, plundering and burning many villages. The Papel responded by attacking Bissau. Near the end of the year, the Portuguese were ravaging Balanta villages in Gole; the Africans retaliated by attacking the Portuguese military post. The Balanta were driven off after Abdul Injai, a Fulani, joined the Portuguese against them.

In 1912, the Portuguese appointed João Teixeira Pinto commander of forces in Guinea. In March 1913, with Abdul Injai and several hundred Africans on his side, Pinto was attacked by the Balanta and Mandingos. By June, he had occupied Mansôa and Mansaba. From January to April 1914, Pinto campaigned against the Papel and Manjaco peoples in the Cacheu region. From May to July, he marched against the Balanta in Mansôa, and sought revenge against the Papel, who had earlier attacked Bissau, killing eighty-eight Portuguese. Abdul Injai was rewarded for his services to the Portuguese with appointment as chief of Oio, but before long, he turned against the Portuguese, who were compelled to mount a campaign against him. The insurgent was exiled from the country.

This was not the end of African resistance to Portuguese colonialism in Guinea. In March 1917, a state of siege was declared in the Bijagós archipelago, and in July troops were sent to Nhambalam. In 1918 troops were sent to Baiote. There was trouble at Canhabague in 1925; at

Bissau in 1931; and again in Canhabague in 1936. Resistance continued until independence was gained in the 1970s.

In Mozambique (or Portuguese East Africa), the colonial government was never without its challengers. In July 1572, Francesco Barreto set out from Sena to conquer the kingdom of Monomotapa. Barreto commanded an army of 800 Europeans and 2,000 Africans. Along the Ruwenya River, toward Mount Fura, the Portuguese expedition came across the main village of the Mongaze people. They fired a few rounds and dispossessed the people of their village. For three days, they remained in the village, experiencing only minor attempts on the part of the Mongaze to regain their homes.

At dawn on the fourth day, however, Francesco de Sousa reported that there came "like a great dust storm with loud clamor, the Mongaze army: Some sixteen thousand men with great intrepidity and noise of drums." The army was led by a doctor carrying spells in a gourd to assure victory. A cloud of arrows and spears flew toward the Portuguese, who responded with a volley of musketry and a barrage of cannonballs. The doctor and 4,000 Mongaze men were killed. The Portuguese lost forty men in the battle.

Although Barreto and his army were decimated by fever before they got to Zimbabwe, Monomotapa's capital, news of their victory over the Mongaze impressed the kingdom's ruler. Chisa Mharu Nogomo, who had problems with his vassals, decided to come to terms with the Portuguese and secure his position on the throne. In 1575, Vasco Fernandes Homem, taking another route, led an expedition of 412 Portuguese soldiers to Zimbabwe. He met only minor resistance. On the throne of Monomotapa now sat Gatsi Rusere, who honored his predecessor's agreement with the Portuguese. However, Gatsi Rusere was succeeded by Nyambo Kapararidze, who was openly hostile to the Portuguese and forced them to retire. Africans were, once more, resisting foreign domination. His army was defeated by the Portuguese in 1628, and Kapararidze's nephew, Mavura Mhande, who was friendly to the Portuguese, was installed as ruler.

At his death, another puppet was appointed; but in 1693, one of his vassals, Changamire, raised an insurrection and routed the *monomotapa*'s army. Changamire then attacked and destroyed a number of Portuguese settlements, including Dambarare. This ended Portuguese political influence beyond the borders of Mozambique.

The Portuguese position in East Africa was once again seriously shaken in the nineteenth century when Nyande, or Joaquin José da Cruz, a half-caste, organized an insurgent force and established inland headquarters at Massangena in the southern region of Mozambique. In 1853, his son Bonga destroyed the colonial post at Tete, and a Portuguese expedition, sent some sixteen years later to regain control of the area, only resulted in Bonga's gaining a still larger territory. When Bonga died in 1885, his brother succeeded him but was captured three years later.

The Shangana, a Nguni people, also challenged the Portuguese in Mozambique. At the port city of Lourenço Marques near the southern frontier, the followers of Soshangana besieged the Portuguese fortress and massacred its garrison. The Shangana also attacked Inhambane in 1834 and Sofala in 1836. They overran Portuguese *prazos*, or estates, south of the Zambezi and occupied Sena. When Soshangana died, however, there were two claimants to his throne. Mahueva, the legitimate successor, was, like his father, opposed to the Portuguese. He lost to Mzila, who maintained official relations with the Portuguese while continuing to demand tribute from them and to raid their settlements. Mzila was succeeded by Gungunyana. He cooperated with both the Portuguese and the British, whose South Africa Company, under the direction of Cecil Rhodes, was eyeing the southern portion of Mozambique.

Wars of resistance also broke out in the eastern Sudan. This ancient land of Kush had in 1805 come under Turko-Egyptian rule. Although the Sudan remained under the official administration of the Egyptian khedive, it came increasingly under the influence and control of the British government.

In 1882, the Anglo-Egyptian consortium suffered a major upset when a Sudanese spiritual leader, Muhammad Ahmad, declared himself the Mahdi, or messiah, and urged his countrymen to rise against the forces of evil. Muhammad Ahmad called for no less than a holy war against the Egyptian government. Before long, the holy war became for the Sudanese people a war of liberation from colonialism, injustice, and economic exploitation.

The British government had strived to avoid active involvement. Its efforts were, however, doomed to failure since the Egyptian government was virtually its puppet, obliged to accept British advice on all matters of importance in exchange for British military protection. Thus, it was only a matter of time before Queen Victoria's agents were actively involved in suppressing Sudanese resistance. To the Sudanese Africans, however, the issue remained always simple and crystal clear; resistance was seen as a duty inspired and sanctioned by their religion. Its success was believed to be ordained by Allah and assured through the appearance among them of the expected Mahdi.

Soon after Muhammad Ahmad had declared himself the Mahdi, the Egyptian government sent the assistant governor-general of the Sudan, Muhammad Bey Abu al-Saud, to talk him into abandoning his claim. When this failed, the government dispatched two companies of regular troops to Aba Island in the Nile, where Muhammad Ahmad and about 200 of his supporters, including members of the militant dervish sect, were gathered.

Muhammad Ahmad offered his followers the choice of either freely joining him in his holy war or returning to their homes. His followers unanimously swore allegiance to his cause and leadership, whereupon he armed them with swords, spears, and sticks. Then, while awaiting the arrival of the army, he trained them in the rudiments of defense and attack.

One night during the fasting month of Ramadan, while Muhammad Ahmad and his followers were performing their prayers, news reached him that the Nile steamer carrying government troops sent to capture him had arrived in the neighboring city of El Fashashuyah.

The government soldiers disembarked on Aba Island at 3:00 a.m. and, ignoring instructions to send the local *qadi* to parley with the Mahdi, marched straight to the village. Meeting a villager, they asked him to point out the Mahdi's house. The villager said he did not know. There followed an altercation during which one of the soldiers fired a gun, whereupon the Mahdi's followers, armed only with their primitive weapons, fell upon the soldiers, killing 126 of them, including six officers. The rest of the soldiers ran away and took refuge aboard the steamer that had brought them. The following day, the twelfth of August 1881, the Mahdi's dervishes completely defeated the government force at the battle of Aba, giving the Mahdi his first great victory.

Emulating the Prophet's flight to Medina, the Mahdi left Aba Island, scene of his first victory, and trekked westward with his followers to Qadir Mountain in the Nuba hills of Kordofan. This was territory inhabited by people who had never completely submitted to government authority.

Hoping that local jealousies and dissension would disintegrate the Mahdi's movement, causing it to collapse of itself, the government decided to take no further military action against the Mahdi. But Rashid, the governor of Fashoda (modern Kodok in southeast Sudan), ignoring instructions, set out against the Mahdi with 350 soldiers, seventy irregulars, and 1,000 Shilluk tribesmen under the leadership of their chief, Kaikun Bey. Rashid's plan was to surprise the Mahdi, so he compelled his men to march long hours; utterly exhausting them. But the Mahdi was not to be taken by surprise. A Qadir chief warned him by lighting large fires on top of a mountain, and a Kinanah woman walked the whole night to report that she had seen the soldiers. It was Rashid who was surprised. The Mahdi laid an ambush for him and completely annihilated Rashid's exhausted force. Only a few Shilluk escaped to tell the tale. The Mahdi had won another great victory, and rumors crediting him with invincibility and the ability to turn bullets into water were related in the Sudan. New adherents flocked to the Mahdi's lair at Qadir.

A new governor-general was appointed to the Sudan. While awaiting his arrival, however, the acting governor-general, a German known as Geigler Pasha, grossly underrated the Mahdi's strength. He reversed the wait-and-see policy of his predecessor and decided to restore law and order in the Sudan by striking the Mahdi's stronghold with a force of some 3,500 men under the command of Yusuf Pasha al-Shallali.

Geigler Pasha also sent Yusuf Agha al-Malik with fifty soldiers and some officers to the eastern bank of the Blue Nile, where Sherif Ahmad Taha, who claimed to be a descendant of the Prophet, was about to declare his allegiance to the Mahdi. Al-Malik met with disaster. All his officers and most of his soldiers were slain. When he saw that all was lost, rather than be disgraced, Al-Malik calmly sat on his sheepskin and ordered his slave to kill him. In May 1882, Geigler ordered another attack on Sherif Ahmad Taha. Sherif Ahmad Taha was once more victorious, killing 210 officers and men. Reinforced by Awad al-Karim's Shukria tribesmen, Geigler again attacked Sherif Ahmad Taha the following day and completely defeated him.

Meanwhile, the government force sent to Qadir

under the command of Al-Shallali traveled via Fashoda, making a long halt at Funqur, where Taifarah, a local chief, reneged on an earlier agreement with the Mahdi and handed over the latter's spies to Al-Shallali. The spies were cruelly and slowly put to death by having their limbs severed, one after another, before a crowd of spectators. But the fortitude with which they met their death, uttering defiance to the executioners and professing a profound conviction in the divine mission of the Mahdi, demoralized the troops. They concluded that the Mahdi must really have supernatural powers if he could make men face death as these spies had done. On June 6, 1882, Al-Shallali's force arrived in the vicinity of the Qadir, fatigued and morally depressed. They hardly had strength to construct a *zaribah* (a thorny enclosure) before falling asleep. At dawn, the Mahdi's men attacked and annihilated them in spite of a heroic stand. The wife of one of the slain leaders of the government forces gallantly beat the war drum to rally her husband's troops. The Mahdi had scored another brilliant victory, and again rumor had it that supernatural forces were working in concert with him. It was said that a mysterious fire had consumed the bodies of the soldiers and had left the Mahdi's name clearly written on eggshells and the leaves of trees.

When the new governor-general, Abd al-Qadir Pasha, took his appointment, he first made

overtures of peace to the Mahdi. Failing in this,
he plotted to assassinate the Madhi by sending
him a gift of poisoned dates purportedly from
an adherent, dispatching a parcel containing
dynamite, and hiring two men to murder him.
When these attempts failed also, Al-Qadir directed
the mufti, Sudan's chief judge of Muslim law, and
other learned men to engage in a propaganda war
against the Mahdi, while soldiers to fight him were
being recruited and trained.

The Mahdi was also changing his course. He
decided to abandon the purely defensive policy
he had hitherto pursued. In the two months after
the annihilation of Al-Shallali's expedition, he sent
troops to attack government garrisons in Kordofan.
One by one, these fell and were occupied by the
Mahdi's men; only Kordofan's provincial capital
at El Obeid and the nearby city of Bara remained.
In August 1882, the Mahdi's troops began their
march against El Obeid, and in September 1882,
the Mahdi sent messengers to the garrison, urging
it to surrender. Authorities of El Obeid arrested the
messengers and hanged them. As a result, many
citizens went over to the Mahdi.

Thirty thousand warriors then rushed El Obeid,
as Father Joseph Ohrwalder, who spent ten years
as a captive in the Mahdi's camp, described in his
memoirs:

> The first ditch was soon crossed, and then

the Mahdists spread out and completely encircled the town; masses of wild fanatics rolled like waves through the deserted streets; they did not advance through these alone, but hurrying on from house to house, wall to wall, and yard to yard, they reached the ditch of the Mudirieh, and like a torrent suddenly let loose, regardless of every obstacle, with wild shouts they dashed across it and up the ramparts, from which the din of a thousand rifles and the booming of the guns suddenly burst forth; but these wild hordes, utterly fearless of death, cared neither for the deadly Remington nor the thunder of the guns, and still swept forward in ever-increasing numbers.

The poor garrison, utterly powerless to resist such an assault, ran to the tops of the houses and kept up an incessant fire on the masses, which now formed such a crowd that they could scarcely move - indeed the barrels of the rifles from the rapidity of the fire became almost red-hot; and soon the streets and open spaces became literally choked with the bodies of those who had fallen. . . . It was impossible not to admire the reckless bravery of these fanatics who, dancing and shouting, rushed up to the very muzzles of the rifles with nothing but the knotty stick in their hands, only to fall dead one over the other. Numbers of them carried large bundles of Dhurra stalks, which they threw into the ditch, hoping to fill it up and then cross over.

The Mahdi lost about 10,000 men and decided to change his tactics. He surrounded El Obeid and Bara. Before long the besieged inhabitants were short of food and plagued by disease. A government relief expedition under Ali Bey Lufti was attacked and completely destroyed by the Mahdi's men. Over 1,127 of its men were killed. Bara surrendered on the fifth and El Obeid on the seventeenth of January 1883. Large stores of military equipment, rifles, guns, and ammunition fell into the Mahdi's hands.

A new governor-general, Ala al-Din, was appointed, and a new army under the command of William Hicks, a British officer, was sent to reconquer El Obeid. The Mahdi let his army - 7,000 infantry, 500 cavalry, 400 *bashbazuks*, or mounted Turkish irregulars, with ten mounted guns, 100 cuirassiers, 2,000 camp followers, and 5,500 transport camels - wear itself out marching. The insurgents cut its line of retreat, constantly harassed it as it came nearer, and then in November 1883, attacked and overwhelmed it.

It was at this point that the British government, believing that the Sudan could not be held against the Mahdi, exerted pressure on the Egyptian government to abandon it and evacuate the capital at Khartoum. In response to public demand, the British government also returned General Charles George "Chinese" Gordon, Britain's hero of campaigns in China and Anglo-Egyptian North Africa and former governor of the Sudan. He was instructed to ascertain the best means of evacuating Egyptian forces from the Sudan. Instead, Gordon tried to hold Khartoum against the Mahdi. The Mahdi delayed attacking the city in the hope that it would surrender without bloodshed.

When in the fall of 1884, a British relief column under the command of Sir Herbert Stewart started for Khartoum, the Mahdi was compelled to take action. He dispatched a strong force to meet Stewart's troops and prepared to assault the capital. Near the Abu Tlaih wells, where the relief column had camped for the night, they encountered the Mahdi forces. Early the following morning, the Mahdi forces opened fire on the British force as breakfast was being served. Stewart decided to take the offensive and ordered the column to march in square formation. As it marched, the column was subjected to heavy fire and frequently came to a halt in order to enable the rear to catch up. At one such halt, Stewart's men were amazed to see a large mounted force of the Mahdi's men emerge from a nearby ravine in which they had been hiding and advance upon them in close formation. In spite of accurate fire from the relief column's Martini-Henry rifles, the Mahdi's army advanced to within eighty yards; then the fire began to take its toll and dead bodies fell one upon another in huge piles. Those still alive veered to the right and attacked the rear of the column, penetrating the square at several points. Sir Charles Wilson, who took over command of the column when Sir Herbert Stewart was wounded, later wrote: "I remember thinking, by Jove, they will be into the square! and almost the next moment I saw a fine old Shaikh on horse back plant his banner in the center of the square, behind the camels. He was at once shot down falling on his banner. He turned out to be Musa, Amir of Dighaim Arabs, from Kurdufan. I had noticed him in the advance, with his banner in one hand and a book of prayers in the other, and never saw anything finer. The old man never swerved to the right or left, and never ceased chanting his prayers until he had planted his banner in our square. If any man deserved a place in the Moslem paradise he did."

The relief column closed the gaps and killed all who had penetrated the square. The rest of the Mahdi's forces recreated. The British column made it to the river near Metemma, where its wounded and most of its able-bodied men were left in fortified positions while Wilson, with British and African troops, embarked in late January 1885, on steamers for Khartoum. Khartoum, which had been under siege for over a year by a force of up to 100,000 men, was beginning to show the strain. There were famine and disease in the town. The low water level of the Nile at that time of the year made breaching the town's fortifications possible. The Mahdi tried to persuade General Gordon to surrender, even offering him a safe-conduct to the British column. Gordon was defiant and determined to fight.

On January 26, the Mahdi forces launched their attack on Khartoum. The fortifications yielded in the first assault and great slaughter followed. General Gordon was killed, and Khartoum captured. The fall of Khartoum had a profound effect in England. Queen Victoria told her ministers that earlier action by them might have prevented the catastrophe and saved many precious lives. After this, it became a matter of Britain's national honor to suppress the Mahdiyya, the Mahdi's resistance movement.

However, on June 22, 1895, the Mahdi died. At his death, his resistance movement had liberated from foreign rule most of Muslim Sudan. He was succeeded by Abdullahi, Khalifa al-Mahdi. But the new leader's position was shaky, for he could not cope with the military might of England. In 1897, at the battle of Atbara (some 200 miles downriver from Khartoum) and in 1898, at Omdurman (opposite Khartoum), British and Egyptian regiments under Sir Horatio Herbert Kitchener finally shattered the Khalifa al-Mahdi's power. The Khalifa himself lost his life on the field of battle at Om Dubreikat on November 25, 1899. Despite the Sudan's prolonged bid for independence, the Anglo-Egyptian Sudan had come into existence.

Resistance continued. Among the Dinka people living between the White Nile and the Sobat River, there was strong opposition to the new order. In 1904, the British were compelled to send an expedition against the Nyima tribes of the western Bahr-el-Ghazal. In 1908, a Halawi tribesman in Sennar declared himself to be Jesus Christ come to expel Europeans from the Sudan. He was hanged by the British. And during 1911 and 1912, two expeditions were sent against the Annak on the Sobat River.

Between 1899 and 1904, and again between 1908 and 1910, Muhammad ibn Abdallah, sometimes called quite wrongly the Mad Mullah, organized resistance to colonial rule in British Somaliland, that portion of the Horn which Britain had administered as a protectorate since 1884. An army of 7,000 men, raised at a cost of over £2 million, was sent against him. After more than one disaster had befallen British troops, however, it was decided to leave the interior of British Somaliland alone and to confine British occupation to the coastal towns along the Gulf of Aden.

South of Anglo-Egyptian Sudan, in the territory of modern-day Uganda, Mwanga, the *kabaka*, or king, of Buganda, and Kabarenga, the king of Bunyoro, responded in 1898 to the rivalries of Europe's empire builders by attempting to massacre British officers and missionaries. For over a year, the British were kept at bay until Captain John Evatt and a detachment of Sikh soldiers from British India captured the African kings in 1899.

In Zanzibar, where in 1890 the sultanate had been placed under British protection and the administration of the islands of Zanzibar and Pemba conducted by English ministers, a palace revolt occurred in 1896 on the occasion of the death of Sultan Hamid bin Thwain. It was really a premature outbreak of resistance to British occupation.

Along that part of the East African coast under German "protection" - roughly the area later designated as Tanganyika - between the Tana and Odzi rivers, African resistance to foreign rule resulted in a British naval expedition under Admiral Edmund Fremantle being sent to the area in 1890. Southwest of Mombasa, Sir Arthur Hardinge was compelled, on assuming control of British East Africa, to fight a long war of skirmishes, ambushes, and raids of resistance until 1896. Kikuyu warriors attacked British settlers and big game hunters in Kenya.

In southern Africa, the earliest resistance to European encroachment on African land rights was in 1659 when Hottentot clans that had always grazed their cattle in the Cape Peninsula were ordered by the Dutch to keep away. Although there was plenty of grazing land to which they could have taken their cattle, they insisted on their right to graze their cattle where they liked. So, the first Hottentot-Dutch war broke out. The Hottentots avoided a pitched battle, and the Europeans were unable to surprise any sizable body of them or inflict a large number of casualties.

The second Hottentot-Dutch war was sparked in 1673 by the Europeans' destruction of too much game on land under the Hottentot king Gonnema. Although Hottentot tribes hostile to him joined the Dutch, Gonnema and his people held on in the mountains until both sides desired peace.

In 1779, the Dutch fought their first war against the Bantu-speaking Xhosa, who resisted attempts to remove them from lands west of the Great Fish River. Ten years later, the Xhosa reoccupied large areas west of this river. The Dutch tried to expel them, and so the second Xhosa-Dutch war was fought. As the Xhosa proved more than able to hold their own, the Dutch finally agreed to make peace with them.

In 1795, the Cape came under British rule. Four years later, Ndlambe, who had been Xhosa's regent during the minority of his nephew Gaika, was forced to hand over power to the younger man. Ndlambe escaped, crossed the Great Fish River, and immediately won the allegiance of most clans between the Great Fish and the Kowie rivers. White people in these areas took their cattle and fled. In a few days, Ndlambe was master of the entire Zuurveld east of the Sunday River.

Ndlambe's forces attacked a British party on its way to Algoa Bay, under the command of General John Ormsby Vandeleur. The Europeans beat them off and then fell back to form a camp so that an approaching patrol of twenty men could join them. But the Xhosa surrounded the patrol and killed all but four of its members. Then they turned to the camp, rushing it with spear shafts broken so short that they could be used as assagais for stabbing. The charges were met with such a volley of musket balls and grapeshot that the Xhosa were forced to retire. General Vandeleur made it to Algoa Bay, sent some of his soldiers back to Cape Town by sea, and ordered burgher commandos to expel the Xhosa. Some Hottentots joined the Xhosa and overran the area. Twenty-nine white people were killed. Once more, Africans had resisted attempts by Europeans to run them off their land.

In 1811, a strong body of European soldiers and a Hottentot regiment were sent to force Ndlambe and his men to abandon the lands they occupied. In a parley with Major Jacob Cuyler, Ndlambe told him, stamping his foot on the ground: "This country is mine; I won it in war, and intend to keep it." Then, shaking an assagai with one hand, he raised a horn to his mouth and signaled his forces, concealed in the thicket, whereupon 300 men rushed on the British party, which escaped solely because of the fleetness of their horses. Soon after this, the *landdrost,* meaning governor, of Graaff-Reinet, and eight farmers were killed by the Xhosa. In 1812, six Hottentot units, with European soldiers in the rear, attacked the Xhosa and succeeded in forcing them northeast across the Great Fish River.

This was by no means the end of Ndlambe. Several chiefs, including an influential seer named Makana, defected from Gaika and joined him. In the ensuing war between the uncle and nephew, Gaika lost and appealed to the white men for help. Believing Ndlambe to be a much more determined and dangerous enemy, Lord Charles Somerset, governor of the Cape Colony, in 1818 sent European troops to fight side by side with Gaika's men against Ndlambe, who was believed to have 18,000 men under arms. Ndlambe's men took shelter in the dense thickets, but their villages were destroyed and 23,000 of their cattle taken.

When the British soldiers withdrew, Ndlambe fell on Gaika and put him to flight. Then he attacked Europeans between the Great Fish and Sunday rivers. A burgher force was called out, but before it could take the field, the British settlement at Grahamstown was attacked on April 22, 1819, by 10,000 warriors led by Ndlambe's ally, Makana.

It was three months later that a strong army of

colonists succeeded in driving Ndlambe's warriors northeastward to the Kei River, slaughtering many and burning their kraals, or villages. Makana gave himself up so that his friends could be spared. He was imprisoned on Robben Island off Cape Town, where he died three years later while trying to escape. As a buffer against further trouble, the colonial government placed Gaika's people between the Cape Colony and Ndlambe. Ndlambe died, and his sons quarreled for the throne. Gaika also died, leaving Sandile, then a child, as heir; Makoma, his half brother, was named regent. Ndlambe's sons allied themselves with Makoma to win his support.

When in 1834, European soldiers near Fort Beaufort wounded a Xhosa chief and took cattle belonging to Tyali, another of Gaika's sons, the Xhosa regarded this act as a declaration of war. About 20,000 warriors rushed into the Cape Colony, seized all the cattle east of the Sunday River, burned houses, and killed every white man they found. Knowing that a white commando force would follow, they herded the cattle across the Kei River to the territory of another Xhosa king, Hintsa, before retiring to their mountain strongholds. Hintsa, seeking to avoid further trouble with the Europeans, agreed to give up the cattle, but was treacherously shot dead by a colonist while en route to carry out the terms. Kreli, his son, succeeded him; he undertook to restore the cattle and concluded a peace treaty with the Europeans, but African resistance was by no means over.

In 1846, a Xhosa man accused of stealing an axe at Fort Beaufort was arrested by white constables. While being taken to a magistrate's court for trial, his compatriots swooped down on the police patrol, overpowering it. They killed a Hottentot policeman and released the prisoner. The Europeans applied to Sandile for extradition of the alleged offenders. Sandile ignored the request. Thus began the War of the Axe. A military force was then ordered to occupy Sandile's kraal. A long wagon train carrying provisions, tents, baggage, and ammunition followed the military force. Xhosa warriors ambushed the wagon train and captured it. The military force was compelled to retreat. Xhosa warriors then took the field and in the area surrounding the town of Uitenhage, burned Europeans' houses, killed all Europeans who could not escape, and seized the cattle. The Tembu people joined the Xhosa and devastated European settlements north of Winterberg. Another wagon train, on its way from Grahamstown to a frontier garrison with supplies of food and ammunition, was ambushed, and the supplies fell into Xhosa hands. It was a long time before the colonists could organize themselves and induce Sandile to submit to their rule.

In 1850, war broke out again. Sir Harry Smith,

then governor of the Cape, received several reports that the Xhosa were preparing for war. He called a meeting of African chiefs and kings, but the most important figure, Sandile, did not show up. Sir Harry Smith then ordered Sandile, who was known to be in the forests at the headwaters of the Keiskama River, to be arrested. On their way to arrest the Xhosa king, the European troops were attacked by warriors at Boomah. Twenty-three Europeans were killed and many wounded. A few hours later, in another part of the country, a patrol of fifteen European soldiers was completely wiped out by Sandile's warriors, and on Christmas day of that year, Xhosa warriors surprised European settlements near Auckland and Woburn, killing forty-six men and burning down houses. European settlements along the frontier districts were devastated once more. Again, the Tembu tribe joined the uprising, and even the Hottentot regiments under colonial arms deserted the Europeans and joined their fellow Africans. This became the longest and, to Europeans, the most costly war in South Africa. The steamship *Birkenhead*, proceeding from Ireland and carrying among its passengers 400 reinforcements, struck a rock off Danger Point, a few miles beyond the Cape of Good Hope. Women, children, and the sick were put into boats; but the soldiers perished in the shark-infested sea.

Not until their food supplies began to run low

did Africans pretend to submit to European rule; hostilities ended, but resistance to European colonialism remained in their hearts and minds. To some of them, it became such an obsession that it led to a terrible tragedy. In May 1856, a girl named Nongqawuse returned from drawing water at a little stream not far from her village and said she had seen men who differed greatly in appearance from the men she was accustomed to seeing there. Umhlakaza, her uncle, went to the stream and found the strangers where his niece had indicated. The strangers told Umhlakaza to return home, perform certain rituals, sacrifice an ox to the spirits of the dead, and then return to them on the fourth day.

Since there was in their appearance something that commanded obedience, Umhlakaza did as he had been told and returned to the stream on the fourth day. The strange people were there as before, and to his astonishment, he recognized among them his brother, who had been dead for many years. It was then he learned that the strange men were the eternal enemies of white men who had come from battlefields beyond the sea; they would with their invincible power assist the Xhosa in driving the Europeans from the land. He, Umhlakaza, was to be the medium between the kings and chiefs of the land and the strange men. Their first message to the kings, chiefs, and people was to abandon the practice of witchcraft and to kill fat cattle and eat them. One of the kings of the land,

Kreli, son of Hintsa, received the message with joy and immediately commanded that the spirits be obeyed throughout his land, and the best cattle be killed and eaten. King Sandile hesitated.

Nongqawuse again went to the river, and in the presence of a multitude of people, strange unearthly sounds beneath her feet were heard. All averred that they were voices of the spirits holding council over the affairs of men. People were ordered to slay and eat more cattle, and more cattle, and more cattle.

King Sandile joined the believers when his brother told him that he had himself seen and conversed with the spirits of two of his father's dead councilors and that they had commanded Sandile to kill his cattle or perish.

Umhlakaza then communicated the final message of the spirits: When not a single animal out of all their herds was left alive, when not a single grain remained in their granaries, supplications would be complete, and the Xhosa would be worthy of the aid of a spirit host. Then, on a certain day, two blood-red suns would fall and crush to dust the bones of every white man in the land, together with his allies the Fingo, a Zulu subtribe that had consistently supported the white settlers, and everyone who opposed the will of the spirits or disobeyed their commands.

Myriad cattle, more beautiful than anyone had

ever seen, would issue from the earth and cover pastures far and wide. Large fields of millet, maize, pumpkins, and monkeynuts, ripe and ready for the pot, would appear. The ancient heroes of the Xhosa, the great, brave, and wise ones long since departed, would rise again to feast and dance with the faithful. Trouble, sickness, and old age would disappear, and youth, beauty, peace, and happiness would reign forever. Thus said Umhlakaza, spokesman of the spirits.

There were some who thought the real aim of the spirits was to throw the full force and might of all Xhosa, fully armed and desperate for food, on the whites in the Cape Colony. Most, however, took what Umhlakaza said as the literal description of what was to happen. Great kraals were built for the expected cattle, and enormous gourds prepared to contain their milk. Huge granaries were erected to hold the marvelous millet, maize, pumpkins, and monkeynuts.

When the appointed day dawned and there were no blood-red suns over the eastern hills, or the heavens falling to crush white men and their Fingo allies, or myriad beautiful cattle, or large fields of millet, maize, pumpkins, and monkeynuts, or a resurrection of the heroes of the race; misery and death stalked the land. Over 30,000 Africans died of starvation.

Ironically, the tragic events did much to reduce, for

a time, the Xhosa's ability to resist white rule. It was not until February 1878, twenty-two years later, that 5,000 Xhosa, the combined forces of Kreli and Sandile, were able once more to take the field against the white man at Kentani. Several months later, Sandile was killed in another action. After his death, his people surrendered to the British. Kreli was driven across the Bashee River and spent the rest of his life in a segregated location at Elliotdale. Thus ended, for a time, African wars of resistance in the Cape Colony.

In Basutoland, which is today independent Lesotho entirely surrounded by South Africa, a different course of resistance was followed in the early nineteenth century. The genius behind it was a Sotho king, the great Moshoeshoe (also known as Moshesh). While he was joining together diverse African societies into a single nation of Basuto people, King Moshoeshoe was compelled to resist European encroachment. With his own position among the various tribes far from secure, he could not risk defeat or a prolonged war with the British. Giving in to European demands was, nevertheless, out of the question; so, he resorted to both fighting and diplomacy.

In 1851, Cape governor Sir Harry Smith sent Major Henry Warden with a force of 162 professional soldiers, 120 armed farmers, and 1,500 Africans against Chief Molitsane, a vassal of

Moshoeshoe. Major Warden's force was drawn into a trap at Viervoet and crushed. Many Boers in the neighboring Orange River Sovereignty saved their skins by promising not to take part in hostilities against the Basuto. Moshoeshoe kept his word not to molest the neutrals, but sought out pro-British farmers and plundered them mercilessly.

It was not until December 1852, that Sir George Cathcart, who had replaced Sir Harry Smith as governor at the Cape, brought together a well-equipped force of 2,000 infantry, 500 cavalry, and some artillerymen with two field guns, hoping that such a force would intimidate Moshoeshoe into acceding to the demands without fighting. The British governor ordered King Moshoeshoe to comply with certain conditions and deliver, within three days, 10,000 head of cattle and 1,000 horses.

Moshoeshoe preferred not to fight, but his people chose to go to war rather than part with so many of their cattle and horses. Moshoeshoe decided to compromise by sending 3,500 head of cattle. He hoped for the best and prepared for the worst by assembling his warriors at a new capital and stronghold at Thaba Bosigo. The compromise was not acceptable to the British, so Sir George Cathcart and his force entered Basutoland.

On Berea Mountain, Moshoeshoe left a large herd of cattle, which appeared easy to capture, and with this decoy drew half the British forces into an ambush. Although this deployment seized about 4,000 cattle, they suffered heavy losses. The other half of the force, personally led by Sir George, was routed by 6,000 Basuto horsemen, some of whom were armed with guns. The British retreated.

Although Moshoeshoe had carried the day, he instructed the Reverend Eugene Casalis, a missionary in his realm, to write what has been called "the most politic document that has ever been penned in South Africa." The communiqué, dated Thaba Bosigo, Midnight, 20th December 1852, began: "Your Excellency, - This day you have fought against my people, and taken much cattle. As the object for which you have come is to have a compensation for the Boers, I beg you will be satisfied with what you have taken. I entreat peace from you - you have shown your power - you have chastised - let it be enough I pray you; and let me no longer be considered an enemy to the Queen, I will try all I can to keep my people in order for the future. Your humble servant, Moshoeshoe." Sir George Cathcart grasped this opportunity to extricate himself with honor from an awkward situation. He announced he was satisfied with the number of cattle captured and considered his obligations fulfilled. He returned to the Cape.

Burghers in the Orange River Sovereignty elected as president Josias Hoffman, a farmer who was a close friend of Moshoeshoe. In 1855, the Boers deposed him because they felt by electing a friend of the Basuto king they had conceded more to Moshoeshoe than was consistent with the dignity of an independent state. Jacobus Nicolaas Boshoff became their next president.

Moshoeshoe began harassing them with a view to recovering land lost by some of the tribes who were now his vassals. In 1858, the Boers decided to invade Basutoland and thus carry the war into Moshoeshoe's territory. The Basuto king let the Boers fight their way to the gates of Thaba Bosigo, where they learned that swarms of Basuto horsemen were at that moment ravaging their farms back home. Since it was impossible to take Moshoeshoe's mountain stronghold by storm, and they had not the means to lay siege, they abandoned the battle and hurried home, leaving Moshoeshoe master of his land once more. Sir George Grey, who had become Cape governor in 1854, was asked to mediate, and he awarded the Basuto king most of the land he wanted.

Meanwhile, in Zululand, in the northern corridor between the Indian Ocean coast of South Africa and the Drakensberg range, political units capable of military resistance to the colonial government were forming. When Chaka, the founder of the Zulu nation, was assassinated in 1828, he predicted the advent of white rule in southern Africa. Dingane, his successor, however, had to deal with the problem. Events were precipitated by the Great Trek, the migration of great numbers of Boer cattlemen into the interior and away from British rule. One such group was led by Pieter Retief. Retief approached Dingane at Umgungundlovu, his capital, and asked for land to settle his party. Dingane indicated his willingness to consider making a grant of land to Retief if, in exchange, the Boers would retrieve cattle that had been taken by Sikonyeia, one of Dingane's rivals. Retief retrieved the cattle without bloodshed and, accompanied by sixty-five other white men and about thirty Hottentots, waited on Dingane to make the grant of land. Instead, Dingane gave the order, "*Bulalani abathakati!* (Kill the wizards!)" and Retief's party was massacred to a man.

Dingane then sent soldiers to wipe out the rest of Retief's group, temporarily settled at Weenen, the "place of weeping," as the Dutch subsequently named it. Two hundred eighty-two white men, women, and children and fifty African servants perished that day. Fortunately for the white people, one man escaped; he was able to ride and warn other groups so that when the Zulu army arrived, they were already in a laager, their wagons drawn up in a defensive circle for the night.

Pieter Uys, Hendrik Potgieter, Gerrit Maritz, and some English leaders then assembled an army of 347 men to fight the Zulu. The English were to attack from one side, while Potgieter and Uys attacked from the other. Maritz was to stay and protect the camp. In April 1838, after a five-day march, the Boers sighted a Zulu army and attacked it impetuously. The Zulu skillfully drew them into a planned ambuscade between two parallel ranges of hills. Retreating into the narrowest part of the gorge, the Boers found themselves surrounded. They were so hemmed in that they could not, as was their usual strategy, fall back rapidly after firing, load again, and charge. The Boers turned back, directed their fire upon a mass of Zulu, cleared a path, rushed through, and escaped, although not without leaving behind many dead and some of their horses, baggage, and spare ammunition. Among the dead were Pieter Uys and his fifteen-year-old son.

The English contingent left the port of Natal with 1,500 Africans, 400 of whom were armed with muskets. On April 17, 1838, some miles south of the Tugela River, they came upon a Zulu regiment. The regiment pretended to take flight; they even left food cooking on fires and a number of assagais and shields lying about. The English contingent pursued with all speed, crossed the Tugela, and took possession of a Zulu kraal on the northern bank before it realized it had been drawn into the horns of a Zulu army, 7,000 strong.

Three times the English contingent beat back the

Zulu regiments that furiously charged upon it. Zulu reinforcements arrived. Another rush was made. This time, the English contingent was cut in two. One half tried to escape by a path along a steep bank of the Tugela. A Zulu regiment cut off its retreat, but four Englishmen and 500 Africans escaped.

The other half was completely surrounded. A young Zulu regiment was selected to charge, while the veterans watched from a hill. Whole masses of young Zulu went down before the withering fire, but still they came and came again, until all the Englishmen and over 1,000 of their African allies lay dead on the battlefield.

During the winter, Dingane sent an army to attack various white groups. The white people, however, were now careful to avoid being lured out of their laagers by any stratagem. In December 1838, Andries Pretorius assembled a force of 464 men and a sufficient number of wagons to form a laager every night. This army vowed that if God gave it victory, it would build a church and set apart an annual thanksgiving day to commemorate the victory. Pretorius sent word to Dingane, offering to enter into peace negotiations if Dingane restored the property of the white people killed by the Zulu. Dingane's reply was to send an army of 10,000 men. The impi, or army, attacked Pretorius's camp at dawn and for hours sent waves of Zulu warriors charging upon it; thousands were felled by the white man's gunfire. When at length the Zulu withdrew, thousands upon thousands of men lay dead, and a stream that flowed near the field of battle was colored with blood. (From that day, this stream has been known as Blood River, and December 16 has been officially celebrated as the Day of the Covenant in South Africa.) Pretorius went on to Umgungundlovu and found that Dingane had set it on fire and fled. His commando force returned with 5,000 cattle.

In September 1839, Mpande, a half brother of Dingane, conspired to seize the throne. This divided the Zulu nation in two. Mpande's supporters sought white people's support against Dingane. Dingane sent Tambusa, his trusted *induna,* or chief, to negotiate with the white people. But the Boers, bent on avenging Retief's death, arrested Tambusa and executed him and his party.

The combined force of Boers under the command of Pretorius and Mpande's impi under Nongalaza defeated Dingane, who fled north toward the Swazi border, where he was later assassinated. Mpande became king of the Zulu and a vassal of the Boers. With great bravery and loss of life, Africans in Zululand had resisted European encroachment, but had succumbed in defeat when internal quarrels divided them in fratricidal strife.

As soon as Mpande was king, he became lethargic both mentally and physically. He grew grossly fat, and discipline in his army declined. His two sons, Mbulazi and Cetshwayo, however, were energetic and brilliant men. It became clear that, as no two bulls can remain in one kraal, these two princes could not both live in Zululand. In December 1856, civil war broke out, and the two princes led opposing forces into battle. The result was a complete victory for the handsome Cetshwayo, who became from that day the real ruler of the Zulu, even though his father lived until 1872. Mbulazi was never heard of again. His followers - men, women, and children - were put to death.

Under Cetshwayo, discipline in the Zulu army was restored, and the Zulu fighting machine became formidable, as it had been in Chaka's time. This was felt by neighboring European settlements, who began to fear for their safety. In 1878, the British governor, Sir Bartle Frere, collected a military force in Natal and sent an ultimatum to Cetshwayo, calling upon the Zulu king to disband his army. Cetshwayo ignored the ultimatum. An army of British soldiers, colonists, and Africans loyal to the colonial government under the command of Lord Frederick Chelmsford entered Zululand in three divisions.

The first division proceeded toward the Buffalo River. One column camped at the foot of Isandlwana Hill. On January 22, 1879, Lord Chelmsford and a small party left camp to attack kraals several miles away. At noon that day, the remaining camp suddenly found itself enclosed within the horns of a Zulu impi. Seven hundred British soldiers, over 130 colonists, and hundreds of their African allies were killed. Lord Chelmsford's party heard of the disaster in the afternoon, marched back to spend the night among the corpses of their comrades, and the next day returned to Port Natal.

A Zulu impi, under the command of another of Cetshwayo's brothers, Dabulamanzi, attacked a column guarding a depot of provisions at Rock Drift about 5:00 p.m. on the day of the Zulu victory at Isandlwana. The 130 soldiers at the depot had been warned of the attack and formed a laager. Waves of Zulu warriors continued to besiege the depot until dawn, when they retired, leaving seventeen enemy dead and hundreds of their brave comrades killed.

Meanwhile, the division commanded by Colonel Charles Pearson crossed the Tugela River and marched toward Ulundi, where the three divisions intended to unite. A Zulu impi, about 5,000 strong, attacked Pearson's column, consisting of 2,000 Europeans and an equal force of African allies, at Inyezane and inflicted heavy losses. When he learned of the disaster of Isandlwana, Colonel Pearson sent most of the remaining cavalry and Africans back to Natal, and with a smaller force fortified a Norwegian mission station near Eshowe, where he remained until reinforcements from England arrived.

The third division, consisting of 1,700 British soldiers, fifty Boer farmers, and 400 Africans under Brigadier General Evelyn Wood, fortified a post at Kambula and made frequent sallies on Zulu villages. At Hlobane, ninety-six of the column were surrounded by an impi and killed.

When news of the British defeat at Isandlwana reached England, 9,000 soldiers - cavalry and infantry - with large quantities of munitions and provisions, were sent out. Among the soldiers was Louis Bonaparte, heir to Napoleon III's throne, who lost his life in Zululand while with a reconnoitering party that was surprised by the Zulu. His companions abandoned him and rode away when he was unable to mount his horse. He was stabbed to death.

Cetshwayo's army was eventually defeated by a British force at Ulundi. The Zulu king went into hiding, and for a long time, no one could be induced to say where he was. At length, one man, threatened with death, revealed the name of a small village where Cetshwayo was found and taken prisoner. In captivity, the Zulu king conducted himself with such dignity that in 1883, after visiting England, he was allowed to return to his throne.

In his absence, a rival named Sikepu had arisen and

won the allegiance of many Zulu. There was civil war. Cetshwayo died and was succeeded by his son, Dinizulu. The war continued, but Dinizulu secured the assistance of Europeans in exchange for land in the Vryheid district in northern Natal. Dinizulu won, but before long fell out with the Europeans and began to resist their rule. In 1889, he was arrested and exiled to the island of St. Helena, and Zululand was put under European rule.

In the area now included in Southern Rhodesia, the Bantu-speaking Mashona also resisted foreign occupation of their country. Europeans entered Mashonaland in 1890. The Mashona, under the impression that the invaders were mere transients interested in trade, were advised by their *midzimu*, or spirit mediums, not to resist, but to trade with them amicably. However, under the auspices of Cecil Rhodes's British South Africa Company, the Europeans began to carve for themselves large farms, mine gold, eject Africans from what they called their property, impress young men into labor gangs, and abuse African women. When, in short, they gave every indication that they had come to stay, Mashona resistance began to simmer.

In 1893, the British South Africa Company also treacherously invaded Matabeleland, a neighboring kingdom whose capital was near present-day Bulawayo. Six thousand Matabele warriors were on a military expedition across the Zambezi when the white men invaded their land in three columns.

The Matabele king, Lobengula, was informed that the *indunas* he had sent to the Cape at the request of the governor had been murdered by white men at Matloutsie. Lobengula was mad with rage and regarded this act as the most despicable treachery. His *indunas* had been sent on an errand of peace, their safety guaranteed by the high commissioner, yet the white men had turned around and murdered his men. "The white men," he declared, "are the fathers of liars." Ordering his army to take up arms, he appeared before them daubed with paint and carrying an assagai. Before thousands of his warriors, Lobengula drove the spear into the earth, signaling war. In response, the warriors gave the royal salute, "*Bayete! Bayete! Bayete!' Uyi Zulu!*" leaping high and striking their shields, causing such a din as to make the whole earth shake. In the excitement, few noticed that the King's assagai broke as it hit the earth - a bad omen.

Although Lobengula's best regiments had been recalled from Barotseland, most of them had contracted smallpox in the north and had been isolated in special kraals so that the disease would not spread. Thus, the Matabele army was not at full strength when it went to meet the European invaders.

Several regiments went out to meet the foe. They were prevented by fog from making contact with the enemy in the thick Somabula forests. Consequently, the Matabele met the invaders on the plains of the Shangani, where conditions favored the white men and their guns. Leander Starr Jameson, who was to gain dubious fame as the leader of the Jameson Raid two years later, was with this force. A. J. de Roos, a Hollander who also fought on the side of the invaders, wrote of the Shangani encounter:

It was full moon, the Matabele had marched all night and were well informed of our movements. Near the laager they waited for the dawn to attack. Their tactics nearly succeeded.

If the Makalangas, who were sleeping outside the laager, had not immediately given the alarm, we would all have gone where the woodbine twineth and the wangdoodtle uttereth its mournful song.

It was still too dark to take in the whole situation, but the surrounding veld was absolutely black with Matabele. On one side the impi was so closely massed that they resembled a stretch of burnt grass in the half light.

However, as dawn approached, the situation changed. De Roos went on to say that the Matabele were so close that it was impossible to miss; he continues: "The maxims and other guns began to speak and within a quarter of an hour one could see that it was all up with them. The sun rose and the surrounding country was strewn with dead and wounded, I estimate that a few thousand Matabele must have taken part in the fight."

Major Forbes pressed on to Bulawayo, the Matabele capital, but on November 18, as the invaders were about to make camp, the Matabele attacked again. De Roos described the battle: "This was also a surprise attack. Most of the men were occupied in preparing their food, when suddenly shots were heard from the horse pickets. The Matabele nearly captured our horses, and draught animals, and this calamity was averted only by the resolute boldness of few Colonials [Cape Colony Africans] who did not retire nor hesitate, but fired as rapidly as possible at the charging enemy. They were soon reinforced from the laager. Within half an hour the enemy were in full retreat. Here also the maxims did their deadly work. A thousand Matabele must have fallen before they retreated. A sortie was made to pursue the retreating enemy. A few wounded Matabele were brought into the laager, but they were killed, when the laager broke up and the column trekked on. I say killed. I know what I am saying, for I saw it myself - without trial or hearing. If there is any question of a "blot" anywhere - here is one. No prisoners of war were made at that time. I don't know what the English parson, who taught us to sing: "Onward Christian Soldiers," had to say about it."

Then this Christian army, which slaughtered

prisoners of war, marched on to Bulawayo. On November 4, they were met by two traders, who told them that King Lobengula had abandoned his town, after instructing an *induna* to see to the safety of the two white men. When the invaders were close, the *induna* told the traders, "I have carried out my king's instructions and must go now, for your people are not far, and they will kill me. If any harm comes to you, it will be from your own people, not mine." Then he set fire to the royal kraal and disappeared. The imperial force arrived in Bulawayo on November 15.

In Bulawayo, De Roos tells us: "The first thing we did was to hold a thanksgiving service, which was conducted by the English Bishop. The subject of his sermon was that we had been led by the hand of God through all those dangers, to the greater glory of His Name, and His Kingdom and the extension of the glorious Empire. 'Onward, Christian Soldiers,' was sung again, for we had not yet captured Lobengula, with his cattle, diamonds, and gold."

Jameson asked Lobengula to return to Bulawayo, promising him safety and friendly treatment, but threatening pursuit if he refused. The king replied that he was prepared to come, but wanted to know what had happened to the *indunas* he had sent on a peace mission to the white men. Finding no satisfactory answer, Lobengula set off in the direction of the Shangani River, with the British in pursuit.

After he had crossed the Shangani, Lobengula told his men: "Matabele! The white men will never cease following us whilst we have gold in our possession; for gold is what they prize above all things. Collect now my gold, and you, and you [indicating two *indunas*], carry it back to the white men. Tell them they have beaten my regiments, killed my people, burnt my kraals, captured my cattle, and that I want peace." Two *indunas* carried the gold to the white soldiers. The gold was taken by two troopers, and the message ignored.

Matabeleland was placed under white rule, but on March 24, 1896, a white man was killed in the Mzingwane district, and an uprising, ably described by Terence Ranger in *Revolt in Southern Rhodesia* 1896–7, had begun. From Mzingwane the uprising spread to large parts of Matabeleland and Mashonaland. Prominent among the leaders of the uprising was the Mashona priest Mkwati. His communications network coordinated moves throughout the area as, for once, the Mashona and Ndebele peoples acted in unison. When the uprising in Mashonaland eventually ended, 10 percent of the white population in the country had been killed, "a staggeringly high figure," which, Lewis Gann has noted, was "infinitely greater than the proportion of casualties suffered by white colonists in the Algerian national rising or the Mau Mau in Kenya in the twentieth century."

In West Africa, the indigenous peoples also struggled to hold their birthright. In the Gambia in 1891, France recognized Britain's claims to both banks of the Gambia River as far as the sea. Soon after this, there was friction between the French and the Mandingos and Fulani. As a result, a chief named Fodi Kabba was exiled to Médine (in present-day Mali), from where he directed a movement against the British. It took a combined British and French military operation in 1901 to destroy Fodi Kabba's movement.

In 1893, another Gambian chief, Fodi Silah, inflicted heavy losses on a British punitive expedition sent against him. He was, however, eventually driven into French-claimed territory, where he died.

In Sierra Leone, the indigenous peoples rose against the British in 1898. They massacred white people, including American missionaries, in their opposition to the "hut tax," a tax charged against every dwelling. The British were compelled to mount an expedition, under Sir Francis de Winton, against them.

In the territory of modern Ghana, the Asante in 1807 attacked and destroyed a British fort at Anomabu and the Dutch fort of Kormantin, and besieged the Cape Coast Castle. They held the area until 1824, when the governor of Sierra Leone, Sir Charles Macarthy, landed at Cape Coast Castle while on a tour of inspection. Impetuously he embarked on a war with the Asante. He was defeated and committed suicide. It took the British imperial government three years to contain the Asante.

Between 1871 and 1872, the Dutch turned over their possessions on the Gold Coast to the British in exchange for certain British claims in Sumatra. The transfer of territory involved the latter in another war with the Asante. The Asante king put 40,000 men in the field. The British allied themselves with the Fante, providing the Africans with British weapons. They were badly defeated twice, before the Asante assaulted the British at Elmina. In 1873, Sir Garnet Wolseley, with a strong force of British soldiers, contingents of West Indian regiments, British seamen, and marines, joined Sir John Glover, who commanded Hausa levies, in attacking and burning Kumasi, the Asante capital.

In 1895, another war broke out. The British captured Kumasi and demanded an indemnity of 357,000 pounds in gold. When this was not paid the *asantehene*, or king, the queen mother, and important chiefs were exiled to the Seychelles in the Indian Ocean. The British looted the Asante palace and dynamited sacred trees and altars.

To add insult to injury, in 1900, the governor of the Gold Coast, Sir Frederick Hodgson, demanded the surrender of the Golden Stool so that he could sit on it. Not even the *asantehene* himself sits on the Golden Stool, which is believed to hold the soul of the Asante nation; rather, the stool is placed on its side, atop a stool of its own. To defend themselves against this sacrilege the Asante revolted and besieged the governor and his wife in Kumasi from, appropriately, April Fool's Day to June 23, 1900, when, with a force of 600 Hausa soldiers and British officers, Hodgson fought his way through Asante warriors to the Gold Coast colony. Later, Colonel James Willcocks arrived from Nigeria with several hundred Yoruba and Hausa troops; these were joined by other African and Indian troops from British Central Africa and officers from England. When the British force eventually advanced on Kumasi in July, it numbered 3,500 officers and men and thousands of African allies from regions hostile to the Asante.

In Nigeria, the British were compelled in 1851 to mount a naval expedition against Kosoko, the king of Lagos. They expelled the king, putting his cousin on the throne. The British met more resistance, however, from Jaja, who had risen from slavery to become a formidable merchant prince of the Niger delta, capable of putting in the field a large force of fighting men. Jaja jealously guarded his independence, and when threatened, engaged the British with armed forces. He was defeated and removed to the West Indies.

Another Nigerian potentate who resisted the British was the king of Benin. In January 1897, he massacred an ostensibly peaceful British expedition under the command of J. R. Phillips, the acting consul general. The *oba* was subsequently exiled, and a number of his chiefs executed. Yet, another resistance flared up in 1899 when a punitive British expedition was sent to Benin,

Between 1900 and 1910, several wars were fought to subdue the Aro, an Ibo people in the northeastern part of the Niger delta. The Fulani kingdom of Nupe also fought wars of resistance to British rule. Colonel T. L. N. Moreland, with a force of 800 African soldiers and British officers, equipped with artillery and maxim guns, was compelled in 1902–1903 to fight not only in Nupe but also in Bornu, Kano, and Sokoto.

French interest in West Africa was stimulated by René Caillié, who in 1827 traveled up the Niger to Timbuktu and across the Sahara to Morocco. At this time, the Fulani conqueror, Al Hajj Umar, dominated this area. He blocked Caillié's route and threatened French settlements on the Senegal River. In 1854, General Louis Faidherbe was appointed governor-general of Senegal, and he conducted skirmishes against African tribes resisting French rule north of the river. He annexed the Wuli country and built a fort at the river port of Médine. Umar sent an army of 20,000 men against him.

In 1864, a French expedition under Lieutenant Abdon Mage reached Segu but was detained for two years by Umar's nephew and successor, Ahmadu ibn Tindani (Ahmadu Seku), who also resisted French forces under General Gustave Borgnis-Desbordes, Colonel Louis Archinard, and other officers.

In 1890, the Tukolor Fulani of Takrur and the Macina Fulani under Ahmadu Abdulei (Ahmadu Cheiku) fought a war of resistance against the French, and the following year a Mandingo king, Samori Touré, also led his people in resisting white rule. In the years 1885 and 1886, the French undertook a campaign against him, but the king's dogged resistance turned it into a seven years' war. In 1894 and 1895, Colonel P. L. Monteil led an unsuccessful military expedition against Samori. Monteil was recalled by the French government, but in 1898, Samori was taken prisoner and exiled to Gabon. Similarly, in Dahomey, King Behanzin fiercely resisted French rule from 1891 to 1893, when he was captured and exiled to the West Indies. Unrest existed as well in other parts of French-held Africa: near Timbuktu in 1894; in the Ivory Coast in 1900; in Mauritania in 1908 and 1909.

In Algeria, Abd al-Kader inflicted defeat after defeat on the French between 1835 and 1837. Only after the French had suffered great losses did they send in an army sufficient to rout the guerilla leader.

Forced to retire to Morocco, he again attacked the French with a large army. The bey of Constantine, who ruled over much of eastern Algeria, repulsed French assaults for many years until his stronghold finally fell to the enemy in 1847. In 1863, the Kabylia Berbers rose in resistance to French rule, and to the south of Oran, there was another uprising under Bu Amama. In Tunisia in 1882, there were uprisings against the French and the bey's government, which had placed the country under French control. A French expedition, led by Paul Flatters, was massacred by the Tuaregs in the Sahara in 1881. In Morocco, Europeans were killed, and Casablanca was sacked by Africans in 1907. In response, France sent 15,000 troops, who fought sporadically until 1911.

In the Congo, the sultan of Bagirmi, who had been induced to accept French protection, was forced to flee, together with the French resident, from the army of Robah Zobeir, sultan of Bornu. It was not until after two years' fighting, in which the French suffered many defeats, that Zobeir was slain. His sons and successors continued the struggle until 1902. To the northeast of Bagirmi, the Wadai ruler attacked French outposts on the Chari River in 1904, thereby opening a war that did not end till 1911.

Relations with the Portuguese, the British, and the French pale before the record left by the Belgians. Few episodes in the history of colonialism in

Africa can surpass the revolting brutality and sordid crimes committed in the name of Leopold, king of the Belgians, on Africans in the Congo. The imposition of Belgian rule is the most miserable chapter of a miserable story.

In less than twenty years after the first Belgian attack, an African population that had been estimated at between 20 and 30 million was reduced to 8 million. Fighting became endemic in the Congo. Belgian officials ordered that recalcitrant villagers be punished by having the hands and sexual organs of males cut off and brought to them for check and tally. In 1892, Belgians were attacked and massacred all over the upper Congo. In 1895, as a result of the murder by the Belgians of Gongo Lutete, chief of the Manyema, there was an uprising at Luluabourg, and another in 1897.

Meanwhile, back on the east coast, the German East Africa Company obtained from the sultan of Zanzibar a fifty-year lease on his mainland territory extending from the Ruvuma River to the Umba River. Over sixty German officials were sent to administer the region. On August 21, 1888, disturbances broke out. A month later, the Germans hardly held any post in the interior. Not only Germans but all Europeans suffered. It took 1,000 Sudanese troops, 200 German sailors, and sixty German officers over eighteen months to put down the uprising.

In 1891, the Wahehe, a warlike people on the Rufiji River, rose against German rule and fought a war that lasted until 1893. In 1905, however, other African tribes between northern Nyasaland (present-day Malawi) and the Kilwa coast rose against the Germans. German officials, male and female missionaries, planters, and traders were killed. It took the Germans nearly a year and a half to subdue the Africans, using not only Masai and Sudanese Africans but also New Guinea, Papuan, and Melanesian troops to fight for them.

In German Kamerun (or Cameroon), cruelties committed between 1887 and 1896 resulted in a mutiny of African soldiers. In 1904 and 1905, African groups rose against German rule and were suppressed after much fighting.

In South West Africa, the Hottentot leader Hendrik Witbooi led his people in several victories against the Germans, who were eventually persuaded to sign a treaty of peace. In 1903, another group of Hottentots - the Bondelswarts living north of the Orange River - took up arms against the Germans and fought them for four years before being exterminated. While this war was in progress, Bantu-speaking Herero tribes also rose up against Germans. Led by Samuel Maherero, they attacked and, killed every white man in sight, burning their houses until they were defeated in the Waterberg Mountains in 1904. Maherero escaped to British territory, where he died while organizing further resistance to the Germans.

Resistance erupted again in the following year, when under Witbooi and his successor Jacob Marengo the Hottentots took up arms. Sixty German settlers in the southeast were killed. By 1908, when the troubles finally came to an end, the Germans in South West Africa had lost 5,000 soldiers and settlers and spent over £15 million trying to hold on there.

The Italians also entered Africa in the last quarter of the nineteenth century. Italy had for a long time cast an envious eye over what it called Abyssinia (Ethiopia, as it is known today). In 1873, Italy purchased the small coaling station of Assab on the Red Sea. After the downfall of Egypt, Italy occupied the neighboring port of Massawa and other areas in the region of Eritrea, and so came to loggerheads with Emperor Yohannes IV of Ethiopia.

The Italians had already occupied Sahiti, an inland town formerly under the Egyptians, when the Ethiopian general Ras Alula moved against them with 10,000 men. An Italian army of 450 men was completely destroyed. In 1895, when Emperor Menelik sat on the Ethiopian throne, the Italians tried again. First, they made secret treaties with one of the vassal kings of Ethiopia - Ras Mangasha of Tigre. Menelik had reason to doubt the loyalty of Ras Mangasha of Tigre, his rival for the emperorship of Ethiopia. In 1891, Ras Mangasha had made a treaty with the Italians: In return for their support, he undertook to detach Tigre from the Ethiopian Empire. This the Italians did, though they were still bound by the Treaty of Wichale to support Menelik.

Ras Mangasha, tiring of an alliance that proved to be meaningless, threw in his lot with Menelik in 1895. He ignored Italian general Baratieri's order to disband, and the Italians, being short of men and funds, did nothing about it. Baratieri went to Rome and succeeded in obtaining money and supplies. He, nevertheless, underestimated the strength of Menelik's troops and counted on some vassal kings rising against the emperor. This did not happen. In September 1895, Menelik had issued a proclamation about the foreign menace, which raised a wave of genuine patriotism among his subjects. All his vassals came to his side.

The Italians staked the reputation of their army on the Ethiopian campaign. Having decided upon a surprise attack on Adowa, the capital of Tigre, Baratieri chose for his attack Sunday, March 1, 1896, a feast day in the Ethiopian Church, with the hope that Ethiopian soldiers would have gone to worship at the holy city of Axum. It never occurred to him that Menelik could move so many troops so quickly from one distant point to another. Nor did he know that Menelik had for some years been importing arms and ammunition. Over and above all, he had faulty and inaccurate maps of Ethiopia.

On the night of February 29 (it was leap year), an Italian force of 14,500 in three columns advanced toward Adowa. Its objective was to occupy three hills commanding the plain. Rain slowed the march. One column, which was to encamp on a hill called Chidan Meret, had far outdistanced the two other Italian detachments. When they encamped at daybreak, there was no sign of the rest of the army, which should have been on its right. Runners, sent to reconnoiter, never returned. The commander's African guides reported that the maps were wrong and that the hill they were on was not Chidan Meret. He seriously considered whether to rely on the map or on his African informants. He decided to rely on his map. The Ethiopians attacked, outmaneuvering and overwhelming the Italian force. A detachment of African troops under Italian command fought well but could not do anything against a determined Ethiopian attack. Finally, they broke and ran, forcing the Italian officers to surrender. The Ethiopians then cut off the other two Italian columns. Over 8,000 Italians and some 4,000 of their African troops were killed. Fugitives not taken prisoner were harried in the gorges, which were their only way back to Eritrea. Had Menelik not ordered all his troops back into camp on the evening of the battle, his cavalry could have cut off the few passes available to the retreating army and exterminated the entire Italian force. The ignominy of this defeat was never to be forgotten in Italy.

From the evidence presented throughout this chapter, it is abundantly clear that the vast majority of Africans responded bravely to the Berlin conspiracy. The European invader enjoyed the advantage of superior weaponry. In all other aspects of the conflict - in generalship, strategy, and battle tactics - it is clear Africans more than held their own against graduates of the best military academies of Europe. It could be said that in these encounters, Africans, armed usually only with spears, displayed greater valor than Europeans firing guns from a safe distance. As a king of the Ndebele once observed: A gun is a weapon that must have been invented by a coward.

What, then, turned the scales in favor of Europeans? It was the assistance they received from a small number of African collaborators, who acted as soldiers, carriers, informants, and food suppliers. Without internal division, then, Europeans would never have been able to win the wars of resistance against them.

Even today, where armed opposition to white rule is taking place, the success of the white man in suppressing this resistance is due in no small measure to the extent and manner in which he has been able to use Africans as soldiers, secret agents, and intelligence gatherers. Perhaps this part of our history illustrates the point of the Zulu saying: *"Isitha somunthu nguye uqhobo Iwake.* (The enemy of an African is he, himself.)" There can be no doubt, however, that these early wars were a source of great inspiration and spiritual strength to the generation of Africans whose destiny it was to carry on the fight against European colonialism and, from the late 1950s on through the 1960s, eradicate it from most of the soil of Africa.

11

UNDER COLONIAL RULE

GEORGE SHEPPERSON

From the West African conference of Bertlin 1884-1885 to the independence of Ghana in 1957, the history of Africa is one of terrifying complexity. The former set the stage for the partition of the continent among the powers of Europe in little more than ten years; the latter touched off the emergence of the new, modern Africa of independent states, also largely within a decade. To employ the adjective "terrifying" in this colonial context is not merely to evoke a sensationally journalistic element that was never far from the surface throughout this intricate story; nor is it a confession of the historian's failure to cope with a diverse mass of detail that often defies analysis and generalization.

There was, to be sure, a genuine touch of terror about relations between white and black in Africa during this three-quarters of a century. It revealed itself in the obvious horrors of the European presence in Africa, such as Joseph Conrad witnessed during his journey into the Belgian Congo in 1890 and which he was to transmute into the terrifying tale, *Heart of Darkness*. It was to be seen in atrocity and counter-atrocity in the many conflicts between European and African, such as the Maji Maji Rising in southern Tanzania against the Germans in 1905, which resulted in the death of some 120,000 Africans. But this terror manifested itself, above all, in the harnessing of almost the whole of Africa, through the hectic period of the so-called Scramble for Africa.

Indeed, the leitmotif of much of the history of Africa in this three-quarters of a century is war; not the localized, so-called tribal wars of old Africa, of which Europeans spoke so disparagingly and often inaccurately when they were flush with the confidence of the virtues of their own civilization, but major wars, mainly of European origin. Five such wars provided a challenge and evoked a response from the people of Africa, whether they came from the sophisticated Islamic societies of the north, from the subsistence economies of central Africa, or from the countries of southern Africa that had experienced European penetration from the fifteenth century onward.

These wars were the Franco-Prussian War, 1870-1871 (although it precedes the period discussed in this chapter, it must be noted because its role in the rearrangement of the European state system in the late nineteenth century was an important factor behind the partition of Africa); the war between the British and the Boers in South Africa, 1899-1902; the First World War, 1914-1918; the Italian invasion of Ethiopia, 1935-1936; and the Second World War, 1939-1945. They span the period of the rise and decline of European power in Africa. They pose the perennial questions in an African context: Is war entirely destructive? Is there not also a constructive element in it? They provide a convenient periodization for the complex history of Africa in the age of European colonial rule.

When the architect of the modern German state, Chancellor Otto von Bismarck, declared, "My map of Africa lies in Europe," he indicated, in his circuitous manner, the background to the conference he convened at Berlin from November 15, 1884, to February 25, 1885, to decide the fate of Africa. This West African Conference of Berlin, at which fourteen European countries and the United States of America were represented, is commonly looked upon as the starting point of the Scramble for Africa (*The Times* newspaper of London, indeed, had popularized this phrase in a leading article only two months before the conference began). Yet, its roots lay in the previous fifteen years of European history - in particular, in the war between France and Prussia that led to the loss by France of the region of Alsace-Lorraine and to the proclamation of the German Empire at Versailles in 1871. A humiliated France faced a new Germany, powerful but not completely convinced of its security. In the decade and a half that followed, Bismarck, the master diplomat, wanted to divert France's ambitions from the recovery of its lost provinces. The best way of doing this was to involve France in rivalries with other European states for overseas territories, especially in Africa.

The old empires of Portugal and Britain and the emerging new empires of Italy and Belgium were, of necessity, involved in the attempt to keep the balance of power in Germany's hands. To political drives were harnessed powerful economic forces: the emergence of industrially based economies throughout Europe, which sought new markets, areas for capital investment, and sources of raw materials overseas. Africa was a convenient field into which this political and economic imbroglio of Europe could extend itself. Although Africa's interior by the 1880s had been charted in considerable outline by European explorers, those parts that were in doubt provided excellent sources of controversy for the powers of Europe, especially Germany, France, and Britain. The extension of European rivalries to another chessboard sometimes had the effect of dissipating them, but more often of exacerbating them. The countries and people of Africa were hardly consulted in the matter, although, as recent historical researches have demonstrated, political and economic forces inside Africa had much to do with deciding where the main thrusts of the powers of Europe into Africa should be directed.

In particular, British and French rivalry in northern Africa converged on Egypt and its hinterland in the early 1880s under the tenuous rule of the Ottoman Empire. The British intervention in and occupation of Egypt in 1881-1882 coincided with the start of the Mahdiyya in the Sudan. The Mahdiyya began with the proclamation by Muhammad Ahmad, son of a boat builder near Khartoum, that he was the Mahdi, the messiah of Islam, who would cast out socioreligious corruption and restore the faith in all its pristine purity. At the same time, but at the other end of Africa, Britain, defeated by rebellious Boers at Majuba Hill on February 27, 1881, was forced to give up its control over the Transvaal. At both ends of Africa, therefore, as well as on the west and east coasts, European rivalries, under the influence of local African problems, were reaching a point of no return.

Bismarck's convening of the Berlin Conference had, no doubt, more than enough of the characteristically Machiavellian motivations of the Iron Chancellor. But his ostensible motive - and that of the powers represented at the conference - was to prevent a European war, and this was serious enough. Much that happened around the conference table at Berlin and in backroom bargaining in those thirteen weeks in 1884-1885 undoubtedly made more certain the Scramble for African territory and concessions by the powers of Europe. It could be argued that it prevented a European war in the mid-1880s, but only at the expense of partitioning and Balkanizing Africa and, ultimately, of ensuring the emergence of a major European war.

It must also not be forgotten that the Berlin Conference indicated a growing American interest in Africa. Some historians would claim that the creation of the so-called conventional basin of the Congo (by which the relatively free sphere of trade was extended beyond the geographical Congo Basin to include the east coast between the boundaries of what is now southern Somalia and northern Mozambique) owed something to the East African commercial interests of the United States. Its representatives at the conference, by their emphasis on America's interests on the East African coast, ensured that these factors would not be overlooked. But the American Senate, under isolationist influences, did not ratify the General Act, as the resultant treaty was known; and United States' interests in the partition of Africa and the subsequent erection of modern types of colonial administration took the unofficial but nonetheless frequently influential forms of trade and investment, especially in the minerals of southern Africa and the Congo.

It was, indeed, the personal empire of King Leopold II of Belgium that profited most notably from the Berlin Conference. Its General Act led to Leopold's recognition as sovereign head of the Congo Free State, although the checking of British and Portuguese expansion in West and East Africa, French gains in West Africa, and the triumph of Bismarckian diplomacy were also important results. The cunning and avaricious Belgian king took every advantage through his own tortuous brand of diplomacy of the requirements of the conference that claims to colonies and protectorates on any part of the African coastline should be formally notified to the other powers that took part in the Berlin Conference and that such claims must be backed by an effective degree of authority. The calling at Brussels in 1890 of a second international conference on Africa to regularize and humanize the partition was used by Leopold to make a breach in the free-trade provisions of the Berlin Conference to the advantage of his Congo possession. By the mid-1890s, the Congo Independent State, a vast area eighty times the size of Belgium, was a reality under the absentee regime of King Leopold.

The Congo Independent State included not only some of the most isolated, culturally traditional peoples of Africa but also the potentially rich rubber territory and wealthy copper country of Katanga. Others besides Leopold had their eyes on this fabulous region where for nearly forty years a Nyamwezi trader, Msiri, had been ruler, presiding from his capital at Bunkeya over a highly profitable commercial network that stretched from Luanda in the west to Zanzibar in the east.

Leopold's most powerful rival for the lordship of Katanga was Cecil Rhodes, the British mining magnate whose British South Africa Company had received a royal charter in 1889. Rhodes wanted Katanga as part of his mining empire in southern and central Africa; he realized also that the area could be made into a main link in his dream of a "Cape-to-Cairo" corridor of British power, spanning the continent from south to north. Katanga at this time was an element in Rhodes's subsidization of British rule in Nyasaland (modern Malawi), over which a British protectorate was defined and declared between 1891 and 1893. (It was known as British Central Africa between 1893 and 1907.) The territory, in Rhodes's opinion, could have become a useful link in a trade route from Katanga to the coast of East Africa. But the Belgian king outmaneuvered him; in 1891, one of Leopold's mercenaries shot Msiri, and the modern exploitation of Katanga's riches was started.

Seven years before, Leopold had been about to

take into his service in the Congo the mystically minded British soldier of fortune Charles George Gordon, who had served the Ottoman Empire between 1874 and 1880 in the Egyptian equatorial provinces and the Sudan. The rise of the Mahdiyya, however, had complicated British policy, particularly as a result of the rapid extension of Mahdist power in the Sudan during the next three years. Gordon was thus persuaded by the British government, which had made itself responsible for the administration of Egypt and its dependencies, to postpone his engagement with Leopold and to go out to Khartoum to evacuate the Turko-Egyptian garrisons that were threatened by Mahdist advances. A year later, on January 26, 1885, while Bismarck and the powers of Europe were attempting to settle the fate of Africa on paper in Berlin, the killing of Gordon by Mahdist forces in Khartoum demonstrated that the people directly involved were determined to have some say in Africa's future.

Shortly after the capture of Khartoum, the Mahdi died. Abdullahi, his general, followed him to power, and was known as the Khalifa, from the Arabic word meaning "successor." He established a strong secular administration that lasted thirteen years. Had the European partition of Africa not taken place, the government of the Mahdiyya in the Sudan, under the Khalifa's rule, might have continued much longer. But British fear of the threat to their strategic interests in Egypt brought an end to the Mahdiyya's rule. In 1896, an Anglo-Egyptian army under Lord Horatio Herbert Kitchener, the British commander, advanced into the Sudan, and in 1898 defeated the Mahdist forces at Omdurman. About 20,000 Sudanese lost their lives.

Kitchener's services to the British Empire in Africa did not end with the defeat of the Mahdiyya. He hastened 200 miles to the south, with a large army, to the Sudanese city of Fashoda (now Kodok), where Commandant Jean-Baptiste Marchand had taken up a position with a force of French-African soldiers. France and Britain were poised on the brink of a war that seemed likely to be something much larger than a localized conflict in the Sudan. After several months, the French gave way and the so-called Fashoda incident of 1898 was solved in Britain's favor. The detente also signaled the closing of a protracted period of Anglo-French rivalry, especially in Uganda, where English Protestant and French Roman Catholic missionaries had been the chief protagonists, largely in Britain's favor. The British government's fear that the headwaters of the Nile would pass into foreign control and that this, in its turn, would jeopardize Britain's suzerainty over Egypt and the Suez Canal was, if only for a moment, greatly diminished.

The same could not be said at this time for the Italians, who two years earlier had received the most resounding defeat that any European power experienced in Africa during the Scramble. In 1896, Italy had seemed in a strong position vis-à-vis Ethiopia, an ancient Christian state that, in spite of a distinctly centralizing process, from the middle of the nineteenth century onward suffered from the problems of maintaining control over a difficult terrain and from traditional border warfare with its African neighbors. To avenge a border defeat in 1887 by Ethiopian troops, the Mahdists invaded western Ethiopia, and in battle with them in 1889, the Ethiopian emperor Yohannes IV was killed.

Meanwhile, the Italians had been gaining: They held a substantial section of the Red Sea coast bordering on Ethiopia, and from 1886 had shared in the divisions of the sultan of Zanzibar's possessions on the mainland of East Africa by claiming a large portion of the Somali coast adjacent to eastern Ethiopia. Yohannes IV's successor, Menelik II, signed with the Italians on May 2, 1889, the Treaty of Wichale (Ucciali), by which he surrendered some of Ethiopia's northern territory; the area was organized the following year by the Italians as the colony of Eritrea.

Menelik believed that this was the last concession he would have to make to the Italians and that the treaty gave him international recognition. Italy, however, used its interpretation of the treaty to notify the other Berlin Conference participants that it claimed a protectorate over Ethiopia. Protesting to the European governments, Menelik abrogated the whole treaty in 1893. Italy invaded Ethiopia two years later in an attempt to compel Menelik to accept its protectorate. But by this time, he had strengthened Ethiopian political unity and had managed to acquire a larger number of firearms. At Adowa, on March 1, 1896, an Ethiopian army of over 80,000 men, outnumbering the Italian forces by about four to one, inflicted a heavy defeat on them: about 6,000 dead, 1,500 wounded, and 3,000 prisoners of war.

Italy was forced to admit that the Treaty of Wichale was void and that Ethiopia was a sovereign and independent state. This gave Menelik the opportunity to return to his mission of extending the boundaries of his kingdom to the south - enlarging them to such an extent that it has been said that he, too, was a participant in the Scramble for Africa, As one of the first occasions in modern times when a non-European army had inflicted a major defeat on a European-led force, the Ethiopian victory also gave heart to Africans all over the continent at a moment when so many of them were losing their ancestral lands and prestige to the might of the white man.

The victory at Adowa in 1896 became an element in what many whites toward the end of the nineteenth century were coming to call "Ethiopianism," by which they meant the Africans' political and religious reaction to European conquest, anticipating pan-Africanism. Many white men at this time, particularly in southern Africa, were fearful that a "Black Peril" would sweep them out of the continent. They believed that this challenge to their supremacy was manifesting itself, to begin with, in the reorganization of African churches, which were breaking away from European tutelage and putting themselves under independent African control. These bodies often called themselves Ethiopian churches, not because they claimed any affiliation with the ancient Coptic Christian Church of Ethiopia but because, in the King James version of the Bible, Black Africa, following the Greek, was called Ethiopia.

The first so-called Ethiopian Church was established in South Africa by black separatist Wesleyans four years before the battle at Adowa. After 1896, therefore, the "Ethiopianism" of the often politically conscious separatist Churches in southern Africa could take pride in the successful militancy of the territorial Ethiopians as well as in their own "Ethiopian" religious self-assertion. The white men, for their part, feared that the day of white domination was coming to an end. Even before the Scramble for Africa drew to a close and Europeans got ready to consolidate and administer their hastily acquired possessions, both the proto-nationalism of the Ethiopian Church leaders and the real nationalism, bloodied in battle, of Menelik and his followers were forces to be reckoned with. Within little more than half a century, they would grow into a movement that would oust Europeans from the political control of the greater part of Africa.

But to this trend, there was one great exception, the other nationalism that was growing in southern Africa, the nationalism of the Afrikaners, or as the British and others called them, the Boers. The defeat of the British at Majuba Hill in 1881 did not stop what seemed to the Afrikaners to be a relentless determination on the part of Great Britain to drive on until it had swallowed up the whole of South Africa. The Afrikaners' isolated, agrarian way of life, bolstered by a devout, if often too rigidly inspired, biblical culture, was at odds with the cosmopolitan capitalism that the discovery of gold in the Witwatersrand in 1886 had encouraged in the Boer's South African Republic (as the Transvaal was then called). The British were in an ideal position to profit from these discoveries. Unlike the Boers, they were a people who were accustomed to the intricacies and intrigues of international capitalism; in the person of Cecil Rhodes, they had a financier and a leader who had the capital, knowledge, ruthlessness, and luck to take every advantage of the gold strikes in the southern Transvaal.

Also bolstering the position of British adventurers and speculators in the Transvaal was the establishment, the previous year, of a British protectorate over Bechuanaland (modern Botswana). Lord Salisbury, the British prime minister, had grabbed this arid territory between German South West Africa and the Transvaal in order to gain access not only to the Boer Republic but also to the territories to the north, where many, including Rhodes, believed that a second Witwatersrand, ripe for plundering, was to be found.

Rhodes's British South Africa Company in 1890 pushed its pioneer column of white settlers into the lands north of the Limpopo River. Within six years, Rhodesia was created. The great Ndebele chief, Lobengula, died after the defeat of his army in 1893. The Ndebele and the Mashona, angry at the loss of their lands and cattle to the victorious white settlers, made a last effort at resistance in 1896 but gave way to superior fire power.

To many Afrikaners in the Transvaal, it must have seemed that Rhodes and his English-speaking followers were all around them, particularly when, from 1890 to 1896, he became the prime minister of the Cape Colony. Rhodes's ideal of a union of all white men south of the Zambezi did not appeal to the majority of the Boers who, although they had ingrained ideas of white supremacy, preferred to live there on their own terms. The Boer president of the South African Republic, Paulus Kruger, and his people angered British immigrants into the Transvaal by taxing them heavily and by making it difficult for them to get the vote.

Rhodes was incensed. With the foreknowledge of the imperialist-minded British Colonial Secretary Joseph Chamberlain and other powerful figures in Britain and South Africa, he supported a sudden invasion of the Transvaal from Bechuanaland in 1895 under the leadership of his lieutenant, Dr. Leander Starr Jameson. The Jameson Raid was a fiasco, easily stopped by the Boers. Rhodes fell from power in the Cape Colony, and while the Fashoda incident was in progress in 1898 far to the north, Britain and the Boers stood at the brink of war.

By 1898, however, the Scramble for the greater part of Africa was largely complete. The French had taken the lion's share of territory, particularly in the north, the Sahara regions, and West Africa. In 1894, Timbuktu fell to them, and in 1896, Say (in the western portion of the modern Niger Republic). And, two years later, their advance down the Niger succeeded in defeating and exiling Samori, the Muslim Mandingo leader whose determined resistance to the French had made him the hero of many African peoples in the huge area between the basin of the Upper Volta and the Niger sources. But Britain was not without compensations in West Africa. Sir

George Goldie's Royal Niger Company, which was chartered in 1885, helped to push British power into the Nigerian hinterland; and from its existing coastal possessions, especially in the northward thrust against the Asante of the Gold Coast, Great Britain extended an already vast empire.

Germany, meanwhile, taking advantage of the bargaining positions obtained by Bismarck, emerged from the Scramble with a sizable empire. It spread-eagled across Africa, from Togo and Kamerun in West Africa, through the extensive possessions of German South West Africa (which, by its closeness to the Transvaal and the obvious sympathy of the Germans to Afrikaner nationalism, was a constant source of worry to the British at this time) to German East Africa. German East Africa's common borders with what later became the British colonies of Kenya and Uganda were defined in a series of agreements in 1890. By this same treaty, British claims to Zanzibar were also recognized. A year later, Britain and Portugal agreed on their Nyasaland and Rhodesian borders; and Portugal, in spite of evident internal weaknesses, succeeded in maintaining its claim to substantial segments of the vast territories in western and eastern Africa, which, with little effective government in the hinterland, it had insisted on calling its own for three centuries.

It seems hardly accidental, then, that in 1898,

at this final stage of the European partition, the Anglo-French writer Hilaire Belloc published *The Modern Traveller,* a satire on the Scramble, a kind of epic poem in reverse, in a sequence of caustic couplets of which the best known are those famous lines that sum up both the confidence and the basic insecurity of the Scramblers:

Whatever happens we have got

The Maxim Gun, and they have not.

The limitations of the Maxim Gun, however, had been demonstrated in the Jameson Raid. A semiautomatic weapon that could create havoc amongst the close formations of Ndebele warriors, and whose praises could be sung by the English officer Frederick Lugard for the "moral effect" of its "long-distance shooting" and its "apparent ubiquity" in the conquest of Uganda, had proved ineffective against the Afrikaners. These skillful sharpshooters did not offer the same kind of target, for they fought a largely guerilla resistance, utilizing every nook and cranny of the land in which they were born. It was this dogged nationalism, harnessed to an almost inborn skill with horse and rifle, that enabled them to stand against the might of the British Empire in the Boer War of 1899-1902. The consequences of this war for Africa were profound.

The conflict was precipitated by the deliberate attempts of Sir Alfred Milner, the British high commissioner in South Africa, to incite the South African Republic to war. The Transvaalers were supported by their fellow Afrikaners in the Orange Free State. Indeed, modern Afrikaner nationalism was consolidated in the fight against Britain. The protracted war led to British reprisals against the Boers, particularly the burning of their farms and the herding of their women and children into concentration camps. The Boers surrendered their independence in the Peace of Vereeniging of May 31, 1902. But, in an attempt to conciliate them, the British bestowed on the Afrikaners in the Transvaal and the Orange Free State the right to decide whether or not the vote should be given to the indigenous Africans. In accordance with their white supremacist traditions, the Boers decided in the negative; and an opportunity was lost to bring about peaceful political change among the nonwhites of South Africa. This British compromise with Boer attitudes continued, helped by former Afrikaner leaders such as Jan Christiaan Smuts and Louis Botha, who were prepared to meet the British more than halfway in order to preserve essential Boer interests. When the four South African provinces united in 1910, it was clear that the block to African political advancement, which had been established at Vereeniging, was to be maintained and, indeed, extended. The Union Act of 1910, while preserving the franchise for qualified Africans at the Cape, ensured that they would have no political rights in the former Boer republics and in Natal. And it also stipulated that not even in the Cape, in spite of all its liberal traditions, should an African be able to stand for Parliament. The Afrikaners may have lost the Boer War on the battlefield, but like the Southerners of the Confederacy in America, they appear to have won it in the council chamber.

A further consequence of the Boer War was that it showed once again how African issues and European diplomacy intertwined and stretched almost to the breaking point. This had been seen in an event that was a minor cause of the Boer War and a manifestation of acute tensions in Anglo-German relations: the dispatch of a telegram on June 3, 1896, from Kaiser Wilhelm of Germany to President Kruger congratulating him on his success in suppressing the Jameson Raid. Looking back on the Boer War, behind the scenes as well as at the overt pattern of assistance and sympathy that was given to the combatants, it is possible to see it as a kind of rehearsal for the First World War.

Out of the Boer War came the stimulus to the first important analysis of that imperialism of which the Scramble for Africa had been a leading but not an isolated example. In the year of the Treaty of Vereeniging, the English author John A. Hobson produced his seminal work. *Imperialism: A Study.* Nikolai Lenin, the ideologist for many of the responses of today's Third World to European colonialism, acknowledged the importance of Hobson's book for his own influential *Imperialism: The Highest Stage of Capitalism* (1917). Hobson spent the summer and autumn of 1899 in South Africa, and he used his experiences and his meditations on them not only for a book entitled *The War in South Africa* (1900) but also for his masterpiece, *Imperialism*. Recent scholars have been critical of Hobson's economic interpretation of the Anglo-Boer conflict, but no student of the colonial age in Africa can afford to neglect it.

Many Africans could not avoid noticing that the Boer War was a major breach in white unity in Africa, but most of them were in no position to take advantage of this for the advancement of their own emerging nationalist movements. They could, however, draw from it conclusions that were often highly embarrassing for the colonial powers. As one African nationalist could later write: "We reason that if the British Government were so generous with the Dutch, will they not also see to it that we of British Africa have just peace and educational treatment, such as the good missionary pioneers assured us of and which we still confidently look for?"

This was the voice of an African who was prepared to reason with his colonial masters. And, to be sure, this was largely the spirit of the first pan-African conference at which thirty-one delegates, mainly from America and the West Indies, met in London in July 1900, to discuss the many problems that confronted men of African descent everywhere as the new century opened. One issue that concerned the delegates was the conflict that had broken out between 1896 and 1898 in Sierra Leone; there, the British, consolidating their rule and imposing relatively heavy taxes on African dwellings, stung many Africans into resistance. Their opposition was stamped out, often with brutality (the systematic razing of African villages was one method). And the delegates to the first pan-African conference protested to Queen Victoria against the treatment of nonwhites in South Africa and Rhodesia. Their feelings were summed up in an "Address to the Nations of the World" that was drafted by the Afro-American scholar W. E. B. Du Bois, in which he first made his famous prophetic statement: "The problem of the twentieth century is the problem of the color line."

Elsewhere in Africa, while the Boer War was being fought, the colonial powers were stamping out much of the old-style resistance to the imposition of their new order. In 1900, the French defeated and killed Rabih, an Arab soldier from the Sudan. He had conquered Bagirmi and much of eastern Bornu, where he had established a slave-raiding state and defied French power in West Africa. By this victory, which came after a long and fierce series of campaigns, the French united their West

African and equatorial empires.

From 1898 to 1900, in bitter warfare, the British eradicated the last Asante resistance to their rule in the Gold Coast. And having halted by 1898 Banyoro attempts to stop their expansion in Uganda, they made the Uganda Agreement of 1900. As a not uncommon consequence of European rule in Africa, the settlement favored one group of Africans (in this instance, the Baganda) over another, thereby setting in motion a train of future difficulties for European and African alike. And, although the British had defeated the Mahdiyya in the Sudan, another Mahdi declared himself in British Somaliland in 1899. During the next two decades, he would gain virtual control over much of greater Somalia. To the colonialists, he was the Mad Mullah; to his countrymen, he was Said Muhammad and a national hero.

By the end of the period of the Boer War, however, the development of modern communications and economies based on Western models in Europe's colonial possessions - a notable example was the Kenya-Uganda railway - presaged the end of much of the old African order, which had neither the resources nor the communications to match the accomplishments of new conquerors. Although Morocco and Tripolitania were independent at the start of the twentieth century, by the outbreak of World War I in 1914, most of Morocco had been swallowed up by France, with a small portion going to Spain, and Tripolitania passed under Italian domination. Only the Afro-American state of Liberia and proud Ethiopia remained independent.

The characteristic patterns of European colonial administration were established in Africa in the two decades before the First World War: Portuguese assimilation; German rational but ruthless "scientific" development; French attempts to create an African elite closely tied to the metropolitan culture; Belgian barefaced exploitation (at least until an international outcry against Leopold II's methods forced the Belgian nation in 1908 to assume direct responsibility for the Congo); and British pragmatism, drawing upon three centuries of British experience of ruling India, respecting - too often over-paternalistically - the local African cultures and their traditional rulers. The combination, and the conflict, of principle and expediency was best seen in Africa in the British method of indirect rule through traditional chiefs and potentates, of which the outstanding example was the fusion of northern and southern Nigeria in 1914 into a viable but volatile state under the watchful eye of its first governor-general, the high priest of indirect rule, Sir Frederick Lugard.

Road, rails, reading, writing, modern medicine, technology, Christianity, and commerce pushed relentlessly into Africa in these years. On both sides of the Sahara, many Africans were won over to the charms of the European way of life. It was, to be sure, essential for the colonial powers to win them over because they could not administer their vast territories without the assistance of literate Africans accustomed to the white man's ways and wishes. Nevertheless, many Africans remained unconvinced of the desirability of the new European order. The Maji Maji Rising in German East Africa in 1905 was an outstanding example of this. In German South West Africa, the resistance of the Herero and other African peoples from 1904 to 1906 led to the destruction of the Herero in the course of German reprisals. In Angola in 1913, there were extensive risings against Portuguese rule. In the French island of Madagascar, the Malagasy people continued their resistance to the rule of the French and their African allies. The last Zulu revolt against the white man in South Africa took place in 1906. A complex web of the resistance of Islamic peoples was spun across North Africa; this embarrassed France, Italy, and Spain. And, in the British-occupied countries of Egypt and the Sudan, the situation was by no means settled, as discontent matured during the First World War, and revolt against the British broke out in Egypt between 1919 and 1920. As if not to be outdone by men of darker skins, a group of pro-German Boers who had still not made their peace with Great Britain revolted in South Africa in 1913.

The First World War rearranged the formal pattern of European colonialism in Africa. Parts of Germany's Togoland and Kamerun were divided between Britain and France, and Germany's East African possessions were split between Britain (receiving Tanganyika) and Belgium (receiving Ruanda-Urundi). World War I also dragged thousands of Africans into a major international conflict against their own choice, dashing the hopes raised by the Berlin Act of 1885. The signatories had then agreed that in time of war among European powers, the African territories would be neutralized and African people spared from the kind of modern conflict of which there had been a foretaste in the Franco-Prussian War.

Although many Germans in East Africa feared that the coming of war into their colony would touch off another African revolt akin to the terrible Maji Maji Rising, the commander of their forces, General Paul von Lettow-Vorbeck, was determined to fight the British in order to embarrass their war effort in Europe. For four years, with remarkable skill, his army resisted combined British and West, East, and South African forces. And Lettow-Vorbeck himself was still fighting when the news of the German capitulation in Europe reached him in 1918. Throughout the East African campaign, the armies relied largely on African porters for their communications, as motorized transport was not suited to the difficult terrain. Many of these porters, especially those from Nyasaland and Kenya, went through considerable hardships, and both they, and later their sons, became increasingly critical of the Europeans. The grievances of the African military carriers of the First World War, indeed, were an important factor in the subsequent emergence of African nationalism.

It was curious, however, that the dispersal of the larger part of the West's armies on the European continent between 1914 and 1918 was not made the occasion for a widespread intensification of African resistance to European rule. Certainly, in northern Africa, where an Islamic power, Turkey, was at war with Britain, France, and Italy, the opportunity was taken to embarrass them; particularly troublesome was the Sanusiyya brotherhood, which accepted Turkish support in its own nationalist drive to wrest Libya from the Italian colonial rule. But in tropical Africa, resistance was the exception rather than the rule. Many Africans seemed stunned by the sight of fighting among white men, who had come into their countries under the banner of the Prince of Peace. As one Christian missionary witness put it: "They can't understand the war, and ask such questions as: 'Why have the Christian countries gone to war? Have the evil spirits got into the hearts of Kings?'"

In West and East Africa, apart from small disturbances - some of which were more the continuation of traditional grievances than a direct response to the war - the outstanding African militant reaction to it was the rising against the British in Nyasaland led by the pastor of an independent African Baptist Church, John Chilembwe, who had been educated in the United States at Virginia Theological Seminary in Lynchburg, Virginia. Even Chilembwe's rising in 1915 was as much, if not more, the result of grievances against harsh practices by Europeans, particularly planters, in Nyasaland as it was the consequence of the coming of the 1914 war; and it was put down quickly with few casualties on either side. Nevertheless, Chilembwe protested against the war in no uncertain terms: "Let the rich men, bankers, titled men, storekeepers, farmers and landlords go to war and get shot. Instead the poor Africans who have nothing to own in this present world, who in death leave only a long line of widows and orphans in utter want and distress are invited to die for a cause which is not theirs." Chilembwe's movement, moreover, represented something of a break with the traditional tribal revolts against European rule in Africa; and it stands out not only as an indication of the disturbing effect of the 1914-1918 World War on Africans but also as a foretaste of the new type of African discontent. The point, indeed, was driven home in Norman Leys's *Kenya,* published in 1924. In one of the first important books to emerge from World War

I, Leys predicted that nationalist movements would increasingly disturb the continent unless Europeans took the opportunity to reform their colonial rule and to live up to the promises implicit in their Christian and democratic ideologies.

The employment of African troops in European armies, whether as labor battalions, as with South Africa, or as combatants, as in the case of the French Senegalese soldiers, opened the eyes of many Africans to the contradiction between European principle and practice. And many of the 200,000 Afro-American soldiers who fought in Europe during the First World War experienced similar disillusion. The ground, indeed, was being prepared for a pan-African approach to the problems of peoples of African descent everywhere.

Leadership was not lacking. There was the fiery Jamaican Marcus Garvey, who had taken his Universal Negro Improvement Association and African Communities League to the United States in 1916; the scholarly Afro-American W.E.B. Du Bois, who had played an important part in the first pan-African conference of 1900; and Blaise Diagne, Senegalese member of the French Chamber of Deputies in Paris, who was given special responsibility by the French during the World War for the recruitment of black soldiers. Diagne's position in France contrasted strikingly with the situation in British Africa, where it was unthinkable that a black man should become a member of a European legislative assembly.

When Du Bois was sent to Europe in 1919 by the National Association for the Advancement of Colored People of the United States to inquire into the grievances of black American troops, it was the influential Blaise Diagne who obtained permission for a second pan-African conference to be held that year in Paris. The congress continued, in the new circumstances of the postwar world, the criticisms of European colonial rule that had been launched by the 1900 conference. And although, like the earlier gathering, it did not ask for African political independence, it insisted that "the natives of Africa must have the right to participate in the Government as fast as their development permits." Du Bois later claimed that the 1919 congress influenced the League of Nations in its mandates system, by which the Allied Powers planned to parcel out the enemy colonial territories among themselves. However, a few other advanced thinkers hoped for a more fundamental approach to the African problem than the League's mandates system: nothing less than a descrambling of Africa. Du Bois favored the establishment of a genuine system of international trusteeships for African underdeveloped countries in which a part would also be played by peoples of African descent settled in other continents.

The following year, Garvey's organization arranged in New York a massive thirty-one-day convention at which Marcus Garvey was elected Provisional President of Africa. It was a grandiloquent and unrealistic title; but it indicated his power over many disillusioned blacks in America (some persuaded by the still more segregationist Afrikaner National Party, which legislated for outright apartheid). Yet, the tendency toward apartheid in South Africa was apparent at least as early as 1936 when the United Party introduced the Natives Representation Act. This legislation swept away the limited multiracial democracy whereby qualified non-Europeans had been able to register as voters on the common roll with whites in the Cape Province. By the mid-1930s, therefore, the leadership of African political movements for greater independence and democracy was clearly passing from South Africa and was moving north. Meanwhile, men such as Nnamdi Azikiwe of Nigeria and Leopold Senghor of Senegal, who were to play leading parts in the securing of independence after the Second World War, were sharpening their wits for the struggle by obtaining an education overseas in Europe and America.

The mid-1930s were for African nationalists, at home and abroad, dark days. Ethiopia, the oldest independent African state, with its ancient history and Christian culture, was invaded and conquered by Italy, then under the brash and brutal Fascist order of Benito Mussolini. Even before the coming of the xenophobic leader, Italy had never been reconciled to its defeat at Adowa in 1896. But it was in no position to take revenge until its war with the Sanusiyya in Libya, which lasted from 1912 to 1931, was at an end. On the eve of the Italian invasion, Ethiopia had just received its first modern constitution. The charter anticipated the increasing modernization of the country at the hands of its own people, assisted but not dominated by foreign advisers. Its architect was Haile Selassie (formerly Ras Tafari Makonnen), who had also brought Ethiopia into the League of Nations in 1923. He had shown his independent spirit when he denounced Britain and Italy before the League. Without consulting Ethiopia, the two powers had decided to support each other in plans to construct a dam at Lake Tana and a railway from Eritrea to Italian Somaliland. In 1928, Haile Selassie signed a treaty of friendship with Italy. It proved of no avail.

As early as 1933, the Italians had decided to conquer Ethiopia. An excuse for invasion was found in a border incident at Walwal in December 1934; and on October 2, 1935, the Italian armies crossed into Ethiopian territory. The Ethiopians experienced the full onslaught of modern weapons, from aerial bombardment to the spraying of poisonous gas over soldiers and civilians alike. Haile Selassie appealed to the League of Nations for action against the Italians; in a historic speech at its headquarters at Geneva on June 30, 1936, three months after the decisive battle in which the Italians had defeated his army, he asked: "Are the States going to set up a terrible precedent of bowing before force?"

An Italian Empire of Eritrea, Somaliland, and, finally, Ethiopia had been created, but nearly forty years after the Scramble for Africa and at a period when most other European powers were reforming their colonial policies and, on paper at least, looking forward to ultimate African independence. Winston S. Churchill, in the first volume of his history of *The Second World War,* commented trenchantly that Mussolini's Ethiopian adventure "belonged to those dark ages when white men felt themselves entitled to conquer yellow, brown, black or red men, and subjugate them by their superior strength and weapons." He went on to describe how Mussolini's show of force had deceived the British government, which might otherwise have stopped him: "Mussolini's bluff succeeded, and an important spectator [Adolph Hitler] drew far-reaching conclusions from the fact." The Second World War, it might be said, really began in Africa.

The Italian conquest of Ethiopia further undermined the confidence of countless Africans in the promises and practices of white men. In London, an association called the International African Friends of Abyssinia was formed, the forerunner of the more widely based International

African Service Bureau, which began in 1937; this, in turn, prepared the way for the Fifth Pan-African Congress, held in Manchester, England, in 1945. The Italian war on Ethiopia, indeed, brought together black men from many different countries and conditions in a fierce crescendo of criticism of white rule in Africa; it precipitated much of the spirit and some of the structure of the African nationalism that was to triumph after the Second World War. And in the destruction of Mussolini's short-lived empire in East Africa in 1941, not only Ethiopian guerrillas but also other African soldiers played their part.

In the three years before the outbreak of the Second World War, the European powers were recovering from the worst ravages of the economic depression of the 1930s. Their African possessions had suffered with them, especially in those territories in which a start had been made on the export of modern primary products. The mining of the potentially rich copper belt of Northern Rhodesia (now Zambia), which had got off to a splendid start in the early 1920s, and the valuable copper production of the Belgian Congo, were hit almost as drastically as those countries with subsistence economies and little export trade, such as Nyasaland and Tanganyika. Even in the more heavily capitalized white settler areas such as Algeria, Kenya, and Southern Rhodesia (which had voted in 1922 for responsible government under Britain, rather than for incorporation in the Union of South Africa) were hard hit.

The colonial governments could do little to remedy the situation until, on the eve of the Second World War and partly as a consequence of it, prosperity began to return to the metropolitan countries. In the interim, nationalism was sharpened not only among Africans but also among white settlers. Many Southern and Northern Rhodesians at this time were critical of the influence of the British South Africa Company over their economic life. A modest proposal by the French Popular Front government in 1936 to admit Algeria's Muslims to the political rights of French citizens was bitterly opposed by whites. And throughout British-ruled East and Central Africa, European settlers fought for closer union between their territories in order to ensure white domination of them. Indeed, the beginnings of the ill-fated Federation of Rhodesia and Nyasaland (1953-1963) may be seen at a 1936 conference at Victoria Falls, when white representatives met to discuss the amalgamation of Southern and Northern Rhodesia.

It was paradoxical, but the outbreak of the Second World War united many black and white nationalists in Africa (if only for the duration of the campaigns) against Fascism, Nazism, and Japanese imperialism. The French in Africa, however, were divided between the supporters of the Vichy government and of General Charles de Gaulle's Free French Forces as France's metropolitan dissensions were exported to its African colonies. The black governor of Chad, Felix Eboué, unlike many white Frenchmen in Africa, supported the Free French Resistance to Germany. He became governor-general of the whole of French Equatorial Africa, which by 1943 was in the Gaullist camp. Eventually, French West Africa and Madagascar also went over to the Gaullist side. But the squabbles, intrigues, and dissensions among white Frenchmen during the Second World War reduced their prestige in the eyes of their subjects all over Africa.

A similar process was at work elsewhere in Africa. Although the British had no Vichy-style problems, and many white British fought as comrades-in-arms with Africans in the African and Burmese campaigns, their prestige was also lowered, particularly when their African soldiers witnessed the force of Asian nationalism against their white masters. "General China," as one of the leaders of the insurgents during the Mau Mau emergency in Kenya in the 1950s called himself, is not untypical in dating his political awakening to his war service with the British army in Burma. The process of disillusion and political awakening among Africans under colonialism, which the First World War had intensified and the Italian-Ethiopian conflict of 1935-1936 had further increased, was completed during the Second World War.

The generation of Africans who had benefitted from the educational policies of the Europeans, particularly of Britain and France, in the interwar years were anxious for political independence. The five years of the Second World War brought forward the date when this could become possible by weakening the colonial powers and by holding before the eyes of African nationalists and their followers a sequence of democratic promises, from the Atlantic Charter of 1941 to the Charter of the United Nations in 1945.

Unfortunately, the colonial powers had not extended education much beyond the relatively small circles of privileged Africans. Yet, this, in its turn, was to sharpen the Africans' appetite for independence all over the continent, whether they had received European-style education or not. The nature of the education given to the subject peoples was different according to the nationality of the colonial power bestowing it. France, by its emphasis on metropolitan-style education, provided exclusively in French, aimed at the creation of an elite of black Frenchmen and produced in them a deep attachment to Parisian norms.

The division between French-speaking and English-speaking Africa, which had begun well before 1939, was not diminished during the Second World War. African independence was to come within little more than a decade and a half after the end of the war, but it was to be an independence following largely the state boundaries the European nations had scored across it with European systems of values and loyalties.

Yet only a month after the surrender of the Japanese at the end of the war, the last pan-African conference to be held outside Africa was convened at Manchester, England, from October 15 to 19, 1945. There were over 100 delegates, primarily from Africa and the Caribbean. They came predominantly from the English-speaking world; there were, apparently, no representatives from French-speaking Africa, although French translations of the main resolutions were provided. Whether this was the result of poor planning and finances in the immediate postwar situation, or of problems of communication, or of deeper political realities is a matter for research and speculation.

Du Bois, the doyen of pan-Africanism, was present at the 1945 congress. but its control and planning were in the hands of younger men - especially Kwame Nkrumah, Jomo Kenyatta, and George Padmore of Trinidad - most of whom were destined within the next two decades to play leading parts in bringing their countries to independence. The spirit of the conference was one of young men in a hurry, and it matched the mood of the ending of the war. It went further than previous congresses in demanding "for black

Africa autonomy and independence"; it spoke out against "a false aristocracy and a discredited Imperialism"; and in its condemnation of "the rule of private wealth and industry for private profit alone," it came close to the concept of African socialism that was to be adopted by many political parties upon gaining independence.

The 1945 Pan-African Congress was a symbol of the rapid and intense achievement of independence throughout most of colonial Africa. The following year, 800 delegates from the colonies of French West Africa and French Equatorial Africa met at Bamako (located in what is today Mali) and formed the *Rassemblement Démocratique Africain*. Although it revealed and represented differences between French-speaking African leaders (especially Leopold Senghor of Senegal, Felix Houphouet-Boigny of the Ivory Coast, and Sékou Touré of Guinea) and asserted a characteristic attachment to French ideals, it manifested a growing spirit of impatience at the slow pace of political advancement in French Africa.

In 1946, the first modern political party was founded in Madagascar, with independence as its objective; the island was shaken by a violent rebellion, which, it has been claimed, took 40,000 Malagasy lives. Until the outbreak of the Mau Mau insurrection in Kenya in 1951, however, the course of independence in the British tropical

African territories was relatively peaceful. Also in 1951, under social revolutionary pressures, tension mounted in Egypt, whose government abrogated the 1936 treaty with Britain, by which British troops were permitted to remain in the Suez Canal zone. On July 23, 1952, a group of young army officers, led by Colonel Abdel Nasser, seized power; and four years later, he nationalized the Suez Canal, forcing Britain to withdraw its troops. Britain and France, assisted by newly formed Israel, attacked Egypt but were compelled to withdraw under international pressure. The coup represented the destruction of the old imperialist pattern in Egypt and the beginning of the end of the European colonial epoch in northern Africa. In 1956, the Egyptians agreed to British proposals for the independence of the Sudan. It was the first formal break in the chain of British colonial power in Africa, and this was emphasized when the Sudan voted to become a republic and not to remain within the British Commonwealth of Nations.

The achievement of independence by the Gold Coast, together with the British Trust territory of Togoland under the name of the old African state of Ghana, in March 1957, made a much greater impact on aspiring African nationalisms than did the achievement of self-government in the Sudan. In the founder of its Convention People's Party and its first prime minister, Kwame Nkrumah, it possessed a dramatic and dramatizing leader who passionately believed: "Freedom for the Gold Coast will be the fountain of inspiration from which other African colonial territories can draw when the time comes for them to strike for their freedom." That time was close at hand. Throughout British, French, and Belgian Africa, the ensuing transfer of power took place at a speed that rivaled the partition in the nineteenth century. As was often said at the time, the Scramble for Africa had become the Scram from Africa. Only white South Africa, Rhodesia, and the Portuguese colonies continued to confront the new Africa of the future with little visible change.

At the threshold of independence for the greater part of colonial Africa, the leaders and the led of the emerging new states could look back over three-quarters of a century of European political domination and ask what it had all been worth. A similar question had been posed toward the end of the Scramble by the young Winston Churchill after his service with the British forces that defeated the Mahdiyya in the Sudan. Writing in his book *The River War* in 1899, Churchill questioned acutely the relation of means to ends in the imperialist process. Though he was convinced that progress had been made, he observed that it was achieved at great cost to both sides, the dominators and the dominated: "The inevitable gap between conquest and dominion becomes filled with the figures of the greedy trader, the inopportune missionary, the ambitious soldier, and the lying speculator, who disquiet the minds of the conquered and excite the sordid appetites of the conquerors. And as the eye of thought rests on these sinister features, it hardly seems possible for us to believe that any fair prospect is approached by so foul a path." Before he asked this mordant question, however, Churchill had indicated the less negative aims of imperialism, which, as he analyzed it, were: "To give peace to warring tribes, to administer justice where all was violence, to strike the chains off the slave, to draw richness from the soil, to plant the earliest seeds of commerce and learning, to increase in whole peoples their capacities for pleasure and diminish their chances for pain." Churchill undoubtedly exaggerated here the underdevelopment of the complex and differentiated cultures of Africa on the eve of imperialism. Nevertheless, even the harshest critic of its role in Africa between 1885 and 1947 would find it difficult to deny that the European presence in Africa during this period had some advantages for the indigenous inhabitants.

Perhaps the colonialists' greatest service was the extension of scientific medicine in Africa, although this was counterbalanced, as a result of improvement in communications, by the spread of new diseases such as sleeping sickness and influenza, causing thousands of deaths. Europe left Africa Balkanized, with the pan-African dreams of political unity far from realization. It could be argued that Europe had reduced considerably the number of separate sovereignties in Africa, but at the expense of overriding old national boundaries and of splitting up once-complete cultures bound together by intimate ties of language, land, and religion.

Modern industry and the promises of an ever-developing science and technology had been thrust into an increasingly wider area of Africa, but, as in Europe, it was introduced with all the attendant disadvantages of a series of severe cultural shocks. And the colonial powers had introduced into their African possessions, often unconsciously and unintentionally, ideas of democracy, socialism, and nationalism that could be employed not only against Africa's own ancient and variegated ways of life but also against European control of the continent. Discontent was inevitable, whether in the form of the older, "tribal" types of reaction and resistance to the white man's rule or in the newer nationalist movements.

Indeed, as the British imperialist Frederick Lugard put it, speaking of the African peoples whom he and other European conquerors had uprooted from their ancient and well-tried ways of life: "Their very discontent is a measure of their progress." But progress, as in Europe where the concept originated, was purchased in Africa at a steep price.

12
AFRICA FOR
THE AFRICANS
IMMANUEL ALLERSTEIN

March 6, 1957, was an important, symbolic date in the history of modern Africa. It was the day on which Ghana (formerly the colony of the Gold Coast) became independent, the first Black African state to do so in the twentieth century.

Ghana was not, however, the first autonomous state on the continent. Ethiopia had been independent throughout its history except for a brief period from 1935 to 1941. Liberia had been founded as a free republic in 1847. Egypt had been independent since 1922. The Union of South Africa had become a self-governing state in 1910 (though under the domination of a white minority).

In addition, a number of states of Arab North Africa had become independent in the six years preceding 1957. Libya had been granted independence in 1951; Tunisia and Morocco in 1956. The Anglo-Egyptian Sudan had become the Republic of the Sudan on January 1, 1956.

Although the Sudan might legitimately be considered by many to be part of Black Africa, it was, nonetheless, Ghana's independence that in the eyes of Africa and of the world represented the dawning of a new era. The countries of the whole world sent representatives to the festivities. Princess Alexandra represented Queen Elizabeth; President Habib Bourguiba of Tunisia came in person. The United States sent its then vice president, Richard M. Nixon.

The independence of Ghana as the "first" had a psychological impact on the rest of Africa that far outweighed the importance of this relatively small African state. It meant that for Africans and for others, a transfer of power to an all-black independent government was a realizable alternative to the continuance of colonial rule in one guise or another.

The effect could be seen in many places. In nearby Nigeria, political leaders of the three regions, into which the country was divided, buried their differences the following month and agreed to work together to achieve independence. In French

Black Africa, the main political movement, the *Rassemblement Démocratique Africain* (RDA), had always eschewed independence as a specific political goal. In October of 1957, however, at the Third Interterritorial Congress of the RDA at Bamako, capital of Mali, the RDA proclaimed that all African states had "the right to independence." In East and Central Africa, leaders of nationalist movements rejected "multiracial" formulas - by which the black African, white, and Asian communities were to be separately represented in the legislature - and indicated their intention to strive for independence on the basis of one man, one vote, and majority rule.

Ghana's independence affected the white-settler-dominated areas of southern Africa as well. The inconceivable - the governance by blacks of an independent state - had become conceivable. At the conferences of the Commonwealth's British prime ministers, the white prime minister of South Africa found as his peer and colleague the black prime minister of Ghana. The sense of the ongoing revolution was felt throughout the white world - in Africa, in the United States, and in the colonial metropoles of the United Kingdom, France, and Belgium.

Ghana saw its role not merely as a symbol of the new possibilities. The government of Ghana immediately began to pursue an active policy of pan-Africanism, of support of the struggle for independence and majority rule in other African countries. One of the first objectives was to convene a Conference of Independent African States (CIAS), which took place in Accra, Ghana's capital, in April 1958. *All* independent states on the African continent, even white-dominated South Africa, were invited to the initial preparatory committee meeting. South Africa demanded as a condition of its attendance that an invitation be extended to the various colonial powers. When Ghana rejected this condition, South Africa declined to come. This was the first and last time the white government of South Africa was to be invited to a pan-African conference.

Eight states came to the CIAS meeting in Accra: Ethiopia, Ghana, Liberia, Libya, Morocco, Sudan, Tunisia, and the United Arab Republic. Without the Arab-African states, there would hardly have been a meeting. A crucial turning point in the history of pan-Africanism had been reached; pan-African meetings would thereafter include the whole continent, not just "black" areas. The geopolitical concept that had seemed immutable during the colonial era, that of two Africas - one north of the Sahara and the other south of the Sahara - was all but banished from the vocabulary and the minds of those living on the continent.

Delegates at the first meeting of the CIAS made two decisions of great importance. They decided to give the liberation of still-dependent territories priority in their political efforts. Specifically, they voted to support the Algerian *Front de Libération Nationale* (FLN), leading what was at that time Africa's most significant war of independence. The support was concrete. The independent African states undertook to send diplomatic missions to potentially sympathetic governments in Scandinavia, Central America, and South America to encourage support for the FLN as the legitimate representative of the Algerian people. Their ultimate goal was to enlist votes for United Nations resolutions, calling on France to negotiate with the FLN and grant independence to Algeria. Indeed, the United Nations was a central focus of African independent states' early politico-diplomatic activity.

The second major decision of the CIAS meeting was to establish permanent consultative machinery in the form of regular meetings in New York of its ambassadors to the United Nations. Thus was formed the so-called African Group, which would play an increasingly important role at the United Nations in the years to come.

Ghana's pan-Africanist thrust did not stop at the convening of the CIAS. Later that same year, in December 1958, Ghana's Africa Bureau, an agency of Ghana's government to promote pan-African ideas, arranged the first meeting of a new group, the All-African Peoples' Conference (AAPC). The invitees represented were not states but movements - political parties and trade unions coming not only from independent Africa but also from the states of colonial and white settler-controlled Africa.

The atmosphere of the AAPC was livelier and more militant than that of the CIAS, which had represented governments. Also, from a pan-African point of view, it represented a far larger cross section of the continent's peoples and ideologies. It was at this meeting of the AAPC that the creation of the Commonwealth of Free African States, an all-African governmental structure, was first recognized as an objective of pan-Africanism. It was at this meeting, too, that "tribalism" was denounced as a barrier to African progress.

On colonial issues, the AAPC called for the recognition of the Provisional Government of the Algerian Republic (known by its French initials as the GPRA), a structure that had been created by the FLN after the April CIAS meeting. The meeting also called for special efforts to secure UN-supervised elections in French Cameroun *before* independence in order to foil what were considered to be French attempts to install a puppet regime rather than one led by the most militant nationalist organization, the *Union des Populations du Cameroun.* This concern with the Cameroun situation caused the African Group to seek and obtain a special convening of the UN General

Assembly in February 1969, solely to deal with Cameroun. However, in what was to be the first of many frustrations encountered by the African states in attempting to use the UN machinery to achieve difficult political goals, the African Group was unable to secure the UN-supervised elections they sought.

Nonetheless, the years from 1958 to 1960 were years of tremendous forward movement for African nationalism and pan-Africanism. The independence of Ghana, followed by the two Accra conferences of 1958 - the CIAS and the AAPC - created a sense of dynamism and optimism that fed upon itself and was to a large degree self-fulfilling.

Events all over the continent reflected this movement. In North Africa, the continuing strain of the Algerian war led to a French internal crisis of major proportions in early 1958, which brought Charles de Gaulle back to power. Although many of the forces supporting de Gaulle were motivated by a desire to halt or slow down the decolonization of French Africa, particularly of Algeria, de Gaulle's accession to power nonetheless set in train a series of events that would bring about within four years independence for virtually all of French Africa, even Algeria.

At first, however, the French sought at all costs to keep Algeria. To consolidate his power, de Gaulle submitted a new constitution to a referendum throughout the French Union. The constitution provided for increased powers to the president and increased political rights for French overseas territories, not, however, including Algeria. For voters in France itself, the issue of the referendum was seen to be the structure of the French government. In Algeria, a vote in favor of the new constitution was interpreted as a vote to keep Algeria French.

In the rest of French Africa, however, the referendum took on another meaning. This was because, as a concession to growing nationalist sentiment, de Gaulle had written into the proposed laws a new autonomous status for the Black African states. De Gaulle actually went to France's Black African territories to seek support for his referendum. There, egged on by nationalist stirrings, he went one step further. He said he would interpret a "no" vote in any African territory as a rejection of the status of autonomy and a withdrawal from the new French community. "Yes" would mean autonomy; "no" would mean independence.

The states of French Black Africa were faced with an important political choice. Few political parties decided to seek a "no" vote, and only one of these succeeded in pulling it off: The ruling party of Guinea, affiliated with the RDA, called for a "no" vote and received almost unanimous backing. After the vote, the new president of Guinea, Sékou

Touré, extended the hand of friendship to France, but President de Gaulle, reacting in pique, abruptly withdrew all French assistance, personnel, and equipment (even some telephone lines) in an attempt to punish and isolate the rebellious state.

As a response to this attempt by France to stifle Guinea's impact on other French African states, Ghana and Guinea announced on November 23, 1958, their union. Although, structurally, the Ghana-Guinea Union amounted to little more than a financial loan by Ghana to Guinea and the establishment of some joint political committees, psychologically and politically it meant much more. The Ghana-Guinea Union was the first real bridging of the linguistic gap that European colonialism had created in Africa.

Meanwhile, the struggle for independence was escalating throughout Africa. As already noted, Algeria's FLN responded to de Gaulle's return to power by creating the Provisional Government, or GPRA. The determination to gain independence without compromise was reinforced. In East and Central Africa, inspired by the CIAS meeting at which they had been observers, the leaders of the nationalist movements of the various British colonies created the Pan-African Freedom Movement for East Central Africa (PAFMECA) on September 17, 1958. The object of PAFMECA was to coordinate the political efforts of the different parties in order to secure a rapid transfer of power.

In French Black Africa, de Gaulle's moves against Guinea were of no avail. Guinea, sustained initially by African and east European assistance, maintained its equilibrium and joined the UN, where it promptly became the most vigorous and radical spokesman of African liberation. Guinea's example spread. By 1960, President de Gaulle was forced to accede by negotiation with the other states within the French community to the independence that he had been punishing Guinea for achieving. The British agreed to grant Nigeria its independence in 1960. Somalia, an Italian trust territory, had long been scheduled to get independence the same year. In the Belgian Congo, thought to be an impervious stronghold of eternal colonial rule, riots broke out in Leopoldville in January 1959, a few weeks following the All-African Peoples' Conference, to which Congolese nationalist leaders had gone. Suddenly the dike broke. The Belgians began to talk of decolonization, and one short year later, on June 30, 1960, they agreed to give the Congo its freedom.

Even in the citadel of white-settler ideology - South Africa - events took on a new face. In February 1960, Prime Minister Harold Macmillan visited South Africa, where he addressed Parliament. This was the famous speech in which he said: "The wind of change is blowing through [Africa], and whether we like it or not this growth of national consciousness is a political fact. We must all accept it as a fact, and our national policies must take account of it."

The next month was a month of crisis. An African demonstration at Sharpeville was gunned down by the police, and by March 30, a state of emergency had been declared. (By the end of the year, South Africa's white electorate had voted to become a republic. The British government deemed that this meant that South Africa had to reapply for membership to the Commonwealth. At first, South Africa did so, but in March 1961, Prime Minister Hendrik Verwoerd withdrew South Africa's application to stay in the Commonwealth as a republic in the face of almost certain refusal.)

Nineteen hundred sixty, often called the Year of Africa, was a year in which much formal political change was occurring on the continent of Africa in the direction of African liberation. Despite this, 1960 was also the year of the first of a series of major setbacks for African liberation. It was the year of the first Congo crisis. On June 30, the Congo became independent. Within one week, the Congolese army, the *Force Publique,* had rebelled - largely against the Belgian officers still in command and against the Congolese government, which countenanced this situation. In the confusion that followed, mineral-rich Katanga, under provincial president Moise Tshombe, seceded, and Belgian troops invaded the Congo, ostensibly to protect Belgian lives in areas controlled by the central government. The Belgians, however, actually landed in Katanga. The Congolese government appealed to the UN for troops, which were sent, the contingents coming, in part, from African countries. The UN troops went to all parts of the Congo except Katanga, where Belgian troops provided a de facto defense shield for the secessionist province. The UN command rather hindered attempts by the Congolese army, partially back under the control of the government, to restore the authority of the central government in Katanga.

Throughout July and August, public order continued to be uncertain in the Congo, and the political strains between the two main central government factions - the one led by Prime Minister Patrice Lumumba and the other by President Joseph Kasavubu - worsened steadily. A special meeting of the foreign ministers of the CIAS in Leopoldville in August solved nothing.

In early September, Kasavubu dismissed Lumumba in a move of dubious constitutional validity. Lumumba challenged the legality of this action. The army, under Colonel Joseph Mobutu, who had ousted his superior officer, announced neutrality, closed Parliament, and then claimed power itself in conjunction with Kasavubu. The UN command also claimed neutrality but acted in a way that many observers felt supported Kasavubu.

African independent states, including those with troops in the Congo, split over the question of whether Kasavubu or Lumumba represented the legal central government. Outside Africa, Western powers generally supported Kasavubu. The Soviet Union supported Lumumba. Meanwhile, Katanga's secession continued.

Beneath the welter of detail and the purely legal-constitutional issues of the Congo crisis lay a fundamental political issue that divided Africa, then and ever since. On the one side were those Africans who felt that the achievement of state sovereignty for African states was merely a minor step in a more basic and revolutionary thrust for African liberation. They drew a series of conclusions from this premise. They felt that political independence was not secure as long as other African states were colonized; hence, active support should be given to the remaining anti-colonial struggles in southern Africa. They felt that most African states were too small to be politically viable; hence, steps toward meaningful African unity had to begin rapidly. They felt that political independence would not bring true independence unless it was coupled with economic independence; hence, states should reject "neocolonial" links to their former colonial power and other Western capitalist states. (The third All-African Peoples' Conference in 1961 denounced as manifestations of neocolonialism: puppet governments; regrouping of states in federations linked to overseas powers; deliberate fragmentation by the creation of artificial political entities; economic interference in a variety of guises, including direct monetary dependence; and the maintenance of foreign military and/or research bases.) They felt, further, that African states should be "nonaligned" internationally, which meant, in their view, cultivation of new diplomatic, political, economic, and cultural ties with the Communist world in order to reduce the primacy of ties with the Western world, and gain a new balance. Finally, they felt that economic development required rapid industrialization and the establishment of socialist modes of organization of the economy. African political theorists of the opposing view worked on a quite different premise: that Africa, being weak, required assistance from the Western world in order to make economic progress, and that such assistance required a political quid pro quo. They placed less emphasis on the liberation of southern Africa (though they lent verbal support). They thought African political federation to be a utopian goal and talked of loose forms of economic cooperation. Far from wanting to break economic ties with the West, they wished to reinforce and expand them. Their version of "nonalignment" was limited to a reluctance to form political alignment with the West. They were highly suspicious of

Communist motives. While sometimes utilizing the term "socialist" to describe their objectives, this group sought to keep African economies open and welcoming to Western capital.

In the immediate Congo crisis, the first group supported Lumumba, and the second Kasavubu. In the parallel debate over what kind of action the UN should take on the continuing Algerian war of independence, the first group unequivocally supported the GPRA; the second group sought to be more conciliatory toward France.

This split was soon to take institutional form. In October 1960, President Felix Houphouët-Boigny of the Ivory Coast invited the states that formerly made up French Black Africa, plus the Malagasy (Malgache) Republic on the Island of Madagascar, to come together in Abidjan to discuss a common position on the Congo and Algerian issues. Soon thereafter, this group of states became the *Union Africaine et Malgache* (UAM), otherwise known as the Brazzaville Group. This group supported Joseph Kasavubu. In January 1961, a counter group was formed. The so-called Casablanca Group included Ghana, Guinea, Mali, Morocco, the United Arab Republic, and Algeria's GPRA. This group supported Lumumba and, of course, the GPRA.

The states of East and Central Africa were placed in a delicate position by this split among African independent states. The nationalist movements of seven states had created PAFMECA. Three of the PAFMECA states bordered the Congo. All were under British rule, and they were hopeful of achieving independence within the foreseeable future. For the time being, they supported Patrice Lumumba.

Lumumba himself fell into the hands of the Kasavubu government and in January 1961, was turned over to the Katanga authorities, who murdered him. The Lumumbists set up their rival central government in Stanleyville. Lumumba became a martyr to revolutionary Africa.

The Congo turmoil had a direct impact on neighboring Angola, which became the first Portuguese territory to experience armed rebellion. On February 4, 1961, there was an uprising in Luanda, the capital, led by the *Movimento Popular de Libertação de Angola* (MPLA), and on March 15, rural guerrilla warfare started in the northern province adjoining the Congo, led by the *União das Populações de Angola* (UPA). The MPLA-UPA split paralleled the Lumumba-Kasavubu and Casablanca-Brazzaville splits, and alliances were made accordingly.

Some attempts were made to heal this inter-African split. Some African states belonged neither to the Brazzaville nor the Casablanca groups. In May 1961, a meeting of all independent states was convened in Monrovia, Liberia. At the last minute, the Casablanca powers declined to come. The resulting organization, which called itself the Inter-African and Malagasy Organization (IAMO), or Monrovia Group, was nothing but an enlarged Brazzaville Group.

The attempt to reunify inter-African political structures was premature. In 1962, however, two events occurred that would make such reunification more plausible. One was the Evian Accords, so named because the agreement was reached in the French city of Evian, which led to the independence of Algeria in July 1962. The second was a temporary internal reconciliation in the Congo. In August 1961, the two claimants to central power in the Congo- the Kasavubu forces in Leopoldville and the Lumumbists in Stanleyville - agreed to a united government under Cyrille Adoula as prime minister. The UN command strongly supported this new regime and, after two false starts, sent in troops to Katanga in December 1962, and finally put down the secession. Congolese sovereignty was thus re-established.

The two immediate thorns to African unity being removed - differences concerning the Congo and Algeria - and an international detente between the United States and the Soviet Union seemingly established, the moment was ripe for new attempts at unity.

But just as independent African states were about

to shelve their differences and join together in an Organization of African Unity (OAU), the first of a series of coups began when President Sylvanus Olympio of Togo was assassinated by army elements on January 13, 1963. Once again, this "first" was not a real first. Egypt's monarchy had been overthrown by a coup in 1952; in November 1958, the army overthrew the government of the Sudan and remained in power until October 1964. However, the Togo coup was the first since the large spate of nations had achieved their separate independences in 1960 and the first marked by an assassination of the top political leader.

Olympio's assassination profoundly shocked the governments of all African states. Many were reluctant to recognize the new regime, and they split anew over the Togo recognition issue. The lines drawn were unexpected. Among the most hostile to recognition were Guinea (of the Casablanca Group) and the Ivory Coast (of the Brazzaville Group). On the other hand, Togo's two neighbors, Ghana (a Casablanca power) and Dahomey (a Brazzaville power), were inclined to work with the new government. Although the Togo recognition issue would not be solved in time for the founding meeting of the Organization of African Unity in May of 1963, and hence, Togo was not invited to that meeting, the new government was eventually recognized by all African states, indeed by all states throughout the world. A clear precedent for further coups was set. De facto control would lead to recognition and full participation in inter-African activities.

Between 1963 and 1971, seventeen African states had successful coups d'état, a few of them several times. In addition, there were abortive coups in many other states. Although the circumstances vary from case to case, there seemed to be two main patterns among the coups, those arising in the Casablanca-type states, sometimes called the revolutionary states, and those in the Monrovia-type states, sometimes called the moderates.

All African states, of whatever bent, faced some basic dilemmas after independence. The state machinery was weak. The bureaucracy was insufficient in size and effectiveness; nonetheless, government administration absorbed too large a part of the states' budgets. The budgets of these regimes steadily expanded under the pressure of demands of the urban middle class and of the workers, both rural and urban. The latter class placed particular pressure on expansion of schooling and job-earning opportunities, while the former pressed for uneconomic expenditures that provided them with greater facilities and perquisites. These expenditures were compounded by the "corruption" that was a widespread feature of the regimes.

However, almost nowhere did governmental

income rise to match increased governmental expenditures - partly because of widespread tax evasion, partly because of political resistance to higher taxation by urban wage earners and foreign investors. The only exceptions were some mineral-producing countries, the high demand for whose products placed them in a relatively better international bargaining position. In any case, the results were simple: Governments suffered a steadily increasing budgetary gap.

The Monrovia-type powers tried to handle this difficulty by maintaining a relatively open economy, and hence continued close economic involvement in the international economic networks of their former colonial overlords, supplemented by new links to the United States and West Germany. As unemployment increased because of the swelling numbers of educated individuals who could not be absorbed into a more slowly developing economy, and Western powers became more reluctant to compensate for budget deficits, governments often attempted mild austerity programs. This tended to alienate the cadres against whom they were directed - the new elite in particular - while irritating the unemployed by the mildness of the measures.

In the tight employment situation of such countries, "tribalism" (that is, giving particularistic preference to others coming from the same "tribe" or ethnic group) became a natural corollary of self-protection.

This often led to outbreaks of violence, which were increasingly met by political or military repression. Often the outcome was a coup.

To the extent that rivalry among Western powers was important in a particular country, coup leaders may have received the support and encouragement of a power displeased by the former regime. Togo in 1963 is a case in point. The immediate precipitant to the coup was Olympio's austerity program. In furtherance of this program, he refused to employ in the Togo army individual Togolese released from service in the French army. Since many of these persons came from the Kabre people, and many of the noncommissioned officers and privates of the Togo army were also Kabre, the Kabre precipitated a coup. It was not without relevance that France had been displeased with the Olympio regime because he had opened the country to United States and German economic involvement and had refused to join the Brazzaville Group (despite the fact that Togo was a member of the Monrovia Group). The government that succeeded Olympio's regime developed closer ties with France and joined the Brazzaville Group.

So-called radical regimes were faced with somewhat different dilemmas. (The first of these governments was not to fall until 1965.) These regimes invested more in job opportunities and had tighter monetary and import controls, which meant less luxury expenditures. They had therefore less unemployment and, consequently, less "tribalism." But the bureaucrats, the armies, and the political classes were increasingly unhappy about the constraints on their style of life. There was also growing displeasure among the Western powers, both because of their foreign policy and because of the difficulties caused to Western firms and their employees. In some of these states, the accumulation of enemies came to be too much for the regime, and a coup ensued.

In May of 1963, at Addis Ababa, Ethiopia, the division of African states came to an end with the creation of the Organization of African Unity (OAU). It momentarily renewed the optimistic atmosphere so prevalent in early 1960. The divisions of Casablanca and Monrovia seemed surmounted, and the assassination of Olympio was not allowed to undo this new drive for unity. Beneath the euphoria of the founding of the OAU could be discerned the crumbling of internal stability of the independent African states. Yet, it was euphoria nonetheless.

Furthermore, unity was based on an unstable compromise between the member states. The Monrovia powers got the kind of loose confederal structure they wanted for the OAU (rather than the United States of Africa some had called for). In addition, they got a promise from the Casablanca states that they would cease giving political support to opposition elements in the Monrovia states. In return, the OAU was officially committed to nonalignment. And most important, all African states were obligated to contribute material aid to the African Liberation Committee (ALC), a body established under the OAU. The function of the ALC was to organize and channel financial, political, and military assistance to liberation movements in the remaining colonies, principally in southern Africa.

Almost immediately, the OAU discovered a knotty problem. Most inter-African organizations disbanded in its favor, including the Casablanca and Monrovia groups and PAFMECSA, which consisted of the earlier Pan-African Movement of East and Central Africa, or PAFMECA, begun in 1958 but expanded in 1962 to include southern African parties. But the Brazzaville powers, or UAM, refused to dissolve. They insisted they were a regional organization permitted within the framework of OAU. They did, however, as a gesture, eliminate their office at the UN to indicate they had no political function, and in 1964, they went further and changed the name of the organization so as to emphasize the primarily economic character of the association. It now became the *Union Africaine et Malgache de Coopération Économique* (UAMCE). Some UAM states, notably the Ivory Coast, were unhappy with this shift and declined to participate in the UAMCE. The spirit of OAU primacy appeared to be gaining ground.

The pace of African liberation also quickened again, and the British timetable for granting independence to its former colonies in East and West Africa was advanced. Kenya, once the great white-settler state of East Africa, became independent under majority rule in 1963. The British broke up the Central African Federation (of the Rhodesias and Nyasaland), which African nationalists had persistently opposed since 1953, and Malawi and Zambia became independent in 1964. There was hope that Southern Rhodesia would follow the path of Kenya.

But the compromise of the OAU was unstable. By December 1963, the internal compromise of the Congo had broken down, and the ex-Lumumbists established the *Conseil National de Libération* (CNL), with headquarters in neighboring Brazzaville (a more radical regime had been installed there after a coup the previous July). Guerrilla warfare broke out in the Congo (Kinshasa). In June 1964, the last United Nations' troops were scheduled to be withdrawn from the Congo. President Kasavubu, fearing the strength of the CNL forces, appointed the former Katanga secessionist leader Moise Tshombe as prime minister. Tshombe returned to the Congo from exile in Angola with his white, mercenary-led ex-Katanga forces.

Civil war broke out again in the Congo, and the OAU sought to put out the fire. It appointed a special committee under the chairmanship of President Jomo Kenyatta of Kenya. As the situation deteriorated, concern focused on the fact that the CNL forces held hostage a group of whites in Stanleyville, attempting to use these hostages to force central government troops to halt their march on the CNL-held city. In the midst of negotiations under the aegis of the OAU committee, Belgian paratroopers with United States logistical aid (consisting of large US air transport planes) invaded Stanleyville. They liberated most of the hostages, an act that had the effect of militarily ending the civil war in favor of the central government. Half the members of the OAU introduced a resolution calling upon the Security Council at the United Nations to condemn Belgian and United States aggression. In the resultant declaration, much weaker than they had hoped, the UN merely "deplored" the intervention and "encouraged" the OAU to continue its efforts toward resolving the Congo split.

Soon thereafter, the Ivory Coast took the lead in re-creating the Brazzaville group in a political form. The UAMCE was replaced by the *Organisation Commune Africaine et Malgache* (OCAM). Several members of OCAM began a campaign against the holding of the next OAU meeting in Accra, Ghana, on the grounds that the government of Ghana was involved in active subversion against OAU states, notably Niger. The compromise of the OAU was cracking further.

In the summer of 1965, the OCAM admitted the Congo (Kinshasa) to membership, thus giving moral sanction to Tshombe's government. In Algeria, Ahmed Ben Bella was overthrown. Whatever this overthrow involved in terms of internal politics, on the African scene, Ben Bella was known as a strong advocate of maximum aid to the liberation movements of southern Africa.

In 1960, the accumulated impact of ten years of struggle in Africa had led to a feeling - both among the African nationalists and the white settlers - that southern Africa was likely to follow the path of the rest of Africa: independence under governments with majority rule. There were small signs in the period from 1960 to 1962 that the Portuguese in their several African colonies and the white regimes of Southern Rhodesia and even South Africa were thinking of making some accommodations to the pressure.

However, the first Congo crisis marked the beginning of the end of what one African leader called "the downward sweep of African liberation," referring to the geographical thrust. The white redoubt of southern Africa stiffened. By the time of the second Congo crisis, there was no longer any doubt that the white rulers would resist to the end.

When the African Liberation Committee came into existence in 1963, they decided on a strategy of liberation that involved the support of guerrilla warfare in Portuguese Africa. (Fighting had begun in Angola in 1961 and in Portuguese Guinea in 1962. It would break out in Mozambique in 1964.) The eventual use of force was also slated for South Africa. However, the liberation of South West Africa was sought through the International Court of Justice. In 1960, Ethiopia and Liberia, as the only African states then recognized by the World Court, had begun litigation against the Union of South Africa, which, they charged, had violated the League of Nations mandate in South West Africa. The issue was still pending, and the ALC hoped for a favorable decision, which it could use as a political weapon. In the case of Southern Rhodesia, the ALC was banking on the assumption that the British would arrange things as they did in Kenya, if only sufficient pressure were put on them by the independent African states who were members of the Commonwealth. This optimism regarding the efficacy of political means for South West Africa and Southern Rhodesia turned out to be seriously misplaced.

The cause of liberation of southern Africa received a series of major blows in 1965 and 1966. The Accra meeting of the OAU was seriously divided, and some members boycotted it. On November 11, 1965, the whites of Southern Rhodesia issued a unilateral declaration of independence of a state they named Rhodesia. The British refused to send troops to put down the rebellion. The OAU was unable to muster any military riposte. Although it voted to respond with a political answer - the breaking of diplomatic ties with Great Britain because of its failure to quell the white revolt - only ten African states actually carried out the resolution.

In January 1966, Nigeria had a coup, which was at first greeted enthusiastically by the population. However, it led to great internal difficulties in Nigeria, which would force Africa's most populous country to turn inward for several years, unable to devote much attention to the liberation of southern Africa. In February 1966, Kwame Nkrumah's regime in Ghana was overthrown, thus removing from the OAU one of the dynamic centers of activity on liberation questions. And in July 1966, the World Court unexpectedly ruled that the complainants against South Africa in the South West Africa case had no legal right to bring suit. The last doorway of peaceful change seemed to have been closed.

The years from 1960 to 1966 can be seen as a shift in Africa from easy optimism to the realization of deep resistance to further change, especially in southern Africa. New tactics were going to have to be developed to meet this new and more difficult struggle. During this same period took place a parallel shift among black Americans. The optimism of 1960, the period of the great sit-ins that would lead to the Civil Rights Acts of 1964 and 1965, came to be displaced by the realization of great resistance to change. Malcolm X was the prophet of this new awareness, and his address to the OAU meeting in Cairo in 1964 marked the first significant attempt in the postindependence era to link the African and Afro-American struggles.

Nineteen hundred sixty-four also was the year of the Watts riots in Los Angeles, the signal of the great frustration of blacks in urban centers. It was the year that the Mississippi Freedom Democratic Party did not receive recognition at the National Convention of the Democratic Party. In 1965, Malcolm X was assassinated, and in 1966, the Black movement took new directions. A more militant leadership took over the most militant student group, the Student Nonviolent Coordinating Committee (SNCC), and the new leader, Stokely Carmichael, proclaimed the slogan "Black Power." In Lowndes County, Alabama, the Black Panther Party came into existence. This shift in Black America involved the beginning of a new kind of interest in Africa, a directly political interest. The fruits of this new interest, however, were not to be seen immediately.

In the years from 1966 to 1970, the questions of inter-African structures moved to the background of African affairs. In southern Africa, it was a time of reorganization and retrenchment for the liberation movements, which sought to find new ways of cracking the strong resistance of the white redoubt. In independent Africa, it was a time of considerable instability, in which the case of the Nigerian civil war is especially notable and important.

In October 1965, nationalist movements from Portuguese Africa met together in Dar es Salaam. It was the third conference of the *Conferência das Organizações Nacionalistas das Colónias Portuguesas* (CONCP), which grouped the radical independence movements of Guinea (PAIGC), Angola (MPLA), and Mozambique (FRELIMO). This loose federation of liberation parties, first formed in 1965, took stock of the situation in Africa and of the setbacks to liberation and African unity. They decided, in the light of what they found, to reinforce their links and plan a coordinated politico-military strategy of the only three areas in colonial Africa then conducting active guerrilla warfare.

Nineteen hundred sixty-six was a year of dilatory activity on Rhodesia. The British, who had refused to use troops against the illegal actions of the white settler government, proposed, instead, a United Nations boycott. Most countries, of course, supported the boycott, but not South Africa or Portugal. Since these two countries controlled the borders of Rhodesia and the outlets for the railway system, their noncooperation made the boycott ineffective. That same year, Great Britain made the so-called NIBMAR pledge, NIBMAR standing for "no independence before majority rule." This meant that they would not negotiate any agreement with Rhodesia that would provide for British recognition of Rhodesian independence *before* the majority of the population - that is, the Africans - had the suffrage. White Rhodesians simply held tight, and no agreement was ever negotiated, nor was the white Rhodesian government overthrown. The settlers seemed to have won their gamble for the moment.

In April 1967, there was an abortive attempt to revive the Casablanca alliance. A so-called Little African Summit was held in Cairo, bringing together the leaders of Algeria, Guinea, the United Arab Republic, and two non-Casablanca powers - Tanzania and Mauritania. The major purpose of the meeting was to discuss ways and means of using force to oust the regime in Rhodesia. Unfortunately, however, the participants did not appear to have uncovered any effective ones.

In May, the United Nations General Assembly reacted to the World Court nondecision on South West Africa by ordering that the United Nations assume direct administration of South West Africa, now to be called Namibia. Since, however, no armed force was to be used to oust South Africa from de facto control of the territory of Namibia, the resolution was as politically efficacious as was the UN boycott of Rhodesia.

At this point in time, the white southern African governments faced a Black African belt of three countries that spanned the continent: Tanzania, Zambia, and the Congo (Kinshasa). Tanzania was the headquarters of the ALC and offered active support to African liberation movements. Zambia was equally militant in its support, if slightly more prudent. Its prudence derived from a geographical necessity. Zambia is landlocked, and historically its outlet to the sea was largely via Rhodesia and Mozambique. Until it could obtain alternate routes to the sea, it had to cooperate to a limited extent on economic matters with Rhodesia. Zambia was anxious to get out from under this yoke and had begun the process of constructing a new rail line through Tanzania to the sea.

The Congo (Kinshasa) saw a shift of government in late 1965. Tshombe was removed from power. Soon thereafter, Joseph Mobutu staged a military coup and seized control. Although Mobutu represented in pan-African terms a centrist and pro-American position, Tshombe had represented a viewpoint of active cooperation with white settlers. Mobutu's government was willing to give support to anti-Portuguese forces, although they preferred the UPA in Angola (the MPLA was the Angolan group backed by Tanzania and Zambia).

Under the circumstances, the governments of Tanzania and Zambia saw Mobutu's regime as a great improvement over Tshombe's, and they moved to create closer links with it.

In 1967, some white mercenary soldiers still in the Congo (Kinshasa), some remaining Belgian settlers, and some remnants of Tshombe's old Katanga forces tried to arrange a pro-Tshombe coup d'état. Thus, the third Congo crisis began. This time, however, the fight was between Mobutu and Tshombe, since the United States gave assistance to Mobutu, and the Casablanca-type groups also gave tacit support to Mobutu, who defeated the mercenaries and solidified his control.

The failure of the mercenary-led coup was a rebuff to the South African counteroffensive against the liberation movements. Another setback was the announcement in August by the outlawed African National Congress (ANC) of South Africa and the outlawed Zimbabwe African People's Union (ZAPU) of Rhodesia of a joint military agreement and of their first common guerrilla action in Wankie in Rhodesia.

The riposte of the White government to joint ANC-ZAPU action was the announcement on September 10 by Prime Minister Ian Smith of Rhodesia that he had invited the cooperation of the South African police in "anti-terrorist operations." That same day, the South African government announced a great diplomatic and political achievement. It revealed its first exchange of diplomatic relations with an independent Black African state, Malawi. South Africa offered Malawi economic and technical assistance. In the years to follow, South Africa would seek to enter into more and more such arrangements - with Lesotho, Botswana, Swaziland, Malagasy Republic, and Mauritius - with the intent to both undermine the support of independent African states for the liberation movements and to develop a new economic network of outlets for its own burgeoning industries.

The South African counteroffensive pushed the liberation movements into closer cooperation. In September 1968, the three members of the federation of liberation parties in Portuguese Africa (CONCP), plus ZAPU and ANC, plus the South West Africa Peoples' Organization (SWAPO), issued a joint statement to the Algiers meeting of the Organization of African Unity. These six organizations were cooperating quite closely. In January 1969, they met together in Khartoum (Sudan) under the aegis of an International Conference in Support of the Liberation Movements of the Portuguese Colonies and Southern Africa. In February 1969, the leader of FRELIMO, Dr. Eduardo Mondlane, was assassinated by the Portuguese, which would lead to an internal political crisis in the Mozambique liberation movement.

In April 1969, the Fifth Summit Conference of East and Central Africa States, meeting in Zambia, issued the so-called Lusaka Manifesto on southern Africa, restating their belief in the equality of men and calling for the reordering of southern Africa to achieve such liberation. It was a moderate statement in view of the events that provoked it but was given no response by these states except the proclamation in March 1970, by the white settler regime that Rhodesia would be a republic. In June 1970, the Sixth Summit Conference of East and Central African States declared that by rejecting the Lusaka Manifesto, Portugal and South Africa had closed the door to the possibility of a peaceful settlement. No progress had been achieved.

This same period (1966 to 1970) saw the acting out of the great Nigerian drama. The first coup in January 1966, was followed by a second coup in July 1966, in which army elements coming from northern Nigeria played a large role. In the turmoil that surrounded the second coup, there were riots and murders of persons coming from eastern Nigeria (mainly Ibo) living in northern Nigeria. Nigeria was faced with a typical legacy of the colonial era in which one segment of the population - in this instance the Ibo - had secured greater access to education and hence to bureaucratic positions than many other segments. As typically happens, this more educated sector then began to monopolize bureaucratic and clerical positions in an educationally backward region - in Nigeria's case, the north. As independence came, the educationally backward region began to regard the monopoly of skilled positions in the hands of "outsiders" as oppressive and hateful. In the turmoil of the coup, this resentment led to bloody riots.

The easterners retreated from the hostile north to their own region and began to talk of secession. The issue was complicated by the fact that the Eastern Region was the focus of recently discovered oil, and the Eastern Region came to feel that it, in turn, was being economically exploited by the rest of Nigeria.

New formulas for governing Nigeria that would reconcile the conflicting interests were sought. In May 1967, they ended in a breakdown of negotiations. The federal government implemented its twelve-state proposal, eliminating the four existing administrative regions of Nigeria and replacing them by twelve states. From the federal government's point of view, this would strengthen the center and eliminate the foci of secession. From eastern Nigeria's point of view, this would break up the Eastern Region into three states and weaken them politically. The leaders of the Eastern Region seceded and proclaimed themselves the Republic of Biafra. The central government immediately sought to restore national unity by military means.

At the September 1967, meeting of the OAU in Kinshasa, the OAU established a consultative commission to help restore peace in Nigeria, carefully refraining from defining the situation as an interstate conflict. This consultative commission functioned throughout the Nigerian civil war with limited effect.

The first nation to recognize Biafra and break the solid African opposition to secession was Tanzania. Tanzania's action, on April 13, 1968, was followed by Zambia's; then came the Ivory Coast and Gabon. Elsewhere in the world, no other state was to recognize Biafra, except Haiti. But many outside forces were sympathetic to Biafra. Indeed, the Nigerian civil war was to produce strange bedfellows. Biafra received various kinds of political and economic support, overtly or covertly, from France, Portugal, South Africa, Israel, and Communist China. Some say the American Central Intelligence Agency also gave support. Biafra also received strong support from the Vatican and from various Protestant relief agencies. The Nigerian federal government received military assistance from Great Britain, the Soviet Union, and the United Arab Republic, and formal support from the US government. Within Africa, Nigeria was supported strongly not only by the majority of states but by the liberation movements of southern Africa.

Ultimately, all initiatives for a peaceful settlement failed. The federal government, however, triumphed on the battlefield, and the secession ended in January 1970. It was followed by a prompt and reasonably effective policy of reconciliation pursued by the federal government.

Elsewhere in independent Africa, there were no civil wars to match that of Nigeria. But political instability remained the norm. In Ghana, the overthrow of Kwame Nkrumah's regime led to several years of army rule, which was replaced by a civilian government in 1969, in which the forces historically opposed to the Nkrumah regime assumed the leadership. Ghana's partner in the Casablanca Group, Mali, also saw its regime overthrown by an army coup in November 1968. The only one of the Casablanca Group regimes in West Africa to survive was Guinea; it was menaced by an abortive Portuguese-led invasion in early 1971, but the commandos were rebuffed.

In the center of Africa, we have already described the political evolution of the belt of states opposed to the white domination of South Africa. The most important event in other states in the region occurred in the Congo (Brazzaville), where the radical regime emerging from the 1963 coup survived various attempts to overthrow it or modify its character. In 1968, the regime took a further turn to the left, proclaiming itself a Marxist state. This outlook led to hostile relations with the Congo (Kinshasa), considered an American puppet, and sympathetic ties with the socialist block, especially China and Cuba. The Congo (Brazzaville) nevertheless maintained close links with France and membership in OCAM, the majority of whose member states were former French colonies.

While the OAU was finding itself in great internal difficulties, OCAM was strengthening itself as an organization. Although it lost Mauritania in 1965, it had been able over the years to add to the original Brazzaville Group Togo, Rwanda, the Congo (Kinshasa), and Mauritius, thus embracing most of French-speaking Africa except North Africa.

In 1969, there was a sudden spurt of radicalization in northeast Africa. There were coups in the Sudan (May), Libya (September), and Somalia (October). In all cases, military regimes came to power. In all cases, the regimes were more anti-Western than their predecessors had been, and they talked of substantive social change at home. The Sudan and Libya moved toward a close alliance with the UAR on the Arab and African scene. About this time, Uganda also moved leftward, but this was reversed by a military coup in early 1971. Britain's Conservative government resumed arms shipments to South Africa in defiance of a United Nations ban and over the vigorous protests of the African members of the Commonwealth.

In summary, the years from 1966 to 1971 were years of political uncertainty and relative stagnation for Africa. The liberation movements of southern Africa worked hard to survive; they succeeded, but did not advance much. Nigeria, Africa's largest country, survived a bloody civil war and was trying to catch its breath. Elsewhere the balance sheet was about even.

The decade from 1960 to 1970 had started high and ended lower. It was the decade to come, 1970-1980, that would more clearly indicate how and to what degree Africa would move forward to political liberation and economic development.

Made in the USA
Monee, IL
18 December 2021

86181830R10344